Praise for
Stelladaur: Finding T...

"Captivating, inspiring, creative and insightful are a few words to describe *Stelladaur: Finding Tir Na Nog* by S. L. Whyte. This fable teaches important lessons about the power of love and the meaning of life. I highly recommend it. You're going to love it!"
> —Dr. Joe Rubino, Author of *The Magic Lantern, The Legend of the Light-Bearers*, and *The Seven Blessings*

"... a very unique and exciting concept ... a very well developed plot and a very intriguing concept."
> —Andrea Hurst, Literary Agent

"In this truly remarkable book, S. L. Whyte has returned me to the dreams of my childhood, dreams that formal education had drummed out of me. Seldom have I come across a philosophical perspective weaved so beautifully into an adventurous love story, easy to read and compelling from start to finish. This is a must read for anyone young or old. If you are open to understanding that dreams create reality, this believably magical story provides profound truths on how to create the reality you yearn for and the dreams you dare to dream. Whether you are a teenager experiencing the awkwardness of first love, or an adult seeking to understand life itself, the *Stelladaur: Finding Tir Na Nog* will give life a whole new meaning."
> —Astrid Witt, Innovative Educator, Speaker, Telesummit Host, Founder of *What the Experts Know*

"*Finding Tir Na Nog*, S. L. Whyte's debut novel and the first book in *The Stelladaur Series*, is a beautiful coming of age story which, at its heart, acts as the reader's very own Stelladaur.... The idea that we each have a reservoir of light within us is not a new one, but S. L. Whyte presents it here in such a unique way that she manages to make a very abstract idea much more concrete and accessible, while still maintaining an effective balance with the ethereal.... I recommend this book for anyone who is searching for a little more strength ... hope and ... magic in their lives ... for anyone who is searching for their own way into Tir Na Nog."
> —Kathryn Lee Moss, Writer and Film Director, *Resistance Movement* (winner of the "Faith Builder Award" at the San Diego Christian Film Festival)

"The plot was intriguing; the action was enthralling; and the romance was tantalizing. Destined to be a hit with teenagers! The message of a practical application of Manifestation makes this a wonderful read for all ages. I hope this becomes required reading for all young people ...!"
> —Andrea Suave, reader

The Stelladaur Series

Book 1

Finding Tir Na Nog

S. L. Whyte

Find your Stelladaur!

S L Whyte

The Stelladaur Series: Finding Tir Na Nog by S. L. Whyte
Copyright © 2013 by S. L. Whyte

ISBN: 978-0-9857523-0-9 (paperback)
ISBN: 978-0-9857523-1-6 (hardcover)
ISBN: 978-0-9857523-2-3 (ebook)
Library of Congress Control Number: 2012942680

Fireglass Publishing
815 1st Avenue, Suite 246
Seattle, WA, USA 98104

www.fireglasspublishing.com
info@fireglasspublishing.com
www.stelladaur.com

Printed and bound in the USA

Cover and interior art by Konohiki Place
Stelladaur logo design and custom lettering by Konohiki Place
Book design and editing by Jill Ronsley, Sun Editing & Book Design
Author's photo by Garrett Wesley Gibbons, Aderyn Productions

Summary: Sixteen-year-old Reilly finds an heirloom treasure and uses it to discover portals to other dimensions in search of his deceased father, and to pursue the man trying to steal the power it possesses.

The Stelladaur Series

Finding Tir Na Nog

S. L. WHYTE

FIREGLASS
PUBLISHING

... to me the imagination is a place all by itself.
A very wonderful country. You've heard of
the British Nation and the French Nation?
Well, this is the Imagination. And once you get there
you can do almost anything you want.

— Kris Kringle
from *Miracle on 34th Street* by Valentine Davies

For Emma, Charlotte and Joshua,
who imagine as everyone ought to do,
and fill me with unspeakable joy

Contents

Gratitude

"Thank you" is insufficient. I wish to express my deepest gratitude to:

My husband, Larry, for refusing to read the manuscript until it was published. And for your patience and strength. I love you forever!

Our sons, Michael, Jeffrey, and Andrew, for believing talking trees exist. I hope you always do.

My sister, Miriam, for giving me the blank journal in which I jotted down characters, scenes and plot ideas years before I began to write the story; and my sister, Amy, for listening with genuine enthusiasm the first time I shared those notes with anyone. Malauri, Makayla, Malachi, and MariAna for your perspective and just plain niceness..

Everyone at Speculative Fiction Writing Cooperative for your helpful critiques, feedback and support when my story began to emerge. Special thanks to Ashley Crandall, Tamara Sellman and Susan Lee for incredibly helpful nitty-gritty.

My editor and book designer, Jill Ronsley, for your expertise, attention to detail, professionalism and good energy. I look forward to working with you on the Stelladaur Series and more.

Konohiki Place, for your obvious gifts of artistic vision, interpretation and expression, and for your commitment to the best things in life.

Diane, for our long walks along the beach and your encouragement. Claudette, for your steadfast faith and love.

Every person, young and old, who finds magic in the Stelladaur.

Thanks to each one of you for shining your light on the story, and in my life.

Chapter One

Eilam

eilly reached the entrance gate to the marina and swung it open with one hand, not bothering to acknowledge the man who glared at him through the giant window of the yacht club. He knew it was Mr. Jackson, the club owner, and passing Mr. Jackson each morning without making eye contact was Reilly's greatest challenge before reaching the water. Most mornings the man stood at the window or on the massive deck, puffing his pipe and looking out over the water as if he owned the harbor itself. There was something creepy about Travis Jackson that crawled on Reilly's skin like disgusting black algae. He didn't know how the muck got there but the grime felt thick whenever Travis was near. Reilly shuddered but kept his focus and succeeded in diverting his gaze away from the man's icy stares. He let the gate shut with a loud clang.

Starting down the dock ramp, Reilly absentmindedly counted each crossbar securing the wooden planks. There were nine but he stepped over the last one, which was covered with moss. He looked across the water, shaking off the lingering feeling of griminess, and thought about a comment his dad often made.

"We live in a postcard, son!"

Reilly paused to take in the pristine view. He nodded and then tugged the side straps of his backpack as he headed for his kayak.

Directly across from a neatly tethered row of one-person sail-boats used for summer classes, Reilly bent down to untie his two-person kayak. He removed the waterproof covering draped over the front seat, threw in his backpack, pulled off the back covering and tucked both covers inside the hull. He lifted the paddle and slid smoothly into the vessel. For almost a year, this had been Reilly's usual mode of transportation to and from town and school, as well as the place for his best adventures.

The kayak was bright orange, with a wide forest-green stripe over the bow and a wide stark-white stripe over the stern, some-what resembling an Irish national flag. It was a putrid pale yellow when Reilly's dad won the bid for it at the Rotary Auction, but they spent the summer sanding it down and then repainting. Since he was a small child Reilly had enjoyed sailing with his dad—being on the water was in his blood—but his kayak gave him a sense of belonging to the sea.

Though completely familiar with his morning routine, Reilly was in awe as he climbed into the kayak and gently sliced through the rippling water, a domino effect created by the departing ferry-boat in the distance. This fifteen-minute ride wasn't just a commute for Reilly. It was a silent meditation.

However, Reilly's morning ritual was never long enough. It ended on the north side of the harbor when he reached Eilam's Kayak Hut.

"Good morning, Reilly," Eilam smiled as he took the paddle.

"Good morning," he said, grabbing his backpack.

"Ahh … and such a nice morning. Love this misty rain," Eilam said.

Reilly smiled and tilted his head to the sky. He closed his eyes and breathed in deeply, then exhaled slowly. "Yes." Opening his eyes, he said, "Are you coming to the bakery this morning?"

"Absolutely! My stomach's been howling. The only thing that will quiet it down is one of your mom's currant scones hot from the oven."

Eilam put his arm around Reilly's shoulder as they headed up the boat ramp, and Reilly reached his arm around the old man's waist. They were more than good friends. Eilam was like the grandfather Reilly never knew, considered part of the family before Reilly was born. Although most islanders knew who Eilam was—and thought him to be a kind man—they also thought he was strange. Even a bit crazy. They were polite to his face, but Reilly was not oblivious to the hum of gossip about his old friend.

Reilly knew Eilam was the oldest local resident, although the man never would say how old. And a curious phenomenon was that no one seemed to remember Eilam looking any younger than he did now. So people could only speculate. The general consensus was that some traumatic experience had caused emotional scarring and left his mind filled with a mumble-jumble of thoughts and ideas. His stories of years past were intriguing, but most occurred so far back that they could not be accurately documented. This only added to peoples' skepticism and reservations about the old man.

Though Reilly did not have all the answers about Eilam's mysterious upbringing and life, he never doubted his friend.

Once, when Reilly asked him how old he *really* was, Eilam simply said, "Age is a myth."

Eilam often said strange things. But if Eilam had said he was 300 years old, Reilly would have believed him. Reilly didn't know for sure, but he felt almost certain that Eilam was from another time and place.

They walked through Waterfront Park and down Main Street through town. Neither spoke on the short journey to the bakery, but they smiled continuously as they breathed in the misty rain.

It was 7:40 a.m. when they arrived at the bakery. Reilly opened the screen door for Eilam, and then let it shut with a single *clap*. Reilly inched his way through the crowded room to the kitchen, where he found his mom brushing a thin layer of glaze on a tray of giant cranberry-orange sweet rolls. She glanced up and smiled. Reilly's dad set down the spatula he was using to scoop lemon poppy seed scones from another tray and moved towards Reilly.

"Hi, son, how was the water this morning?" he asked.

"Perfect."

"Great! What'll it be today?" His dad went back to scooping the scones onto a serving platter, and then left to the dining area, while Reilly wandered around the room sniffing.

Pecan pull-a-parts and pumpkin chocolate chip muffins were his favorites, but today Reilly was looking for something different. He found a clean plate, put a large currant scone on it for Eilam and continued to meander around the worktables. He seriously considered the blueberry bagels. The sugar-sprinkled cherry turnovers made his mouth water. But he finally chose a big slice of hot pumpernickel bread and smothered it with honey butter from a large crock on the side table. He grabbed a lemon yogurt from the fridge and left the kitchen.

As he stepped through the doorway into the crowded room, Reilly accidentally bumped into a man waiting at the end of a long line. Annoyed, the man turned around.

"Get out of my way, kid!" It was Travis Jackson.

Their eyes met. Reilly froze.

"Well, don't just stand there," Travis commanded. "You're in my way!"

"Uh … I, uh … Sorry, sir."

Reilly ducked to the right, but he felt the man's searing gaze on his back.

Annoyed with himself for stammering, he quickly found Eilam seated at their usual corner booth, inhaling steam from a cup of raspberry tea.

"Ugh! I wish he'd stayed at the club," Reilly said as he set the food on the table. "He makes me nervous." He decided to wait before getting his hot chocolate and sat down.

Typical for a Friday morning, the bakery was packed, and Reilly noticed his dad multi-tasking to help the employees assist customers. He could see Travis getting impatient with the wait.

Trying to ignore Travis, Reilly nibbled his bread and turned to look out the window. The misty rain turned to a drizzle as it landed gently on the benches and soaked into the surrounding flower beds. He inhaled the soothing smell of coffee mixed with salty air. But his attempted reverie ended abruptly.

"… and you'd better do something about that *crazy* man!" Travis's voice bellowed above the customers' chatter.

Reilly turned and saw Travis standing at the counter across from his dad—pointing directly at Eilam. Then the obnoxious man pushed his way through the crowded room and stormed out of the bakery.

The boisterous buzz in the bakery subsided; numerous people began to whisper and glance warily at Eilam.

"What a jerk," Reilly muttered. His usual smile had disappeared when he bumped into Travis. He didn't usually let the customers' whispers bother him, but Travis had created a scene that brought unwanted attention to their corner booth.

"Remember, Reilly, gossip is just people's insecurity and fear of what they don't really understand," Eilam said. "It is unconsciously propagated to feed their egos."

"Doesn't it ever bother you?" Reilly asked as he pulled the top off his yogurt.

"I've lived much too long to put any stock in the external judgments of others, or to take anything personally."

Reilly looked intently at Eilam as he tried to understand what the old man had said. He glanced at his friend's thick, silvery hair, which he kept in a loose braid over his left shoulder. He liked Eilam's scruffy-looking beard. It tapered slightly as it fell to his breastbone, the soft gray color of a Northwest seagull. The man's eyes were emerald and perfectly round. His hunched back, gangly legs, crooked hands, slender nose and wide ruby lips never made Reilly feel uncomfortable. This was the only Eilam Reilly had known.

Reilly left the table to get something to drink. He wanted to ask his dad about Travis but knew he was too busy.

He filled an oversized mug with milk, placed it in the microwave for one minute and then pumped a squirt of thick chocolate from the syrup dispenser into his beverage. Using a single-serve hand whip, he whisked the liquid together until it was frothy on top. Finally, he grabbed a banana from a basket near the espresso bar and pushed gently through the crowd once more. When he had made his way back to the booth, he and Eilam sipped their hot beverages and silently observed their surroundings.

To Reilly, the scene was so familiar he could see it without really looking. Most people who came to Blackberry Bakers at this time of the morning were regular customers, many on their way to catch the 8:45 ferry to Seattle with a coffee in one hand and a freshly baked bread or pastry in the other. They were enjoying a latte, reading *The Bainbridge Review*, talking on their cell phones, or just staring out the picture windows.

Reilly watched customers come into the bakery shaking the rain off their clothes and cupping their hands in anticipation of a hot mug to occupy the space. No one bothered to shut the main door, and the screen door released the constant sound of clapping.

In addition to the whispering voices of gossips and the groans of commuters who were miffed about having to rush to catch the boat, the usual chatter picked up. Through it all, the employees remained pleasant and cheerful, doing their best to accommodate each customer. This was a strict staff requirement outlined by Reilly's parents, Kevin and Monique McNamara.

Sipping his hot chocolate, Reilly relaxed as he thought about the fact that he'd basically grown up in the bakery. His smile returned as he reviewed his story. His mom had grown up in a small town in France, helping out in a third-generation family bakery. Restless to see the world, she left home at seventeen, and later moved to Seattle to work for a large accounting firm. One of the firm's main clients was the inventor, Travis Jackson, owner of Imperial Plastics.

Reilly squirmed, just as he did the first time he realized that his mom had known Travis before she met his dad, Kevin. He tore a chunk of crust off his bread and shoved it in his mouth. Chewing hard, he zoned out and continued daydreaming.

Kevin McNamara had come from a rich heritage of maritime folks—lovers of the sea—and like Reilly, he loved the water more than just about anything. Reilly knew the name McNamara meant "hound of the sea," which he thought was ironic, since neither he nor his dad had ever owned a dog. His dad grew up in a family-owned and operated lighthouse in Puget Sound, Washington. But the changing Coast Guard regulations left a bleak future for the family business. Always fascinated by how and why things moved—especially the sea—he decided to study physics at the University of Washington. Reilly's parents met at a benefit dinner hosted by Imperial Plastics, then dated for nearly two years while Kevin worked on his Master's thesis—*Understanding the Displacement and Conductivity of Salt Water Relative to Various Foreign Substances*. They were married the week after he earned his degree.

Early one Tuesday morning in late August, on their two-month anniversary, Monique woke with a sudden urge to go sailing.

The sun rose over the Seattle skyline, sending illuminating rays across Bainbridge Island, beckoning them. Impulsively, Kevin and Monique sailed west for just over an hour, eased into Eagle Harbor, and lowered their sails in the marina just past the ferry terminal. Later, Reilly's dad told people he and his wife didn't know why they were there, but both felt it was a magical place.

Reilly blew into his mug and shifted on the bench.

He thought of his parents walking along the waterfront, picking a few blackberries, when an old man came up from behind them and said hello. Kevin returned the greeting and asked the man if he knew of a place for a good cup of coffee and a bite to eat.

"That is precisely the thing this island needs," the man said. "I've been around these parts for a long while and I've seen a lot of shops come and go. It would be nice to have a spot to sit and rest, sip a cup of tea, and chat with folks." He paused and pointed with his gnarly finger. "But if you head up the hill that way, turn right on Main Street and walk a block, you will find a little diner on the right side of the street." Kevin held out his hand to thank the man and asked his name. "Eilam. Just Eilam."

Later, Reilly's dad said that in that instant, he thought the man looked familiar. Now, watching Eilam drink his tea, Reilly wondered why he'd always thought the same thing.

Turning right on their walk up the hill towards town, Reilly's parents noticed a placard hanging on the wall of an old brick building in the center of town: COMMERCIAL SPACE FOR SALE. It was as if the sun's rays had moved from the harbor to shine right on those words. To the newlyweds it was a sign! So the McNamaras left the city life, a stifling accounting career and the potential for fame and fortune in the field of physics, and opened Blackberry Bakers. Over a quarter of a century later, the bakery had become one of the island's most famous icons, providing Reilly's parents with the small-town lifestyle they truly wanted. Neither of them ever regretted their decision to marry or to venture out as bakers. Petit fours and cappuccinos sprinkled with Irish chocolate were quite a combination.

Shifting slightly so he could see the clock above the door, Reilly realized with a start that his thoughts had carried him away—as usual—and that school started in 15 minutes. He stuffed the last half of banana in his mouth and took a gulp of now warm hot chocolate before he scooted along the bench.

"See ya this afternoon," Reilly said, smiling at Eilam.

He poked his head into the kitchen.

"Bye Dad! Bye Mom!"

"Have a great day, Reilly," his dad shouted.

Reilly hoisted his backpack over his shoulders and headed out the back door. He perched on the seat of his ten-speed, which he kept locked behind the bakery, and started out in the mist.

For reasons Reilly didn't understand, he knew he often saw things differently than others did. Sometimes he could see with his ears … speak with his eyes … or hear with his heart. Or just *know* things. A quintessential dreamer, he welcomed each day as an invitation for his dreams to come true. Oddly, they often did. He didn't know why this was so, or why he felt compelled to look for the good and expect the best, or what made his thoughts connect his reality to what others considered unreal, impossible or ridiculous.

Adults said he had a keen imagination. His peers thought he was just plain different. Regardless, this was how Reilly had lived his life. Up to this point.

Chapter Two

Time

School was a good ten-minute bike ride from the bakery, and Reilly knew he had to hurry if he was going to make it before the first bell rang. He zipped up his favorite sky-blue Mariner's sweatshirt, pulled the hood over his wavy blond hair and tucked in the ends. With the blond now mostly covered, his eyes sparkled like sapphires. His fair skin was healthy and covered with freckles, a trait his mom told him he'd inherited from his Irish ancestors on his father's side. Reilly's nose was small and pug-like. His mouth was wide with slender lips; faint lines had appeared prematurely around it from his almost constant smile. Though Reilly was one of the shortest kids in the entire sophomore class, wearing a sweatshirt that was too small accentuated his upper arm definition. But he barely noticed. What to wear was only a matter of comfort and convenience to Reilly, not an attempt to win the approval or acceptance of others. Reilly was not conscious of his advanced awareness of self; the fact was he just didn't care what he wore.

He pedaled quickly through the city offices parking lot and headed up Madison Avenue to the roundabout in front of the library, where he snuck in front of an elderly woman driving an old Buick. After rounding the curve to head west, he glanced back and noticed the lady still waiting to inch her car into the traffic.

Reilly's mind wandered to Eilam, who had never obtained a driver's license and said he never had a need for one. Eilam went everywhere he needed to go by foot or by water. Though his feet were long and awkward, he claimed they were solid and dependable for walking. As for traveling by water, he had done so in many types of vessels: canoe, sailboat, submarine, kayak, and large ships. Eilam had told tales of endless sea adventures with alluring detail and passion that invariably left Reilly wanting to hear more. Once Reilly asked Eilam what was the longest distance he'd ever traveled by water, and the old man only replied, "It's quite remarkable how far a person can go by sea."

Reilly's thoughts were interrupted by the horn of a school bus honking at a car that had swerved in front of it while turning into the parking lot. He picked up speed as he pedaled the last hundred feet downhill towards the school's side entrance and saw students still unloading from three or four buses, so he knew the bell had not rung yet. He locked his bike in the usual spot and turned to enter the building.

"Hey, *Smiley Reilly*, what's happ'nin'?" chanted Todd Petrowski. He and Frank Bingham towered over Reilly with their usual following of students close behind.

Todd was the tallest kid in the sophomore class; Frank was only slightly shorter. They were both on the basketball team and could easily be mistaken for juniors. As school jocks—stars in their own minds—the boys prided themselves on the fact that a gathering of giddy girls was always nearby.

"Yeah, what's to smile about on a soggy, pathetic school day?" Frank sneered.

The boys were more annoying than harmful; however, harassing Reilly seemed to be a favorite pastime. They'd never thrown a punch at him, but they'd threatened to do so regularly for one stupid reason or another. Every day they did their best to provoke him, or at least ruffle his feathers but the fact that they hadn't ever successfully done so only added to their irritation.

Like Eilam, Reilly wasn't usually bothered if people made snide remarks. He tried not to take the comments personally.

"I like the rain." Reilly smiled, though not intentionally, and started to move past the small but growing crowd.

"You would, you moron!" Frank shouted.

"Punk!" Todd hollered.

The bell rang as Reilly entered the school and headed towards Room 115. Not bothering to stop at his locker, he sprinted into Pre-Calculus. Reilly liked the fact that Ms. Lamar allowed her students to sit wherever they wanted, so he took the first available seat. Today was "B" day so he had four of his seven classes. Math was every day. The next seventy-five minutes passed quickly as Ms. Lamar handed back the assignments she'd graded over the weekend and used them as a review for the upcoming test. Reilly had aced the assignments and he had no questions about concepts from the three previous chapters. So his thoughts drifted, as usual.

What was Mr. Jackson talking about with Dad this morning? Travis rarely came to the bakery, unless he was placing an order for an event at the club. Years ago, the men had made an agreement so his dad could use a slip at the marina for his sailboat, where Reilly now kept his kayak, too. Up until that time, his dad had kept his boat across the harbor at the public marina, which was much less expensive than docking at the yacht club. According to the agreement, Reilly's dad would supply a variety of artisan breads for the club's monthly luncheon and desserts for their annual black tie affair, which the McNamaras attended as a professional courtesy. But the monthly luncheon was last week, and the gala event wasn't until September. So why did Travis come to the bakery this morning?

The agreement also included full membership in the yacht club, with all its perks. Reilly's dad never officially joined—yacht clubs weren't his style. He simply agreed to Travis's proposal because he thought it would be good advertising and it might attract a few new customers from Seattle. And an immediate financial benefit was not having to pay the docking fees at the public marina for several years.

Reilly remembered overhearing his mom and dad talking about the proposal when the offer was first made, and his mom said she didn't think Mr. Jackson's motives were pure. At the time, Reilly wasn't sure what she meant. But over the years, he watched the way Travis looked at his mom whenever he came into the bakery—and every year he became increasingly uneasy around the man. Reilly's mom often retreated to the back room and let his dad deal with Travis, who often said weird things like, "Tell Monique I say hello, and if she ever gets tired of baking, I've got just the thing for her" or "Be sure to tell *my* Monique hello."

Reilly's dad never seemed threatened by these overtly lame comments, but he promised his wife he'd never join the club. Still, if there was one thing that irritated Reilly, it was Travis Jackson.

Travis Jackson was a world-renowned scientist and international entrepreneur, one of the wealthiest men in the Pacific Northwest. Married and divorced three times over the past decade, he was often seen with different women. And he had a problem with alcohol. Around the island his reputation was questionable, but outside the community his success and influence over others kept most people thinking it was no big deal. He had no children, but Frank Bingham was his nephew.

Thinking about the way Travis flailed his arms around the bakery earlier, Reilly was certain the man was drunk. And he couldn't forget the look in Travis's eyes when he pointed deliberately at Eilam, shouting. *What did Eilam have to do with anything?* Reilly decided to ask both his dad and Eilam about it after school.

For a few minutes he zoned back in to what Ms. Lamar was saying. Something about coefficients and plugging constants into the quadratic equation.

Oh, yeah, that was covered in the last chapter. Got it. No need for review there. When is she going to get on with the next concept?

Math had always been easy for Reilly. He was fascinated by the precision of numbers, and he was always anxious to learn something new about how they worked. Like when Eilam showed him how to take one times 9, plus 2, to get 11. Then make the 1 a 12, multiply it by 9, and add 3 to get 111, and so forth. Reilly drew it out on the back of his test paper. Soon the final equation was clear in his mind: Take the number 123456789, multiply it by 9, add 10, and the answer is …

$$1 \times 9 + 2 = 11$$
$$12 \times 9 + 3 = 111$$
$$123 \times 9 + 4 = 1111$$
$$1234 \times 9 + 5 = 11111$$
$$12345 \times 9 + 6 = 111111$$
$$123456 \times 9 + 7 = 1111111$$
$$1234567 \times 9 + 8 = 11111111$$
$$12345678 \times 9 + 9 = 111111111$$
$$123456789 \times 9 + 10 = 1111111111$$

He looked at the pyramid of numbers for a few minutes, remembering the exact moment Eilam explained it to him. They were sitting on the dock at the kayak hut on a hot summer day with their feet dangling over the water, when a tiny crab scurried up the piling beside them.

"Some may think that little creature is useless," Eilam said. "But even the very smallest of all creations is essential to our existence. Every single one adds to the whole."

It was the way he emphasized *one* that caught Reilly's attention. Then he watched Eilam carve something into the wood on the dock with his pocketknife. Its pattern was similar to the mathematical picture Reilly had just scribbled on his test paper, but it fascinated him even more.

Reilly lifted his head and stared blankly out the side window while he drew it out in his mind. Everything started with ones. One times one equals one. Then start with 11 times 11 and get 121. He kept adding ones to both sides of the quotient until multiplying nine ones by nine ones revealed …

$$1 \times 1 = 1$$
$$11 \times 11 = 121$$
$$111 \times 111 = 12321$$
$$1111 \times 1111 = 1234321$$
$$11111 \times 11111 = 123454321$$
$$111111 \times 111111 = 12345654321$$
$$1111111 \times 1111111 = 1234567654321$$
$$11111111 \times 11111111 = 123456787654321$$
$$111111111 \times 111111111 = 12345678987654321$$

It really was just as Eilam had said. Perfect. No disputing its authenticity. It was a fact.

"Every*one* is vital to the whole. And every*one* has a purpose and place in this world," Eilam had told him as he folded up his pocketknife.

"Reilly … Reilly, do you have the answer?" Ms. Lamar interrupted his numerical daydream.

"Huh? Um, yeah, it's … uh … I think it's something ending in a one?"

"That's right. Pages 231 through 251 will be covered on the test next Monday. Be sure to study carefully and answer all the questions thoroughly. I will be available 40 minutes before school for anyone who needs a last-minute refresher." With that the bell rang and Ms. Lamar dismissed the class with the wave of her hand in the direction of the door.

Reilly's next class was P. E. He looked forward to his senior year when he could take kayaking as an elective, but for now he was stuck in regular 10th grade P. E. right in the middle of a four-week unit on basketball. Since he was shorter than average, the next hour and a quarter would be near torture for Reilly. He was quick and could dribble reasonably well, but he struggled to get the ball high enough in the air to make a decent pass. As a matter of fact, he could count on three fingers the times he had made a basket. Worse yet, Todd and Frank were both in the class.

"Oh, well. I managed to get through volleyball with those creeps. I'll survive basketball, too," he mumbled to himself as he made his way to his gym locker.

Most of the kids in the class were average. Not everyone was a jock like Todd and Frank. Still, Reilly thought there should be a rule that kids who played on school teams should not be required—or allowed—to take regular P. E. classes. It just put everyone else in the class at an unfair disadvantage! But Reilly knew it was what it was; there was no changing it.

Fortunately, his locker was on the opposite end of the locker room from Todd and Frank, so there usually wasn't time for any conflict until after they were dressed. Today, Frank inched his way between Reilly and another kid as they headed to the gym floor.

"So, Smiley, my uncle told me your dad isn't keeping up his end of the deal they made," Frank chided as he yanked on Reilly's ponytail.

"I don't know what you're talking about," Reilly answered honestly, but he couldn't help wondering if it had anything to do with what had happened in the bakery that morning.

"Yeah, right. You're a lyin' freak!" Frank mocked Reilly as he gave his bicep a shove.

"You'd better ask your dear old dad about it," Todd sneered as he rammed Reilly from behind. "Better yet, why not see if your kooky kayak guru will *enlighten* you." Frank and Todd headed onto the court leaving a trail of profanities echoing off the lockers.

Reilly began to wonder if there was an agreement between his dad and Travis that he was unaware of. Something that had nothing to do with ordering artisan breads for the yacht club luncheons or keeping his kayak docked at the club's marina. *But what did it have to do with Eilam?*

The students took their places in two lines to do the usual sets of dribbles, passes, and shoots. Reilly was the last one in his row, and Frank and Todd were the first two on the opposite row. This suited Reilly fine until he realized his row was short by one person which, over the course of five or six minutes of warm-ups, put Reilly even with Frank on the next set up to the basket. They dribbled together at an angle, one from the left, the other from the right, until they met nearly in the middle to take their shots. Frank raised his arms with the grace of a pro and flipped his hand effortlessly to make a perfect basket. Reilly tried his best. Using both hands he propelled the ball into the air like a volleyball, then raised his brows high as the ball brushed the bottom of the net.

"You throw a ball the same way your dad keeps his word. Bad form," Frank said. "Always coming up short." He looked at Reilly with disgust as he sauntered to the back of his row.

By the time Reilly retrieved the ball and passed it to the next in line, Frank's team had moved up in the row, and he was relieved that the two boys would not be up together again to shoot.

After thirty minutes of drills and Frank repeatedly gawking at Reilly, they began a real game. Todd and Reilly were on one team and Frank was on the other. Now it was Todd's turn to be annoying.

"When are ya gonna get it, Smiley? Everyone in this town knows Eilam is crazy. Why do your parents even let him in the bakery?" Todd sneered. "There should be laws against people like him going into public places." He hovered above Reilly and intercepted the ball in mid-air.

Todd took the ball down mid-court and passed it to another team member, who took the shot. He missed but it rebounded right in front of Reilly, who grabbed it and began dribbling back down the court, with Frank towering over him the entire way. Eyeing each other intently, Reilly still had complete control of the dribble and he wasn't about to give it up to Frank.

"Yeah, you think you're fast. But you're not quick enough to see what's right in front of your pathetic face," Frank panted. He frantically grabbed for the ball, irritated that he wasn't able to take it from Reilly, who kept the dribble under check and then passed it sharply to a teammate at his left.

Frank grunted, "You moron! Don't think your dad can keep his secret from Uncle Travis the way you keep a lousy basketball from me for a few measly seconds." With that he sprinted off to the far end of the court leaving Reilly to wonder what on earth he was talking about.

What secret? What's right in front of me? What does Eilam have to do with anything between my dad and Mr. Jackson?

The whole thing annoyed Reilly more than usual, but he was determined not to let it get the best of him. He knew he could get the truth from his dad and Eilam, so he tried to put it out of his mind while he showered and headed to his third-hour class. Science.

In addition to math, science captivated Reilly. He loved discovering how things worked, why they existed, what could be done to change the way they appeared, and what "cause and effect" actually *did* affect.

"Come in, come in!" Mr. Ludwig sang in a high-pitched voice while stretching up on his toes and rubbing the palms of his hands together gleefully. "Hurry now! Find your seats. Let's get started. Much to do ... much to do!" He alternately clapped his hands numerous times and rubbed them together, while repeating his brief commands. He virtually danced about the front of the class until the students were in their chairs and all eyes were up front.

Mr. Ludwig lived and breathed science. As a result, he came to class every day acting as if it was Christmas morning—hardly able to contain himself with the thrill of it all—and overly anxious to tell his students what they'd be learning that day. Or what totally amazing experiment they'd be doing. Or what plant or small amphibian dissection they'd have the opportunity to perform. Sometimes he'd literally jump up and down with excitement. Reilly appreciated his zeal; most just found it amusing.

"Excellent!" he began again. "Today we are going to shift from our recent discussions on igneous and sedimentary rocks, and talk about something else ... but something equally fascinating!"

Mr. Ludwig's philosophy was that anything could be related to science in one way or another. That's why he thought just about *everything* was *fascinating*. Without fail, he used the word "fascinating" every day in class. Sometimes he used it in every sentence. And it was not unusual for him to deviate from the regular curriculum because his mind simply wandered off in so many directions at one time. This was precisely why Reilly, and most every student, loved his class so much.

"The science of time," Mr. Ludwig continued. He moved behind the large lab desk at the center front of the room and pulled out an enormous clock, a good three feet in diameter, and propped it up in front of the tall sink faucet. Then he pulled out a common kitchen timer, twisted the knob until it ticked for a moment, turned it back again so it would give a *ding* and placed it on the counter. He reached in his lab coat pocket, pulled out a runner's stopwatch and dangled it by the cord in an almost hypnotic motion. After setting the stopwatch on the desk, he took off his wristwatch and placed it beside the other time devices. Finally, he opened the left drawer and retrieved a two-foot hourglass.

"What is time? How is it measured? Why do we measure it? Is it always the same? What is its purpose?" He posed each question while touching the items he had just set up for display. "Let's try an experiment. When I say 'go,' we will each do something to try to capture time for one minute."

Mr. Ludwig paced back and forth slowly … methodically … behind the desk four times without saying another word. He looked deliberately at each student.

"Go!" he finally blurted out.

Most students looked around with bewildered expressions on their faces. Some started to chat with each other. Others wiggled uncomfortably in their chairs. The girl to Reilly's left inhaled, puffed out her cheeks and held her breath. The boy next to him pulled out a cell phone in a desperate attempt to send a text message before the teacher would notice.

Reilly looked intently at Mr. Ludwig and imagined what might happen next. With Mr. Ludwig, the possibilities were unpredictable. The fact that he looked somewhat like the stereotypical mad scientist only added to the mystique.

"Stop! Time's up!" he commanded with a single clap of his hands. "Uhm … *time's up*. Now that's an interesting phrase." He smiled thoughtfully. "What do you suppose that means?"

"Duh! It means we don't have any more time," a kid from the back shouted.

"It means the one minute you gave us is gone," added another.

"Maybe it means after time is gone, it goes up?" Reilly laughed.

"Ah … now there's a thought. But where does it actually go? How do we know it's really gone?" Mr. Ludwig inquired with a glint in his eye. He reached for the large clock and placed his right pointer finger over the second hand to make it stop moving. "What if we could stop time?"

"But you're not stopping time," the boy with the cell phone insisted. "You're just stopping the clock."

"Fascinating observation! And very accurate, too," Mr. Ludwig responded. "So, is there a way to capture time? Make it stand still? Can we understand its true properties and functions? I'm asking all of you: Who thinks it is simply *not* possible?" Over half of the class raised their hands. Many shrugged their shoulders.

Reilly continued to grin and watch his teacher intently.

"So then … a few of you think it is, or could be, possible," he said. "Let me ask another question. If I take this bottle … and …" He reached under the lab desk and pulled out an empty glass bottle that looked like a small container for chocolate milk. "… If I put this egg on top of it, can the egg fit into the jar without breaking?" He placed a hard-boiled egg on the lip of the bottle.

"No, the egg's too big," someone in the front row declared.

"Yeah, it's not possible," another kid reaffirmed.

"Oh, so quick to decide what you think you know. What we think is possible is often limited by what our eyes perceive," Mr. Ludwig said, as he lifted his pointer finger and raised his brow.

Mr. Ludwig removed the egg from the lip of the bottle and set it on the lab desk. He took a box of matches from the drawer, lit one, and tossed it quickly into the bottle. Then he quickly replaced the egg on top of the bottle.

"Hey, I've see this trick before," someone whined.

The class watched as the egg slid gently into the bottle, contracting to fit the narrow space and then plopping to the bottom of the glass container.

"No trick," insisted Mr. Ludwig. "This is elementary science. Who can explain what happened?"

The girl two rows to Reilly's left and up one seat raised her hand. "Well," she began, "it's an example of a partial vacuum. The fire heated the air molecules inside the bottle and made the molecules move further away from each other. Some of those molecules even escaped past the egg. That's why it wobbled on top. Then after the flames went out all the molecules cooled down and moved closer together again. The air pressure—well, the pressure of the air molecules—pulled the egg into the bottle."

"I couldn't have explained it more precisely!" Mr. Ludwig squealed. "Extra credit points for you today."

"Okay, so it's not a trick," the whining kid said. "But what does that have to do with time?"

"That was my next question. Any thoughts?" said Mr. Ludwig.

Reilly's brain was spinning. There could be lots of connections. Obviously, the teacher proved his point that some things that at first appear to be impossible are, in fact, possible when we understand the laws that govern them. And sometimes proof is shown in very simple terms. Perhaps Mr. Ludwig just wanted his students to consider that even time has elements that are not visible, but still very real. What about the partial vacuum? Did that have anything to do with time?

Mr. Ludwig began again. "If time represents the egg, how can we change the conditions surrounding it to change its functionality? Can we hold time? Balance it? Force it? Move it?" He did not provide answers to the questions. No one raised a hand to give a response. Everyone sat still and waited.

Finally, Mr. Ludwig asked a seemingly irrelevant question, which only added to the tangible anticipation in the room. "Who wants to go to New York City at the end of May?"

Eyes shifted back and forth. The students' grins looked like frowns, and everyone raised an arm.

"Super! You each have an equal opportunity to go on an all-expenses-paid trip to New York, with a parent or the adult chaperone of your choice." He produced a stack of stapled packets.

"The top page is a flyer from the National High School Science Fair Competition," he continued. "It will be held on May 3rd at Columbia University in New York City." He moved across the front of the room quickly, handing a stack of papers to the first person in each row. "It's open to all students in the 10th through 12th grades who have won competitions at their regional levels. We'll cover that info on the next page. Notice the theme of this year's competition: *The Time Is Now: Using Science to Expand, Extend and Expose.*"

After handing the last stack to the student in the end row, Mr. Ludwig walked behind the lab desk.

"Next page. Here you will see the location and dates for the upcoming regional competition to be held at the Seattle Convention Center on Friday, April 26th. Next page. The two students from Bainbridge High with the highest scores will represent our community and present their experiments at the regional competition. However, *everyone* is required to prepare an experiment and project for the school competition in three weeks. This doesn't give you much *time*." Mr. Ludwig chuckled at the clever pun. "So you might want to figure out a way to capture that *time*."

A dozen students' arms shot up in the air, competitively waving their hands.

"The bell is going to ring in one minute. Let's *hold* that minute."

A few students sighed and lowered their arms.

"I will need your thesis statements in class on Monday. Check out the parameters the judges will be using to determine the winners. Also, remember what a hypothesis is, how to conduct an experiment, draw conclusions, etc., and the entire model for the Scientific Method, which you will be required to follow strictly. I've included a list of questions to get your brains thinking about possible projects. And finally ..."

The bell rang and most students stood up immediately on cue.

"… don't forget to have the parent permission forms filled out and signed," Mr. Ludwig said over the sound of the bell.

Everyone left the room flipping through papers and talking about how cool it would be to miss a day of school to go to Seattle, and how much more cool it would be to fly to New York City. Most admitted they'd never been there. Reilly had only been as far east as Yakima, and he had never been on a plane.

The rest of the day was a blur of excitement, which made it difficult for Reilly to focus. At lunch, he had no idea of what he was putting on his tray—in fact, later, he couldn't remember if he had even eaten a thing. He totally zoned out during English class and spent the entire period brainstorming possible project ideas, jotting them down on the back of the packet Mr. Ludwig had given him. By the end of school, Reilly had made a list of a dozen or so ideas, but he'd scratched most of them out. He kept only two possibilities to run by his dad.

He reached the bakery in record time, left his bike behind the building as usual and bounded through the back service door waving the packet in the air.

"Mo-om … Da-ad!" He dropped his backpack near the walk-in refrigerator and scanned the kitchen, but he didn't see either of them. He walked into the dining area and saw his mom serving the last slice of pear-glazed tart and a latte to a customer at the counter.

She turned to Reilly with her usual warm smile, and greeted him in her French accent. "Hey, how was your day?"

"Great! Wait till I tell you and Dad what happened in Mr. Ludwig's class. By the way, where *is* Dad? He wasn't in the kitchen."

"It was a little slow around here so he took the boat out. You know Dad—if the sun is shining, he'd rather be sailing. Let's go sit down and you can tell me." Heading towards the corner booth, Reilly grabbed a sticky bun from the display case.

"Look at this, Mom." Reilly pointed to the flyer for the National Science Fair and bit into the bun. "I could go to New York City! Wouldn't that be cool?"

"That would definitely be cool," she said.

"Yeah! First I'd have to win the school competition and then the regional competition—and maybe I wouldn't even get to go to New York—but it *is* a possibility! I *know* I could make it to the regional in Seattle. My idea for a project just came to me and I think it's very original. The judges would like it, but there isn't much time. The school competition is the day before my birthday—in only three weeks! How will I get it all done in that much time?" Reilly finally took a breath and used it to inhale another bite of sticky bun.

"Whoa, slow down!" His mother gently pulled the papers from Reilly's hand. "You chew. I'll read."

She read the entire first page and, without bothering to flip through the other pages, agreed that it was an awesome opportunity. "And you could see Chantal!"

Reilly's sister, Chantal, was ten years older than he was. Because of the difference in age—not to mention the physical distance between them—she felt more like a close cousin than a sister to him. Reilly was barely eight years old when Chantal graduated early from high school and accepted a scholarship to Columbia University to pursue a degree in marketing. Brilliant, she had left home at seventeen with her mother's zeal for exploring different people and places. Six years later, she had already received her Master's degree and was working for a large advertising firm in the heart of the Big Apple. During that time, Chantal only came home for Christmas, the occasional spur-of-the-moment weekend and a week-long break in mid-July each year.

"Yeah, I know. Look! I can take one adult chaperone," he added as he pushed the flyer across the table towards his mom. "Do you think you *and* Dad could come with me? We've never all been in New York together. It would be so much fun!"

"Yes, it sure would," she said, dreamily looking at the poster. "It's been over three years since I've been there myself." She moved the flyer away with a sigh. "But it's just so hard to get away."

"Aw, c'mon, Mom. You and Dad hardly ever close the bakery. We should do it!"

"I appreciate your enthusiasm, Reilly, but even *if* you win … well, I doubt we could afford it."

"That's always the excuse," Reilly snapped.

"I'm sorry."

Reilly frowned but didn't press any further. "I know." He flipped through the papers in an effort to hide his frustration.

"It looks like you've got a lot to do to get ready," his mom said as she handed him the poster. "I'll be home in an hour or so. Let's go over it again then."

"Okay, Mom. I think I'll head to the library and start some research."

Reilly left the bakery without his typical broad smile. He had hoped his mom would be more open to the idea and silently lamented her uncertainty about the possibility of anyone going with him to New York.

Fueled by determination, Reilly focused with acute intensity on his science fair project, which consumed not only his spare time but almost every waking—and perhaps every non-waking—thought. Even he was surprised by his obsession.

Welcoming his preoccupation as a measurable, exhilarating energy, he concluded that it was not so much about the experiment itself, but rather, about a subtle feeling that something remarkable was about to happen in his life.

Chapter Three

The Spell

Reilly's emotions vacillated between the thrill of waiting for Christmas morning and the exhilaration of imagining what it would feel like to fly. He remembered experiencing both feelings as early as age four, and as recently as a month ago. He wondered if others did, too.

Lately, he had been propelled by the euphoria of preparing his science fair project. This was precisely why he forgot to ask either his dad or Eilam about the situation in the bakery with Travis over a week ago.

When Reilly presented his thesis statement to his dad, he was sure his idea was both original and totally awesome.

"Your idea is super," his dad said. "Measuring the speed of refracted light rays relative to its distance traveling through water mixed with other substances is great. But, what if you added the element of salt water to the equation?"

"Salt water?"

"Uh-huh. You could do the same thing, but do it with sea water."

"I didn't think of that!" Reilly was surprised it hadn't crossed his mind. "Yeah. Then the thesis could be 'Energy in the form of light rays travels through salt water at various speeds causing varying distances of refraction.'"

Reilly wrote it down while repeating the words. He glanced up from the paper and stared across the room. "That makes more sense because salt is a conductor of energy, or light, itself." He spoke the words as if it was a secret only he was privy to.

Later, when Reilly told Eilam about his project, he had a sudden epiphany. "Eilam, do you think it's possible to travel through time … through water?"

Eilam tugged gently on his chin, pulling at his scruffy beard, and then repeated something he'd said before. "It's quite remarkable how far a person can travel by sea."

The day of the fair was one of those rare occasions when Reilly had to forgo his morning kayak ride. He awoke earlier than usual and had everything ready to go when his mom returned from the bakery to take him and his project to school.

"I can hardly believe you'll be sixteen tomorrow, Reilly," she said as she lifted his tri-fold display board from the kitchen table. Reilly hoped she wouldn't start getting all nostalgic about past birthdays—or worse, begin her next sentence with, 'remember the time when …' and then bring up some embarrassing thing that happened when he was young. "You've been so busy getting ready for the science fair that we haven't talked about your birthday."

"Weird." He paused, surprised by the direction of the conversation. "I almost forgot about it."

"So, does anything come to mind? Any last-minute birthday requests?" She folded the five-foot by three-foot cardboard in thirds.

"Uhm ... well, not really." He was lying. Reilly secretly hoped his parents would find some way to get them all to New York ... *if*, by chance, he won the regional competition. They were silent as they walked out the front door, their arms loaded with paraphernalia. "I guess we'll just have Eilam come over for cake and ice cream, as we usually do."

Reilly's mom smiled. "That's easy. Anything else?"

Loading everything into the car, Reilly silently debated asking her again if she and his dad could go with him to New York. But he was already feeling out of sync, so he let it go. It was more than just the jitters—so much of his future depended on today's success at the science fair.

"No, just whatever," Reilly said, discontented with his own lack of enthusiasm for his birthday.

They got in the car and pulled out of the garage. "Well, your dad and I just *might* have something else special planned."

"What?" Reilly asked with renewed excitement.

"What ... *what*?" she teased.

"What are the plans?" he insisted.

"Hey, I just said we *might* have something planned. Birthdays are for surprises, are they not? You're not going to get anything more out of me." She turned an invisible key in front of her lips.

"Party pooper!"

The school gymnasium was in chaos when they walked in. Students clumsily bumped into each other as a virtual sea of arms juggled poster boards, notebooks and apparatus. The perimeter of the room was lined with a continuous row of long, conference-style tables. In the center was a small platform with four smaller tables arranged in a square. A staff member at each small table directed students to their assigned locations.

Reilly found the "M" row and waited in line. He noticed Frank Bingham directly across from him. Frank wrinkled his nose and turned up the left side of his upper lip when he saw Reilly. Awkwardly holding a massive box that looked something like a diorama, Frank puffed out his chest and lifted his head higher.

Finally, Reilly was told to go to the far east corner of the gym, where he found his name card fixed to a table. His mom only stayed long enough to open the display board and place it on the table.

Reilly carefully unpacked the contents of his project: prisms of various sizes, eye droppers, a container of salt, a roll of paper towels, a measuring tape, latex gloves, a gallon jug filled with sea water, empty beakers, stirring rods, sealed glass bottles filled with various liquids and sediments, and a thick spiral bound report. He meticulously placed each item at its predetermined spot and hung a banner that read "How Fast Can Light Travel Through Salt Water?" over the entire display area.

Reilly stepped back to critique the overall visual effect. The banner was an attention grabber and the display board was eye-catching, though not overdone. Every step of the Scientific Method was clearly visible, with the results easily identifiable. His report included pages of research, data and analysis, an explanation of the experiment and thorough conclusions. Equally impressive was the apparatus showing the experimental processes and comparative results.

Reilly glanced around at the neighboring exhibits and noted that some looked really cool. But he felt renewed confidence and decided he had a good chance of representing his school in Seattle.

The school buzzed with commotion and excitement throughout the entire day. Students could hardly focus in class, so some teachers chose to show DVDs. Reilly zoned out completely in history class as the movie narrator droned on about the impact state legislators had had on government policy throughout the early part of the 20th century.

It was an assembly-day schedule, which meant shortened class periods and added distraction. Rather than attending an actual assembly, students were allowed to go to the gym during the period following their lunch to look at the displays. This was also the time when the judges questioned the students on their projects. School ended fifty minutes early so everyone could go home and get geared up to return with their families that evening.

Reilly stopped by the bakery to get a muffin and a loaf of cinnamon swirl bread. He stuffed the bread in his backpack and ate the muffin in three big bites. Then he left for the kayak hut.

It was a sunny spring day, which was a nice change from the rain that was typical at this time of year. Within minutes he was at the head of the dock. He leaned his bike against a tree, and with his usual smile picked up his pace when his eyes met Eilam's.

"Hi, Eilam. I brought you some cinnamon bread."

"Ah, you must have read my mind. Thank you." Eilam gently held out both hands in an awkward cup to receive the bread, the way he always did. "I was just ready to take a little break. Let's paddle over to my place and have some bread and cheese with a cup of tea." He stood up from his Adirondack chair and walked behind the counter.

"School got out early today so I've got more time than usual."

"I'd love to hear how things have come together for tonight's big event." Eilam looked Reilly in the eye as he fumbled for something under the counter. He pulled out a small sign and propped it up in front of the cash register: *Be back soon. Fill out paper work. Help yourself to a kayak. Pay later.* He put a few "Consent and Release" forms next to the sign and placed his palm on the papers for a brief moment.

Having watched Eilam put the sign up several times, Reilly figured people probably questioned Eilam's business practices. But Reilly knew Eilam came from a time when a person's word was good and honesty was valued. The fact remained that Eilam had never had a kayak stolen, and Reilly had never heard him say he felt cheated.

They got in a double kayak and eased out across the water. Reilly savored the salty air. He thought this was as perfect as life could get.

They pulled up to Eilam's place and looped the kayak rope around a spike secured to the small dock. For as long as the McNamaras had known Eilam, he had lived in the small thirteen-by-twenty-foot structure that floated a quarter of the way across Eagle Harbor. Reilly stepped inside and scanned the two-room home. Everything was just as it had always been: a small living area combined with a much smaller kitchen, a dresser and a single bed in one corner and a door that led to a tiny bathroom. All was simple and tidy.

They sat at a small round table, Eilam on the only kitchen chair and Reilly on an empty, upturned five-gallon bucket sometimes used for holding live crabs. A pale yellow hand towel was draped over the top to serve as a cushion for Eilam's only regular visitor—Reilly.

Eilam set out a block of cheddar cheese and Reilly removed the twist tie from the cinnamon bread.

"Is everything ready for tonight?" Eilam asked.

"Yeah, it's all set up. Wait till you see how many projects there are! Some of them are pretty cool."

"I'm looking forward to it." Eilam handed Reilly a chunk of cheese.

They ate in comfortable silence. Then, Reilly remembered he was going to ask his friend about Travis and his dad in the bakery a few weeks earlier.

"Eilam," he began hesitantly, "do you remember a few weeks ago when we were in the bakery before school and Mr. Jackson showed up?"

"Yes."

"When I came around the corner on my bike, I could see him yelling at my dad. And then he pointed his finger at you."

"Yes."

"What was that all about? I mean, Frank Bingham keeps telling me Dad isn't keeping up some kind of an agreement they made, but I know Dad always has everything ready to go with the bread orders for the club. And I've never heard anything about Mr. Jackson not wanting me to keep our sailboat or my kayak at his marina, although he does give me creepy looks. It makes me sort of nervous."

"Yes, I imagine it would."

"So, what do you know about an agreement between Mr. Jackson and my dad? Does it involve you?" Reilly started on his second piece of bread and waited for a reply.

"Of course, I cannot speak for your dad. You will have to ask him about anything between him and Mr. Jackson. But I will tell you a story that may help you better understand Travis Jackson." He took a sip of tea and continued. "I used to know a good and honest man who lived in a town overseas. He was the town's magistrate."

"A magistrate?"

"Like a mayor ... someone who was elected by the people to represent them and help keep their town safe. The people in the town were very poor but the magistrate did all he could to assist them, though he himself was not very well off."

"One day his daughter was playing in the town hall, waiting for her father to finish his day's work. The girl discovered a secret passageway, which twisted and turned under the building, and led her to a very unusual place filled with beauty and wealth like nothing she had ever imagined."

"Really?" Reilly whispered.

"She would visit that place often and bring back riches to share with the people of the town. Possibilities and opportunities became abundant; poverty and deprivation all but disappeared. The people began to have hope and started to believe dreams really could come true."

Reilly stopped eating just to listen.

"But there was also an ornery and mean man who lived at the edge of town. People called him the Griffin because he was so beastly, selfish, and greedy. The Griffin wanted access to the hidden wealth, and he spent many years trying to figure out how he could get it all for himself." Eilam paused to take a drink.

"Did he figure it out?"

"No. Never."

"Then what did he do?"

"He defamed the name of the magistrate and his daughter. Using deceit and trickery, he convinced some of the people that the place of endless beauty and wealth did not actually exist. He told the people that the riches had come from the magistrate's personal stash and someday it would all be gone, and everyone would be destitute again. Over time, many people became fearful; only a few still believed in their dreams. Then a stranger named Malie came to town and offered to help the magistrate do something with the Griffin."

"What did he do?"

"How he did it no one knew, but Malie turned that selfish man into a gargoyle, chiseled out of obsidian because his heart had been so hard and dark. The people gave the stranger the honorable title of Malie the Magician. But Malie did not stay long in their town, and after he left, the secret place of endless beauty and wealth was closed. The girl and her father could no longer help the people as they had been doing. Meanwhile, the gargoyle sat motionless outside the entrance to the town hall. Until the spell was broken, the Griffin was cursed to remain a statue."

"What would break the spell?" Reilly peered at Eilam.

"Only one thing can break the spell of all evil." Eilam's green eyes looked deeply into Reilly's. "Love."

Reilly grimaced. "You mean like romance and fairy tale stuff?"

"No. This would require the deepest kind of love, that of compassion and forgiveness—the very essence of love."

"Oh."

"The people of the town would need to feel compassion for the Griffin and forgive him for his lies, unkindness and greed. Whenever anyone harbored ill will towards the beast or said he'd got what he deserved, the spell increased and the evil grew stronger and stronger in the gargoyle. It became more and more difficult for the people to forgive—and love—not only the beast, but each other, as well. This, too, made the evil increase. But the people didn't know this—not even the magistrate or his daughter did. Only Malie the Magician understood it." Eilam took another sip of tea.

"But how could the people learn to love such a horrible creature if Malie didn't tell them how to do it?" Reilly asked.

"It was up to each of them to search his or her own heart."

Now speechless, Reilly could not take his eyes off Eilam. Finally, he replied. "Mr. Jackson is kind of like a gargoyle."

"Yes."

"And when he was yelling at my dad and pointing at you, you knew it wasn't really about you. It was coming from a man who didn't feel any love inside of himself."

"Yes," Eilam smiled. But Reilly noticed the old man's eyes looked sad.

They sat in silence for a few more minutes before returning to the kayak hut. Reilly told Eilam his family would pick him up for the science fair, and then he left for home on his bike.

The McNamaras ate dinner earlier than usual and although Reilly had intended to ask his dad about the agreement with

Travis, he decided to wait until after the science fair. Eilam's story had given him more than enough to think about.

The gym was packed! Everyone moved clockwise around the perimeter of the room, following the giant black-and-neon-orange arrows painted on the walls that guided people to *MOVE THIS WAY, PLEASE* .

People pretended to be interested in all the displays, but the truth was most parents were anxious to find their own child's project and listen for any glowing comments about it. Rows and rows of chairs, set up for the awards ceremony, filled the center of the room.

The McNamaras and Eilam moved slowly around the gym, taking their time as they gave each project an honest critique. When they reached Frank Bingham's diorama, showing the depth of the ocean floor in the Puget Sound, Frank and Travis Jackson both stood behind the table with wide grins, looking eager to receive compliments. Reilly thought it was an impressive 3-D art display, attractively covered in a shiny lacquer, but he noticed that Frank had left out a clear hypothesis and thesis statement.

"Cool display," Reilly offered. "What did you use to make it so shiny?"

"Uncle Travis's sailboat resin. It makes anything it sticks to as solid as rock," Frank said, puffing out his chest.

"Yeah, you remember when I invented my patented resin, don't you, Kevin?" Travis said, stealing a glance at Reilly's mom, who purposely busied herself looking at Frank's research paper. "The resin gives the boats an advantage in racing. It'll likely take Frank to the regional competition." Travis patted his nephew's back so hard the boy had to catch himself to keep from falling into the diorama.

Reilly's dad nodded to Travis as Eilam and Reilly exchanged a quick glance. But Reilly's mom kept facing the Admiralty Inlet on the diorama until they moved with the flow of traffic towards Reilly's display.

Eilam had not seen Reilly's work yet and quietly took the time to look over his project. Reilly stood by while his parents continued on to reserve chairs for the ceremony, which would start in five minutes.

When Eilam finished reading the report, he paused to look again at the banner. Then, putting both hands firmly on Reilly's shoulders and looking deeply into his eyes, he said, "Yes, it is remarkable how far a person can travel by sea."

To confirm his earlier epiphany, Reilly opened his mouth to ask Eilam if he was saying what he thought he was saying. But the sentence was halted by a screeching noise from a microphone set at too high a level and a blaring voice asking everyone to please take a seat. It took a long minute for the tech people to adjust the microphone and sound system; meanwhile, the noise level in the room raised additional decibels with moaning comments from numerous people as they covered their ears. Eilam and Reilly quietly made their way to their seats.

The principal thanked the people who had adjusted the sound and offered the usual welcome-and-we're-glad-you-could-all-be-here-this-evening speech. He then introduced Mr. Ludwig, who would present the awards, and the team of judges. The awards presentation began with honorable mentions and third- and second-place winners for each grade level. Mr. Ludwig held the microphone closer to his mouth to make the final presentations.

"As you may know, we will be sending two students to the regional competition next week in Seattle," Mr. Ludwig began. "The judges have given these students the highest overall scores in every category of the contest. They have demonstrated not only a firm understanding of the Scientific Method, but have been thorough in their research, data, and conclusions in an organized and creative manner. Additionally, these students have exhibited an innovative interpretation of the national theme, *The Time is Now: Using Science to Expand, Extend and Expose.* Most significantly, these individuals have expanded our minds to reach interesting possibilities and allowed us to consider unique approaches to science, which we may not have explored before. Is that not what science truly is?"

Noticeably restless, the students grew worried that Mr. Ludwig might go on and on, as he often did in class. There was an audible sigh as he turned to the table behind him and picked up two large blue ribbons.

"The first first-place winner, with an overall score of 95, is ... Malauri Jacobson!"

Applause burst forth in the room as Malauri found her way to the portable stage to receive her ribbon and certificate. Reilly smiled as he clapped, but he sighed, too. He began to wonder if he'd be going to New York after all.

Mr. Ludwig waited until the applause ended before clearing his throat.

"Our top first-place winner, with a score of 99, is ... Reilly McNamara, with his project titled, *How Fast Can Light Travel Through Salt Water?*"

Cheers erupted and everyone stood to applaud.

"I won?" Reilly looked at his parents and then at Eilam. "I won!"

"Well, get up there," his dad said.

Eilam laughed. Reilly's mom gave him a quick hug before he walked to the stage to receive his award.

The two winners were asked to pose with Mr. Ludwig for an official acceptance photo taken by a photographer from *The Bainbridge Review.* The McNamaras and Eilam made their way to the stage, along with a number of other people, to congratulate Reilly.

Handing an information packet to Reilly, Mr. Ludwig interrupted their chatter on the stage. "Make sure you get this filled out and faxed to me tomorrow," he said. "Reilly, you're going to Seattle!"

"Thanks, Mr. Ludwig. I will." Reilly took the packet and shook his teacher's hand.

As the crowd dispersed and the commotion created by students dismantling their projects dissipated, Reilly saw Frank and his uncle heading up the main aisle. Frank's giant diorama in his arms did not hide his seething stare. Travis stopped directly in front of Reilly's dad and looked him straight in the eye.

"Nice work, Kevin," he oozed. "It's obvious whose idea *this* project was. But the thing is you're no closer to realizing your dream than you were twenty-five years ago. You should've taken my offer back then." He leaned in closer. "As far as I'm concerned, our deal is off. Someone else will have to fund your expedition. Not that you'll *ever* pursue it!"

Frank had stared at Reilly with disgust during the entire speech. He and his uncle turned to leave before Reilly's dad could say anything. Then, when they were about ten feet away, Travis turned and added, "It's funny that you're in the *dough* business and know so little about making any real money."

Reilly scowled. "What was *that* all about?"

His dad paused briefly. "Let's gather your things and we'll talk about it in the car, son."

Reilly clenched his jaw, knowing there was no point in pressing the matter right then. "Okay," he said.

He noticed Travis and Frank exiting the room at the far end, and turned to Eilam for reassurance.

Eilam nodded gently and whispered, "Gargoyle."

When they got in the car, Eilam asked to see Reilly's blue ribbon.

"Eilam, would you go with me to the regional competition?" Reilly said. "My parents can't go cuz they've got end-of-the-month accounting and a huge order for a wedding dinner that day."

"Of course, Reilly. I would be delighted to join you."

Pulling up to the dock near Eilam's place, Reilly got right to the point of what had been on his mind during the past week.

"Dad, do you believe a person can time travel through water? Like through some kind of portal in the ocean? Is that what your thesis paper was about?"

Reilly watched his dad glance at his wife in the front passenger seat, and then at Eilam, who met his gaze in the rearview mirror.

"Some things really *are* simply a matter of time," his dad replied. Then, turning to face Reilly, he said, "Yes, I do." It was spoken with conviction and without apology. "Would you like the whole story?"

"Yes, I would."

"Let's walk Eilam down to the kayak hut and I'll tell you the whole thing there."

Reilly turned to look at Eilam, but the man had already opened the car door and was standing outside.

Under the extended awning of the hut, Eilam sat in his usual chair and Reilly's mom pulled up a stool. Reilly sat next to Eilam on the arm of the Adirondack, and his dad straddled the end of an overturned kayak.

"As you know, I grew up near the sea and I've always loved to sail, as did my father and my grandfather," Reilly's dad began. "My grandfather, your Great Grandpa Alistair McNamara, lived in a lighthouse on the coast of Ireland. He had been alone until he was nearly forty, when he met a young woman who came to their town to teach school. She hadn't been given accurate directions to the schoolhouse, and on the first day of her new job, she got lost on a country road that took her to Grandpa's lighthouse. From the moment their eyes met, they knew it was a love that was meant to be. Grandpa Alistair loved his wife more than life itself. Later, she died giving birth to their only child, my father. Grandpa Alistair was overcome with a grief so deep that he could hardly get out of bed. He didn't have the strength to care for his new son. Neighbors and members of the local parish came each day to help with the baby." Reilly's dad paused, but he kept his eyes on Reilly.

"After a few weeks, someone he didn't recognize came to offer assistance. It was an older man who said he was passing through the town. He asked if anyone might be willing to give him room and board in exchange for his services. Grandpa Alistair accepted the man's help, though he thought it was strange that a man older than himself—who did not seem to have a family of his own—would know much about taking care of an infant. But the man was a natural, and the baby was very content in his care."

Shifting slightly, Reilly's dad continued.

"One morning, about two months later, Grandpa Alistair woke to the sound of his son crying. He wondered why the older man wasn't taking care of the baby. Finally, he got out of bed, but couldn't find the man anywhere. He went to the baby's cradle, and as he picked up his son—who was your Grandpa Angus—something fell from the blanket. It was a glistening stone, chiseled like a misshapen star. Luminescent—whiter and brighter than anything he had ever seen—it sparkled like a giant diamond. It was so clear that he could see right through it. Holding his son in one arm, he reached to pick up the stone. When he touched it, he felt a sudden urge, a compulsion, to go out to sea. So he bundled up his son, placed him in a small wooden crate, which he used as carrier, and took the child on his first sail."

Reilly's eyes widened. "Where did they go?"

"I remember my father telling me the stone worked like a compass, showing his father the way through a portal in the water—a doorway to where Great Grandma McNamara had gone. Apparently, they went back and forth to that place a number of times, but my father was too young to remember. As my father grew up, Great Grandpa Alistair told him stories of their adventures through time and space, and of using the stone to guide them."

"But how—?" Reilly interrupted, but his dad raised his hand and continued.

"One day, when he was old enough to appreciate its significance, Great Grandpa gave his son the stone, called a Stelladaur, as a gift. 'The Stelladaur will lead you to your greatest desire,' he told his son. 'Most everyone has a wish, but only some have a true *greatest desire.*' When my father asked Great Grandpa how he would know if he had a greatest desire, he replied, 'A wish becomes a greatest desire at the very moment when a person's belief in the seemingly impossible is stronger than any doubt.'"

Reilly didn't move. He hardly breathed.

"By holding the Stelladaur at a certain angle to the sun, a person can look into it and realize that belief *is* the key that unlocks the door of uncertainty. That's when imagination becomes tangible."

Reilly's mind raced with more questions but he felt a strange stillness.

His dad paused a moment to look at his wife and at Eilam. Then he began again.

"There's more, Reilly. Great Grandpa Alistair never remarried, and he died when your Grandpa Angus was only nineteen. More than anything, my father wanted to leave Ireland and come to America. He believed the Stelladaur would work for him, as it had for his father. And it did. One sunny day, while he held the stone up to the window and watching the colors of the rainbow dance off the walls of the lighthouse, the moment that turns a wish to a greatest desire *happened*. A strange thought came to his mind: he should go immediately to the local mercantile. Without hesitation, he left for the store. Wandering around the mercantile for a while, he wasn't quite sure what to do next. He picked up a pound of nails that he needed to repair a picket fence and went to the counter to pay. There, near the cash register, was a newsprint flyer advertising a lighthouse for sale in America—in Puget Sound, Washington. When your Grandpa Angus asked the clerk where he'd found the flyer, he said an old man—someone he didn't recognize—had brought it in a few minutes earlier.

"Through this series of events, based on my father's belief that the impossible was his for the asking, his greatest desire—to come to America—became a reality. And that's where I grew up, in a little house beside the lighthouse your grandpa purchased."

Reilly adjusted his position on the arm of the Adirondack, but kept his focus on his dad. It was dark now, and a gentle breeze came in off the water.

"So Great Grandpa Alistair *did* find a portal through the water to another time or another world ... or something?"

"Apparently so."

"But your dad never showed you where it was?"

"He never knew himself. But he believed his father had told him the truth about their adventures together when he was just a baby. That's one of the reasons the Stelladaur worked for him. He believed. My dad's greatest desire was to come to America, not to find the portal. A person only finds a *true* greatest desire when he follows his own heart."

Reilly looked at Eilam, remembering the story he had recounted earlier that day. Was there a connection? He reviewed in his mind what Eilam had said: *It was up to each of them to search his own heart.*

He still had so many questions, particularly one he had already asked but did not get an answer to.

"So Mr. Jackson knows that you think there is a portal in the ocean somewhere?"

"Yes. When I first met Travis Jackson, the same night I met your mother at the benefit dinner at the Elliot Bay Yacht Club, he overheard me talking with my professor about my thesis. My professor and I were discussing some of the scientific aspects of the project. I told him I had reason to believe there was a portal through the ocean off the coast of Ireland and that my father had been through that very portal. My professor was interested, and not at all surprised. But we were interrupted, and it wasn't really the time or place to continue the conversation anyway. Unfortunately, the next week my professor died of a heart attack. I wished then that I hadn't told him what I knew."

"Why?" Reilly asked.

"Well, truthfully, I wished I had told him about it sooner. I knew he would believe me," his dad continued, "but I was careless when I told him about it at a place where others might hear. Anyway, a short time later Travis approached me with a business proposition. He had obtained a copy of my thesis and said he believed his fiberglass resin used on the hull of racing sailboats—"

"—the resin Frank used on his diorama," Reilly interrupted.

"Uh-huh. Travis said the resin had the necessary chemical properties to hone in to unusual stimuli in water, maybe even a portal. He had big plans for us to become partners. He saw dollar signs, but I knew better."

"What did you tell him?"

"I told him I wasn't interested."

"That's all?"

"Well, I knew my grandpa had used his Stelladaur to open a portal, but it worked because he was motivated by love, not by greed."

"Right."

"Travis said if I ever changed my mind he would fund the expedition to Ireland and give me a thousand shares of *Imperial Plastics*. That would be worth an awful lot of money today! And over the years he's convinced himself that I had agreed to tell him what I might know about the portal."

"Did you tell him anything else?"

"No. I only told him he'd have to find it on his own. He's spent two decades and millions of dollars searching."

"No wonder he's so frustrated." Reilly thought for a moment, and everyone else remained quiet. "But who was the old man that came to help Great Grandpa Alistair with his son? And who was the man that left the flyer at the hardware store?"

"His name was Malie," Reilly's dad said.

"Malie?" Reilly turned quickly to Eilam. "You mean like *Malie the Magician*?"

"Malie is one of his names," Eilam nodded.

"And he also goes by Eilam," his dad interjected.

Chapter Four

A Wish and a Knife

It was true. Eilam really *had* lived a very long time.

Reilly lay awake that night for some time, reviewing everything his father and Eilam had told him. He rewrote the name in his mind: E-I-L-A-M, and then backwards. It was a realization of profound proportions. M-A-L-I-E!

Questions raced through Reilly's mind. He decided to ask his dad the next time they had some quiet time together, or perhaps some answers would come to him when he least expected it. He fell asleep wondering what else he might have missed.

The next morning Reilly's decision to question his dad for more answers was diverted when he found a note stuck to the refrigerator: "Happy Birthday! We'll be home early to go sailing!" With so many unusual things to think about, his birthday hardly seemed important. Nevertheless, for Reilly, sailing was truly magical, and he went with his dad every chance he could. His mom usually stayed at the bakery, so sailing as a family, and with Eilam, was exciting, and his mind filled with anticipation.

During the summer months, Reilly and his dad sailed more frequently on Sundays, if it happened to be a good-weather-day. Fortunately, this April 21st not only landed on a Sunday, but also it was unseasonably sunny with only a few high clouds, and there were perfect winds for sailing at a comfortable three knots.

When Reilly's parents returned in the early afternoon they loaded a cooler and headed to the marina. They motored to Eilam's place, and on their arrival, the old friend handed Reilly's mom a bag of red grapes, his contribution to the birthday picnic. Eilam took Reilly's elbow to board *The Ark*. Reilly's dad took the wheel and they sailed out of Eagle Harbor, heading towards Blake Island. Two seals perched on nearby rocks barked noisily.

"Listen," Reilly laughed. "They're singing Happy Birthday to me." He started barking out the melody and the others joined in.

After docking, they spent an hour walking trails and then stopped to catch the matinée showing of a Native American dance festival at the resident long house. Following the presentation, they found a picnic spot east of the marina and pulled everything out of the cooler. All of Reilly's favorites: smoked salmon, potato salad, chips with mango salsa, fresh dinner rolls and red grapes. His mom presented a German chocolate cake and carefully placed 16 spiral candles on top.

Later, when the candles were lit and Reilly had taken a deep breath, Eilam interjected, "Remember, a wish is different from a greatest desire Reilly."

Reilly slowly let out his breath to the side and watched the tiny flames flicker. He wasn't sure he had a greatest desire, or if he'd know when he did have one. But he *did* have a wish—something he'd wished for on every birthday since he was four years old.

So, on his 16th birthday, Reilly made the same wish again. He wished for a dog. It didn't matter what kind of dog—any dog would do, unless of course it was a little yapper. The truth was that Reilly wanted a big dog like a husky or a retriever. Logically, it wasn't feasible because his dad was allergic to dogs. But Reilly took a deep breath and made the wish anyway, blowing out all the candles but one. He stared at the single flame and watched the wax drool down the candle.

"That's weird," he said. "I've always blown them all out on the first try. Maybe it means something." He sighed and gave a gentle *poof* to blow out the final one.

"Naw, it just means you're getting too old," his mom said, pulling off the candles before the wax melted onto the coconut frosting.

"When you're as old as Eilam you'll need a blow torch." His Dad laughed. Eilam winked at Reilly as he attempted to straighten his hunched shoulders.

Reilly devoured a big piece of cake and then finished off another more slowly.

"We ought to start heading back before sunset," his Dad began. "What do you say we pack up?"

"Sounds good, Dad. This has been a great birthday. Thanks."

"Aren't we forgetting something?" Reilly's mom looked at her husband.

"What?"

"What? You know *what*, you big tease."

"Oh, right. We do have a small surprise." Reilly's dad grinned as he pulled a plain envelope from his jacket pocket and handed it to him.

Reilly couldn't imagine what it would be. He turned it over to examine the seal, trying to decide which direction to tear it open, or if he should just rip off the entire end of the envelope.

"Wait," Eilam began, reaching into his pocket, "this may help."

Eilam handed Reilly a knife, unlike any he had seen before. About seven inches in length, it did not fold in half like the pocketknife Eilam usually carried with him. The blade fit perfectly in a thick leather sheath and had a handle made of intricately carved ivory. He carefully pulled the blade from the sheath and paused to look at the shiny metal. He noticed the top of the handle was made of silver with a faint engraving of a star.

"Wow!"

"You like it!" Eilam declared.

"Yeah! It's awesome! Where did you get it?"

"The magistrate's daughter brought it back from the place of endless beauty and wealth. She gave it to me as a token of gratitude for keeping the Griffin from destroying the dreams of her people. I have saved it all these years to give to someone who would appreciate it and use it wisely. It's yours now, Reilly. Happy birthday."

Reilly couldn't think of anything to say. He tucked the envelope under his arm and examined the knife closely, running his fingers over the blade's surface and over the ivory handle. When he traced his finger over the star, he felt a gentle electric zap.

"Thank you," he whispered. "I'll take good care of it."

"I know you will."

No one said anything for a minute. It was a solemn moment, during which something from the pages of history that had never been written connected to pages that may never be believed.

Tentatively breaking the silence, Reilly's mom suggested that he open the envelope.

Reilly handed the leather sheath to Eilam, and then, holding the envelope in his left hand, carefully placed the tip of the blade at the corner of the paper. The knife slid effortlessly along the top of the envelope, making a perfect slice.

He passed the knife to Eilam and pulled out a piece of cardstock with the words **American Airlines** written across the top.

He scanned the computer-printed information. It was a round-trip ticket to New York City.

"Huh? I don't get it."

"Well, we starting thinking," his mom bubbled. "It's been much too long since you've seen your sister. We decided whether you go on to the national competition or not, you're going to New York City!" She nearly sang the words.

"I'm sorry we can't afford for us all to go," his dad said. "But we were able to get a great Internet special on a ticket for you." Just then, his cell phone rang. "Hi, Chantal. Yeah, perfect timing … Reilly just opened the envelope." He handed the phone to his son.

"Hey, Chan." The 'ch' was soft like her name.

"Happy birthday! Wow! Sixteen, huh? That's getting up there, brother. Bet the girls are gaga over you, huh?" She couldn't resist teasing him right away.

"No, they're not," he insisted.

"Right."

"Whatever."

Plenty of girls flirted with Reilly but he just wasn't interested in anyone in particular. No one seemed to capture his attention the way he thought it ought to feel when a guy really likes a girl.

"So what do you think about your gift?"

"It's way cool! Can you believe it? I'm coming to see you!"

"Yep, and my gift to you is that I'm taking a few vacation days to hang out and escort you to the competition—*if* you win next week in Seattle. I'll show you all the sights: Ellis Island, Ground Zero, Fifth Avenue shopping, a Broadway show, Central Park … the works! How does that sound?"

"Wow! I'm going to New York! I can hardly wait to see you."

"Me, too. It's going to be great," she agreed. "Look, I've got to run. I'll call you in a day or so. Think about what show you want to see, and anything else that sounds fun. We're going to have a blast, Reilly. Bye."

"Bye, Chan."

Reilly smiled his typical broad smile.

"Thanks, Mom. Thanks, Dad. This is the best birthday ever." Reilly gave his parents quick hugs and then turned to Eilam.

Eilam handed the knife back to Reilly.

"Thank you." He hoped Eilam knew how much he loved the gift.

"You are welcome."

The following week, it was a drizzly ferry ride to Seattle for the competition. Reilly and Eilam didn't go out on the upper deck so they could keep Reilly's display items dry. They took a cab from Colman Dock at Pier 52 to the convention center and meandered up three flights of escalators to the main exhibit hall.

The sheer numbers of people and displays was chaos times ten. However, things flowed smoothly for Reilly as he signed in, found his name tag, reached his assigned set-up area and actually got everything ready to go in the forty minutes they had before the exhibit opened to the public.

The regional competition was conducted differently than his school science fair. Every hour between 10:00 a.m. and 4:00 p.m. a different judge interviewed each student, making a total of six adjudications. The judges asked numerous in-depth questions to test the students' knowledge of their own findings and how their discovery related to other aspects of the scientific world. The remainder of each hour was spent observing the students' responses to comments and questions from the public who wandered around the massive hall.

Only one thing about this process made Reilly nervous. He was given a three-page list of judges, each of whom had different science-related expertise. Scanning the list, Reilly noticed Travis Jackson's name—staring at him like a halogen flashlight in a dark tunnel.

The students didn't know which judges had been assigned to them and the uncertainty of it caused Reilly to be on the verge of hyperventilation every hour, before the new judge showed up. Eilam told him not to worry and that things would work out. However, Reilly's anxiety overshadowed his ability to remain hopeful.

As the last hour of the competition approached, Reilly felt optimistic that his luck with the assigned judges would hold out—until he spotted Travis heading directly towards him. Reilly held his breath and turned to look at Eilam, who smiled and simply said, "It will be all right."

Much to Reilly's surprise, Travis walked right past them and stopped at a display two tables down the row. Eilam nodded at Reilly and smiled wider.

At the end of the judging period, a voice over the loud speaker announced a 90-minute break for a catered dinner in the grand banquet hall on the second floor, after which the awards ceremony would begin in the adjacent auditorium.

Reilly ate heartily, famished from the judges' rigorous questioning. Everyone reconvened for the awards, and Reilly and Eilam found two seats only a few rows from the stage.

"I'm glad you could be here with me, Eilam," Reilly said after they sat down. "Thanks."

"Of course. I'll always be here for you, Reilly."

"I know."

Reilly looked around the room at the hundreds of competitors, each full of anticipation, hoping to place in the competition. Reilly's stomach was doing somersaults, and his brain was caught in a maze of confusion. *I think I'm going to win. But doesn't everyone else think they will win? Am I just wishing? No, this is more than that. Is it a greatest desire? How the heck am I supposed to know? I must be going crazy!*

An Honorable Mention would have satisfied him, except that he knew it wouldn't be in sync with the impending feeling that something greater was happening in his life. Something out of the ordinary. On the other hand, he knew only one First-Place winner from each grade-level would be chosen to go to the national competition. He was annoyed with himself for mentally vacillating between the two points, and he wished his stomach would settle down and his brain would shut up.

After announcing the Honorable Mention awards—none of which Reilly received—the emcee drew out the final announcement almost longer than Reilly could tolerate. The man presenting the awards reminded all the students that each of their efforts was to be commended; he talked about the difficult judging process; he thanked each of the financial sponsors of the competition by name; and he gave instructions on how the disassembling of the displays was to happen efficiently.

Finally, Reilly held his breath for the 10th grade winner to be announced. Filled with anticipation, excitement and that confusing impending feeling, Reilly tapped his fingers nervously on his knee.

"Relax," Eilam said, gently tossing his braid behind him.

Reilly let out his breath and sat on his hands.

"And the first place winner for 10th grade is …" the emcee paused "… Reilly McNamara from Bainbridge Island, Washington!"

At that moment, Reilly's stomach met his brain halfway—in the middle of his chest. Somewhere inside his thumping aorta, Reilly knew this was indeed the beginning of an unusual adventure. A journey that would not take him only to New York City—but elsewhere.

As Reilly stood on stage to receive his award, his eyes met Eilam's. The expression on Eilam's face told Reilly that Eilam knew exactly where *elsewhere* was.

Chapter Five

Interrogation

To his utter dismay, and since it was his first time flying, Reilly's mom insisted she and her husband get an escorting-a-minor pass and go right to the gate with Reilly. Waiting in the boarding line for the flight attendant to call his row number, Reilly stepped away from his mom.

"Mom, stop hovering," he insisted. "You can go now."

"C'mon, Monique," his dad added as he pulled at her elbow. "He'll be just fine. This is an adventure we should have let him go on some time ago."

Reilly turned to face the gate as the passengers ahead of him started to move forward. Not turning to wave goodbye, Reilly heard his mom's voice trail off in the distance.

"… I know, I just have this feeling … something … much tougher … competition …"

Reilly brushed it aside and moved down the breezeway to board the plane. After finding his seat and opening the air vent above his head, he looked out the window until takeoff, and then watched everything below him get smaller and smaller. As the altitude of the plane increased and the Puget Sound began to look more like a series of puddles, Reilly remembered the fun he'd had as a kid stomping through mud puddles on rainy days. *Wouldn't it be cool if I was a kid again but as big as a giant and could go from Lake Washington to the other side of the Tacoma Narrows Bridge in one step?* He felt silly with the thought, as he continued to watch the Earth below disappear into the white clouds. Closing his eyes, he smiled, knowing that he was actually going to New York City—to see his sister!

It was a nonstop flight. The passenger next to Reilly put earplugs in the minute he sat down and slept the entire flight. Reilly was content to look out the window at the wisps of clouds and daydream, or think about the sights he would see with Chantal. However, he spent most of the time contemplating all he had recently learned about Eilam, his grandfather, his great-grandfather and portals. The five-hour flight seemed like only forty-five minutes.

Reilly saw Chantal waiting at the gate and smiled broadly when their eyes met. He ran to meet his sister and threw his arms around her.

"Chan!" he squeaked. "I'm here! Can you believe it?"

"Yep, you're here!" She hugged him tightly. "And I *can* believe it, cuz I've been thinking about it nonstop since your birthday!" She loosened her hold and held her hands at his shoulders, squeezing his biceps. "You've grown, kiddo. How was the flight? This was your first time on a plane, huh?"

"Yeah," Reilly pulled away and picked up his backpack. "It was way fun and it seemed really quick but they didn't feed us much. Can we get some food? I'm starved."

"Absolutely. There's a pizza place around the corner from my apartment. New York has the best pizza anywhere … You do still love pizza, right?" she teased.

"Of course!" He smiled.

After waiting twenty minutes for the luggage, they stepped outside the terminal to hail a taxi. Fortunately, a driver was waiting at the curb with the passenger door and trunk already open. The man took Reilly's luggage from his hand, and with a Jamaican accent and a great deal of gusto, he said, "Welcome you to New York City, sir!"

Reilly hopped in first and scooted over behind the driver's seat. Waiting for Chantal and the driver to get situated, he noticed a photo of a young boy—maybe seven years old—and a woman, taped to the dashboard. The driver asked Reilly and Chantal where they were headed and then began to whistle. Using the steering wheel as a percussion instrument, he whistled, hummed or bebopped as he drove. Reilly wanted to ask the man about the photo—about the boy in it, staring back at him. But he was distracted by Chantal's continual tour-guide comments as she pointed out numerous places of interest, so he decided not to inquire about the boy.

When they arrived at the pizza place, the driver assisted Reilly with his luggage and offered him his business card. "Now you enjoy this day! And please, sir, I would appreciate it if you would call me again."

Chantal paid the man with a generous tip and thanked him for his help. Reilly smiled and turned to wave goodbye as he pulled his luggage towards the restaurant. The man's cheerfulness helped Reilly feel more at ease in his new surroundings but claustrophobia engulfed him as they entered the packed restaurant. He had the sudden urge to be gliding in his kayak across Eagle Harbor.

Chantal sensed his anxiety. "Once you get some food, things won't seem so overwhelming. The sun-dried tomato with olives and artichokes is delicious." She smiled. "It has a fabulous home-made pesto sauce and they load it with Feta and Gouda. What sounds good to you?"

Reilly wasn't sure. Once they were seated, he glanced over the menu quickly, but didn't actually read it. "I guess I'll have that pesto kind, the one with the artichokes."

They ordered a large to share and spent the next hour catching up as Chantal rattled off questions: How are Mom and Dad? Do you wish they could have come, too? Have they tried any new reci-pes for the bakery? What recipes? Were they a hit? How is Eilam? Are you nervous about the science fair?

Reilly relaxed as he ate and talked about familiar things. He told his sister about the school competition and Travis's outburst, the regional event and how glad he was that Travis wasn't one of his judges, and his birthday sail over to Blake Island. It wasn't until they finished eating, walked the two blocks to Chantal's apartment and sat down on her couch that Reilly told his sister about Malie, the knife, their grandpa and portals.

"You didn't already know about this, did you?" he finally asked.

Chantal scowled. "It's strange," she began, "but I've often won-dered if there was more to Eilam's past. On the other hand, I've heard him tell some incredible stories, too. He has quite an imagination."

"He didn't just *imagine* that stuff, Chan!" Reilly protested.

Chantal raised her brow. "Nonetheless, he's a very genuine per-son. I've always admired that about him."

Reilly sighed.

"Remember when Dad and Mom hosted a party for me at the bakery, just before I left for college?"

"Yeah. The place was packed."

"You overheard someone say something rude to Eilam, and you walked right up to the guy. With the innocence of your eight-year-old self, you said, 'Please don't say that about my friend.' The guy didn't know what to say, but I remember what Eilam said to him. Do you?"

"No. What did he say?"

"True friends love you just as you are. I hope you come to know such friendship."

"I remember that now." Reilly nodded.

"The thing is, Reilly, I know you and Eilam are true friends. I might not understand all his stories, but to me, he's sort of like the grandpa I never knew. And I love that about him."

"What I love about Eilam is that he makes me feel like I matter," Reilly added. "Just like grandpas are supposed to."

Reilly was glad for the common ground he had found with Chantal—their feelings about Eilam—and felt relieved that his claustrophobia from the restaurant had vanished. Later, he fell asleep easily on the couch, and he woke the next morning completely rested.

It was Friday and the competition wasn't until Saturday, so they had a full day to see the sights, which began with a side trip to Chantal's office.

Chantal had been with Premiere Advertising for two years, hired right after graduation. It was one of the top marketing and advertising firms in the country and there were rumors someone had pulled strings for her to get the job, but she didn't know who or why. The rumors died down after a few weeks because she was so competent and confident in her work. After she introduced Reilly to her coworkers—and bragged about his scientific brilliance— they left the building for a walk through Central Park.

By mid-afternoon they had packed in two days' worth of sight-seeing including Ground Zero and Ellis Island. Though Reilly was only in kindergarten on September 11, 2001, he grew up knowing its ongoing effects. They spent three hours taking in the view from

Lady Liberty, looking out over the water and imagining what it must have been like to be alive when she first arrived at her new home. Reilly wondered where Eilam would have been at that time … and what he was doing then.

By the next morning, delayed jetlag caught up with Reilly, and he might have slept right through the competition if his sister hadn't awakened him. As it was, they arrived at the massive convention hall at Columbia University in plenty of time.

The sheer number of people overwhelmed Reilly.

It wasn't until his display was perfectly arranged that he sat down to try to relax. He flipped through the information packet, and his anxiety increased when he read that each student was pre-assigned to six judges. Last on his list was Travis Jackson's name.

"Oh, no!" he gasped, and he dropped his hand to his lap, barely holding on to the papers. "It can't be!"

"What's wrong?" Chantal scooted her chair closer to Reilly and took the papers just before they slipped from his fingers.

"Anyone but Mr. Jackson! What will I say? What will he do?" Reilly shook his head and stared blankly ahead. "This is not good."

"Don't worry about him, Reilly." Chantal tapped the bottom of the pages on the table to straighten them into a pile. "You're going to do fine. Just do your best."

"Why did they pick *him* to be a judge, anyway?"

"They probably have one or two from each regional competition. Besides, he's a well-known businessman—you can hardly pick up a *New York Times* without reading something about Travis Jackson, owner and CEO of Imperial Plastics and a dozen other companies. He's basically a celebrity, you know." Her sarcasm was obvious. She stuffed the papers back in the packet envelope and added, "But we know the guy; and we know how incredibly arrogant he is. He likely donated a bunch of money to the national committee."

"Yeah, probably. But now I'm *really* nervous," Reilly admitted. "He's just so rude all the time. I mean, does anyone even like the guy?"

"Hey, look!" Chantal shifted to her encouraging voice and put her hand on Reilly's leg. "He's the last one on your list, so try to put it out of your mind until later this afternoon. Besides, you know this stuff inside and out. Don't let that jerk get to you."

Reilly sighed again. She was right. It wasn't worth stressing about it now. After all, there were five judges ahead of Travis that Reilly needed to wow.

"You're right. He's just an old gargoyle anyway."

"A what?"

"Never mind. I'll tell you about it later."

A woman wearing a yellow name badge with the words *Committee Member* on it approached. She asked Reilly if he was ready for the competition to begin, then pulled out a map of the university, pointing out the campus eating establishments, emergency exits and restrooms.

"Just relax and have fun with it," she bubbled, as she waltzed to the next booth.

"Easy for you to say," Reilly muttered under his breath.

A few minutes later a general welcome announcement was broadcast and Reilly's first judge promptly appeared.

"Good morning, my name is Ashton Webster. And you are ..." The judge glanced at his paper as he held out his hand to Reilly.

"Reilly. Reilly McNamara from Seattle." Reilly shook the man's hand. "Well, Bainbridge Island, actually."

"Ah, yes, here you are. Reilly McNamara," Mr. Webster said, glancing at his judging sheet. "Well, Mr. McNamara from Bainbridge Island, tell me about your project."

It wasn't really a question and it took Reilly a few seconds to gather his thoughts. He had thought the judges would ask the pre-assigned questions. But he relaxed as he started to explain how light travels, how to measure the distance and speed of light, and what stimuli can slow down or speed up the distance of light travel.

"You were awesome, Reilly," Chantal said after the judge left. "And I sort of accidentally caught a glimpse of the scores he gave you."

"You did?" Reilly looked surprised. "And?"

"He gave you 10 out of 10 on every area but one."

"Which area?"

"I couldn't tell. Like I said, it was *accidental*," she said winking.

"Thanks, Chan. I'm more encouraged now," Reilly said. "I guess I should just chill, huh?"

"Yeah, just have fun."

By noon three different judges had interviewed Reilly; each was friendly, complimentary and engaging. Lunch hour passed quickly and soon Reilly was chatting with the next judge. Chantal left to wander and privately critique the other displays.

"You can see here, as I add obsidian sediments to the test tube," Reilly said, demonstrating for the fifth judge, "that the light's ray creates a much shorter arc; therefore, the distance from the indigo light to the red is much shorter."

"According to the statements in your findings, you've concluded that light traveling through salt water is slowed down when dark sediments are added," the judge observed.

"Correct."

"Tell me what happens when you add other liquids to the water."

"The same thing. There was no change in the distance of the light's rays with clear liquids but when dark liquids were added— like the molasses in this one—the light's rays bent at a much shorter distance." Reilly moved test tubes about effortlessly as he talked.

"What impact do these findings have on plants, animals or humans?"

Reilly knew this was a pre-assigned question and he was ready to answer.

"Our oceans need to be kept free of harmful sediments and pollutants that can block the sun's rays from penetrating the surface and prevent them from bringing much needed energy to plant life. Just as humans need light to be energized, so does marine life. You might not think so because most of the ocean life lives in darkness. But the energy from the sun fuels the surface plants and fish, which the creatures further down feed on. All living things are made of the same energy. All need to be fueled by the same energy source—light."

"Interesting."

The judge made some notations on his paper, asked a few more questions which Reilly answered with ease, then shook his hand before moving on.

Reilly looked at the clock next to the nearest exit sign and suddenly realized he had only ten minutes before his final judge— Travis Jackson! Ten whole minutes to just breathe deeply—to keep from hyperventilating—or ten minutes to escape through the exit door! Somehow he knew he had to keep from getting flustered and tense. Fortunately, Chantal returned with just the right antidote.

"I brought you a snack." She smiled and handed him a chocolate milkshake.

"Thanks!" Reilly took three deep slurps from the straw. "Do you want some?"

Not bothering to respond, Chantal whipped out a plastic spoon from her pocket and plunged into the cup. "You've done really well, you know. Regardless of whether you win or not, from what I've seen, your project is one of the coolest by far." One of the things Reilly loved about his sister was her optimism. She usually knew when to tease and when not to, when to give honest but gentle criticism, and when to simply pile on the praise.

"Thanks, Chan."

They finished the milkshake in silence, enjoying the simple pleasure of people-watching. Reilly often did that if he needed a distraction from something he couldn't resolve simply with a ride in his kayak. This time it worked only until the thing he was nervous about appeared.

"Mr. McNamara!" Travis Jackson bellowed from behind. Reilly choked on his last mouthful of milkshake and coughed as he stood up, trying to catch his breath. Travis gave him a snide look and continued. "We meet again. I was disappointed I didn't have the opportunity to critique your project in Seattle. However, it will be my pleasure to do so now."

Reilly gave a final deep cough and handed the empty cup to his sister. Chantal scooted her chair out of the way and gave him a "chin-up" look as she sat back down. Reilly stepped in front of the display.

"Good afternoon, Mr. Jackson."

"We'll see, won't we?" The scoring sheet with Reilly's name on the top already had several markings on it. "I'm quite familiar with your project, having reviewed it both at your school and the regional competition. Frankly, I'm unimpressed that you've come so far in the competition."

Reilly's chest tightened and he choked on residual phlegm from his milkshake.

"Explain to me, Reilly, how you decided on your hypothesis, as it is obviously not your original work."

"Uh … well … I, um … I just thought of it when Mr. Ludwig presented the theme. It kind of popped into my head."

"Just like that?"

"Yes, sir."

"And you didn't receive prompting from anyone else? Your parents, perhaps?"

"I thought of using regular H2O. My dad suggested I use salt water."

"I see. So in other words, this is *not* your own work?"

"Yes, sir, it is. He simply suggested I try my experiment with salt water instead. Other than that, I've done all the research and work myself."

Travis's eyes narrowed as he continued to press Reilly. "And what were the main resources for your research?"

"Well, I used the Internet a lot. And books, of course. I found all the sources on my own." Reilly tried to sound confident but knew his words fell on deaf ears. "Everything I used is correctly cited in my bibliography."

"Did you come across any masters or doctorate works from UW that you found helpful?"

"No. However, I did find a published article by a Professor Johnstone from Miami State who studied the effects of refracted light on porpoise behavior."

"Mmm …" Travis looked down and scribbled something on the scoring sheet. "Are you aware that your thesis statement parallels your father's graduate work?"

"No, I didn't know that."

"But you do know of your father's interest in various unusual phenomena of the sea?"

"What do you mean?"

"You surely know precisely what I mean! Don't pretend that you don't!"

Reilly's heart thumped in his chest and he swallowed hard.

"My dad has always loved the sea. He's an expert sailor, like you, sir, and he knows many things the average person might not know. But that's because he's spent so much time on the water. Ever since he was a kid," Reilly added.

"Yes, and I understand when he was a young boy his father told him something very interesting about light traveling through the sea. Something about a portal through the ocean. What do you know about portals, Mr. McNamara?" Travis demanded.

"My project isn't about portals, sir. It's about understanding how light can actually travel at different speeds with varying degrees of refraction relative to those speeds."

"So it is." Travis took a step closer to Reilly. Then spoke slowly and deliberately. "However, with your understanding of this subject, do you think it's possible that light refracted a certain way could unveil a portal in the ocean?"

The interrogation made Reilly's stomach churn, but he did his best to keep his cool.

"Uh, perhaps. I'm not sure. That's not what my research is about."

"Maybe not, but that *is* what *my* research is about!" Travis bellowed. "For the past twenty-some years I've been dumping millions of dollars into the study of time-travel through the medium of light, all the while searching for a portal in the ocean your dad once talked about. Everything else I do is superfluous—irrelevant!" He jammed his pen into his clipboard and his face burned with rage. "If such a possibility does exist, then what I want to know is how a kid can come up with such a supposition, all on his own!"

Reilly could feel the eyes of others looking their direction but he kept his focus directly on Travis.

"But I didn't make that supposition in my research, Mr. Jackson. You did."

"Don't get smart with me, Reilly McNamara. That's no way to get points on *my* scoring sheet." He scribbled on his paper with short jerking motions, and then lowered his voice speaking each word slowly and deliberately. "Now I ask you again, what do you know of any portal through the sea?"

Reilly took a deep breath, glanced quickly at Chantal, and then spoke calmly. "A friend of mine told me that people would be surprised by how far they can travel by sea. But I've only ever been on a sailboat as far north as Vancouver Island. I suppose one could call the Puget Sound a portal to Canada."

"There you go with your cheeky remarks again. I suppose the *friend* you're talking about is Eilam. What he has to do with this, I don't know yet. But there *is* a connection and I intend to find out what it is." Travis leaned in even closer to Reilly, who noticed beads of sweat forming on the man's forehead. "Here's the thing, Reilly: I have all the power to award you the national championship of this competition. Winning would mean college scholarships, opportunities for travel, future internships. I could go on and on. But the only way that's going to happen is if you give me a straight answer right here and now." His black eyes widened with obsession. "So, I'll ask you one more time. Do you have any knowledge of time-travel portals through the ocean … anywhere … anytime … from any source?"

Reilly did not hesitate with his answer. "I've told you what I know, sir."

"Very well." Travis shuffled his papers. He turned to leave but stopped in front of Chantal, who had been standing behind him a few feet away.

"Ah … Miss McNamara, nice to see you again. How are you enjoying your work at Premiere Advertising?" But he walked past her without waiting for a reply.

Reilly noticed a confused look on Chantal's face but ignored it and collapsed in his chair. Neither of them said a word. It was over. He had lived through it. What happened after this would be a piece of cake.

Finally, Chantal broke the silence.

"You were amazing, Reilly," she said. "You really kept your cool with that creep."

"Thanks. I don't remember what I said, but I've never been so scared in my life."

"I bet. And guess what I just figured out?"

"What's that?"

"Travis Jackson is the man responsible for getting me hired at Premiere Advertising."

"What?"

"It all makes sense. There were rumors about why I was hired without any previous experience."

"Huh?" Reilly frowned.

"I'd heard about the 'T. J. Account' but I wasn't assigned to work on it, so I never put it together."

"What are you talking about?"

"It's no coincidence. Travis wants me there for a reason. It probably has something to do with his obsession to find the alleged portal."

"Alleged?" Reilly blurted. "What? You still don't believe there is one?"

"I'm not saying that."

"Then what are you saying?"

"Travis only *thinks* he knows what he's talking about, that's all."

"But you think *I* know what *I'm* talking about, right?"

"Of course."

"And you believe Dad—and Grandpa?"

"Look, Reilly, it's been a challenging day. We've got a couple of hours before the awards ceremony, so let's walk around outside."

Reilly scowled at his sister but suddenly felt too frustrated to argue. Outside, he breathed in the early spring air in a feeble attempt to ease his irritation. After eating a sandwich at a café on the edge of campus, he finally felt rejuvenated.

Back in the auditorium, Chantal spotted a half-empty row of seats near the back of the room and pointed towards them as they made their way past dozens of people moving in and out of the aisles. It was too noisy to carry on a conversation. Reilly's mind wandered to his first flight a couple days ago.

The clouds looked so still and peaceful. I didn't even feel the plane moving. I wonder if I would feel any movement if I travelled through a portal. Would it be fast? Or slow? Would it be noisy? What color would it be? How long would it take to get where I was going? And where would that be?

A welcome announcement from the president of the National Science Fair Foundation interrupted his stream of questions. As before, the usual pleasantries seemed to drone on: words of thanks to Columbia University for providing the venue, introduction of the judges, recognition to top sponsors—of which Imperial Plastics and Travis Jackson Industries were named first—and complimentary praise to all participants.

Fifteen minutes later, the Honorable Mention Awards for each grade level were presented. Because the auditorium was so large, it took some time for the winners to reach the stage to receive their certificates and ribbons, and to be escorted to the side of the stage where they were seated.

"Now, for the top three winners of the competition," the emcee began again. He waved a white envelope in the air, opened it carefully and pulled out a note card. "The third-place winner, with a $500 scholarship, is given to … Makayla Feldtman from Nashville, Tennessee."

Reilly clapped loudly, mostly to try to rid himself of the jitters. A feeling of *déjà vu* presented itself with a noticeable twist in his stomach. He tried to imagine hearing his name called as the first-place winner and receiving the $5000 grand prize. With college just around the corner, the scholarship would ensure that he could actually attend. He didn't care about the celebrity of winning, but he knew there would likely be a big to-do back home with banners and balloons, and the staff from *The Bainbridge Review* waiting for him as he got off the ferry—an uncomfortable reality he was willing to deal with.

"Reilly! Reilly!" Chantal nudged him and pulled at his arm. "Reilly, they called your name! Get up there!"

"Huh? They did? Are you sure?"

"Yes! You won second place, Reilly! Get up there!"

Reilly jumped up and squeezed his way down the narrow row then ran down the aisle. *Second place! Wow!* He paused briefly at the steps of the stage to take a deep breath. He'd never been in front of so many people before, and for a second he thought he might throw up. Inhaling stale auditorium air didn't bring the relief he'd been hoping for and suddenly his legs jiggled like a jellyfish. The emcee noticed Reilly's apprehension and stepped to meet him; they shook hands. Reilly turned his head to alleviate the nausea, and it subsided briefly, but only until he stood in the center of the stage and glanced down at the front row.

Blinking to deflect the glare of the bright lights and to keep the queasiness at bay, Reilly's moment in the spotlight went strangely dark. There, in the front row, sat Travis— looking up at him with a nefarious grin spread across his face and a wicked gleam in his eye. He seemed to be shouting at Reilly, *You could have taken first!*

Reilly froze momentarily with the realization that Travis Jackson was truly an evil man.

The announcer escorted Reilly to center stage, where he re-ceived numerous handshakes, a large ribbon, a framed certificate, a silver-cup trophy and a $2,000 scholarship. Cameras flashed re-peatedly and Reilly had to blink several times to see his way to join the other students already seated on stage. The first-place winner was announced, a Michael someone from Richmond, Virginia, but Reilly didn't hear the full name because he was distracted by the continual glares from Travis.

Reilly wasn't sure how he kept from losing his lunch on stage, but somehow he got through the congratulatory formalities, retrieved his project and got into a cab with Chantal. He was exhausted and anxious to return to Bainbridge.

The next morning on the flight to Seattle, he unzipped his back-pack to pull out the packet with the judges' scoring sheets and take a closer look at the results. There he found the business card from the Jamaican taxi driver. Reilly and Chantal had used several different taxis throughout his stay. *Darn, I wish I had remembered to call him.* Reilly unzipped the small front pocket of his backpack and put the card inside. Then he zipped it shut.

He opened the packet and discovered that four of the six judges had given him perfect scores. One judge had given him the highest possible scores in every area but one, where he was marked down two points for lack of sufficient graphs and data to support his hypothesis. Most of the judges wrote numerous positive comments and notations.

Travis Jackson, however, gave Reilly a 5 out of 10 rating straight across. And his only notation was scribbled in red ink across the entire bottom of the page: *I know where it is!*

Chapter 6

The Ark

Reilly's parents met him at the airport and he was relieved to see that only Eilam came to welcome him home at the ferry terminal. There was, however, a large banner across Main Street just as he had expected: *Reilly McNamara—2nd Place Winner, National Science Fair.* Below, in smaller lettering: *Congratulations from all of us!* And a reporter from the newspaper called to request an immediate interview. The article was the main feature on the front page later that week. At school the next day Reilly was lauded as somewhat of a celebrity with an assembly in his honor, where he was asked to give full details of the competition. On Friday evening, his parents held an open house at the bakery, where he received tokens of congratulations in the form of firm handshakes, cards, a bunch of "Way to go, Reilly!" and "We're sure proud of you, Reilly!" comments, and even gift certificates from local businesses.

It was all a bit much for him.

Sunday morning, a week after his return, his dad made an announcement at breakfast.

"The storm that was forecast for today apparently passed us by. It turned south towards Rainier and is headed into northern Oregon. Looks like it's going to be one of those rare sunny Sundays," he said. "Let's get out on the water!"

"Best idea I've heard all week, Dad!"

"I'll pack you a lunch," Reilly's mom said.

"Aren't you coming?" Reilly asked.

"I've got some things I want to do around here," she said as she opened the fridge. She made sandwiches and packed a bag of chips, two apples, a handful of string cheese sticks and four bottles of their favorite beverages. With lunches packed, Reilly and his dad walked out the door, but they barely made it across the front lawn when Reilly's mom came running.

"I thought you might want to take this with you." She handed Reilly the knife Eilam had given him for his birthday. "You left it on the counter."

"Thanks. I meant to pick it up," he said as he took the knife.

"You guys have a great time. I'll see you later."

Reilly pulled his belt out of the side loop and threaded it through the back of the knife's sheath. It fit snugly and hung at the perfect distance from his hip.

"I wonder how old it really is," he whispered to himself as he refastened the prongs on his belt buckle. He touched the star engraved on the tip of the handle and felt a slight jolt through his body.

"What's that?" his dad shouted above the roar of a passing truck. "You know how old I am."

"Not you, Dad. The knife."

"I couldn't say for sure, son. I doubt Eilam knows. Age and time don't seem very relevant to him, if you know what I mean."

"True. But still, I wish I knew more about it."

"One thing I know is that Eilam could have saved it for who knows how many more centuries and then given it to someone else. But he didn't. He gave it to you." His dad picked up his pace. "He must have a good reason."

"It's a real treasure." Feeling the knife bump at his hip as he walked was a steady invitation to daydream about other things he treasured: an unexpected hummingbird outside his bedroom window, snow on Christmas morning, giant leaves in the Grand Forest, his kayak …

Reilly's peaceful thoughts were abruptly interrupted as he and his dad approached the marina dock, where Travis stood directly in front of the main gate down to the boat slips. It was the first time Reilly had seen Travis since the haunting moment when their eyes met on the stage in New York.

"Ugh!" He sighed. "Why does he keep showing up in the middle of otherwise pleasant events? It's so annoying."

His dad shrugged his shoulders, pursed his lips and shook his head twice from left to right. They approached the gate but had to make a complete stop, as Travis would not step aside.

"Excuse us," said Reilly's dad, as he attempted to step around the man.

Travis leaned forward and breathed heavily. "Yep, it does look like a *fff*ine day for a sail." He over emphasized the "f" and the stench of stale liquor mingled with rancid tobacco permeated the air. "How *far* you headed out today? *Blake* Island? *Poulsbo* Marina? Up to *Port Townsend?*"

"Excuse us, please," his dad repeated more firmly.

Waving both hands in the air, Travis shouted, "How about a new horizon! Through a *portal* perhaps?"

"Travis, please. Step aside." Reilly's dad looked him directly in the eye but turned his head slightly to avoid the ripe odor.

"Step aside?" Travis moved even closer to the gate. "You want *me* to move out of *your* way? This is *my* marina. *My* dock. And you've been using it rent-free for years. For what? Some lousy bread for a few lousy parties." He swung his arms to his side and added, "I've had it with you, Kevin McNamara. Our deal is over!"

Reilly's dad handed the sack of food to his son and pulled out his cell phone. "You're drunk, Travis. If you don't step aside, I'm calling the police."

"Hell, there's no need for that. You just tell me where that *portal* is and you can *keep* your damn *boat* here as long as you like." The drunk's eyes wandered as he spoke, and his gaze landed precisely at Reilly's right hip. "That's a damn fancy knife you got there!" Reilly tried to cover it with his free hand but Travis had already stepped directly in front of Reilly and taken a good look. "Is that a star carved on the top?"

"I'm dialing the number, Travis," said Reilly's dad.

"Oh, all right!" Seeing the knife had momentarily distracted him and he fumbled backward a step, just enough for Reilly's dad to push the gate open.

Reilly squeezed between the two of them and headed quickly down the ramp. Still mesmerized by the knife, Travis remained silent.

A few minutes later, Reilly and his dad stepped aboard *The Ark* and prepared to sail. They both knew the routine: untie the lines, pull the fenders onto the deck, steer backward out of the slip, and ease the sail toward the wind. Every movement was deliberate, yet graceful, as they made their claim. His dad could have done it blindfolded. Although Reilly had never taken the boat out by himself, the thrill of sailing rushed through his veins with the same beat that echoed through his soul when he kayaked. They were a great team: Reilly and his dad ... his dad and the sailboat ... Reilly and the kayak.

The old vessel was thirty-two feet long, a fairly good size considering it was mostly used for day sailing on the Sound. Reilly's dad had purchased it almost three decades earlier as a reprieve from the demands of grad school. The ad in the classifieds had read: BUSY SURGEON HAS SUDDEN AND PAINFUL REALIZATION HE HAS NO TIME TO SAIL. LOOKING FOR SOMEONE WHO PROMISES TO DO SO FREQUENTLY. SHE'S A BEAUTY.

Reilly's dad called immediately and spoke to the owner, who indicated he'd had the boat for five years and only taken it out twice. He was willing to sell it at a ridiculously low price to the right owner. The day Reilly's dad met with the surgeon to inspect the boat was a day he'd always remember.

"I bought it brand new from a seasoned sailor who agreed to sell it to me for almost nothing ... but with one condition," the doctor had said. "She's called *The Ark* and whoever owns the boat must agree to retain that name. There was no written agreement, nor did he give me a receipt. He simply asked me to give him my word, which I did. Then we shook on it." So *The Ark* was sold to Reilly's dad in the same manner—with a firm handshake and a promise to sail her often, which he did.

As a small boy, and on one of Reilly's earliest sails, he asked his dad what the word "ark" meant, so his dad told him about the surgeon and the original owner's request. It was the first time Reilly learned about animals marching two-by-two and forty-day-and-forty-night floods. At the time, Reilly wondered when the friendly four-legged beasts and creepy-crawly snakes would arrive. But to his disappointment, no animal had ever stepped aboard *The Ark*.

Passing the No Wake Zone sign on their right and an incoming ferryboat on their left, *The Ark* picked up speed as she peeked out of Eagle Harbor into the Puget Sound. The wind from the north caught her sails.

The mainsail was bright yellow and the headsail was indigo, with a hickory-colored hull. Looking up, Reilly remembered doing a fifth-grade research paper on endemic birds of Peru and discovering that the Chestnut Breasted Coronet existed. At the time, he thought the vessel looked more like a giant version of that bird than it did an ocean liner for a plethora of mating animals. He often wondered if *The Coronet* would be a more fitting name for the vessel. Or perhaps the two names could be combined and she could be called *The Coronark*. But her given name remained.

The Ark moved effortlessly east towards Seattle with Reilly sitting on the upper deck, his feet dangling over the galley door.

"What a great day, huh, Reilly?" His dad smiled from his position at the wheel.

"Perfect."

His dad nodded then added, "You've had quite a whirlwind of events lately. Exciting, no doubt, but a bit overwhelming, I'd imagine."

"It's been fun. Sometimes I can hardly believe I took second place … and went to New York!"

"It's a real accomplishment."

"Thanks, Dad." Reilly looked out across the water. "Hanging out with Chan was the best part."

They sailed towards Seattle for twenty-five minutes then tacked to the north, the wind catching the boom faster than expected. Reilly looked south at the grey clouds hovering over Mount Rainier. He was glad they were sailing north towards Edmonds and he smiled at the sight of the clear sky spreading past Mt. Baker. He watched the sun's bright rays sparkle on the rippling water. By the time Queen Anne Hill pressed on them to the right, Reilly's stomach started to growl. He left his spot on deck and went below.

"Let's eat. I'm hungry," Reilly announced as he emerged from the galley with the two bags of food.

"Me, too." His dad smiled. "What've we got?"

Reilly pulled items from the bags and set them on the bench near his dad's foot. His dad stood on one leg with his right hand on the wheel and his left arm draped by his side, as relaxed as someone driving a classic convertible on a summer's day.

"Looks like turkey and avocado. Do you want the rye or the wheat?"

"I'll take the rye. What's there to drink?" His dad took the sandwich.

"Soda … or juice?" Reilly held up two cans, one orange-colored and the other red.

"Whatever. That's good." He pointed to the red beverage as he took a big bite of the sandwich. "This is life," he said with his mouth still half full.

They enjoyed lunch while chatting about New York, Chantal's upcoming visit for the 4th of July, plans to go camping on the far coast and inviting Eilam to join them. Then Reilly's dad asked Reilly if he'd like to start working at the bakery in the summer— for pay! In the middle of munching his last handful of chips, Reilly agreed whole-heartedly.

Reilly wiped his hands on his pants and pulled the knife from its sheath. He ran his fingers over the intricately carved handle, turning it over a few times. Then he traced the shape of the star with his pointer finger. The same prickly sensation he'd felt the first time he touched it tingled through his fingers into his palm. Reilly knew it was time to ask his dad the question that had been on his mind for weeks.

"Dad," he began in a serious tone, "what happened to Grandpa Angus's Stelladaur? Did he bring it with him when he left Ireland?"

Reilly figured his dad must have known the question was coming because he answered as if he'd been rehearsing for weeks.

"He did. He kept it on the inside ledge of the watch room at the top of the lighthouse, in a small wooden box he had carved out of yew wood. Grandpa was an artisan, as well as a sea lover, and as a young boy he took up whittling to help pass the time on watch in the lighthouse with his dad."

Admiring the blade of his knife, Reilly wished he had a piece of wood just then.

"In ancient times, the best bows and spears were made of yew wood because of its strength and durability. Yew trees were a religious symbol, and throughout Ireland they were often planted near churches, but they also grew on the rocky cliffs. An unusually large one grew right beside their lighthouse. One night, a terrible storm raged across the coast, the worst storm in over fifty years. A window of the lighthouse shattered from blowing debris, and the yew tree was uprooted. They tried to replant it but it never recovered."

"Sad."

"Well, Grandpa used the wood to build things. He built a small bookshelf—yew wood is a beautiful reddish color, and it was commonly used to make ornate cabinetry. He fashioned a toy, similar to a boomerang. And he made the box, intricately carved with an engraving of a Stelladaur on the lid, which fit perfectly without hinges."

A sudden gust of wind blew a piece of plastic wrap off the bench and over the galley door. Reilly jumped up quickly and pierced it with the tip of his knife.

Turning to look south, his dad changed the subject.

"The wind has changed. We need to head back." He gave a slight nod to the south as he moved towards the wheel. "Those clouds that were supposed to move into Oregon are coming our way."

Though it was sunny where they were, white caps dotted the waters towards Seattle.

"You gotta always respect Mother Nature, Reilly," he said, putting both hands on the wheel.

Reilly placed the knife back in its sheath, gathered up the pop bottles and other remnants of lunch, and left to store them below. By the time he returned on deck, *The Ark* was headed south and the wind had picked up.

Contrary to the non-locals' belief that it always rains in Seattle, Reilly knew the weather was, nevertheless, quite unpredictable, especially in the spring. Reilly mused, *One minute it's sunny, then it's overcast, then blue sky peeks through again. Overcast again. Misty rain. No rain. Wind. No wind. Some rain. Lots of rain. Sunny. High clouds. Low clouds. All in one day, or sometimes within a few hours!* Reilly sighed and his mind sloshed just thinking about it.

"Darn. So much for our sunny Sunday sail," he said. Pulling a heavier jacket out of the storage bin, he added, "Do you want yours, Dad?"

"Naw, I'm good." His dad tugged at his long-sleeved shirt and zipped his fleece vest.

Maneuvering the oncoming wind fairly easily for about thirty minutes, they passed the Agate Pass Bridge to the distant right and then Port Madison closer by. Then the wind blew in from the southeast more strongly and it started to rain. Reilly zipped up his jacket and pulled the hood over his head. Within ten minutes the grey clouds turned a charcoal color as they headed around Manitou Beach. It rained harder and the sun hid. By the time they approached the tip of the bay into Eagle Harbor, they faced a strong wind head on and Reilly coughed at the salt spray spatting him.

"Ready to jibe?" his dad called out.

Reilly jumped on deck and removed the top warp of line on the winch to free the jib sheet.

His dad unfastened the line from the bow to the end of the boom and started hauling in the main close to *The Ark's* centerline. "Jibe-O!" he hollered.

Reilly let go of the jib sheet carefully, most of the way, allowing the sail to pass through the fore triangle. His dad turned the vessel to its new sailing point. As Reilly began to sheet in the jib on the new side, his dad released the mainsail.

The sail was almost fully set when his dad did something he'd never done before under such conditions.

He stood up.

Hundreds, maybe thousands of times, he had jibed, waiting for the sail to be fully raised before standing.

But this day, he stood up.

A second later the boom jerked violently into place. With the sail whipping mercilessly in full extension, the boom struck the seasoned sailor with a fierce blow to the back of his head.

Reilly's dad plummeted overboard.

"Dad! DAD!"

By the time Reilly reached the edge of the boat and leaned over the side, he saw nothing but a faint whirlpool camouflaged by black waves, which had swallowed his father whole.

"DAD!" he screamed into the relentless wind.

Chapter Seven

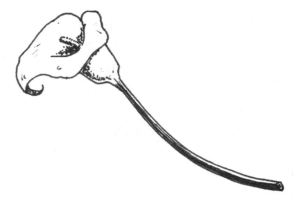

Solemn Vow

Reilly had no recollection of exactly how *The Ark* returned to its slip or when his dad's body was recovered. The sun remained buried under layers of rain clouds—something Reilly was painfully aware of. It rained on and off every day for a week, falling in sheets on the day of the funeral. Crowds of people attended the viewing, a grueling two-hour ordeal that served no purpose to Reilly.

Don't people know my dad needs to stay dry? Why do they come in here dripping wet?

After following in numb procession behind the casket to the front pew of the church, Reilly was oblivious. Everything was a muddy blur.

It wasn't until they were leaving the chapel hall, again in solemn procession, that Reilly's eyes met with Travis Jackson's. Reilly froze for a very long second.

Why are you here? Reilly wanted to scream. *Get out of here! Go away and leave me alone! You're a horrible man and I hate you!*

For the first time in seven days Reilly suddenly became aware of something other than the weather. At the end of that long second, still staring at Travis, Reilly made a firm vow: *I will NEVER let you know what I know about the Stelladaur!*

The ground was too soggy at Port Blakely Cemetery for the caretakers to dig a hole. They set the casket to rest on top of a decorative brass stand, with the rain ricocheting off the metal like bullets. Reilly was relieved that the excavation wouldn't take place until after everyone left, but he shuddered as he pictured his dad's body being lowered into the cold earth. The graveside ceremony was short: the pastor quoted a scripture, a prayer was offered and a piper played "Amazing Grace" and "Mo Ghile Mear" on the bagpipes. Reilly's mom placed a single long-stemmed white calla lily on the massive spray of red roses covering the casket lid. She stepped back under the oversized umbrella where Reilly and Chantal clung to each other. Eilam stood beside them, his gnarly hand on Reilly's back.

It kept raining. Numbing water pellets rebounded off the umbrella.

Reilly's mom closed the family bakery for three days. Reilly stayed at home with Chantal until she returned to New York a week later.

He did not go to see Eilam.

The rain continued like an angry sea refusing to be still.

For hours at a time Reilly sat on the front porch wrapped in a blanket, staring out into the incessant rain. *Why didn't I yell when*

I saw the boom begin to jerk? Why didn't I move faster to grab him? Why ... didn't ... I ... Why? Sometimes he cried gushing, flooding raindrop tears. Sometimes there were no tears. Only dry, desert-like heaves.

And the rain just kept coming.

Maybe everyone is right. He wrapped the blanket more tightly around him. *It really does rain all the time here. I've just never noticed.*

Until then the pitter-patter of rain had been music to his ears; breathing in its freshness had brought him full satisfaction. Now it pounded the earth in the day and lambasted the skylight above his bed at night, like a barbaric sledgehammer chiseling away at his heart. A deafening reminder that his life had been forever changed.

A reminder he did not want to hear.

Still, he would listen for hours.

Reilly's mom picked up his schoolwork and he gave the assignments a half-hearted effort—but only in an attempt to block out the everlasting rain. Reilly finished the last two weeks of his sophomore year at home.

His mom busied herself more than usual at the bakery and the two of them avoided talking about the accident. The silence between them screamed at Reilly with confusing heaviness. Adding to his grief, his mom had put *The Ark* up for sale and forbade him to step foot on it again. And while sitting those long hours listening to the discordant rain, guilt clung to Reilly with such tenacity that he made another solemn vow: *I'll never again slide into the seat of my kayak.*

One afternoon in early June, the rain finally softened to a heavy drizzle.

The entire summer stared at him with haunting emptiness. Finally, he put on a rain jacket and a beige cap with a rust colored emblem of a wildcat, stepped off the front porch and went to see Eilam.

It felt good to stretch his legs after sitting on the porch for so many hours at a time. He pedaled fast down the hill and welcomed the wind as a refreshing substitute for tears.

When he arrived at Waterfront Park, he leaned his bike against a tree and walked slowly down the long dock towards the kayak hut. He could see Eilam talking with a customer who was getting into a kayak. Two more people waited at the counter. Drizzle did not keep tourists from checking out the popular island attractions, and rain rarely stopped locals from doing anything.

A small group of people approached on Reilly's left and a woman who looked familiar stopped in front of him.

"Hello, Reilly. I'm so sorry about your father. How are you doing?"

Reilly knew she was sincere but he didn't recognize her, and he hadn't spoken to anyone besides his mother or sister since the tragedy. Suddenly his mouth felt stuffed with cotton.

"Uh." It was more a guttural moan than a verbal reply.

"I know this is a difficult time, but it's good you're getting out. That helps things a bit." She paused. "I am truly sorry."

Gagging now on the intangible cotton, Reilly simply nodded.

"Well, have a nice time kayaking." She squeezed his forearm and moved on past him.

Suddenly Reilly felt like shouting at her and everyone else in the marina: *I'm NOT going to have a nice time kayaking! EVER! Never again!* He might have actually blurted it out, if it hadn't been for the cotton. Instead, he just expelled dry, spurting coughs until the gagging subsided.

The two tourists who had been waiting filled out paperwork while Eilam rummaged through the lifejackets. Reilly sat in the Adirondack and glanced over the edge of the dock, mesmerized by the continual formation of raindrop rings on the surface of the water. He watched them spread out and bump into one another, then diffuse and disappear into the sea as more emerged.

An unexpected loud bark broke Reilly's trance.

He lifted his head and did a quick scan of the place; the two tourists were in a double kayak, already fifteen feet out, and no one else was coming down the dock. But Reilly could have sworn he'd heard a dog bark, too close to be aboard even the nearest boat in the marina.

Just then Eilam walked around the counter with outstretched arms. "Reilly." Spoken with such affection, it was the only word Reilly needed to hear and he welcomed the tight embrace. "Oh, Reilly."

After a minute, Reilly pulled away gently and wiped both cheeks with his palms.

"Did you hear a dog bark a minute ago?" He tilted his head to one side. "It sounded like it was right here."

"I did. It is." Turning to walk behind the counter again, Eilam called, "Here, Tuma."

Before Reilly's eyes a dog as large as a full-grown Golden Retriever appeared, with paws as broad and chubby as a Saint Bernard's. The dog's ears looked soft like a Labrador's and her long, thick tail wagged gently. Her eyes glistened the color of shining silver. And like a winter rabbit—head to tail and top to bottom—the dog was pure white.

"Why is she so white?" Reilly asked. He reached out his hand for Tuma to sniff.

"She is an albino dog, which is very rare."

"Wow!"

Tuma nuzzled her white face against Reilly's leg, and then sat while Reilly stroked her fur.

"She's so soft. I've never felt anything so soft. Hey, Tuma, how are you, girl?" Reilly rubbed the dog's neck while she licked his face. Without turning to look up at Eilam, he asked, "Where did she come from?"

"The morning after the accident, I found her waiting outside the front door of my houseboat. She's quite a swimmer, too, followed right beside my kayak. When we reached the hut, she was breathing gently, like a napping baby."

Almost laughing, Reilly pulled away. "She doesn't have a collar. I wonder who she belongs to."

There was a moment of silence.

"She belongs to you, Reilly."

"What do you mean?"

"She came here for you."

"For me?"

"Yes. Tuma is not from around here. She came through the portal to be with you. I think your dad sent her."

Reilly looked up at Eilam, wanting to believe his friend.

My dad is somewhere beyond the portal, he thought.

Reilly wrapped his arms fully around Tuma's neck and, burying his face in her plush fur, let the tears fall again. The dog sat still, entirely contented.

"How do you know her name?" Reilly finally asked Eilam.

"I gave her the name. It is an African word that means everlasting."

"African?"

"I first met Tuma in Africa. We were there to help a young girl whose father, mother *and* older brother had died."

"That's terrible!" Reilly winced and then hugged the dog again.

"It is what it is, Reilly. There is no terribleness in it when you understand death is merely a door to another existence."

"But the little girl."

"True, separation may cause pain but there is no real separation when we see things as they are—everlasting." Eilam turned to the dog. "Tuma will help you perceive the door and see the everlasting."

Reilly squinted and continued to stroke the dog in silence.

"Tuma. That's a good name."

Three kayakers pulled up to the loading dock, interrupting Reilly's contemplative moment.

"Your mom hasn't met Tuma yet." Eilam smiled. "Take her to the bakery. She'll love Tuma."

"I'm not sure about that." Reilly stood up slowly. "Tuma really is beautiful. I love her."

As Reilly walked his bike on his right side, Tuma stayed close to him on the left. The albino kept near her new owner as if he had trained her since she was a pup. For the first time in weeks, Reilly smiled.

Entering the bakery through the side door, Reilly nearly bumped into his mom, who came around the corner from the kitchen carrying a tray of macadamia nut cookies. Reilly stopped near the swinging door that led to the dining area. Tuma sat at ease.

"Oh, my! Where did *he* come from?" Reilly's mom said lifting the tray above her head.

"*He* is a *she,* and Eilam said she came through the portal. He said Dad sent her to me!" Reilly stroked the dog's head as he spoke. "Her name is Tuma."

Reilly's mom caught her breath. He could see in her eyes that she considered a connection between her husband and the white dog. Her eyes watered slightly but she quickly blinked the possibility away. After turning to set the tray on a table behind her, she bent over to pet the dog. "Hello, Tuma. What a *beeuteeful* dog you are." Reilly smiled at his mom's French accent but felt an added twinge of guilt about the recent distance between them.

"I can keep her, right, Mom?"

"Of course you may. Your dad always wanted you to have a dog."

"She's an albino dog. Isn't that cool?"

"That's very cool." She scratched behind Tuma's ear.

Reilly squatted beside Tuma and held the dog's face in his hands, looking into her silvery eyes. "Mom, I know the portal Grandpa used with his dad was in Ireland but maybe that isn't the only one. Tuma must have come through a portal around *here* somewhere. There could be more than one, right?"

"Well, uh … I suppose … if there actually was a p—"

Reilly had seen the doubt in her eyes before she stammered.

"Tuma knows. Don't you, girl?"

The dog gave a single bark as she lifted her haunches off the ground. She stood beside Reilly with perked ears and a forehead wrinkled with apparent awareness. Tuma's eyes glowed.

"Look, I can see it in her eyes. She knows!"

"Hmmm." His mom stared deeply into Tuma's glistening eyes then reached for the tray of cookies. "I need to get back to work, Reilly." Pushing the back of her shoulders against the swinging door, she added, "Stay off *The Ark*, Reilly."

"But, Mom—"

She ignored him and stepped into the dining area. Reilly grabbed the swinging door in front of him and held it open slightly to follow her. But he stopped when he saw Travis walking out the front door.

"What did Mr. Jackson want?" Reilly overheard his mom ask James, an employee.

"He didn't say. Just that he wanted to talk with you," James said. "I told him you were in the back room and asked him if he'd mind waiting a few minutes. It's been crazy out here and I didn't have a chance to get you."

Reilly's mom shrugged. "Anything else?"

"Well, he wasn't drunk this time, if that's what you mean." James said. "He just stood right by the kitchen door flipping through a magazine."

Taking the cookies from the tray, Reilly's mom placed them in the glass display counter while James continued.

"Just before you came in the room, he put the magazine down. He smiled at me—a weird, creepy smile—and then he left."

Reilly let go of the door and stood still while it swung to a close. He caught the worried look on his mom's face as their eyes met between the flapping of the door. Then he bolted for the back exit.

The rain slowed to a light drizzle with a hint of blue behind the grey clouds. He pedaled down Wyatt Way with Tuma in the lead. The dog's pace increased rapidly and soon she was running way ahead of the bike. Though Reilly pedaled faster, Tuma's speed continued to increase and she passed the turn towards Reilly's house.

"Hey, slow down!" Reilly shouted. "Where are we going?"

Filled with renewed excitement and eager to see where Tuma was headed, Reilly pedaled with determination. His growing sense of anticipation brought an awareness of emotions quite different from the sublime satisfaction he used to feel kayaking or sailing. But he welcomed the contrast with relief. Again he repeated his silent vow never to kayak again, yet he felt a strange yearning to go back on his dad's boat.

For nearly three miles past the turn, Reilly's eyes stayed focused on his new friend. It was all he could do to keep the white dog in sight.

He didn't notice the car following a quarter of a mile back.

Soon Tuma turned down the gravel road to Gazzam Lake, more a marshy sanctuary for nesting cranes and various birds than a lake.

Reilly dropped his bike at the trailhead but Tuma had already bolted down the path. "Hey, slow down, Tuma! Wait up!"

This time, with her tail wagging and her ears slightly perked, the dog stopped and obediently waited. Reilly caught up and stroked the dog's back. "Let me catch my breath, okay? How can you run all that way and not even be panting? We must be five or six miles from town!" Reilly ran his hand from the top of the dog's head, over her ears and down the middle of her back, three times. "I can barely feel you breathing."

Then he thought he heard something. He looked towards the trailhead but saw no one. Tuma raised her ears higher and barked once before darting towards the lake. Reilly followed, running hard again in an attempt to keep up.

Tree limbs, fallen from a recent windstorm, were strewn along the narrow trail. With his shoes now caked in mud and leaves, Reilly's pace slowed considerably and he pushed low-hanging branches out of his way to jump over a few logs. Tuma, however, shot ahead like a streak of lightning against the brown and green earth.

Soon the lightning-bolt dog stopped, then looked straight ahead and barked three times. She paused to wait for Reilly to catch up but then barked again.

"What is it, Tuma?"

She walked slowly off the trail and headed into the thickest part of the forest, coming up on the south side of the lake. Reilly was only a step behind. Tuma stopped and perked her ears.

A jackhammer noise intruded on the stillness of the forest, growing louder as they neared the lake. Reilly looked around, half expecting to see a logging crew using some heavy equipment or perhaps a dozen woodpeckers hammering on a single tree. But still he could see nothing unusual.

Reilly and Tuma stopped ten feet from the water's edge. Tuma sat and watched Reilly turn in every direction. Reilly took another step closer, tilted his head, and listened. He could have sworn the sound was echoing off the lake.

"It's not coming from the water," Reilly finally decided aloud.

He turned to face Tuma, then walked slowly towards a massive, moss-covered tree that leaned towards them slightly and seemed to beckon him forward.

Is that cedar making the tremendous noise? he wondered.

Reilly carefully touched the thick moss on the giant tree with both palms. The sound stopped abruptly, and at the same moment a strange vibration jolted through his hands and up his arms. It wasn't an electric shock, but an invigorating physical sensation—a tactile awakening in a split-second pause—like a musical eighth-note rest in the middle of incessant staccato notes.

Then the tree began to rumble.

Spreading his arms wide open, Reilly stepped closer and wrapped himself around its enormous trunk as far as he could reach. The vibrational sensation surged through his entire body and he lifted his head to the sky.

Then the din in the woods ceased.

Reilly rested his head against the moss, wondering for a moment if he had imagined it all. He listened with one ear pressed against the trunk, then the other. Ever so faintly now, he heard a subtle creaking sound. He stepped back, looking for signs of wind. Perhaps the bent tree was rubbing against another one. He looked up. No other trees were touching the furry trunk or any of its limbs, and there was no wind. Tuma barked once. Reilly put his ear back up to the tree. When he again wrapped his arms as far around as he could, the creaking changed to a relaxing, moaning sound.

"Ahhhh! Thank you," the tree sighed.

Startled, Reilly dropped his arms and looked at Tuma who barked, again only once.

"I needed that hug. Sometimes it's not easy for me to wake up. Takes a while for me to stretch and get all the kinks out." The tree shimmied its branches and Reilly noticed an opening resembling a mouth on the trunk, some distance up from the ground. "But hugs do help—like a nice massage down to the old roots."

Reilly stepped back and looked up past the tree's mouth to where the sky met the tree. He knew he believed that Eilam was from another time and place. He believed portals existed. He even wanted to believe his dad had sent Tuma to him. But never once had he imagined an actual talking tree. Tuma, however, did not seem at all surprised about the tree.

Reilly wrapped his arms around the tree again and held tightly.

"No need to squeeze so hard! I'm awake now."

Reilly loosened his hold but kept his ear to the trunk, the dense moss tickling his cheek.

"I'm called Sequoran," the cedar said. "It's been many years since anyone has come to me seeking an answer. I'm happy you are here, Reilly."

Reilly had often assumed living things have feelings and that somehow all nature communicates in the same language, but he wondered how the tree could know his name. This was not the only question on his mind. He looked to Tuma for assurance. The dog barked softly, confirming Reilly's thoughts and reminding him that Eilam had said Tuma would help him 'perceive the door and see the everlasting.'

"Do you know where my dad is?" Reilly asked Sequoran tentatively.

Without hesitation, the tree answered kindly but firmly. "You will find your father in *The Ark*. You must seek him there." As if exhausted from delivering the message, the mighty pine rumbled noisily again and became still.

"Wait! You don't understand. He's *not* there. Wake up!" Reilly rubbed the thick moss vigorously, as his tears flowed into Sequoran's furry mane. "Please, wake up! Tell me more!"

But Sequoran only snored loud woodpecker sounds.

"He'll *never* be in *The Ark* again! He fell off and drowned … He's gone!" Reilly sobbed, clinging to the tree as a child clings to his mother's legs when she leaves him with someone who feels like a stranger. Reilly dropped his arms, relinquishing the mossy trunk. He knew the tree wasn't a stranger.

Turning his back to Sequoran, the boy slid down the wide folds of the trunk to the partially exposed roots and the soggy earth. Tuma nuzzled her nose under his hand until he buried his face in her soft, white fur. Soon the dog's hair was as wet as the damp earth.

Reilly tried to drown out the snoring with his crying and heaving for nearly an hour as he clutched to his dog as a child clings to a stuffed animal. Finally, the cloudburst of pent-up emotions subsided until there were no more tears to squeeze out.

"Let's go, Tuma." Reilly loosened his grip on the dog and stood up.

Rounding the trailhead near the parking lot, Reilly spotted Travis's black truck and the tires spinning on the gravel as the vehicle pulled onto the main road.

Later that evening, he told his mom about Sequoran. She listened intently but the conversation turned when he told her about seeing Travis's truck.

"If he *did* overhear us this afternoon, and it seems quite obvious that he did, then he'll likely be keeping a close eye on both of us. On Tuma and Eilam. Mr. Jackson has spent years trying to find a portal in Ireland and if he thinks there's one around here, too, he'll do most anything to find it." Reilly's mom took a deep breath. "I can't imagine he'd really hurt anyone, but if he *ever* threatens you—"

"Mom!" Reilly interrupted and ran his hand down Tuma's side. "I can take care of myself."

"Well, you're going to have to, Reilly," she blurted. "I mean I've got the bakery to take care of ... and, well ... I just can't think about things I've never even seen before."

"Like what?"

"Portals and Stelladaurs!" Exasperated, she lifted both hands to shoulder length. "It's all ridiculous!"

Reilly bit his tongue hard and tasted blood trickling down his throat. "What about Tuma?" he insisted.

"Perhaps Eilam is just telling another story."

"How can you say that, Mom?" Reilly shouted. "Why would you—?" His voice cracked and he turned to leave the room.

"Wait, Reilly." She grabbed his arm. He jerked it away but stayed to see what she had to say. She took a deep breath. "It's just that with your dad gone … I … I can't …" Her voice broke and she blinked away the tears. "If anything happened to you, too, I just couldn't handle it, Reilly." She threw her arms around his neck and began to sob.

Reilly put his arms around her waist. "It's okay, Mom, nothing is going to happen to me."

They held each other tightly for a minute and then he pulled back. "Now that I know what Mr. Jackson is after, for some reason he doesn't freak me out as much. He must have figured I really *didn't* know anything about the portal until this morning when he overheard us talking."

"Maybe," she sniffed.

"Besides, he *doesn't* know anything about Stelladaurs. There's no portal without a Stelladaur." Reilly did his best to sound convincing, but he secretly realized he would have to face his fears without involving his mom anymore.

Turning to leave the room, he shuddered with the sudden awareness that Travis Jackson would not give up until he got what he wanted.

Chapter Eight

Keystone

Reilly and Tuma were inseparable. The dog went everywhere with the boy, and slept next to him, sprawled across most of the bed. Together they searched the island for evidence of a portal, exploring trails in the Grand Forest, Fay Bainbridge Park, city parks and public beaches. Even Reilly's own yard.

"I know you know where it is, girl. Why won't you just show me?" He asked Tuma the same question numerous times. Tuma did not bark in reply.

Reilly returned to Gazzam Lake a few times in the hope that Sequoran might have something more to say. But the tree only snored in loud woodpecker staccatos. Reilly began to wonder if it had all been in his mind.

Maybe grieving causes hallucinations. Whoever heard of a talking tree anyway? Or maybe the tree told me what I wanted to hear: it had all been a horrific nightmare … Dad is still on The Ark and will be home soon. Reilly considered each scenario over and over while he continued to search the island for anything that might lead him to the portal.

Customers at the bakery welcomed Tuma warmly and often made comments about the dog's unusual beauty. Reilly could tell the locals seemed happy that he had a new friend, but he also sensed they might be hoping the dog would take the place of the old man. Nevertheless, he and Tuma continued to spend a great deal of time at the kayak hut.

One rainy afternoon at the end of June, Reilly sat on the arm of the Adirondack, pondering his quest to find the portal.

"We *still* haven't found a single clue," Reilly said sullenly. "I can't get that darn tree to wake up, and I think Tuma has laryngitis."

Eilam laughed. "Well, sometimes answers are not so obvious."

Reilly sighed and folded his arms in frustration. "What do you mean, Eilam? Why won't you just tell me where to find it?"

He hadn't meant to sound irritated, but he had grown impatient.

Suddenly, he knew precisely what Eilam meant. It made him feel awkward—like he was a boy and a man all at the same time.

They sat in silence for a few minutes, watching the falling rain.

"It's really coming down hard," Reilly finally said. "We haven't had this much rain since—" He turned his head to avoid looking at Eilam.

"It has been a while," said Eilam.

"Sometimes I don't like the rain," Reilly said again. "I used to. But I don't as much anymore. Now it's … different."

"The rain is different?"

"Well, no, I guess the rain is the same. But it doesn't feel the same anymore."

"I see."

"It's just wet and soggy, and … it's so loud. I can't hear myself think anymore." He shifted in his chair and looked back at Eilam. "Why can't I hear music in the rain anymore, Eilam? Why does it look so gloomy now?"

"We see what we want to see, Reilly. Rain is rain. Rain is wet … it is soggy. Rain is loud … it is music. Rain is gloomy … it is refreshing. All is merely a reflection. What we see in the reflection depends on our ability to truly look." Eilam smiled. "You must look, Reilly. You must seek."

"Where? How?" He raised his voice and turned away again.

"Just as you always have … inside yourself."

Reilly stroked Tuma and looked into the rain coming down heavily over the harbor. He blinked to resist the hypnotic steady downpour.

"What do you see?" Eilam asked.

At first Reilly didn't answer. Minutes later, he stopped blinking and stared. He shook his head to rid himself of the subtle trance.

"*The Ark?*" he said softly, pointing towards the marina across the harbor.

Tuma barked.

The dog's confirmation was all Reilly needed.

"I need to go there!" He jumped up out of the chair. "Now!"

Tuma barked again and Reilly didn't wait for a reply from Eilam. He ran down the dock and hopped on his bike. He pedaled hard, trying to keep pace with the dog, who seemed to move as swiftly forward as the rain came downward. They reached the marina in twenty minutes and Reilly dropped his bike at the gate. He raced down the ramp and out to the end of the dock, then turned left towards the slip where *The Ark* was secured.

He slowed his pace as he watched the boat sway and bob on the water. The movement of the vessel absorbed his entire body like a thick, dark wave. He blinked and took a deep breath to keep the sudden nausea in check. But he continued to walk forward slowly with Tuma at his side. When he reached the bow, he stopped.

Closing his eyes, he let the rain cleanse his tearless face.

Slowly he opened his eyes and stared at the name painted in black on the reddish hull. Tentatively reaching out, Reilly barely touched the word *Ark*. A subtle jolt seared through him like a tingling electric shock. At precisely the same moment, Reilly heard Sequoran repeat the words it had told him before. "You will find your father in *The Ark*. You must seek him there."

Reilly stood perfectly still as he looked into the rain, trying not to blink. He tilted his head to listen more carefully. Had he really just heard the tree speak? Part of him wanted to run back to Gazzam Lake to see if Sequoran was awake again. He reasoned it would be a justifiable distraction to the formidable task at hand. The tree would understand. So would Eilam. Reilly could ask the tree to confirm what he had heard—just one more time, so he would know for sure. After all, no one was *making* him get back on *The Ark*. It was his choice, independent of anyone else. He could run away from it—now!

Tuma began to bark incessantly.

"Quiet, Tuma!"

The dog would not be quiet.

Reilly knelt down and held Tuma's face in both hands, staring into her silvery eyes. The raindrops reflected off the dog's irises in flickering rainbow colors.

"Oh, Tuma, will I really find him here? In *The Ark*?"

Tuma gave a single bark.

Then Reilly stepped aboard and the dog jumped on deck behind him.

Reilly walked cautiously to the wheel and gripped it firmly with both hands. His body moved involuntarily with the rocking motions of the water.

Closing his eyes, he tried to erase the moment before his father disappeared. Yet, strangely, he also wanted to replay it over and over. Maybe if he replayed it, he could stop it! Then somehow he could quickly jump to the edge … grab a hold of his dad … and pull him back into the boat! Perhaps if he could expand time, stop it, hold it, rewind it—just like Mr. Ludwig had said—then things would be different.

But how do I do that? How? Reilly silently asked the rain. He walked around the outer deck of the vessel, repeating the question in his mind. But he only heard *patter-splat-patter-splat-patter.* Desperately, he wished the noise would sound like familiar music. But it rang with discordance and an elusive melody.

For a long while, Reilly wandered around the deck retracing his steps. He watched the rain slap the water like a reprimand for his inability to bring back his dad.

Finally, soaked and emotionally drained, he sat down on the bench behind the wheel and peered through the top spoke of the wheel into Tuma's eyes. She had been sitting near the galley door waiting patiently without making a sound.

The rain still reflected in his dog's eyes, and Reilly wondered, again, if he was hallucinating. What was he seeing in Tuma's silvery gaze?

Confused, he stared into his dog's eyes. "Life used to be simple, Tuma. Everything used to make sense."

Twice Sequoran said Reilly would find his dad on *The Ark.* But he wasn't there! Reilly had only found emptiness and fear. He thought it through again and again and felt his brain would explode from thinking so hard.

He remembered his mom talking about her own mother's death: she could feel her mother's presence near her for some time after her passing. Was it all just a metaphoric analogy?

That would be a cruel trick! There must be more!

Deep within his muddled thoughts, Reilly still believed Sequoran was talking about something tangible. Perhaps it was the portal itself, though the boy had no idea of what a portal looked like or if he would recognize one if he saw it.

What would you do, Dad?

Somewhere in the midst of his attempts to hear what the rain was telling him through his stream of unanswered questions— somewhere between staring into Tuma's eyes and blinking away the tears—Reilly remembered more specifically what Sequoran had told him.

You must seek him there, the tree had said. It was the word *seek* that rang in Reilly's ears.

Tuma stood up and barked, then turned her nose towards the door that led below deck. Reilly stepped around the wheel and through the galley door. He reached for a towel from the counter and wiped his face and dripping hair. Then he rubbed Tuma's fur and threw the drenched towel in the sink. Reilly began his search. He looked inside every cupboard and drawer, behind curtains, under cabinets and in the ice chest. Nothing. He moved into the dining-living area and turned over each cushion. He looked inside the storage cubby where the table was kept when it wasn't in use. Nothing. Next he moved to the head. The toilet was empty. The shower was bare. Nothing in the sink or in the cabinets.

Reilly saw nothing that looked like it could be a portal.

He checked the stern of the boat, carefully running his hand over the cushions, checking on every shelf and in every storage container. Still nothing.

"What does a portal look like anyway?" Reilly yelled as he threw a pillow across the room.

He moved to the navigational board but didn't see anything out of the ordinary, and he didn't dare push any buttons. He looked in the first aid kit on the wall to his right. Then he moved towards the bow and stepped into the stateroom.

The sweater he had given his dad for Christmas two years earlier lay on the bed. It was his dad's favorite sweater. He threw himself on the bed, grabbed the sweater and hugged it tightly. He closed his eyes and breathed in slowly and deeply, over and over.

When Reilly opened his eyes he was confident his dad must be close by—just beyond a portal, through a twist in time and space. A place between here and there. A dimension right in front of Reilly, but one that he could not see. Yet he felt it was nearby.

Suddenly, Reilly bolted upright on the bed, and rather than plowing through the nooks and crannies of the stateroom, sat solemnly and listened.

The rain, a series of constant staccato notes, tapped on the two small windows on each side of him and on the larger one above his head.

He listened, breathing to the rhythm of the boat; together they yielded to the motions of the sea.

He leaned forward to face Tuma, who sat on the floor at the foot of the bed. Still searching for answers, he held Tuma's face in his palms again and looked deeply into her glistening eyes. But the rainbow flickers were gone. Perhaps the rain had simply caused a reflection in Tuma's silvery eyes. Just then, something caught Reilly's peripheral view from behind the curtain on the ledge above the bed.

Reilly moved as if in slow motion to the edge of the curtain and touched it with his right hand. He paused. Gingerly, he pulled the curtain back. In awe, he inhaled a sudden and deep breath. Directly in front of him, an intricately carved box beckoned. Reilly instinctively knew it was made of yew wood.

Leaning in for a closer look, he carefully ran his finger around the misshapen star carved on the lid of the box. His finger vibrated gently, as it did when he first touched the Stelladaur on the tip of his knife.

Holding the base of the box in his left hand, he placed his right thumb on one side of the lid and stretched his index finger across to the other side. He began to ease open the lid of the box. As he did so, exquisite yet haunting music filled the boat. He glanced around the stateroom to determine the direction of the familiar music but could not place it. Solemnly he raised the lid.

There it was! More magnificent than a giant talking tree, more spectacular than an ancient knife, more intriguing than the mysterious eyes of an albino dog—his great Grandpa Alistair's Stelladaur nestled in the box his Grandpa Angus had carved.

Reilly looked at the brilliant stone, mesmerized, as the music faded into the distance.

With history pounding in his heart and flowing through his veins, he heard his dad's voice echo through *The Ark*: "*It was a glistening stone; a rock chiseled like an arrowhead but shaped something like a misshapen star. Luminescent, whiter and brighter than anything… sparkling like a giant diamond.*"

The Stelladaur was larger than Reilly had imagined it would be, about three inches long from tip to bottom, and two thirds as wide. It was an awkwardly shaped star with points of unequal lengths, each multifaceted on both sides. Blunt at the tips, not sharp. Reilly could see right through the jewel to the golden silk fabric lining the box. Though he was eager to hold the Stelladaur, its radiance left him momentarily paralyzed with awe.

Tuma barked and jumped up on the bed. Reilly blinked and shook his head. With reverence, he lifted the gem from the box. He expected to feel a sudden jolt of electricity surge through him, or a vibration of some kind, or perhaps a tingling feeling. Instead, a calm wrapped around his body like a warm blanket, enveloping him with stillness. All the tranquility he'd felt before while gliding in his kayak did not compare to the peace emanating through him as he held the Stelladaur.

Reilly lifted the stone towards one of the windows, searching to illuminate it with a bit of light. In the dimness of the stateroom, light bounced off the facets of the Stelladaur and danced in white and silver reflections off the walls.

He examined the Stelladaur for a very long time, turning it over and over in his hands. After touching the facets individually, and noticing the smooth surface of each one, he let the gem rest in one palm … then in the other … then in both hands at the same time. He held the treasure between his thumb and forefinger, feeling its thickness. Next, he clutched it with a finger nestled in the vortex of each point and twisted his wrist as if turning a doorknob. He balanced it upright on the lid of the box.

Gripping the Stelladaur at its longest point, Reilly gazed through the center and blinked to focus his vision through the mystical magnifying glass. He held it up to his dad's sweater. The woolen fibers looked like colorful limbs of a sinuous tree. The limbs started to move and make noises like a herd of sheep! Reilly looked again and watched a farmer shear a sheep, while the animal bleated as if in relief to be rid of its heavy winter coat. Splashes of what looked like paint—forest green with bits of auburn and gold—speckled the stateroom as he watched the woolen yarns being treated with dye. After the coloring process he saw the threads wound together on large skeins. Next, he watched hands knitting the sweater. Then, right in the center of the Stelladaur, Reilly saw himself at Pike Place Market, purchasing the gift for his dad.

The scene changed quickly: Reilly heard laughter and music and saw twinkling lights on a tree. He watched as his dad tore open a package and smiled. *Thank you, son,* his dad whispered. *This will be a great sweater for sailing.*

Reilly thought he felt someone hug him from behind and turned to see if anyone was there. No one was.

The entire experience overwhelmed him with a euphoric sense of peace, but he feared the scene would fade without the Stelladaur in his hand. Testing his hunch, Reilly dropped the Stelladaur onto the bed. Sure enough, the scene disappeared. Eagerly he picked up the star again and held it in front of the wooden box.

As if listening through the opening of a giant conch shell, he heard sounds of a raging coastal storm echo throughout the stateroom. Looking into the jewel, he saw a boy intently whittling the branch of a fallen tree. Then the image broadened to show a lighthouse with a small yew wood box set on its ledge. Reilly watched the scene unfold: a young man packed his belongings, left Ireland and settled on the coast of the Pacific Northwest. Finally, he heard the man say: *It's a Stelladaur. My father used it to take me to a place called Tir Na Nog, where my mother was. It was his greatest desire to be with her, but I used it to come to America. Now the Stelladaur is yours. With it, you can also find your greatest desire; and if you believe, you shall have it. But you must never allow the Stelladaur to be discovered by anyone who does not believe, or who will use it for evil.*

Indeed, the Stelladaur *was* everything his dad had said. And more!

Reilly suddenly noticed the sound of Tuma panting and looked at the dog through the center of the magnificent gem. He saw Tuma swimming in a vast ocean. There were no boats, no shore and no people. Only water. Soon, a skyline of tall buildings in one direction and pine trees in another came into view. Tuma swam towards the trees as a ferryboat passed by, and Reilly saw a panoramic image of Eagle Harbor. The dog swam past smaller boats and kayaks with her bright white head gliding effortlessly through the water.

Tuma reached the kayak hut where Eilam greeted her. *Ah, Tuma, you are here.* As Reilly watched Tuma stand on the dock to shake her wet coat, he simultaneously felt a spray of water in the stateroom. He moved the focus of the Stelladaur from Tuma's fur to her face.

A magnetic force pulled on the Stelladaur through Tuma's glistening eyes. There, flickering beyond the dog's silvery irises, was an arch of color—a rainbow that began somewhere beyond what Reilly could see in the Stelladaur and reached high in the sky before it plunged into the harbor. Where the rainbow's stripes met the water, the colors faded slightly and a gossamer veil revealed the words *The Ark*. Instantly Reilly knew he must go.

Placing the Stelladaur safely in the box and carrying the box with both hands, he climbed off the boat, with Tuma beside him. They ran down the dock, turned at the corner, and found his kayak tied to its usual spot just inside the main gate of the marina. As Reilly approached the kayak, he slowed down, his sudden enthusiasm waning quickly with doubt.

Can I actually face it? Even if I can, what do I hope to find there? "Am I crazy?" he whispered.

Gripped with fear, he halted beside his kayak and tried to forget his vow. Scenes of the horrific accident flashed before him, leaving him frozen on the dock.

Tuma began to bark incessantly, snapping Reilly out of his temporary paralysis. Reilly turned and saw Travis walking down the ramp towards him. Vow or no vow, Reilly slid into his kayak. He rested the box on his lap and reached for his paddle.

Travis came up from behind. Reilly quickly moved the paddle closer in an attempt to cover the box with his forearms.

"What's in the box, Reilly?" Travis demanded.

"Nothing."

"I'd like to see that nothing." Travis, at well over six feet tall, towered over Reilly like a giant on the dock.

Tuma continued to bark. "Ah, shut up," Travis shouted. Tuma growled.

"I've seen that carving before." Travis paused, searching his memory. "Yes, on that knife of yours. Where are you headed, anyway, Reilly? You haven't been out here in weeks. Why now on a gloomy day like this?"

Reilly ignored Travis and pushed off before the man could come any closer. Tuma jumped in the water and swam ahead.

"I'm on to you, kid! I heard every word at the bakery, and I saw you at Gazzam Lake. You can't hide it from me!"

Twenty feet away from the dock, Reilly tried to block out Travis's threats.

He paddled faster, racing his pounding heart. The calmness he felt in the stateroom seemed to have vanished. He saw Eilam in the distance, standing near the hut and waving encouragement. Tuma swam in front of the kayak, leading the way. By the time they reached the head of the harbor, the clouds had broken and the Seattle skyline had come into full view. They crossed the wake of a passing ferry, rising in elevation with each crest. Reilly paddled north for another twenty minutes, painfully aware that this kayak ride was hardly the tranquil glide over the harbor that he typically enjoyed.

The Stelladaur rested in the box on his lap, but the responsibility of keeping it from Travis felt like a lead weight in his kayak. Reilly's arms ached.

The late afternoon rain turned to mist, and the clouds continued to clear away. The further north he paddled, the more he felt his arms would break. Swimming ahead in the water, Tuma showed no signs of fatigue. The dog returned to the kayak and propelled herself out of the water as she lunged for the rope coiled at the bow. Reilly tossed the rope overboard and Tuma bit hard on the end. She towed the kayak forward, increasing her speed as she swam.

Reilly rubbed his biceps as he looked at the box on his lap. Lifting his head to check on Tuma, a full arched rainbow broke through the scattered rain clouds and plummeted to the sea at the very spot where the captain of *The Ark* had been gulped into a watery grave. Tuma pulled the kayak directly into the light of the rainbow.

Everything started to change colors: the sea turned purple and the sky changed to yellow. Tuma was no longer white but violet. Reilly rubbed his eyes at the swirling colors emanating from the box. As he lifted the lid, he heard the haunting music again, and Sequoran's voice echoed across the waves: *You will find your father in The Ark.*

"That's it!" Reilly gasped. "Not *in* the boat but where she sailed." He held the Stelladaur with both hands and peered into it as he traced the rainbow in the distance to search for the exact spot.

Flashes of colored light ricocheted in every direction. Reilly's eyes stung from the intense white beams shining through the Stelladaur as he tried various angles. The music grew louder but the melody paused as clouds hovered near the top of the rainbow and caused a break in its arch. Reilly quickly shifted the Stelladaur to the other side of the clouds, inviting the colorful symphony to return.

Back and forth, tracing the outline of the rainbow with the mystical magnifying glass, he searched for the portal.

Sequoran's voice echoed through the music. *In The Ark … in The Ark.* At that precise moment, Reilly felt a breeze from behind, and the clouds at the top of the arch parted to reveal a complete rainbow. Finally, he understood. The portal was indeed in the arc—of the rainbow!

Reilly lifted the keystone up high, aiming it towards the very apex of the rainbow. The sun reflected its light in a startling beam of white.

And the portal opened.

Chapter Nine

Sketches

Like a luminous, iridescent magnet, a mighty force pulled Reilly from his kayak. The surge of a strange electric current between the Stelladaur and the apex of the rainbow propelled him. Still holding the keystone with both hands, he moved ahead with his arms fully extended in front of him, through a swirling violet vortex into the sea. The tunnel spun at such an accelerated speed that everything around him appeared to move in slow motion. Or not move at all. Merely suspended.

Reilly felt only an exhilarating feeling of floating on air. Complete weightlessness. Encompassed by water, he, nevertheless, stayed dry inside the vortex. He noticed that the half-circle curvature of the rainbow above the water continued below the surface, making a half circle into the depths of the sea and forming a complete ring. He was somewhere in the cross-section of that rainbow ring—somewhere far beneath his kayak—sailing through water as he never had before.

Everything he saw under the water was a beautiful vivid violet color: the fish, kelp, seaweed, keels of passing sailboats in the distance, marine life, shells and bubbles. All violet. Reilly blinked rapidly. Then everything intensified, making the molecular structure of the living things around him visible. Pulling the Stelladaur closer to his eyes, the mysterious magnifying glass transformed the undersea world to the millionth power. He could see the cells of the fish's scales, the algae's chlorophyll and the DNA strands in the crabs' vertebrae. Every detail manifested in pure, radiating violet energy. Reilly could even discern the synergism of water—every two atoms of hydrogen melding with every one atom of oxygen.

With each blink, Reilly also heard remarkable sounds—a symphony quite beyond the capability of the seven-note scale. A separate, different tempo beat a rhythm from each living organism, yet synchronized effortlessly. The waves swirling just beyond the tunnel created a visible melody line that all the sea creatures harmonized with. Reilly had never heard such music!

Parallel to the tunnel he moved effortlessly through were similar tunnels in every color of the rainbow. Seven spinning vortexes touched each other on their sides and barely overlapped, where endless shades of violet and indigo mingled together. The violet vortex he was in floated closer to the surface, while the red one farther away extended much deeper into the sea, but each connected at the apex of the arc beneath the water. A brilliant white beam joined the apex below the water with the apex above. And the closer he reached the lower apex, the more movement he began to feel.

A gentle, steady pull made it increasingly difficult for Reilly to keep the Stelladaur close to his eyes. A warm breeze wafted around him and made his body wiggle with fluttering sensations.

The breeziness increased as he floated from the violet vortex at the apex below the surface into the white beam where suddenly everything was a blinding white. But Reilly kept his eyes open. Like a bolt of lightning stretched across a dark night sky to the Earth below, Reilly's body, now infused with light, streamed through the vertical tunnel up to the arc above the water and far above the ground.

As he moved past the center point of the arc, the vortex appeared to remain infinitely straight but was now filled with an almost imperceptible violet mist. He sailed beyond the Earth, beyond the atmosphere and into the universe.

His ears twittered in perfect vibration to the celestial notes coming from a chorus of endless intergalactic formations. Often when Reilly watched and listened to the tides come in and out at the beach near his house, he supposed he felt the Earth breathe. Recently he heard a tree talk. But listening to the music of solar systems and galaxies brought elation beyond his imagination!

Through the mist he saw iridescent flecks of color emanating from stars, planets, suns, moons, and more. Everything zipped past him in an infinitesimal measure of time, but he was exhilarated with his ability to observe all of it at once.

And then he landed on his feet.

The Stelladaur dangled around his neck from a tightly braided, golden cord that had not been there before.

Reilly stood in a thick violet fog.

Am I alive? he wondered.

The realization that he was actually conscious *and* breathing came with repeated exhalations that blew the fog away from him and into the distance, until it completely disappeared.

He blinked. What—or who—was in front of him? A fairy? Too tall. An elf? Too beautiful. A nymph? Too violet.

Her skin was translucent with a faint plum hue. She wore a long, violet dress with a flowing purple sash, revealing bare shoulders and bare feet.

"Welcome," she said, with arms open at her side. "I am called Fiala."

"My name is Reilly McNamara," he said tentatively.

"Yes, that is what you are called." Her bluish-red hair wrapped around her in a flowing mass sprinkled with lepidolite. The violet gems glittered like diamonds.

"Where am I?"

"You have come through The Arc of Color to a place just outside of Tir Na Nog. Here it is called Jolka."

"Tir Na Nog? But that's where ..."

"Yes, the One you call Grandpa Angus and the One you call Great-Grandpa Alistair often traveled there together before it was their time to make residence."

"Are they there now?" Reilly looked around. "Can I see them?"

"It is not your time to make residence there."

"When will it be?" he scowled with confusion.

"I am here to assist you on your journey through Jolka." The lavender irises of her deep orchid eyes penetrated through Reilly. "All questions whose answers are for your best good will be answered."

"What about my dad? Is he here?"

"The One you call Dad is not in Jolka. He, too, is now in Tir Na Nog. The place of endless beauty, endless wealth, and endless peace."

"But I thought I'd find my dad through the portal," Reilly said, lowering his head. "Isn't that why I'm here?"

"The One called Reilly will come to know his purpose here." Fiala took a few steps closer. "I will offer perspective so you can discover your greatest desire. And then it shall be granted."

She raised her arms from her sides and brought her hands together, cupping them in front of her and reaching towards Reilly in an offering gesture.

"Look."

Reilly took a step forward and peered into her hands. He gasped in horror as the water she cupped displayed virtual images of his dad falling over the side of *The Ark* and plunging into the sea.

Reilly turned his eyes away. "Why are you showing this to me?"

"Look," Fiala implored.

Reilly hesitated but looked again. His dad was under the water now. Everything was still. There was no gasping for air, no struggle.

"It was his time to make residence," Fiala said gently. "Now listen."

Reilly strained to listen in the silence of the mist gathering around him.

Hey, Reilly, how was the water today? It was his dad's voice! Was he trying to be funny?

"Dad?"

No answer.

"Dad! I'm here!" He turned completely around. "Can you see me? Do you hear me?"

Fiala raised her hands higher and then opened them. Violet rain sprinkled over Reilly.

"He is always near," she said. "Now, let us glide."

Fiala led the way, her bare feet touching the ground with such grace that it looked to Reilly as if she were floating.

Though they walked in silence, Jolka was no longer quiet. Reilly heard music again, this time coming out of the ground. The melody flowed peacefully and seemed to circle around him. He felt a strange urge to spread his arms out, close his eyes and spin around. So he did. Around and around he went, spinning faster to the increased tempo of the music, yet feeling no dizziness.

The music began to fade and Reilly slowed to a stop as the music ended. He opened his eyes.

"This time whoever catches ten in a row by their stems gets to lead the next movement." A girl taller than Reilly jumped up and down with excitement.

"Okay. Who has the Tah-dah Twig?" Another young girl asked a small group of people.

"I've got it," shouted a young man, shorter but obviously older than Reilly. The man walked over to a gigantic tree—larger than Sequoran—covered with multi-colored leaves in numerous shapes and sizes. He raised the twig in his hand and shouted, "Let the music begin!" Then he tapped the tree's massive trunk and sang out, "Tah-dah!"

Right on cue, the leaves began to fall from the tree, first a few at a time, then like a steady rain. Everyone danced and skipped and jumped and twirled around the tree. Each person was barefoot, trying to catch the leaves.

"Oh, I missed it. Slipped past my hand."

"I just caught one by the stem!"

"Me, too! This is fun!"

"Here comes the wind. Don't let them get away."

"I just stepped on one."

"I've got a whole handful now!"

"The stems keep turning before I can catch one."

Every time a person made contact with a leaf, or when a leaf landed on the ground, a different musical note from an array of instruments sounded.

Reilly watched and listened in utter amazement.

"What are they doing?" he asked Fiala.

"They are playing in the leaves," Fiala smiled. "And making music."

"Huh?"

"It brings them joy."

Reilly smiled and watched the game. The players danced under the tree, trying to catch the falling leaves while music permeated the air. He could hear each instrument, though some of the sounds came from instruments he had never heard before. If someone caught a leaf at the stem a long crescendo echoed around the tree. If a leaf landed on the ground there was a rest. And when one was stepped on, there was clashing of cymbals or beating of drums. Violins played steadily as leaves were caught by the handfuls.

Soon all the leaves had fallen from the tree and everyone's arms were full. Many leaves lay on the ground, so the drums kept beating. Everyone smiled while dancing; some sang or whistled or hummed to the music. But all the sounds blended together in perfect harmony, and their dancing synchronized effortlessly.

One by one, each player sat down on the ground with a lap full of leaves and listened to the decrescendo until the music stopped with a single sustained note. All the dancers closed their eyes and lowered their heads. Finally, the person holding the magic twig sang "One, two, three," and they all looked up to the sky and waited for the "Ta-dah!" command before throwing their piles of leaves back into the air. Reilly watched as the leaves spiraled upward to a clamor of instrumental outbursts. The leaves whirled up from the ground, to the top limbs of the tree, and took their places on the branches just as they had been before the game began. Then silence.

"Lovely," said Fiala, clapping her hands. "Simply lovely and delightful."

All turned to face the violet lady as she spoke.

"I have brought you the One called Reilly," Fiala announced. "Reilly McNamara. He, too, is here to play."

The people waved and offered hellos and welcomes. Some clapped their hands and shouted hooray while others skipped or jumped in place. Each spoke genuinely and moved without inhibition. Reilly accepted their welcome with a smile but he felt like he was suddenly six years old again, not sixteen.

"What other joyful imaginations can you create?" Fiala asked the group.

"Let's make the leaves much bigger!" the one nearest Reilly suggested.

"Fabulous idea!" agreed another.

"Let's ride them in a friendly game of tag."

"As a leaf floats to the ground we must jump on it without falling off."

"Yes, but before it touches the ground!"

"Then kneel on it and use the stem as a steering stick."

Each person chimed in with a suggestion.

"The first person to circle around the tree on a leaf three times without falling off is the leader. Everyone else follows behind until the last one in the line takes the Tah-dah Twig from its holding place and calls out, "Topsy-turvy-upside-down-swervy!" Then all the leaves will turn upside down."

"We'll all laugh and scream as we try to hold on to our stems and steer our leaf so we don't tumble to the ground."

They all nodded in agreement and squealed like children at an amusement park.

"Where shall the holding place be for the Tah-dah Twig?"

"How about there, in that knoll in the trunk?" Reilly offered his suggestion and pointed to a spot about four feet up from the ground.

"Excellent! The One called Reilly is in the game," cheered the one holding the twig.

"All right then, let's gather," said another.

Reilly joined in as everyone held hands around the base of the tree, barely able to circle its trunk.

"On the count of three," announced the one who instructed everyone to gather. "One … two … three!"

They raised their arms in unison, let them drop to their sides and looked up, waiting for the leaves to fall. Each leaf grew larger as it floated downward. Giddy pandemonium struck as people jumped up to land on a leaf. Most missed. To Reilly, it looked as easy as slipping into the seat of his kayak. And it was. He jumped onto a leaf with his first attempt. Grabbing the thick stem with both hands he tried to adjust the steering but nearly fell off before he'd gone halfway around the trunk. Three others jumped on their leaves and hurried to reach the tree to catch up with Reilly. Quite by accident, Reilly discovered that squeezing the stem made the leaf go even faster. He zipped around the massive trunk three times before the others had circled it once.

Reilly relaxed his grip to slow down for others to catch up. Some were still on the ground, trying to master the art of jumping on a leaf. Reilly led seven players around the trunk in a bobbing motion. Up and down, up and down, as if they were going across water in kayaks on a blustery day. But here, the wind felt warm as it blew through Reilly's wavy hair.

When everyone had finally perched on a leaf, Reilly shouted, "Hold on tight and squeeze hard!" Like connected cars of a roller coaster, they zipped and zoomed up and down, over and under branches and limbs, steering hard to the right, then hard to the left, around the trunk, rocketing to the top of the tree and then plummeting in a spiral turn towards the ground, but pulling up on the stems inches before touching. Then back up they soared to do it all again. And again. Reilly reached the top of the tree and hovered on his leaf, waiting so everyone could make the dive at the same moment, rather than in a row behind him.

Unexpectedly, the person at the end of the row grabbed the Tah-dah Twig and hollered the chant. "Topsy-turvy-upside-down-swervy!"

Bodies fell to the ground like water from a sieve and leaves flurried about everywhere. A few players with exceptionally quick reflexes and good balance were able to hold on to their stems without being dumped off. Reilly struggled to pull himself onto his leaf, but he couldn't steer it in the upside-down position. With the increased turbulence, he plummeted. Down he floated, bumping into others, all of whom were twisting and turning with no sense of falling, and all laughing uproariously. They all landed on their feet, still laughing as the leaves shrunk to their original sizes and floated to their original places on the tree.

Fiala clapped and cheered. "Bravo! Hooray! Magnificent!"

Everyone clapped, many bowed and a few girls curtsied.

"Now, I must take the One called Reilly on his journey through Jolka." Fiala stepped next to him and took his hand in hers. A calm, like the calm he had felt when he first touched the Stelladaur etched on the yew box, wrapped around him. Fiala raised both their hands.

"What is the first step to discovering a true greatest desire?" she asked the crowd.

"Imagination!" All but Reilly cheered in unison.

Fiala let go of Reilly's hand. She cupped her hands again, lifted them high and quickly spread them open. Violet raindrops sprinkled everywhere, and everyone welcomed the rain with outstretched hands.

Reilly followed Fiala along a path covered in violet-colored moss. Watching her bare feet brush across the moss, he had a sudden urge to walk barefoot, too.

"May I take off my shoes?" he asked, still uncertain of what was expected of him or what might be acceptable.

"If you believe feeling the moss beneath your feet would bring you joy, then that is what you must do."

Reilly kicked off his shoes and stripped off his socks. Leaving shoes and socks on the path, he stepped gingerly onto the moss.

"It tingles!" Reilly giggled. "It's radiating from my toes up the arches of my feet and heels … up my shins and calves. Now it's going through my belly and spine ..." Reilly kept walking, "... and down my arms to my fingernails. Whoa, it's vibrating my hair!"

"The One called Reilly enjoys the violet moss?"

"Yes! What is it? Does it have some kind of magic spell?"

"No, not a spell. It is the feeling that accompanies pure imagination, though it is not that."

"I don't understand," Reilly said.

"When one is ready to experience pure imagination, he or she is infused with an accompanying feeling. But imagination is not the feeling—it is what creates the feeling."

Fiala glided effortlessly as she moved. Reilly wondered whether the feeling would leave him if his feet were not touching the moss. He tried hopping on one foot, then on both feet. The tingling feeling continued to emanate throughout his body. He marched and then tiptoed, but still the feeling pulsed through his body. Realizing he had fallen somewhat behind Fiala, he walked quickly to catch up.

Soon Fiala stopped in front of a huge ornate silver gate that blocked the pathway.

"Jolka provides many forms of imagination. Come, see." All Reilly could see through the gate was rolling hills of violet moss.

Fiala lightly tapped the gate and it swung open.

In front of them was a very unusual village. Or was it a town? Or a city? Reilly was only sure that he did not know *what* to call it. They stepped through the gate. Strange buildings, each one different and unique, lined both sides of the grassy road where they stood. Only the moss remained violet.

Reilly took six steps, stopped and looked up at a towering glass skyscraper. Right next to it was a double-wide trailer with a tin roof. Beside it stood a stucco townhouse ... a thatched roof building ... a brick apartment complex ... a large tent ... and then a houseboat floating on a lake. Beside the lake, a barn, then a Georgian-style mansion, then an igloo, followed by a large cardboard box ...

another mansion, a park bench, a log cabin, a yacht, a mud hut, a castle, a spot of cement under a highway … and a cedar-shingled cottage. The village extended into the distance as far as Reilly could see, and the moss beneath his feet turned to pavement with his every step.

In front of each building a person busily drew on the sidewalk with thick pieces of rock that changed colors frequently. A myriad of objects jumped out of the ground and then disappeared from view. A few of the people jumped into the ground and disappeared.

"What are they doing?" Reilly asked Fiala.

"Sketching dreams."

"Huh?"

"Sketching dreams brings perspective to desire."

"How does it do that?"

"By bringing feeling to the imagination. It is feeling that brings form. When form is manifested in an undesirable way, it jumps out at them as a warning that the truest self is not being honored."

"Where does the undesirable thing go then?"

"Back into the drawing, to be erased and recreated into a new form."

Reilly tried to comprehend everything he saw and heard. If he thought about it too hard, it boggled his mind. He breathed deeply. *Am I dreaming? Did I fall out of my kayak and drown, too? Is this all a hallucination of some kind?*

"It is not necessary to comprehend, my friend. It is only necessary to believe." Fiala had read his mind.

Reilly pinched himself hard. "Ouch!" he muttered.

He decided to ask questions the answers to which he hoped would be easier to understand.

"How did these people get here?"

"The same way you did."

"But I didn't see anyone else in the vortex."

"Each One came through the violet light reflecting from The Arc of Color nearest his or her own habitation."

That makes sense, he thought.

"Yes, it does." Fiala smiled.

Reilly smiled back.

"Yet all is One Arc," she added.

Confused, Reilly scowled.

Stepping into the space between the sidewalk and the man who knelt in front of the skyscraper, he discovered that, though he and Fiala were taking steps, they actually glided on the outer edge of the sidewalk. It was an invisible moving pathway, taking them past each building and allowing them to peer into each drawing.

"Can they see us? Do they know we are here?"

"Oh, yes. But they are not easily distracted. Focus is required to bring perspective to one's greatest desire."

Without warning, a Leer jet skyrocketed out of the ground at the base of the 50-story building, where an artist frantically scribbled on the ground with a Chalk Drawing Rock. The jet circled upward and then plummeted towards the ground nose first. Reilly gasped and held his breath, hoping the jet would not crash before his eyes. It spiraled past him with a tremendous gust of wind. He cupped his hands over his ears and his hair blew straight out behind him from the force. The artist raised his chest and shoulders, let out a deep sigh, and then hung his head.

"It is not what you want, is it?" Fiala asked the man.

"No, it isn't," he replied. "I've been so foolish."

"Perhaps. But you are here to allow imagination to replace such foolishness. Draw."

As the man touched the Chalk Drawing Rock to the sidewalk, vast lush pasture appeared beneath the surface of the drawing. Horses ran around a large field. There were stables, barns and out-buildings, and a dog. Coming through the door of a ranch-style home, a lovely woman and two small children waved. The man on the sidewalk jumped into the drawing and disappeared.

"Where did he go?" Reilly asked, as he leaned over to look further into the sidewalk.

"To the place of his greatest desire," Fiala replied.

"Does everyone leave Jolka when they've found their greatest desire?"

"One leaves when One is willing to receive what Jolka has to offer."

"So he won't be back?"

"His purpose in Jolka is complete. He will not return."

The skyscraper vanished and a three-story wooden plank home appeared in its place.

"This spot is now being prepared for another artist who will soon come to the Drawing Path. Come." Fiala held out her hand towards the other buildings, and they moved effortlessly along.

They passed the double-wide trailer with the tin roof and the stucco townhouse. Reilly recognized how intently both artists worked. *Why does it seem to take such effort for them to find their greatest desire?* He wondered. *I already know what mine is. I want to be with my dad. I want to see him. I want him never to have drowned. I want it to be as it was before he died.*

"Ah! It is not so easy," Fiala said as she stopped to look at Reilly. "The One called Reilly has just identified four of his desires. But which is the greatest?" She did not wait for a reply, but turned to continue moving ahead.

Knowing that Fiala could read his thoughts, Reilly suddenly felt unsure of himself. It was strange to feel such personal unease, yet at the same time, such trust in her.

They stopped to watch another artist, a young girl, drawing in front of the thatched roof hut. A wooden bucket and an empty cup leaped out of the ground and hung upside down in midair.

She quickly touched her Chalk Drawing Rock to the ground, and both items were sucked back into the sidewalk. She continued to draw. Soon a chicken appeared in the 3D cement, hopping around a pond of clear water. The girl smiled at her reflection and laughed. She dipped the bucket into the water, added a rope to the handle and pulled it up towards herself. She set the bucket down and scooped some water into her mouth with her hands again and again. Then she dove into the water. Water splashed onto the sidewalk and showered Reilly's feet.

"Has she been to Jolka before like the man with the jet and the horses?"

"No, this was her first time in Jolka. But she allowed imagination to expand her greatest desire rather quickly. Although people who live in the place of her habitation suffer from lack of food and water, she has now discovered the way to create the changes she desires."

"She only needed imagination to do that?"

"Imagination gives great power to envision and believe."

"Why wasn't belief in the power of imagination enough for the man?"

"He had many realizations to discover before imagination could assist him. Each colored vortex provides a specific education for the attainment of one's greatest desire. One perspective, and then another, and then another."

A comfortable silence that reminded Reilly of quiet moments with Eilam now settled upon him. They moved along for a while without talking as he continued to digest what Fiala had told him. In front of each of the buildings or homes an artist was busily at work, but none of them jumped or dived into the sidewalk. And none looked up to observe them. Still trying to absorb the extraordinary experiences, Reilly was, nevertheless, certain it was all very real. He broke the silence between them.

"Can a person have everything he or she wants, or does it only happen if it is a greatest desire?"

"Every desire is for receiving and enjoying. One must only be in alignment with the law that manifests the desire. Most beings from the place of habitation where the One called Reilly resides do not allow such understanding."

"Then what is the purpose of a greatest desire?"

"To reveal the endless potential within every One."

Reilly was immediately reminded of a conversation he'd had with Eilam.

"My friend, Eilam, told me every *one* is essential to our very existence."

"Yes, Eilam always speaks truth. *One* is not singular, it is All. In All. Through All. For All. Every desire that is identified and expressed expands the realm of desire for all." Fiala paused for a moment, then touched both of Reilly's shoulders with her hands and looked deeply into his eyes. "The One called Reilly imagines and believes easily. It is a rare gift you must share. In so doing, you will know your greatest desire, and it will be given."

Reilly felt exhilarated as Fiala's hands rested on his shoulders. The Stelladaur around his neck vibrated visibly, beating against his chest and shining beams of white light in every direction.

"How?" he asked hesitantly. "How can I help others imagine and believe?"

"The Stelladaur."

Reilly reached for the stone around his neck and covered his hand over it, allowing its vibrations to penetrate more deeply through his body.

"Yes, you will need to protect it but also to extend its light to each One."

"Are there other Stelladaurs?"

Fiala gently dropped her hands to her side.

"In abundance. Yet many remain buried because of lack of belief, anger, stubbornness, discouragement, selfishness and greed. A Stelladaur is found only by One who seeks truth and whose desires are in alignment with it. The One called Reilly is given the assignment to expand imagination and belief throughout the habitation called Earth, by helping others find their own Stelladaur. This expansion occurs One at a time, but simultaneously with All."

"How?"

"As each One lives by *The Law of Invisible Truth*—the principle that operates a Stelladaur—there is increased power to move away from that which destroys belief."

"And what destroys belief?"

"Fear," Fiala said, looking directly into his eyes. "Fear is generated from *The Law of Absolute Opposites*: Happiness and sorrow, riches and poverty, confidence and diffidence, kindness and cruelty. Most beings of your kind view this law as a frustration and impediment because they only see what they don't have. In the not having, they fear that what they desire will never be. And so it never is. Fear remains, and truth is rejected. Fear and faith cannot function in harmony with one another. However, *The Law of Absolute Opposites* is essential to the never-ending expansion of the One and All."

"So fear is a good thing?"

"Fear has a purpose if One's own fear brings One to the opposite of such. Otherwise, fear empowers disbelief and consumes imagination, without which, no desire can be granted." Fiala touched Reilly again, this time only on his right shoulder. "Come."

He followed her, watching the drawings inside the sidewalk come to life and a few random things jump out, only to be scribbled over or thrown back. Reilly was particularly aware of a mansion: it towered between a cardboard box and a cement wall drawn by artists who were small children; and between them was another artist busily sketching on the walkway in front of the mansion's door.

It wasn't the mansion that caught Reilly's eye, but rather, the artist.

Reilly had never *really* been interested in a girl before. None had ever intrigued him as he thought a girl who captured his heart would do. Until he saw her!

"She's beautiful," he muttered, more softly than a whisper.

He stopped a short distance from the girl, and he could not take his eyes off her. She, on the other hand, did not look up at him.

The girl knelt beside a picture in the sidewalk but held the Chalk Drawing Rock in her lap, as if uncertain what to do next. Her head was lowered slightly but Reilly could see her eyes gazing into the images below. Shining like a fine harvest moon, her long auburn hair was a complimentary contrast to her rosy complexion, dotted with a few freckles. As Reilly watched the girl's long lashes blink at the scene in front of her, he suddenly felt awkward, as if he might be intruding on her privacy. He stepped back and noticed a Stelladaur tied on a golden cord around her neck.

Fiala interrupted Reilly's thoughts, as well as the girl's transfixed focus.

"Exert energy from that which you cannot see," Fiala instructed the girl. The girl paused before she lifted her eyes to look at Fiala. She glanced at Reilly and their eyes met. Mesmerized by her dark, spruce-colored eyes, he felt a shyness he had not experienced before, and he was relieved when Fiala spoke again.

"The One called Norah must draw."

So her name is Norah, Reilly thought.

Norah shifted her glance to the Chalk Drawing Rock in her hands. As if all she needed was Fiala's encouragement, she lifted the rock to the sidewalk and began to draw.

Fiala smiled at Norah and then moved along. Reilly was reluctant to follow—staying to watch Norah would have suited him just fine. But as he walked slowly past her, he glanced over his shoulder and their eyes met for another moment. This time she smiled at him. Embarrassed, Reilly looked towards Fiala and moved on.

Fiala continued to lead the way past other buildings and artists, none of which interested Reilly. For the moment, nothing seemed as fascinating as Norah's mesmerizing smile. He nearly bumped into Fiala when she stopped in front of the last structure, an exact replica of his home on Eagle Harbor Drive.

In an attempt to put Norah out of his mind, Reilly peered into the sidewalk, but saw only cement. Stepping closer for a better look, his foot bumped something. A small rock tumbled to the center of the sidewalk.

"The One called Reilly may now draw," said Fiala, inviting him to pick up the rock.

Reilly slowly picked up the Chalk Drawing Rock and squatted to the cement. "What should I draw?"

"That which you cannot see but want most."

"My dad?" he asked with renewed focus.

"The picture will bring perspective."

With innocent hope, he touched the rock to the sidewalk. Immediately, a scene came to life in a massive diorama beneath the surface.

But what he saw was not at all what he had expected.

Chapter Ten

New York Again

Cars, buses and taxis with horns honking and radios blaring, hundreds of people walking along crowded streets, rap music, shouting and a saxophone in the distance—all surrounded Reilly in the scene. Buildings towered above him, so many that he strained to see which direction the sunlight came from. He knew the place looked familiar but couldn't immediately identify it. Then, in the far corner of the diorama, Reilly saw Lady Liberty, her torch ablaze with a fire that wafted a sweet-smelling violet smoke into the sky, and then out of the ground where he squatted. The smoke swirled up from the sidewalk, circled around him three times and then floated back into the scene. It meandered around Central Park, Times Square and Madison Square Gardens, and then it hovered above a taxi parked by the curb. The driver stepped out to assist a woman. With the door now held open for the woman, Reilly could see into the cab, where several packages and luggage were on the seat beside her. He recognized something on the dashboard: a photo of a young boy and a woman.

Reilly leaned over to get a better look and tumbled through the sidewalk onto the backseat of the taxi.

"Let's get some food," Chantal said to Reilly as if he'd been sitting beside her all along.

"Welcome to New York City," the driver said with a Jamaican accent. "Where you go?"

"Frederiko's, please. Corner of Sixteenth and Jackson," Chantal said.

"Yeah, yeah. Everyone say that be the best pizza in town." With that, the man began to whistle, hum and bebop as he drummed his hands on the steering wheel.

Chantal chatted about all the fun things they were going to see and do while Reilly was in New York. He tried to listen but the boy in the photo, who seemed to be staring right at Reilly, distracted him. He noticed something he had missed before. Hung on a golden cord around the boy's neck hung was what looked like a Stelladaur. Reilly tugged at the cord around his own neck, feeling for the bump the jewel made from under his jacket.

Interrupting Chantal as she rambled about a museum she wanted him to see, Reilly leaned over the front seat and blurted out, "Is that your boy?"

"Yes, yes. That is Dante, my son. He is six years old, and that is his mama. I keep their picture here so they can be near me. But they are in Jamaica until I can send for them."

"What do you mean?" Reilly pressed.

"Reilly!" Chantal nudged him hard with her elbow.

"Oh, no worries. I like to talk about my boy and his mother. Most people do not ask, and so I do not tell. Dante cannot be here with me until the paperwork is completed. Then he and his mama will have to wait until there is enough money."

"You must miss them," Reilly said.

"Yes, but someday we will be here in America together."

Reilly turned to glance at Chantal, who looked confused. With a wrinkled brow, she pressed her lips together and shook her head slightly. They were silent for a few minutes while the driver went back to humming and drumming. Reilly leaned back, but the boy in the photo continued to stare at him. Reilly knew he had fallen through the sidewalk into *that* taxi for a reason, and he intended to find out what it was.

"What's that cool thing around his neck?"

The man stopped humming and tapping his hands on the wheel. "Dante found the rock in the tall grass behind our home. His mama tells him it is a good luck charm—there are many old, superstitious beliefs in our country. It is all nonsense to me. But my son has a wild imagination, and he believes it will bring him and his mama to live here, with me."

"And you don't believe that?"

"It is a happy thought, yes. But young children do not understand about life. I will need to drive this taxi for three more years before I will have enough saved. For now, I send all I can to them."

Reilly felt the Stelladaur again through his jacket and his heart beat faster. He didn't know what to say next, though his assignment from Fiala to *expand imagination and belief ... by helping others find their own Stelladaur ... one at a time* played over and over in his mind. He struggled to sort out his thoughts despite his thumping heart. He hoped Chantal would believe him about Malie, the knife, their grandpa and portals. Would she believe he had met Fiala in Jolka? What about his Stelladaur? It was possible that she wouldn't believe *any* of it. If his own sister didn't, how could he expect this taxi driver—a stranger—to believe him?

Chantal changed the subject and pointed out more landmarks. Reilly pretended to listen but continued to battle his indecision. The driver went back to humming and whistling.

When they pulled up to Frederiko's, the man opened the door for his passengers and retrieved Reilly's luggage from the trunk. "Now you enjoy this fine day," he said with a smile. Handing Reilly his business card, the driver added, "And please, sir, I would appreciate it if you would call me again."

"I will, Mr. … Mr. Jones," Reilly said, as he took the card and looked at it more closely than he had.

"Please, Khenan … Khenan Jones," said the driver.

"Okay, Khenan."

Chantal snatched the card from Reilly while he secured his backpack with one hand. "Here, I'll put it with your things." She quickly unzipped his pack on his back and dropped the card in, while he simultaneously grabbed a luggage handle. "It's in the folder, okay?" she added.

"Sure."

Chantal thanked the driver and gave him a generous tip.

As he walked into the restaurant, Reilly felt more claustrophobic than he was when he was there before. Chantal attempted to ease his anxiety by telling him that as soon as he'd eaten some food he would feel much better. The pizza helped, but Reilly was anxious to get to his sister's apartment so they could talk without being surrounded by crowds.

Chantal's apartment was just as he'd seen it in photos she'd sent home: larger than a studio, with a separate bedroom and bath and a tiny kitchen. They sat on two high-backed bar stools at the end of the cook-top counter. Reilly unloaded his recent discoveries.

Chantal listened without interrupting. She did her best to grasp everything Reilly said, but couldn't quite wrap her mind around it all. "So, you're saying that *you've* been through a portal to this place called Jolka, outside of Tir Na Nog?"

"Uh huh."

She raised both eyebrows and frowned. "I want to believe you, Reilly … really, I do. But it's a lot to take in."

"Yeah, I know. It *is* confusing."

"Just a little," she said shaking her head. "I thought you were here for the science competition."

"I am. I mean … I *was*."

Chantal frowned again. "Let me see if I've got it right. You're here … in the past … even though I don't remember you ever coming here before?"

"Yes—I think."

"Reilly, uh, maybe …" She got up from her stool and moved to the other side of the counter to look directly at Reilly. "Maybe Eilam really *is* just an old man who tells fascinating stories, you know?"

"No, I don't know!" Reilly retorted. "Are you saying Dad lied to me? *He* told me about the Stelladaur!"

"Of course not, Reilly. But if he hasn't seen this portal himself, or shown anyone the Stelladaur, I mean—what do you want me to believe?"

"The truth!" Reilly shouted and pounded his fist on the counter. "Eilam is *not* crazy and Dad *didn't* make it up!" With that he jerked on the zipper of his jacket and revealed the glistening stone.

Chantal gasped loudly and covered her mouth with both hands.

Looking at the stone and then up at his sister, Reilly continued. "I don't understand all of this either."

Chantal slowly lowered her hands and whispered, "It's amazing!" Taking a step closer, with her hands clasped tightly behind her back, she added, "And this Stelladaur is like a guide? It helps you … or whatever … somehow?"

"It does. According to Fiala." Reilly turned to look intently at Chantal. "And I *do* believe her, Chan. I really *was* there."

Chantal didn't say anything.

Reilly frowned and attempted to explain it another way. "I'm not sure what day this is. I think it's the past, happening all differently in the present. It doesn't really matter. How do you explain the picture of the boy? And the fact that *he* has a Stelladaur, too? It looks exactly like mine." He lifted the stone away from his chest to make his point, but kept it on the cord around his neck. "Dante believes it will bring him and his mom here to America, to be with his dad. Fiala said the Stelladaur only works—to bring a person his or her greatest desire—*if* that person believes it *will*. He believes! Apparently, I need to help his dad believe, too!"

"How are you going to do *that*, Reilly?"

Reilly ignored her slight sarcasm.

"I'm not sure. What are the plans tomorrow?"

"I thought we'd go to Central Park and then head to Ellis Island, but now—"

"No, that's perfect," Reilly interrupted. "But this time let's call Khenan to drive us around. Maybe it will come to me."

Chantal raised her eyebrows and shook her head. "All right, Reilly, but this is all too weird, you know?"

"I know."

Reilly slept on the couch but felt surprisingly rested the next morning.

"Hey, hurry up with those eggs, Reilly. Let's get going." Chantal said anxiously. "There's so much to see."

"I'm hurryin'," he muttered between mouthfuls.

"You eat up and I'll give Khenan a call."

She picked up Reilly's backpack, found the card where she had thrown it in the day before and called for the taxi. Suddenly, something unusual occurred to Reilly.

"Chan, let me see that card."

She held it out for Reilly, but he just looked at it.

"What?" Chantal asked warily.

"The first time he gave me his card, we didn't call him. We forgot to call him."

"So?"

"Later, the card fell out of my folder on the plane. So I put it in the front zipper of my backpack!"

"What are you talking about?"

Reilly didn't answer. He walked over to his backpack and quickly unzipped the small, front compartment. He pulled out an identical card to the one his sister had in her hand.

"See … this is the one he gave me before! I put it there. It fell out of the folder on the plane when I flew back home after the competition."

Stunned, Chantal compared business cards. "Weird. Very weird." She handed Reilly the card she was holding as if she might suddenly become possessed because she had touched it. "You really *are* in some kind of a time warp!"

"That's what I've been trying to tell you."

"Okay, Reilly. I'm going to go with it." She shivered. "It's just too weird … but for some unexplainable reason, I *do* believe you."

"Thanks, Chan."

The taxi's horn rang out. Reilly grabbed his jacket and zipped it up to cover the Stelladaur around his neck. Chantal grabbed her purse and they hurried out of her apartment onto the street.

"Good morning. Nice to see you again so soon." Khenan greeted them cheerfully as they got into the taxi. "Where to today?"

"Uh, Reilly, I'd like to take you to see my office first. Is that all right with you?"

"Sure."

"Okay. The address is 64 Third Avenue please."

"You bet," Khenan replied. He pulled into traffic and immediately started humming, bebopping and tapping on the steering wheel, as he had before.

"You really like music, don't you?" Reilly asked.

"Oh, yeah! Food for the soul, I call it. Keeps me going in life. Makes everything seem brighter."

"I like music, too. I play the piano some. What about you? Do you play any instruments?"

"Oh, yeah! I play the saxophone. And I sing. Well, not at the same time." He laughed.

"How long have you been playing?"

"Ever since I can remember. My granddaddy gave me his horn when I was only seven years old, just before he died. I used to love to hear him play. I'd imagine how wonderful it would be to play like he did."

"Who taught you how to play?"

"Well, no one, really. I learned it on my own. Just puttin' my fingers over the keys … closin' my eyes … listenin' to the songs in my head—and the ones my granddaddy used to play. Then just blowin'. Oh, at first it sounded awful—my poor mama. But I heard it in my mind, and she always encouraged me on. 'You just play what you feel, Khenan, and it will come to you,' she would say."

"Did it come to you?"

"Yes, sir, it did. I play real fine, if I do say so. Makes me smile. Sometimes it makes others smile, too. I keep it here with me … cuz on slow days, I can pull it out and play a tune on the street." Khenan reached his hand to the front passenger side, and Reilly leaned forward to see him pat the instrument case at his side. "But I don't play as much as I used to. Life changes, you know. I've got to work long hours now."

Reilly noticed Khenan glance at the photo on the dash, and he felt his chest burn as his Stelladaur vibrated gently. He knew he needed to keep the conversation going with this man who, for some reason, didn't seem much like a stranger.

"So, when you were a little boy, maybe the age of your son, you imagined what it might be like to play the saxophone. And you felt something inside tell you that you could do it? Is that right?"

"Yeah, I suppose that's about how it happened."

Reilly took a deep breath. "Maybe your boy has a feeling like that, too. Maybe something inside told him the stone he found can bring him to be here with you."

Khenan glanced at Reilly in the rear view mirror. "Well, maybe … when you put it like that." The taxi pulled up to a curb at Chantal's office and Khenan turned around to look at Reilly. "But I just can't know how."

"Khenan, I'd like to show you something."

Reilly slowly pulled the Stelladaur out from under his jacket. As the stone came into full view, Khenan dropped his jaw and his eyes widened. "That looks just like the rock Dante found! What is it? Where did you get that?"

"It's called a Stelladaur and it belonged to my great grandfather. I found it on my dad's sailboat … shortly after he … just a while ago."

There was an awkward silence. "What's it for?"

"When a person finds a Stelladaur it can help them figure out what they want most, *if* they believe what they want is possible." Reilly paused to make sure Khenan was really listening. "Just as you imagined that you could learn to play the saxophone—you felt the music in your soul. It was that faith in yourself and in what you were feeling that taught you how to play."

"But my boy doesn't want to play the saxophone. He wants to be here with me. Those are two very different things."

"Maybe. But, Khenan, your son *believes* the Stelladaur will bring him what he wants. That's the only real difference."

There was a long pause as Khenan touched his finger to the photo. "I used to believe like that."

Reilly wasn't sure what to say next, if anything.

"Uh … we should be going," Chantal interjected. "Khenan, will you please meet us at the corner of 68th and 5th at one o'clock? We'll need a ride to Ellis Island."

"Of course." He turned back around and gripped the steering wheel. "I will be there."

Chantal paid him with another generous tip.

The taxi pulled away slowly as they turned to walk into the building behind them.

Reilly enjoyed the tour of Chantal's office and the walk around Central Park, both of which were as fun as the first time. Still, his thoughts kept wandering to Khenan.

I'm going to be stuck in this time warp until I can help him believe. Showing him my Stelladaur is one thing, but how do I get him to believe that the Stelladaur his son found can bring them together?

They went to another of Chantal's favorite spots for lunch, an upscale grill a block away from the corner where she'd told Khenan to pick them up.

After ordering, Reilly looked around the room at the eclectic mismatched chairs, the brick walls and wide plank floors. They sat next to an empty rock fireplace with a solid wood-beamed mantel. There was a bar beyond an open doorway at the back of the room. Off-white linens covered each table, complete with linen napkins and silver settings. In the center of each table was a different colored glass vase filled with fresh flowers. The place was packed and noisy.

"This place is great, huh?" Chantal began.

"Yeah, it's cool, I guess." Reilly didn't look at her, but continued to scan the room.

"Hey, Reilly, what's up?" She waved her hand in front of his face. "You've been quiet all morning."

"Huh?" He blinked and shook his head.

"What's on your mind? Are you nervous about the competition?"

"No, not at all. Remember, I know exactly what's going to happen. I'm going to take second place."

Chantal rolled her eyes. "Right. What a stupid question." She took her napkin from the table and unfolded it. "Look, Reilly, I don't know exactly what's going on here. You may know what you are doing, and I'm trying to believe what you told me, but I just don't know what *I'm* supposed to be doing. Is there something you remember about where *I* fit into all this?"

"No, that's one of the weird things. In some ways it's like déjà vu, but in other ways, it's completely new. For example, I don't remember coming to this restaurant at all. Your office was the same, the park was familiar, and I know we're headed to the Statue of Liberty next. But this place … we didn't come here before."

"Not as far as I know, we didn't."

"But I think we were supposed to," he said as he touched the Stelladaur through his jacket.

"What do you mean?"

"Shhh …" Reilly strained to hear a conversation near the doorway to the bar.

"Well what would you like me to do about it?" said a woman slightly older than Chantal.

"It's part of your job, Kate. You keep the entertainment booked, no matter what!" A large-bellied man wearing a suit and tie stepped in front of the woman as he spoke. "It's not my problem to find a replacement. It's yours." He pointed his finger at her and started to move past her.

Reilly noticed other people stopping their own conversations to listen, too.

"But I've contacted all the temps, and there's no one available for tomorrow night."

"Look, Kate, you get somebody here at seven o'clock—somebody good, who meets the standards of this establishment—or you're fired!" The man emphasized the last three words by pointing his finger three times in her face before walking out the main door.

A chill shot down Reilly's back. The man reminded him of Travis Jackson, and Reilly felt his Stelladaur vibrate at the thought.

"Chan, did you hear that?"

"Not really."

"That guy, the one who just walked out the front door. Did you hear what he said to that lady?"

"I didn't catch it all. I just heard him say she was fired."

"No, she's not fired yet. If she doesn't find a musician to play in the bar tomorrow night, *then* she's fired. Don't you get it?"

"Get what?"

"Khenan! She can hire Khenan."

"Reilly, why would you think she'd hire him, just like that?"

"Why not? It sounds like she's out of options. What does she have to lose? I need to go talk to her!"

With that, Reilly stood up and headed to the bar.

"Reilly, wait!" Chantal followed. "You can't go in there. You're not old enough." She caught his arm just as he approached the doorway to the bar. "Hold on! I'll go get her. You wait here."

Reilly watched Chantal walk into the bar and turn down a short hallway. Minutes later, she and Kate stood in front of Reilly.

"Hello, I'm Kate Nelson." She reached to shake Reilly's hand. "I understand you'd like to speak with me."

"Yes, my name is Reilly McNamara. I don't live here, but my sister does," he glanced at Chantal. "And … uh … well … er …" Reilly felt the Stelladaur vibrate again.

"Look, Reilly, you seem like a nice kid. But I'm a very busy woman and—"

"—and you need to find someone to play tomorrow night, someone really good, or else … or else you're fired!" he blurted out with new courage.

Kate sighed, but now she gave Reilly her full attention. "Well, if *you'd* like the job, I'm sorry, you're too young."

"No, not me. A friend of mine, a man named Khenan Jones. He plays the saxophone. He's been playing since he was a kid, and he's really amazing."

"And how is that you know this Khenan Jones?"

"Well, we sort of just met. All I'm asking is that you listen to him play. Let him audition for the position, so to speak."

Kate sighed again. "I have no idea why I'm saying this, but okay. Where is this guy?"

"We're meeting him in twenty minutes, just across the street," Chantal interjected. "Would 1:10 be a good time for you?"

"That will be fine." Kate turned to walk back into the bar. "Meet me here then."

Reilly and Chantal returned to their seats and ate quickly.

"I still think it was awfully bold of you," Chantal said as they walked out of the restaurant and down the street.

Then, at precisely one o'clock, Khenan pulled up to the curb on the corner of 68th and Fifth Avenue.

"Khenan, can you park your car for a few minutes?" Reilly asked him through the open passenger window.

"What … now?"

"There's a woman who wants to hire you to play your saxophone. She wants to hear you play."

"What do you mean?"

"It doesn't matter," Chantal interjected, and she pointed down the street. "Just go park the car at that thirty-minute loading zone." Reilly smiled at his sister, relieved that she knew she didn't need to understand the weirdness that was happening that day.

Khenan parked the car, grabbed his instrument case and sprinted back towards Chantal and Reilly, beaming. Reilly explained the details as they walked back towards the restaurant.

"I've never been hired to play before," Khenan said as they approached the restaurant door. "I'm kinda nervous."

Reilly put his arm around Khenan. "To quote a famous person, 'You just play what you feel. It will come to you.'"

Brief introductions were made and Kate escorted them to an office behind the kitchen. Khenan carefully set up his sax and blew a few squeaky notes.

Kate raised her eyebrows. "Whenever you're ready," she said impatiently.

"Yes, ma'am."

Then Khenan Jones began to play his saxophone.

It was a ballad, something Reilly was unfamiliar with but which made him immediately think of his dad. He closed his eyes and let the music fill him with happy memories of sailing. Reilly imagined his dad standing beside him as he listened to the clear notes of the sax resonate through the room.

Somewhere in the middle of the piece, Reilly opened his eyes with a strange epiphany. Perhaps he was here in New York City at this restaurant in this particular moment because he had come from a past that hadn't yet happened in this dimension of time. Could it mean that if he did something differently—what it was, he did *not* know—he could relive life from this moment forward, as if it were happening for the first time? Maybe then he could somehow prevent his dad from falling overboard!

"… you'll need to be here at 6:30 so we can take care of the paperwork and get the lighting and sound adjusted. Is there anything else you'll need?" Kate asked Khenan.

Reilly shook his head, trying to grasp where he was and why.

"No, I can't think of anything else. Thank you kindly, ma'am," Khenan said as he extended a hand.

"No, thank *you!* And please, call me Kate." She continued to shake his hand. "Mr. Jones, you are an exceptional musician, better than any I've hired before. Quite frankly, you're far too accomplished to play only here. But I'll be happy to take you. And as far as I'm concerned, you have top priority every Friday, Saturday and Sunday night."

"Thank you, again." Khenan dropped his hand. "Kate, could I just ask—?"

"Yes, anything."

"Uh, how much does the job pay?"

"Wage plus tips. The others typically make $100 to $150 a night. But you're truly gifted and you'll likely do much better than that. Will that meet your needs, Mr. Jones?"

"Yes, Kate, that will be just wonderful."

"Six-thirty then. Tonight." They shook hands again, quickly and firmly.

Khenan packed up his instrument and the three of them walked back to his taxi. He could not contain his excitement. "Reilly McNamara, you were right! If I had not met you this very day, and you had not shown me that rock around your neck … what did you say it's called?"

"A Stelladaur."

"Yes, that Stelladaur—just like the one my son found—well, I never would've believed it, but you're right! And so is Dante! This will be more than twice the money I make driving taxi. Do you know what this means, Reilly?"

"Yes, it—"

"It means my family won't need to wait much longer! They can come as soon as the paperwork is done." Khenan laughed through his tears as he opened the door to the taxi for Chantal and Reilly, and then he got in on the driver's side.

"So you believe that Dante—" Reilly began as he leaned forward to look at the photo of Khenan's son. "Hey, where's the picture?"

"Oh, the strangest thing happened this mornin'. I picked up a customer shortly after I dropped you off, a man who'd flown in from Seattle. He noticed the photo and asked about the rock. Said he'd seen something like it before and wanted to know where my son got it. But for some reason, I didn't think I should tell him anything. He was persistent and seemed annoyed. He gave me his card and told me he'd be very interested in paying me good money for the rock. I felt real uneasy, ya know? So I took the photo down and put it here in my pocket." Khenan patted the side pocket on his jacket. Then he reached in. "Here's the card. Looks like his name is …" Khenan held the card closer to his eyes. "… a Mr. Travis Jackson, with Imperial Plastics."

Stunned, Reilly turned to look at Chantal, whose jaw had dropped.

"Do you know this man?" Khenan asked.

"Yes, we do," Chantal said.

"He's not a nice man." Reilly felt anxious. "You didn't tell him anything, did you?"

"No, like I said, it all made me real uneasy. But when I looked at the picture of Dante, it was … well … it was strange, almost like he was telling me *not* to say anything. So I didn't. Who is he, anyway?"

"He owns the yacht club near my house," Reilly said.

"He owns a number of companies. He must be here on business," Chantal added.

"Of course!" Reilly said. "He's here to judge the science fair competition."

"Right," Chantal agreed with a look of understanding that encouraged Reilly.

"I'm glad you didn't tell him anything, Khenan. Things would've worked out very differently if you had," said Reilly.

They rode in silence for a few miles and Khenan began to hum the song he had played on his saxophone.

"I love that tune," Reilly said, leaning over to the front seat.

"My granddaddy used to play it for my grandma. Took me years to learn to play it, but it's my favorite. Takes me away to happy times."

Me, too, thought Reilly. But suddenly, he wasn't sure which time dimension he was in. If he was there from the past, restructuring the present for the future, then Chantal didn't know about the accident yet. And maybe it hadn't even happened yet! *But that's ridiculous ... of course it had!*

"It's beautiful," Chantal chimed in. "You really do have a gift, Khenan. I'll definitely have to come hear you play on the weekends. I'll bring my friends, too. They're going to love you."

When they reached the ferry dock to Ellis Island, Khenan jumped out of the car and opened the back door for Chantal. Reilly got out the other side.

Walking around the car, Khenan said, "My shift ends in an hour. I'm going home to call my son and his mama, and tell them the good news." He grabbed Reilly in a tight hug. "Thank you. Thank you. This is a day I will always remember." He let Reilly go and added, "Will I see you tonight at the restaurant?"

"Maybe, I'm not sure what our plans are," Reilly said.

"If not, I'll be there next weekend with some friends, for sure," Chantal assured him.

"When are you headed back to Seattle?"

"Sunday," Chantal answered for Reilly.

"Call me when you're headed back?"

"Yes, I'll give you a call," Reilly said with conviction.

With that, Khenan got back in his taxi and Reilly and Chantal waved. As the car pulled out and drove off, Reilly could see Khenan drumming his hands on the steering wheel.

Forty minutes later, Reilly and Chantal stepped out of the elevator on to the observation deck of the Statue of Liberty. They spent three hours taking in the view, looking out over the water and talking about their remarkable day.

They tried to imagine what life would have been like when Lady Liberty first arrived in America, where Eilam might have been at that time and what he was doing. Reilly was thrilled that Chantal was considering such possibilities.

In the middle of imagining, a violet smoke drifted down from the torch above them, swirled around Reilly, and swept him off his feet. He disappeared from the observation deck in an instant and whisked through a violet tunnel with a mighty rushing force.

Chapter Eleven

More Questions

Reilly landed back in his kayak, sitting perfectly still. He blinked and turned his head to determine where he was. Tuma tread water beside him in calm waters. The clouds had cleared, and the rainbow had vanished. The box carved of yew wood sat on his lap and the Stelladaur hung gently around his neck from its golden cord. Reilly lifted the jewel away from his chest and looked at it.

"Amazing," he whispered.

Tuma began to bark repeatedly as a boat pulled up from behind and stopped on the other side of the kayak. Reilly had neither heard nor seen the boat coming, and he wondered if it had approached before he landed in his kayak. Shifting through the time warp, he couldn't be sure. Regardless, it was now obvious that Travis had followed them.

"How'd you do it, Reilly?" Travis stood up in his boat.

"Huh?"

"Ah, shut up, dog! Tell your dog to be quiet," Travis yelled.

With the combined rumble of the boat engine, Tuma's barking and Travis's shouting—not to mention a whirlwind trip to New York and back—Reilly was rather befuddled.

"Tuma, shhh!" She barked once more and was silent.

"So, how did you do it?" Travis demanded again.

"Do what?" Reilly asked, not turning to look at the man, but reaching over his kayak to stroke Tuma's head.

"Look, don't be smart with me. I saw you dive into the water fifteen minutes ago. I was back forty feet or so and saw you do the strangest looking dive I've ever seen. Then you were gone under the water, until just now. I didn't take my eyes off this kayak but you didn't come up for air once! And I'm not sure how you got back into your kayak."

"I ... uh ..." Reilly started to turn towards Travis's boat.

"Wait a minute. You're not even wet! What's going on here?"

As Reilly shifted to face Travis, the man's dark eyes widened and he stared at Reilly's chest.

"It's that rock! That rock!" Travis pointed to the Stelladaur with his outstretched arm and reached awkwardly for Reilly.

Reilly lifted the Stelladaur and quickly slipped it down the neck of his shirt. Travis backed off slightly.

"Oh, you can't hide it, Reilly. I've already seen it. Not only that, but I have one, too!" Smirking, Travis unzipped his jacket and revealed a Stelladaur on a golden cord around his own neck.

Reilly was too stunned to speak!

"Surprised? Well, so was I—pleasantly, I might add. I tracked it down in a little town in Jamaica. Stole it, actually, from a kid. Aw, don't look so shocked. He'll get over it, probably just a stupid rock to him, anyway. Hey, but I've got you to thank, Reilly. If it weren't for you, I would've never recognized it."

"Recognized what?" Reilly was trying desperately to put all the pieces together, but it still didn't make sense. *How did Mr. Jackson find a Stelladaur?*

"Your knife, Reilly. Your knife with the star on it. It caught my eye because it was so unusual. Then, I saw a photo of the same star, hung on a necklace. Actually *this* very necklace." He touched the Stelladaur around his neck. "It was a fluke thing in a taxi cab in New York, of all places. Unfortunately for him, the man didn't give me much information, but I got my team on it right away. By the time you and I had finished up at the competition, the rock was mine," Travis sneered. Reilly shuddered.

"But I ...." Reilly felt dizzy. He couldn't sort it all out with Travis blabbering on and on. His brain felt like puzzle pieces scattered across a table, some upside down, and some right side up, but only a few fit together. And there was no puzzle box cover to see what it was supposed to look like.

"For decades, I thought there was only one portal, somewhere near Ireland. But I was wrong. There's at least one more, and it's practically right in my own back yard! Probably one in Jamaica, too, but it's going to be so much easier now having you nearby to help me." Travis laughed a deep, hollow laugh.

"I'm not helping you with anything!" Adrenaline kicked in and Reilly's mind started to clear.

"Ah, but you already have! You already have!" Travis turned away from Reilly and jerked on the steering wheel of his speedboat. He gave the engine a burst of fuel and spun around the kayak, laughing like a wild hyena.

With the force of the wake, Reilly had to grab the paddle to keep it from sliding into the water. A wave splashed over the kayak and soaked him. He shook his head to dispel the spray and rode out the swells until they were only ripples, as the speedboat raced into the distance.

"Here, girl." Reilly patted the space in front of him, encouraging his dog to jump aboard. Though he knew Tuma was capable of swimming the distance back, he wanted his dog close. Tuma lifted her front paws to the edge of the kayak and smoothly heaved her hind legs up to reach Reilly. Reilly wrapped his arms around her and buried his face in her neck.

"Oh, Tuma, now what?" He wished Tuma could speak like Sequoran. "I can't figure this out." He paused. "The Stelladaur showed me the way through The Arc of Color … into the violet tunnel to Jolka, a place somewhere near Tir Na Nog. Fiala was there, and a girl named Norah. Then I fell through the sidewalk— back in time to New York City—so I could help Khenan get a job and his family could come and live with him."

Tuma barked once.

"But, Tuma, I don't understand. I led Travis to Dante, and that put Dante and his family in danger. Now Travis has a Stelladaur, too, and he knows there's a portal right here! I thought I was supposed to help others believe. That didn't include Mr. Jackson, did it?"

Tuma tilted her head and gave a soft whine. Reilly pet her thick, wet fur.

Confused and discouraged, the boy took hold of the paddle and started for Eagle Harbor. He reviewed everything in his mind again. Tuma sat quietly.

With each stroke of the paddle, Reilly tried to piece everything together. But now there seemed to be only more questions: Would he go to Jolka again? Why did Travis want to find the portal? And would he? How could Reilly prevent Travis from doing so, now that he had a Stelladaur, too? Was Reilly still supposed to help others imagine and believe, or just Khenan? How could he be in New

York for days, but return only fifteen minutes after he left? If he hadn't gone back to New York would Travis have been able to steal Dante's Stelladaur? And what did all this have to do with finding his dad?

Tormented by the unanswered questions and heavy guilt, Reilly paddled hard.

As the left side of the paddle plunged into the water, he wondered *What*? Then dipping to the right side, he wondered *Why*? *What ...? Why ...? How ...? When ...? Would ...? Who ...?* Stroke after stroke, only questions. No answers.

Gliding in his kayak across Eagle Harbor for sheer enjoyment seemed to be a completely foreign concept, and the brutal realization increased his anxiety. Reilly felt so confused that at that moment even the Stelladaur around his neck could provide no answers.

However, as he moved closer to the yacht club, one thing became crystal clear. Turning his kayak away from the marina, he decided he would never dock there again. And if he ever saw Travis again, for any reason, it would be too soon. Feeling frustration mixed with the tenseness and uneasiness building inside him, Reilly tightened his grip on the paddle. He had never felt such anger directed towards another person before. And it scared him.

If only I'd let the jib sheet out more slowly. Or hollered more quickly when Dad stood up. If only I'd done something. Anything! Reilly couldn't tell if he was angrier with Travis or himself.

The kayak hut came into full view, and Reilly's melancholy mood shifted to relief as he saw Eilam waving from the edge of the dock. He paddled faster. As the kayak pulled up, Tuma jumped out.

"Good girl." Eilam stroked Tuma's head as she stood beside him.

Reilly handed the paddle to Eilam and slid out of his kayak, the box made of yew wood in hand and the Stelladaur still around his neck.

"Welcome back, Reilly, I've been expecting you."

"You have?"

"Yes, when I saw Mr. Jackson follow you out, I knew your first journey in the portal would create a broader, more challenging view of your relationship with him, so I've been watching for your return."

"Relationship? I don't have a *relationship* with that man! I never want to see him again," Reilly said, louder than he intended. "Can I keep my kayak here from now on?"

Eilam put his arm around Reilly's shoulder and turned with him towards the Adirondack.

"Of course you may. Let's go sit down."

Eilam sat in his chair with his long legs protruding over the edge. Reilly sat on a stool next to it.

"So, you've been to Jolka and back. What's next?"

"I was hoping you'd tell me, Eilam."

"Hmmm."

"Apparently you know all about Jolka … and how I got there … and what I was doing … and who else is there … and when it all happened …"

It wasn't a question. Eilam did not respond.

"I guess I'm more confused now than ever. Fiala said I'm supposed to help people believe in the power of imagination. If I did that, I could have what *I* want."

"Perhaps your wanting is changing, and that causes you inner conflict."

"I don't think so. I just want things to be the way they used to be. With my dad here."

"And do you not see how your imagination is making that possible?"

"No. I want him to *really* be here, not just in my imagination."

"But what is imagination? What is real? Did you not go through The Arc of Color to Jolka?"

"I did, yes, but—"

"There is no *but*. Either you did or you did not."

"I did."

"And was that imagination? Or real?"

"I'm not sure. It seemed magical, but very real."

"Ah, yes. Some imaginations are very magical. Every imagination is real."

Reilly usually understood Eilam but now his philosophies only created more questions and irritated him. "How do I help others believe the power of imagination is real and that it can bring them what they want, when I'm not sure it will bring me what *I* want."

"You already have." Eilam answered the first question but ignored the second.

"You mean with Khenan and Dante?"

"Yes."

"But what did I actually do?" Reilly asked somewhat disappointed. "I showed him my Stelladaur. Was that it?"

"No, you prepared him to find his own by simply asking about his son. It was the asking that opened his mind to receiving more. If you had never inquired, he, likewise, would not have shared. But because you did, he took the opportunity to share with you, which in turn prepared your mind to receive more, as well. More information."

"Information about Mr. Jackson?"

"Yes. You see how all things are connected? Now you know that Mr. Jackson will go to any extremes to get what he wants. He will steal. He will put others in danger. But what Mr. Jackson does not realize is that the power of imagination comes from within, and is independent of the actions of others. Imagination is creation itself in embryo."

Some of Reilly's bitterness and frustration subsided. Tuma had been lying on the ground next to Eilam, but she stood up and walked over to Reilly. Reilly stroked Tuma's soft head continuously, allowing the calmness he usually felt to emerge once again. He gave a long sigh.

"What do I do now?"

"What you did for Khenan, you can do for others. One at a time. Remember, every *One* is important, and every *One* makes a difference for many. Nothing more is required, Reilly; only that you listen when the real you speaks, and then act accordingly."

"The real me?"

"The you who always guides to a place of greater desire, greater being, greater knowing and greater creating."

Tuma barked once.

"And the Stelladaur will continually remind you of the real you … when that is your desire."

Reilly was silent.

He knew his mom would be wondering where he was, so he thanked Eilam, told him he'd be back sometime in the morning and left with Tuma for the bakery.

His mom had already gone home so he sent her a text and waited for her on the wooden bench out front, stroking Tuma and trying not to think too hard. Fifteen minutes later, his mom pulled up in their Jeep Cherokee and he and Tuma jumped in the front seat.

"Whoa, Tuma, get in the back." Reilly's mom hugged the dog and then gave her a shove. "Over you go." Tuma jumped to the back seat and sprawled out.

"Thanks for coming to get us, Mom."

"Yeah, no problem. Hey, I called in some pizza. Should be ready by now." She fumbled in her purse with her right hand and pulled out a twenty. "Here, do you mind running in to get it?"

Reilly took the money and nodded. That's A Some Pizza was only two blocks away. The restaurant was mostly a take-out place and only had four small tables inside. Three customers were waiting in line ahead of Reilly to pick up their orders. The place was so small that he had to stand right beside two older teenagers seated at one of the tables. He felt awkward, but they didn't seem to notice him at all.

"Yeah, right, I don't have a chance," the guy said.

"What do you mean?" the girl asked.

"My grades are horrible, and my ACT wasn't very good either. With everything going on at home … well, you know … it's just hard to figure it all out. Besides, my dad said he isn't going to pay for a penny of it. He says he got along just fine without going to college, and he doesn't understand why I would even want to. He wants me to work in construction with him and take over the business someday."

"Wow, that's tough."

"Tell me about it."

"So what are you going to do?"

"Obviously, I didn't qualify for any scholarships. Without financial aid, well, it just won't happen … even if I ever get accepted."

"But you have applied, right?"

"Yeah, I'm still waiting. At this point, I can't imagine it happening."

The customer at the counter got his pizza and the next in line moved up. Reilly took a step away from the table. Something the guy at the table had said stood out in Reilly's mind: "I can't imagine it." Reilly felt the Stelladaur gently pulsing at his chest.

I should say something, he thought. *But what? They would think I was totally weird.*

"What about other financial aid? Like grants or loans?" the girl asked.

"Again, it all requires a parent to sign papers and stuff. It's just another way my dad wants to control my life and make me do things his way. Besides, he's so anti-anything-government, he'd never ask for money anyway, even if it was a grant."

"That doesn't make any sense."

"I know. But you don't know my dad the way I do."

"Well, there must be other options."

"If there are, I'd sure like to know what they are."

The next person in line paid for his pizza and turned to leave. Reilly stepped up to the counter.

"Order for McNamara," he said.

The girl at the counter found the pizza box under the warmer, picked it up with one hand, and glanced at the ticket in the other. "That'll be $18.69, please."

Reilly handed the girl the twenty, thinking about what he was going to say to the person who couldn't imagine his dream ever becoming a reality. Normally, he would never think to interrupt someone's conversation, certainly not a stranger's. The pulsating Stelladaur nagged him. Reilly held out his hand for the change, shoved it in his pocket and then picked up the pizza box with both hands. He turned to walk out the door but stopped just in front of the table.

"Excuse me, um … well, I know this seems weird but, I mean, I couldn't help overhearing your conversation. And …" Reilly took a breath. He knew he was stammering. The two strangers looked at him as if to say, "And what?" but they remained silent. "Well, maybe you could work in the day, and take a few night classes at a community college for a year or so. That might up your chances of getting in to the university. Imagine what can change when your dad realizes how committed you are to your dream. Stuff works out when you imagine it can." He blurted it out, hoping he hadn't sounded completely psycho. Reilly held his breath as the pizza box began to wobble.

Then the awkward silence ended as a faint look of hope appeared on the teenager's face. "Huh! Thanks, kid," he said. "I didn't think of that." The girl giggled.

Reilly tried to smile and walked quickly out the door, exhaling a sigh of relief.

He was quiet on the drive home. Pulling into the driveway, his mom finally broke the silence. "Mmm, that pizza smells great. Let's go eat."

After three bites, Reilly put down his slice of pizza and for a brief moment debated whether to tell his mom anything at all. Suddenly, he started to talk and he continued non-stop until he'd told her everything: about finding the Stelladaur, going through The Arc of Color and the violet vortex, Fiala, the tree games, the drawing sidewalk, going back in time, Khenan and Dante, Mr. Jackson and the Stelladaur he'd stolen, and the two people at *That's A Some Pizza*. He talked until he couldn't think of anything else to say.

"Well, Reilly, you've had quite an adventure." His mom paused and pushed the box of pizza out of the way. "You're so much like your dad, you know."

Reilly took a short, deep breath. "In what way?"

"Your imagination—"

"You, too? You sound like Chan." He sighed. "I didn't imagine this, Mom."

"That's not what I mean. You just believe so easily, that's all." She placed her napkin on the table.

Reilly felt dumb for having so quickly forgotten about the purpose of imagination and for becoming defensive with his mom.

"Sometimes I wish I was more like that." She stopped speaking and Reilly waited for her to continue. She took a deep breath and began again. "Your dad planned to give you the Stelladaur on your birthday, but when Eilam gave you the knife, it just wasn't the right time. Dad always believed in the Stelladaur's power, and that his own father and grandfather used it to bring them their greatest desires. But he used to wonder why he never had a dramatic experience with it as they did. Then, on your birthday, something changed for him. He realized that the power of the Stelladaur had been bringing him what he wanted all along. It guided him to

The Ark when he was looking for a sailboat to purchase. It gave him courage to change his career path. It steered him into Eagle Harbor and helped him recognize his connection with Eilam. And it told him there is purpose in the timing of everything. None of those things came about simply because he had a Stelladaur in his possession. They all came about because he always believed in its power."

Reilly listened carefully. Hearing his mom talk about his dad brought a lump to his throat.

"But you don't believe in its power?"

"It's not my Stelladaur. I'm not sure there is one for me. But, for whatever reason, I believe it did make a difference in your dad's life."

His mom paused, but the silence caused still more questions to flood Reilly's mind.

"Why didn't Dad give it to me when I got back from New York?" His voice choked.

"I don't know." She reached for her son's hand, resting on the table near the cold pizza.

The warmth of her hand felt good. "Why, Mom? Why did he have to die? It's all my fault." Reilly began to sob.

His mom stood up and moved to embrace Reilly with open arms. "Oh, Reilly, no ... no ..."

Reilly jumped up from his chair and flung his arms around his mom.

"It's not your fault. It's *not* your fault. It just happened." She held him tightly, rocking back and forth. He clung to her, crying as his body heaved. She wept silently. When the sobs subsided into deep sniffles, he pulled away.

"I got your shoulder all wet," he said as he wiped his nose with his shirtsleeve. He sniffed and wiped with the other sleeve. His mom reached for the box of tissues. He took two and blew hard. Then he took two more, blew again, and wiped his eyes.

Reilly breathed in, yawning widely, before he exhaled, welcoming the sense of release. "I'm really tired, Mom. I'm going to bed. Maybe I'll read for a while."

His mom hugged him again. "Good idea, son. I love you."

"I love you, too."

Tuma followed Reilly to his room and jumped on the bed to settle in her usual spot. Reilly didn't bother undressing. He collapsed on the bed, kicked off his shoes, pushed them to the floor with his feet and pulled the blanket over his head. For a few minutes he lay there with his eyes closed, hoping sleep would come immediately. However, with the skylight just above him and the late-June night barely starting, it wasn't dark yet. Sleep did not come. He brought the covers down to his waist and stared straight up. Nothing. Just a cloudless sky at dusk.

For hours and days between the funeral and finding the Stelladaur, Reilly had begged for the rain to stop beating—endlessly beating. But now, he looked up and wished for a summer shower.

Rain to gently wash everything away. To clear his mind. To soothe his heart.

Rain to launch another rainbow, and bring him closer to his dad.

Chapter Twelve

Frequencies and Scruples

For the next eight days there was no rain. The skies were blue and it grew unseasonably warm. At the hut, Reilly helped Eilam, busy now with tourists, many of whom were eager to know about his unusually white dog. Tuma had a way of relaxing the uneasy responses of the locals towards Eilam. Still, no one could get Eilam or Reilly to say where the dog had actually come from. "She just showed up one day," was all either of them would say.

When the boy and the dog weren't at the hut or the bakery, Reilly kayaked or biked around town, or whittled with his knife. Somehow he and Tuma managed to avoid running into Travis.

Even so, Reilly was continually preoccupied with two things. First, although he took his assignment from Fiala seriously, attempting to carry it out often left him wondering if others had started to think about him the way they did about Eilam. Second, every day he hoped it would rain. He spent hours waiting for heavy clouds and an appearance of The Arc of Color. Finally, he decided it proved to be burdensome work, and that the rain would come when it was darn well ready to come. And no sooner.

On the eighth day of straight sunshine, as he walked down the dock to the hut, it occurred to him that his Stelladaur was useful with or without a rainbow in sight. Chagrined that his anxiety had kept him from remembering that his Stelladaur was multifunctional, he consciously touched it, and immediately he knew what he needed to do. Reilly and Tuma went to see Sequoran.

The trail to Gazzam Lake was anything but deserted. Hikers and bikers came in and out of the forest, most with a dog or two. As Reilly smiled at passers-by on the trail, he hoped no one else felt inclined to saunter around the lake that day. He turned off the main trail, and with Sequoran now in full view, he felt relieved that no one else was around.

The forest was quiet—no rumbling or jackhammer sounds. Reilly was disappointed not to hear Sequoran snoring, but he hoped the tree was awake and even, perhaps, waiting for him. Reilly moved quickly to the base of the giant tree. He felt the Stelladaur pulsating gently under his shirt as he stepped up to the trunk. He waited. Nothing. He put his ear to the moss and felt a gentle, steady beating in synch with the pulsating of the Stelladaur.

"I can hear him breathing," Reilly whispered to Tuma. "Maybe he's sleeping quietly today." No answer. "If he's awake, why won't he say so?"

Reilly moved in closer and stretched his arms out to give a wide, firm hug to the tree. He felt a sudden jolt and stepped back.

"Pardon me. I didn't mean to jump," Sequoran said. "But that tickled!"

Reilly smiled broadly. "I'm sorry. Didn't you hear me coming?"

"Of course, I did—you and everyone who comes into the forest. However, I was busy watching the waves roll in on the far coast and I got carried away, blissfully listening to all their chatter. Quite helpful, I must say."

"You can see the waves on the far coast? And they chatter?" Reilly asked.

"Absolutely! All living things communicate in a language understood by all other living things, except by most humans."

"What do you mean?"

"People often lack the awareness and consciousness that other living creatures enjoy naturally. The energy in the waves is the same energy that's in both you and me. Most humans have forgotten this, so they don't really look. They don't really listen."

"But you can always hear the waves talking?"

"Every time I tune in to their frequency."

"Frequency?"

"It's the energy wavelength that communicates understanding from sea to tree. There is a language frequency for communication between all living things. That's why you can hear me, Reilly. You're on the tree-to-human frequency."

Reilly was glad to finally understand how it was that he could hear Sequoran talk.

Sequoran heard Reilly's thoughts. "And that's why you know when the Stelladaur is speaking to you, too."

"But the Stelladaur isn't a living thing. Is it?"

"Oh, yes."

Reilly paused. "My Stelladaur told me to come and see you."

"And so you have."

Reilly didn't know what to say next. He looked at Tuma who, though silent, wagged her tail swiftly. In the silence, a pure and mysterious place, similar to the space between inhaling a deep breath and letting it out, opened up in Reilly's consciousness. *The waves.*

"What did the waves say?" he asked Sequoran.

"Ah, the chattering waves. They're getting organized, lined up, tucked in and around each other, some high, and others down low. They're communicating perfectly with each other and with the wind to prepare ..."

"Prepare for what?"

"To receive."

"Receive what?"

"More water from the rain clouds gathering beyond."

"Is the rain headed this way?" Reilly touched the tree in anticipation.

"Yes. It will be here after the moon grins once and before the sun smiles southeast on Eagle Harbor. You must now prepare for your next journey."

"How?"

"Tonight, look at the moon out your window. Watch. Listen. Be still."

"Okay, I will. Thanks, Sequoran." Reilly hugged himself to Sequoran's mossy trunk. "I'll come again soon. Thank you."

"Ah, thank *you,* Reilly. As I've said before, so many walk by without tuning in."

Reilly touched the tree again and turned to leave the forest with Tuma beside him.

"Hi, Mom, I just talked with Sequoran," Reilly said, as he snitched a slice of raw potato from a pile she was arranging in a casserole dish. He tried to act as if their last interaction had cleared up the recent rift between them. "He said it's going to rain tomorrow. Isn't that great? I'm hoping The Arc of Color will be there again. If it is, I'm headed back through the vortex."

"Reilly, we need to talk." She held her hands under some running water for a moment and wiped them on a paper towel.

"What's up? It sounds serious."

"It is." She picked up the newspaper at the end of the counter and handed it to Reilly.

Reilly gasped as he silently read the front-page headline:

Inventor of Imperial Plastics Announces Patent for a Time Travel Device.

"What?" Reilly shouted. "Does this mean what I think it means?"

"Read it."

Reilly read the article aloud.

Following the success of Imperial Plastics' innovations in industrial robotics, sustainable automotive engine oil, performance-based sailboat hull resins, Jupiter satellite technologies and the first fully functional plastic eye, Bainbridge Island-based innovator Travis Jackson has announced his proprietary claim to a patent for a new device he says is designed to transcend the time-space barrier.

The device, known as the ROCK (Reaching Our Cosmos Kaleidoscope) promises to transport individuals through dimensions previously unknown.

"I've been searching for this discovery for over a quarter of a century," Jackson said at a recent press conference held to announce the patent. "Our team of experts has worked around the clock for the past month to prepare for the premiere unveiling of the ROCK's first functional prototype."

Skeptics decry Jackson's latest invention as nothing more than "pure science fiction," though the inventor is quick to point to the more than 200 other inventions he's birthed, most which were declared as "impossible," as evidence that this innovative new device will be the greatest scientific marvel since astronauts walked on the moon in 1969.

The core structure of the device is fashioned from a lab-generated material that resembles zirconium. The core, measured with a Mohr's scale hardness rating to be as hard as diamond and treated with a patent-pending resin, is shaped in the form of a chiseled three-dimensional star that emits color and sound frequencies. Jackson asserts that the stabilized molecular structure of the ROCK channels the same frequencies related to the color and sound spectra that were only discovered by quantum physicists as recently as last year.

The ROCK has the capability of magnifying the intensity of endless colors in the light spectrum at a rate much faster than the speed of light, eliciting visible vibrations that facilitate what Jackson describes as "travel into another dimension" for the person utilizing one of his ROCKs.

The unveiling of the device will take place at the Fairmont Hotel on Saturday, June 27th, at 8:00 p.m., by invitation only. Footage of the unveiling and possible activation of the device will be broadcast live by Channel 5 News.

If the prototype is shown to definitely replicate time travel in controlled environments, Wall Street analysts project a substantial rise in Imperial Plastics (IPL) stock.

"Mom, this can't be! What are we going to do?" Reilly was panic-stricken. "It's all my fault! It wasn't supposed to happen this way! If I hadn't gone back in time, he wouldn't have that Stelladaur … and now he's used it to make a prototype! It says here that he can prove it works!" Reilly's voice grew louder as he waved the newspaper in the air. "This is terrible!"

"Reilly, calm down," his mom said. "First of all, none of this is your fault. I'm not sure exactly what your Stelladaur can do, but I know it's a rare, treasured gift from your dad. And I don't know what Mr. Jackson plans to do with his ROCK, but I can guarantee you, it's not the same as your Stelladaur."

"But what if he *did* find a portal?"

"I don't know."

"This is horrible! What are we going to do?"

Reilly's mom took the newspaper from his hand and set it on the counter behind her. "Reilly, you've told me your Stelladaur sort of tells you what to do, with some kind of signal, right?"

"Yeah, I guess."

"Well, if that's the case, what is it telling you now?"

Reilly stopped ranting long enough to consider her question, and the fact that she was asking it. "That's weird," he said. "It's not doing anything. It's perfectly still."

"What do you think that might mean?"

Reilly thought a moment and then turned to Tuma. "Well?" The dog did not respond. "I don't know. It's almost like I shouldn't do anything right now." Tuma barked.

"Uhm …" His mom nodded as she patted Tuma's head. "Maybe something will come to you later."

Reilly couldn't tell if she was relieved or worried. "I hope you're right," he sighed. "But I'm nervous."

He went to bed early that night, but lay awake for some time trying to get on the moon-to-person frequency. He stared at the crescent moon until after midnight, listening and waiting, though for what, he wasn't sure. Even after he fell asleep, he stirred throughout the night, reaching for the Stelladaur around his neck and for Tuma at the foot of his bed.

The next morning, they waited at Eilam's for the storm to hit. With colder weather and dark clouds blowing in from the west, it was a slow day for kayak rentals. Reilly spent hours quietly whittling on a piece of pine.

And waiting for the rain.

Eilam broke the silence. "That's very good, Reilly. You have a gift for carving wood, as your grandfather did."

"Do you really think so?" Reilly held the piece of wood away from his body to look at his work. "I didn't realize it was turning into something," he said as he turned it around for Eilam to see. "Look, it's going to be a feather."

"Yes, I noticed," Eilam said. "It is significant that you are carving a feather." He pulled gently on his beard.

"Why?"

"When a person finds a fallen feather on the ground, it means he is on the right path in life for his or her highest good. But you are *creating* a feather. The creation is coming out of complete awareness of the anxiety you are facing. It is not the anxiety or nervousness you feel that dictates inability to provide a desired outcome. It is the unwillingness to allow such a feeling to increase awareness. Allowing brings awareness. Non-allowing promotes a continual state of unconsciousness."

"I'm not sure I follow you."

"You are creating your own path, Reilly. It will be whatever you are willing to allow, through inner awareness."

Reilly kept whittling. "You know what I'm aware of right now?" he grinned.

"What's that?"

"I'm fully aware of my stomach growling, and I'm completely willing to allow food to take care of it!"

They laughed out loud, and Reilly welcomed the concomitant release of his anxiousness for rain. He replaced the knife in the sheath looped to his belt and tucked the piece of wood in his pocket.

At the bakery, Eilam ordered his usual tea and a piece of salmon quiche. Reilly had hot chocolate, a cup of seafood chowder and a thick slice of sourdough bread. Tuma, who usually lay sprawled under the table, sat by the door. Halfway through lunch, Reilly's mom took a break and came to sit by him.

"What's Tuma doing over there?" she asked as she sat down next to Eilam.

"She's waiting," Eilam replied.

"Well, yes, but doesn't she usually wait under the table for any nibbles you might share with her?"

"Today is not a usual day," Eilam said as he took his last bite of quiche. "She's on watch."

"What's she watching for?" Reilly asked.

"For him." Eilam nodded slightly as Travis walked past the large window and approached the front door.

Reilly's mom sighed and excused herself to the kitchen. She'd barely made it into the back room when Travis opened the main door. Tuma growled. Hearing her greet Travis with such disapproval, everyone turned to see what was going on. Reilly held his cup of hot chocolate with both hands and watched.

"Shush!" Travis held his hand out with a "stay" command and walked past the dog. Tuma stood up and sounded a second warning, but she did not leave her post at the door.

Two customers in the center booth waved at Travis. A man who was trying to decide what to order from the display case turned and said hello to him. Simultaneously, a woman at the far end of the bakery lifted her hand to wave. Like an arrogant politician, Travis waved his hand high with a sweeping motion, then stepped in front of the customer who was first in line.

"I need to see Monique," he announced in a loud, obnoxious voice. "I've got a tight schedule today, so let her know I'm here. I'll have a black coffee to go." He turned away from the counter and Tuma growled again. Travis faced the register and impatiently fidgeted with the dish of spare pennies.

Reilly's heart pounded and his cheeks were flushed. He clenched his jaw and gripped his hands more tightly around the mug. Few things brought Reilly more anxiety than observing Travis Jackson interact with his mom.

When Reilly's mom entered the room, Travis whirled around and marched over to meet her on the far side of the display case, directly opposite the booth where Reilly and Eilam were sitting. Tuma growled louder than before and almost nipped at Travis's heels, stopping beside Reilly's mom. Most every eye in the bakery turned to watch. Though some people pretended to ignore the scene, Reilly knew they were eavesdropping.

"Nice to see you, Monique." Travis extended his hand, but she simply nodded and stroked Tuma's head while she kept direct eye contact with Travis. "I'm sure you're aware that I'll be holding a press conference on Saturday to introduce my latest and most valuable invention, the ROCK." She still did not respond. Travis glanced briefly at Tuma and then continued. "Following the official release, I'll be hosting a private reception—you know, for investors, potential shareholders, presidents of major international corporations and a few select friends—about one hundred guests in all. Pacific Northwest Catering will handle the hors d'oeuvres and drinks. Monique, I'd like you to provide a bread buffet—all my favorites, which you make for the club's annual affair. I'll need a dozen of your Chocolate Raspberry Cheesecakes, as well."

"That will be no problem. What time would you like my driver to deliver the order to the venue?"

"Everything needs to be ready to go by six."

Reilly knew most billionaires did *not* take care of ordering bread and desserts for a business event. Or any event! But he also knew Travis always had ulterior motives whenever he stepped inside the bakery. Today was no exception.

"Monique," Travis said in a softer tone, "I'd like you to come."

"Excuse me?"

"I'd be honored if you would attend the event."

Honored? Though Reilly's perception of Travis was limited to his own experiences with him, *honored* was not a word he had ever heard the man use. Tuma growled at the request, which confirmed in Reilly's mind that, once again, Travis had ulterior motives.

"I ... uh ... thank you for the invitation, but I ... don't think I will be able to attend." She quickly regained her composure. "However, I will make sure everything is there by six. Excuse me, please."

Flustered, she turned quickly and exited the room. Travis was noticeably annoyed and left the bakery without his coffee. A few customers raised their eyebrows, but most resumed their normal conversations. Reilly jumped from the bench and ran to the back room.

"Mom," he nearly yelled as he sprinted to her side. "Why did he do that? What's his problem, anyway?"

"Calm down, Reilly." She put a hand on his shoulder. Reilly could feel her hand shaking slightly.

"Mom, I can see it in your eyes. He has no right to come in here and make a scene like that. What makes him think you would ever go *anywhere* with him?" He paused briefly. "You wouldn't, would you?"

She lowered her hand and reached behind her back to tighten her apron.

"Of course not, Reilly. I don't like Mr. Jackson any more than you do ... but maybe he was just being cordial."

"Cordial?" Reilly nearly shouted.

"Polite."

"Mom, please."

"You know he's one of our biggest clients, Reilly. I need to keep my cool. Besides, anytime we've catered an event for him in Seattle, we've always had additional accounts come out of it. It's just business."

"We don't need his business, Mom! He's up to no good. There's some other reason he wants you at that reception, besides the fact that he obviously *likes* you."

"Reilly!" She folded her arms to emphasize the reprimand.

"Mom, I'm not stupid. It's so obvious—to everyone. I've known that for a long time. And I never understood why Dad didn't just tell the guy to take his business somewhere else. Why didn't Dad do something about it?"

Reilly's mom's voice tightened. "Is this about your dad?"

"What do you mean?" Reilly knew he sounded childish.

"You know what I mean. Are you looking for a reason to justify being angry with your dad—for not being here?"

Reilly knew she would wait for a response.

"No ... I guess not. I just get so irritated whenever I see Mr. Jackson. And especially when I see him talking to you."

"Mr. Jackson has never been a threat to your dad or to me. While it's true the man lacks scruples, he's never posed any real harm."

"Scruples?"

"Moral and ethical decency. As far as the moral part of it goes, you're right, he's a flirt and a womanizer. He always has been. But I'm a big girl, Reilly, and there's nothing to worry about."

"I know you would never ... it's just that ..."

"Just what?"

"It's that ethical part of the scruples. I just don't trust him. He's up to something with this ROCK thing, and whatever it is, it's not good."

"Reilly, he's fabricated something in a lab. Whatever the ROCK can do, it's *not* the same as a Stelladaur. That being said, the man is a brilliant scientist who has done many great things for humanity. Maybe what he's introducing will be of some benefit to—"

"There you go again. Taking his side."

"Reilly, please! You're not making this any easier," she said putting her hands on her hips. "I've got the business to think about now, and everything else. I just can't worry about all this, too. Besides, you said the Stelladaur only works according to certain conditions, which are different than the laws of science. And that's something Mr. Jackson will likely never know or understand."

"I don't know, Mom. Whatever he's doing, it's got my stomach turned in knots."

"Just breathe, Reilly. It's going to be all right. Of course, I'm not going to the reception. We can watch the live coverage together, okay?"

He tried not to but he rolled his eyes anyway. Just then he felt the Stelladaur pulsating, giving him a burst of courage.

"Mom, I just had an idea! What if I go with James to make the delivery? Maybe I could find something out, something that won't be shown on TV. You could hire me to help make the delivery!"

"Now wait a minute! You basically just said that whenever you're around Mr. Jackson, you feel nervous and even sick to your stomach."

"Yeah, but *you* just said he isn't a real threat."

"I don't know about—"

"Mom, I've got to. Please! I'll come right back with James. He'd love the company. Besides, I handled Mr. Jackson just fine in New York, didn't I? Twice actually."

"No, Reilly. Absolutely not!"

"If Dad were here, he'd say it was a good idea. You know he would."

"That's not fair." Tears welled up, but she blinked them back. "I can't think about this. Not *today*!" She turned to walk away. "I've got work to do. You may *not* go with James."

Reilly grunted as she left the room, but then he remembered *today* was his parents' anniversary, which would explain his mom's sensitivity to the whole situation. Feeling like a jerk for not remembering earlier, Reilly left the bakery, frustrated because for some reason he could communicate with a talking tree just fine, but he and his mom seemed to be on completely different frequencies.

Chapter Thirteen

Awareness

Reilly, Tuma and Eilam barely had made it back to the kayak hut when the downpour hit. Sheets of heavy rain hammered on the metal roof. They sat watching the rain pellets ricochet off kayaks and boats secured to the dock, peppering the harbor. It gushed like a river from the rain-gutter spout. For over an hour the skies deluged the earth without letting up. Reilly watched intently, anxious for the clouds to part and reveal The Arc of Color again. Finally, the raindrops appeared less plump and the spaces between them more distant; the noise softened. Five minutes later, Reilly put on his jacket and headed to his kayak, showered by just a light rain. As he pushed away from the dock, he felt the rain turn to a drizzle. Smiling, he waved to Eilam as he and Tuma drifted out.

Seeing the clouds move quickly, Reilly paddled fast past the ferry terminal, and then to the far right of an oncoming vessel. The rain diffused to mist, and the clouds parted, showing a patch of blue to the north towards Kingston. He paddled hard, anxious to get past the ferry so he could have a better view of the skyline.

Then, in full view, The Arc of Color materialized before his eyes. A complete arch, it appeared thicker than the first but the point where it landed in the water seemed further away.

Reilly paddled as fast as he could, watching the dreary sky begin to clear.

"Tuma, what if it disappears before I reach it?"

Tuma jumped in the water and positioned herself at the back end of the kayak. With her head pressed up against the hull, the dog moved all four legs rapidly, and the kayak gained significant speed, propelling ahead like a sleek, two-passenger powerboat. Within minutes, Reilly and Tuma arrived at the point where The Arc of Color intersected the water.

Reilly unzipped his jacket and pulled the Stelladaur out from under his shirt. Holding it in both hands, he gently moved it around, aiming it towards the apex and trying to catch the light shining off the water from Seattle. Several times he tried but failed. Frantically, he maneuvered the stone while simultaneously keeping an eye on the grey clouds that were rapidly transforming into white, or disappearing alltogether. Reilly began to panic.

"Tuma, what should I do?"

The dog barked once, but Reilly did not understand the instruction. On the verge of hyperventilating, he manipulated the Stelladaur in numerous contorted angles. *It happened so easily the first time*, he thought. *What am I doing wrong?*

Then, from beyond the harbor, he heard Sequoran.

"Hold still and the light will come to you."

Reilly stopped moving his hands and held the Stelladaur still, pointed directly at the apex of the Arc. His breathing deepened.

Within seconds a beam of light struck the Stelladaur from behind and reflected off the stone to the top of the Arc. The illuminating force propelled Reilly out of the kayak and into the water, arms first with the Stelladaur in his hands. He plummeted into a whirling vortex in the sea.

This time, everything around him was a deep indigo, but he could see the violet vortex beside him, closer to the surface of the water. As before, he moved ahead in a floating fashion, surrounded by water, yet remaining completely dry. Reilly considered moving his legs or arms, or doing something to help propel him through the purple tunnel. But at that moment he heard Sequoran again.

"Just *be*. You don't have to *do* anything."

He relaxed. Shooting ahead at a tremendous speed, the only movement he felt was the air passing through his lungs. Everything around him was moving … spinning … turning … gyrating … dancing—all in a strange under-the-sea conglomeration. Yet he was still and safe in the indigo tunnel.

The vortex met with a white beam of light at the apex of the Arc, under the sea. Reilly shifted effortlessly into the white beam and was propelled straight up—up towards the surface of the water, up out of the water, up towards the apex of the Arc above the water, up past the tip of the Arc and up past the Earth. Up, up, up! Still, still, still! Faster, faster, faster!

Reilly blinked to try to adjust his focus on everything that was zipping past him. In a mesmerizing trance that left him feeling weightless, he became acutely aware of his surroundings. As before, he could hear and see the intricacies of the universe and beyond, but this time it was more encompassing. Somehow he could actually feel it through the awareness of it. Blended together, it became an energetic audio-visual symphony coursing through his veins.

Then, quite without warning, Reilly landed as he had before, on his feet, surrounded by a warm indigo mist. The mist was soothing and refreshing, not stuffy or humid. He heard nothing but a gentle whoosh of air as he breathed. Instinctively, he inhaled the stillness and exhaled slowly. Every breath filled him with an intoxicating calmness. The purple mist began to dissipate, and his breathing returned to normal.

He blinked slowly and saw a strange-looking creature a few feet in front of him.

"Welcome to Just Beyond Jolka. I am Porfino," the purplish creature began. "We have been looking forward to your arrival."

In an instant, Reilly observed numerous details about Porfino. He looked like a man, with dark, short and curly hair, olive skin, full brows and lips, and a well-built physique. He wore a purple, straight tunic that opened with an indigo chord laced loosely at his neck revealing a smooth chest. His arms and legs were hairy. Like Fiala, Porfino did not wear anything on his feet. But what intrigued Reilly most were Porfino's eyes. He had three. One was positioned on each side of the bridge of his nose, like human eyes. Both eyes were closed gently, an aubergine glow emanating from under the lids. The third eye was positioned just above the nose, in the center of his forehead. It sparkled like a dazzling azurite. It had no eyelid. There was only a socket that kept the gemlike eye perfectly still in its place but open and glittering.

"I've been waiting for the Arc to appear again, so I could come back," Reilly said, trying not to stare at the azurite eye.

"The Arc is always there, but only visible to those who are mindful of its never-ending presence. In Just Beyond Jolka, you will become aware of the oneness and purpose in all things."

It was difficult for Reilly to decide which eye to look at or if he should just watch Porfino's mouth.

"When awareness of what *is* permeates one's existence, stillness amidst opposition is welcomed. Stillness expands the soul's ability to understand the divine in all living things."

Reilly wanted Porfino to repeat what he had just said, so he could try to comprehend what it meant. Instead, he remained silent and simply nodded.

Unlike Jolka, Reilly could see no path from where he stood. No roads, sidewalks, trails or directional routes. He felt solid ground under his feet, but for as far as he could see there was only vast, open space with a swirling of opaque purple clouds. There were no visible formations except the creature with three eyes.

Porfino took a step forward and gazed with his azurite eye at Reilly's Stelladaur, creating a ray of indigo light between the two of them. Suddenly, Reilly felt something wrap around him. He reached out but his finger bumped into an invisible wall. At his touch, the wall lit up in an iridescent indigo light like a giant soap bubble, reflecting rainbow colors from the sunlight. But the bubble did not pop when he touched it. Instead, it made an *ahhm* sound, like a meditating Tibetan monk. Both the light from the bubble and the tonal frequency lasted only a few seconds after Reilly touched it. With intention, he touched it again and the bubble lit up, accompanied by the single chant. Then he placed his entire palm on the invisible wall and it lit up much brighter, making his hand radiate in a purple glow. The *ahhm* continued in a series of prolonged notes.

Reilly wondered if it was a game, like one of the imagination games of Jolka. But the sensation was different in this experience, so he wasn't sure.

"No, it is not a game."

Of course, Reilly thought, *if Fiala could read my mind, I should have guessed Porfino could, too.*

"What is it?" Reilly asked as he touched the bubble again with his palm.

"It is not named," Porfino said, "but it represents the awareness in all you experience and all that you are." The bubble reflected in his middle eye.

"You mean like understanding why something is the way it is?"

"No, simply being aware that it is."

"I don't understand."

"Before you touched the screen of the bubble—which is not really what it is, but I only give it a label so you can identify it—you did not know it was there. However, it was always there. You were just unaware of its existence. Is it now necessary for you to understand it, to know that it is?"

"I guess not."

"It is only necessary that you are aware of its existence."

Reilly scowled, confused.

"How do you know it is there?" Porfino probed.

"I can see it when I touch it."

"Yes, but what if you did not have eyes to see? Would that mean it did not exist?"

"No."

"How would you know it exists?"

"I can hear it."

"Yes, but what if you did not have ears to hear? Would that mean it did not exist?"

"No."

"Then how do you know it exists?"

Reilly thought before answering. "Well … something sort of wrapped around me. It's hard to explain. But it felt protective, not restrictive."

"Why do you think you so quickly forgot the feeling that first told you of its existence?"

Reilly thought again before responding. "I don't know. Maybe because I just wanted to see if it was really there, so I reached out to try and touch it."

"You thought your eyes or your ears would be a better guide than your feelings to tell you of its existence."

"Yeah, I suppose so." Reilly's voice had gained an introspective tone.

"Feelings are an indicator that awareness is awakening within. When you learn to trust your feelings you will begin to recognize yourself."

"You mean I will know what I want?"

"No, you will know *you*."

Reilly raised his eyebrows.

"Awareness is the space between what you think you know and what actually is. Some people catch glimpses of this power. However, it is not awareness of self that brings this realization, but attention to the awareness."

Reilly slowly lifted both hands to touch the bubble. This time he had to take two steps forward to reach it. Then it lit up very bright, and the *ahhming* echoed in surround-sound.

"What happened? Why is it further away?"

"It's not further away. You have allowed awareness to encompass a broader space. You have expanded it because of your attention to the awareness of you."

Reilly stood very still and tried not to think. He started to feel the way he did when he was going through the indigo vortex—weightless, with no need for exertion, just conscious of breathing without thinking. Feeling that the boundaries had moved again, Reilly walked a few steps past Porfino and reached out to touch the bubble. It enclosed both of them. The *ahhming* grew bolder and Reilly knew it was now composed of two voices, though it was one sound. Porfino turned to face Reilly's back.

"There are no boundaries when you are still enough to give space. Then awareness continually expands to include all."

Reilly turned around, but the echoing continued. "Ah, I think I get it. I mean, I *feel* like I understand."

"Yes, you are beginning to."

Porfino smiled and his open eye gazed at the Stelladaur around Reilly's neck. In that moment, there was an intense flash of light.

Reilly lowered his chin to shield his eyes. He blinked a number of times, and then closed his eyes for a few seconds, giving them a reprieve from the brightness. When he opened his eyes, he saw nothing. It was completely dark. He blinked again, rapidly, but saw nothing. Instinctively, he reached his hands out for something to hold on to, and with his head tilted up, took a few awkward steps forward.

"When there is resistance to stillness within, awareness is limited. However, beingness—independent of external otherness—creates awareness of what divinely is."

Reilly knew it was Porfino's voice, but he could not see where he had gone. Then all was silent.

Reilly reached out again, then tilted his head and turned his body. His equilibrium was off so he sat down crossed-legged and closed his eyes, hoping the darkness would become less dark. He breathed gently, shallowly. Then, he consciously inhaled deeply, held his breath to the count of three and exhaled slowly. It felt good. He did it again … and again … and again. He felt his abdomen and lungs expand a little more with each breath, and calmness claimed the space between exhalation and inhalation.

Trying to put all logic and reason aside, he slowly opened his eyes again, calmly blinking to adjust to the darkness. He started to see a faint purple hue.

He put his hands on his knees and inhaled again before exhaling a soft tone, *"Ahhm."* This felt good, too. He repeated it several times, letting the sustained note deplete the air in his lungs before inhaling again. Now completely relaxed in the stillness around him, he felt the Stelladaur pulsating to the beating of his own heart.

Standing up and not stopping to analyze his next action, Reilly visualized Porfino's azurite eye and lifted the Stelladaur to touch his forehead. The stone instantly melded into the skin's surface, leaving a sparkling white jewel protruding slightly. It was Reilly's third eye. His other two eyes closed, leaving a purplish hue glowing from under the eyelids.

He watched as the purple clouds dissipated, revealing numerous giant screens draped from invisible hangers in front of him and circling around him, only a few feet away. Like ornate Persian rugs displayed on a movable rack in a store, each screen portrayed a one-dimensional painting that looked strangely familiar.

Reilly stepped forward and touched the edge of the screen directly in front of him so he could move it out of the way and take a closer look. Instantly, the screen lit up in an iridescent indigo, and the images within the scene became animated. It was like watching a giant suspended IMAX movie. Reilly saw himself and his dad at the Rotary Auction, strapping the putrid green kayak on top of their Jeep. Reilly grinned widely due to the emotion the memory evoked. He walked alongside the screen and watched the two of them sanding the hull of the kayak. Reilly's nose twitched with the permeating smell of sawdust and paint. He heard his dad laughing and felt exhilarated by it, relishing the happiness and security he felt in the moment. The scene changed to his dad and him floating in the kayak along Eagle Harbor, with a ferry horn blowing and a cluster of seagulls squawking in the distance. Reilly breathed in the salty air.

Eager to see what the other painted scenes revealed, he walked back to the center of the hanging screens and flipped through a few of them the way he'd tapped apps on a smart phone. At first they seemed random: building a tree house, walking along the beach, playing Frisbee with Chantal, swimming lessons, dinner with his family, hanging out at the bakery, hiking in the Grand Forest, flying a kite. Each one evoked in Reilly real delight, and he found it easy to just be still, to observe the delight.

Enjoying the elation that all the scenes were evoking, Reilly continued to touch them, one at a time—watching and listening—and moving each one out of the way to reveal the next. He flipped quickly past a few unfamiliar scenes but stopped at one when he thought he saw Norah, from Jolka, standing in front of an ornate door. But when he looked again, she was gone. He caught a glipse of the number 10 above the closed door and wondered why it wouldn't open.

Moving a few more of the strange paintings out of the way, Reilly felt compelled to stop at another one. Doing so changed his emotions immediately from delight to dread. He watched himself peer over *The Ark* into nothing but darkness. All blackness—with only the noise of his own suffocation.

But his third eye shone its light into the abyss, and he heard his dad's voice washing over him like a warm August rain. *You will find me in the Ark.* Reilly lifted his head and breathed in the renewing warmth, as his dad's voice echoed deeply into Reilly's soul, filling him with the sudden realization that his dad had never really left him. It was a sacred space between here and there, then and now, life and death, which brought him the awareness of his continual and ever-connectedness to his dad. An awareness of *was* and *is*.

Reilly moved slowly along the hanging scene, allowing the feeling of peace, unknown to him before, to linger.

Coming into the center of the hanging screens again, he simply stood there ... and breathed ... and smiled.

He turned around twice, glancing at the circular rack of giant screens. He stepped closer to one that pulled at him like a magnet. Aware that his feeling of peace had now been swallowed up by unease, he moved towards the screen anyway.

With every step, the unease increased ... to anxiety ... then fear ... and, upon approaching the scene, impending doom. Yet, somehow, Reilly did not relinquish the space of stillness that gave awareness to the doom. He touched the edge of the scene and swung it open so he could see it in full view.

There before him was a giant gargoyle, its mouth gaping open to an infernal cave of darkness. The Stelladaur eye shone from his forehead like a miner's headlamp lighting the way through the darkness. He stepped into the beam of light, which extended into the thick blackness in a straight path through the scene. The stone mouth closed with a loud, echoing BANG!

The sudden contrast between light and dark was harrowing. Seeping through the darkness from every direction, the shadows threatened to engulf him. Depravity, harm, calamity, misery, pain and deceit—they all taunted him in horrendous hooded black forms. He saw a grotesqueness he had never witnessed before. He clenched his jaw and felt the perspiration bead on his brow. In an attempt to ward off the evil hooded creatures, ready to consume him, he lifted his head higher, as if to propel the light from his Stelladaur further in front of him. He caught glimpses of the nefarious monsters, hundreds of them, lurking in the shadows past his third eye, but retreating when the light shone directly on them. Some reached their arms out to grope at him from behind, attempting to pull him towards them.

Reilly had experienced extreme fear and pain when he helplessly watched his dad drown, but this dark tunnel emitted an all-consuming terror. Oddly, Reilly remained acutely conscious of his steady, calm breathing. His heart beat with a subtle pulse. Within the beam of light, all was calm. Yet, beyond the protective aura, hideous noises oozed in hellish disharmony from under the hoods of the beasts. Moaning … cackling … taunting … mocking. The sound waves reverberated in swirling motions off the unseen walls of the cave then ricocheted off the ray of light in a mass of tormented chaos. The stench of decay assaulted his nostrils. The taste of blood stung his tongue and drooled down his throat.

But he walked steadfastly through the scourging cave towards a point where the light shone beyond the fading blackness.

As he reached the exit, he turned to look back. Instantly, the Stelladaur vanished from his forehead and was back on the cord around his neck, leaving no visible sign that anything had ever been implanted in his forehead. His natural eyes opened wide and, with utter horror, he saw the faces of each of the malevolent demons. They all laughed at him in voices edged with insanity. Each was the distorted and contorted face of … Travis Jackson!

No longer feeling any sense of stillness or calm, Reilly bolted from the cave.

With his first step, he landed effortlessly back in his kayak.

A black feather lay beside him. He picked it up and held it to the sunlight. Shades of iridescent indigo bounced off its soft plumes, and Reilly remembered what Eilam had told him about feathers.

Chapter Fourteen

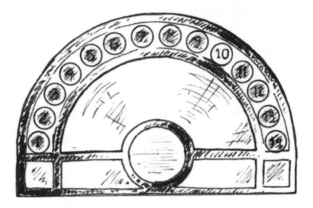

Tenth Floor

Reilly put the feather in his pocket right next to the piece of wood he had been whittling earlier, and grabbed the paddle. Though the feather provided some reassurance, it was, nonetheless, fleeting and seemed miniscule in comparison to the images of Travis he had just witnessed. He stroked frantically, half expecting the hooded demons to have somehow followed him through the warp in time and space, so they now lurked in this world. His pounding heart thudded like a mallet against a bass drum. His breathing grew labored. His head was spinning.

"Tuma," he gasped. "Tuma, help!"

The dog swam up from behind to propel the kayak forward. Completely exhausted, Reilly relaxed his arms and rested the paddle across his lap, allowing Tuma to bring them into the harbor.

Reilly closed his eyes and breathed in deeply, letting the warmth of the setting sun penetrate his eyelids and the sweet smelling rain replace the tightness in his lungs with fresh air.

It was difficult for him to cope with the extreme contrast of emotions. A part of him longed to forget what he had just seen and pretend it never happened. But then he would have to ignore the growing conviction that his dad would, in some unexplainable way, always be near him. And that awareness was something he wouldn't trade for anything—even if it meant facing a thousand Travis Jacksons!

The epiphany lit his consciousness as nothing had before.

Though Reilly had thought he wanted to be with his dad again, now, more than anything, he wanted this fear of Travis to leave him and never come back or torment anyone else. He started to understand what Fiala meant when she said it wasn't easy for a person to find a true greatest desire. Circumstances change. Perspectives change. Ideas change. He also began to realize that his Stelladaur had many purposes.

Yet, he had many unanswered questions. *What is Mr. Jackson planning to do with the Stelladaur he stole from Dante? What will he really be presenting to the world on Saturday evening?* Everything inside of Reilly told him that Travis knew nothing of the Stelladaur's real power.

Reilly grabbed the paddle and plunged it into the water. "It's only a replica. A fake!"

Tuma lifted her head higher above the water and gave her usual single-bark response.

"Okay. Then all we have to do is let people know it's a fake so they won't buy into his scheme. Right?"

Tuma did not bark in reply.

It sounded so simple.

By the time Reilly and his dog had reached the kayak hut, the boy was confused and discouraged.

"But what can *I* do about Mr. Jackson? No one is going to believe me. And why should they?" he asked Eilam as they sat on the dock.

"Reilly, it is not necessary to have knowledge of the end at the beginning of the journey. You only have to know the next step." Eilam put his arm around the boy and paused before continuing. "The Stelladaur will be your guide, just as it was through the dark cave, and as it always has been. Focus on the feelings the Stelladaur's light brings to you. When you do this, you will not give in to fear of the unknown ... or of the known."

Eilam's words calmed Reilly. "I liked the feeling I had when the Stelladaur was stuck in my forehead. It was amazing—and weird— to experience so much calm even though darkness and those evil creatures surrounded me. And I'll never forget how awesome it was to feel my dad close by."

"Good."

Reilly reached in his pocket, pulled out the feather and stroked the quills back and forth to smooth it out. "So ... should I do the delivery on Saturday to see if I can find out more information?"

"You must do what you believe is best."

"But my mom said I can't go."

"Then it will be more difficult to decide what is best."

Reilly left the hut, still vacillating in his decision.

When he got home, he told his mom he'd spent the afternoon in his kayak looking for another rainbow but not finding one. She listened half-heartedly and reminded him that she'd forbidden him to go on *The Ark*. He knew there was no point asking her again about going to Seattle with James. And he tried to brush away the guilt that crept over him for keeping the truth about his afternoon from her.

The next morning, Reilly assisted his mom with the cheesecakes Travis had ordered. Typically, he helped out at the bakery by cleaning up, stocking shelves and serving customers, but that day, he felt a sudden urge to bake.

"You're a natural, Reilly," his mom said as they put the first four cheesecakes in the oven. "A real chef."

"You think so?" He beamed, grateful for the break in the awkward silence that had hung between them all morning.

"You bet. You catch on as quickly as your dad did. He'd never baked a thing in his life before we opened the bakery. I taught him how to make his first loaf of bread and first batch of scones. And he just took off from there."

"Really?"

"Uh-huh. I think it was the scientist in him. He liked combining ingredients—testing different combinations to get different results and whipping them all up. And *voila!*" She closed the oven door and spun around with her hand in the air. "A sumptuous creation!" Reilly laughed at her sudden spontaneity.

"Wow! I didn't know that."

"Your dad had an acute sense of taste and flavor. He could tell if a batch of cookies had a half teaspoon too much baking soda."

"I didn't know that either."

"Fifty-five minutes," she said as she set the timer. Then, turning to look at Reilly, she added, "Since you seem to have inherited your father's ability as a baker, you are now officially promoted."

"Promoted? What do you mean?"

"I mean, instead of your usual jobs around here, would you like to take over some of the baking? I'll teach you." Her eyes lit with optimism but then she sighed. "Actually, I could really use your help."

Noticing the shift in his mom's mood, Reilly paused before responding. "Yeah, uh, that would be great. I'd love to. But do I have to come in at 4:00 in the morning with you?" He frowned.

She laughed. "No, but if you could come between 6:00 and 7:00, even a few days a week during the summer, that would be fabulous."

"Okay, I could probably do that. I'll try … if you really think I'd be helping."

"Very much so. Now, let's get those other cheesecakes together."

Reilly stayed in the kitchen the rest of the afternoon, amazed by how much fun he had baking. He measured the flour for a batch of cookies but threw in an extra handful of pecans, and then worried if he had put in too much almond extract. He smiled at the conscious connectedness he felt to his dad.

Exhausted by the end of the day, he slept well that night, and then woke early the next morning to get a good start at the bakery. His mom showed him how to make baguette-style French bread, and again, he caught on like a pro.

Working hard all day for his mom helped him reconcile his earlier indecision and relieved his guilt over the recent strain between them. He told his mom that he and Tuma were going to bring Eilam some bread. Then he left his dog at the kayak hut and met James on the 4:40 boat to make the delivery for Travis's press conference.

James studied at the University of Washington but lived on the island and worked weekends at the bakery. Reilly often watched James joking around with customers, or just being funny when he wasn't trying to be. There were times when Reilly wished he were more like James— that he didn't take life so seriously or think about things so deeply or worry about stuff that wasn't his to worry about.

They waited in the delivery truck on the ferry to Seattle, snacking on some of the pecan cookies Reilly had baked earlier in the day.

"Your mom tells me you've got a real talent for baking. She's right." James bit into another cookie. "My culinary skills stop at pushing the knob on the toaster and pressing the defrost-for-two-minutes button on the microwave. But, hey, it keeps me alive."

"Yeah, I just started. It's fun."

"I like fun, probably a little too much. I'm dragging school out as long as possible. All work and no play makes for a dull life, you know?"

Reilly nodded.

"Don't get me wrong, I'm not a real partier. I just have a difficult time focusing on the books because, well, there are too many other more interesting things to explore in life," James said, wiping a few crumbs from his mouth with the back of his hand.

"Yeah, I know what you mean."

"I like marine biology and all, but this graduate program is a pain in the keister. A mongrel crab that pinches my otherwise exuberant yen for greater adventures … like scuba diving, beach hiking and rock climbing on the cliffs at Cape Flattery. Have you ever done rock climbing, Reilly?"

"Uh, no, I haven't."

"Ever been under the sea? Ya know, scuba-dooba-dooing?"

Reilly laughed at James's imitation of Scooby Doo. "No, I've never been scuba diving, but I have been through a tu—" He stopped abruptly, surprised that he almost blurted out his secret. Pretending to choke on a cookie, he added, "Uh … what I mean is, I've been going through a tough time, you know, since my dad died. I was just thinking the other day about how much fun it would've been to go scuba diving with him."

"Yeah, kid, that's rough. My dad died when I was almost three. I barely remember him. He died of a sudden heart attack when he was only 35. My mom remarried a couple of years later, so my step-dad is the only dad I really know. And he actually adopted me, so I don't even have my real dad's name." James was now more serious than Reilly had known him to be. "But it's kind of weird. Sometimes I get these flashbacks. I don't know what it is, but I can remember my dad holding me on his lap and telling me stories … about stuff under the sea. Or going through the sea … or something."

Reilly's jaw dropped as he considered the possible meaning of what James was saying.

James misread his reaction. "Yeah, it's crazy, I know. Like I could remember something that happened when I was three years old!" He laughed nervously. "Heck, that was almost twenty-five years ago, and I can hardly remember what I read in my micro-organism book just yesterday!"

"No, I don't think it's crazy. It's cool. Is that why you like scuba diving?"

"Maybe, kid. My mom never really talks about my dad. They were only together a few years. But she did tell me he used to read a lot of books about sea adventures. You know, *Moby Dick, 20,000 Leagues Under the Sea, Master and Commander*—stuff like that. He wasn't a treasure hunter or anything. Actually, he was a physicist, but apparently he always thought there were unsolved mysteries under the sea." He chuckled. "So, yeah, I must have inherited that passion from him."

"James, what was your dad's name? Your real dad's name?"

"Jamison. William Jamison."

"Your name is James Jamison?"

"Yeah, my dad used to call me J.J. But my mom prefers James."

"You said he was a physicist. So was my dad, before he opened the bakery. By any chance was your dad a professor at UW?"

"Yes, he was. How would you know that?" James looked back and forth from the road to Reilly.

"I think your dad may have been my dad's professor when he was in graduate school. They were good friends."

"What? Are you serious? Did your mom know him, too?"

"I'm not sure. But I think she may have. About a month before my dad died, he told me about this professor friend of his. They were at a fancy party at a yacht club, which is also where my mom and dad met. Anyway, my dad told his professor about a discovery he had made. About a tunnel under the sea that went through time and space. The professor told my dad that he, also, had reason to believe it was very possible. They'd barely started talking about it when someone who they did not want to include in their conversation interrupted them. Guess who that was?"

"I don't know. Am I supposed to know?"

"Think about it!" Reilly's voice raised a few notches.

"Uhm …"

"Mr. Jackson! Travis Jackson!" Reilly hollered.

James swerved the van too hard to the left and corrected his move seconds before hitting an oncoming vehicle. "What?"

"He invited your dad because he thought your dad would be a potential investor in a new product he'd invented. My Dad was there because he wanted to get ideas for his thesis—which was about time travel—and because his professor had personally invited him."

"Okay, hold on just a minute, kid," James interjected as he waved his hands. "You think *my* dad was *your* dad's professor and good friend? *Your* dad told him about a discovery he made—about some tunnel under the ocean—and *my* dad believed him?"

"Yes."

"But they never got to talk more about it before my dad died?"

"Right."

"So your family has something else in common with Travis Jackson besides a love of cheesecake and bread."

"Very funny. Yes."

"So what is it? What's the connection with Travis? Besides his obvious obsession with your mom."

"I wouldn't call it a *connection*, and I don't like the word *obsession*," Reilly snorted. James raised his eyebrows at Reilly's defensiveness.

Reilly felt his Stelladaur pulsating again. Or was it his nerves that made his heart pound harder? Either way, he'd found his next step.

Taking a deep breath, he reached for the Stelladaur around his neck and began to pull it out from under his shirt.

"If Travis Jackson is obsessed with anything, it's this." He held up the Stelladaur for James to look at.

"Whoa! What the heck is that?" James's forehead looked shorter as his eyes widened.

"It's called a Stelladaur. It was my great grandfather's," Reilly answered matter-of-factly. "It's what my dad was talking to your dad about, before Travis interrupted them."

Reilly gave James a few minutes to gawk at the Stelladaur and digest what he'd said. Then he saw a light bulb turn on in James's brain, as his expression turned from flabbergasted to one of shocked epiphany. "And you think Travis has one, too! Some kind of magic rock that can take someone through a tunnel under the sea, right?"

"He does have one, but I don't think he'll unveil a real Stelladaur tonight."

"What then?"

"I think he's been making fake ones."

"Why? Money?"

"C'mon … he's a billionaire! There's a lot more to it."

"And that's why you wanted to come with me to make the delivery. You're hoping to find out what this is all about." James's forehead relaxed and his pupils shrunk to normal size. "Unbelievable."

Reilly ignored James's last word of skepticism. "We're *going* to find out!"

The boat pulled into Coleman Dock and they watched the crew direct the cars ahead of them off the boat. There was a break in the line of vehicles, and the driver behind them honked its horn.

"James, we've gotta go."

Giving his head a quick shake, James started the engine and quickly drove off the boat. Distracted by the city traffic, he struggled to stay focused on the conversation.

"This is too weird, kid." James turned north towards the Fairmont Hotel and drove three blocks before commenting further. "It's strange though ... because I remember my dad telling me about a cool star ... it's hard to remember exactly ... but I think I always figured he was talking about wishing stars, or something to do with magic. Make-believe, you know? Nothing more."

Reilly reached for his cell phone. "Let's find out for sure if your dad was my dad's professor." The phone rang five times and Reilly drew in a quick breath.

"Blackberry Bakers, this is Monique."

"Mom, hey, how are you?"

"I'm great, Reilly. What's up? I've only got a minute."

"Okay, Mom. Well ... uhm ... I—"

"Reilly, what? I'm in a hurry."

Reilly took another deep breath and spoke quickly. "I'm in Seattle with James and I need to know the name of dad's physics professor, the one who was at that party where you and Dad met."

"What? What are you talking about? I told you that you couldn't go with him!"

"I know, Mom, but I had to."

"We'll talk about this later, Reilly. I can't believe you—"

Ignoring the reprimand, he interrupted. "Mom, the professor? What was his name?"

"Professor Jamison? His name was Bill Jamison. Why?" she demanded.

"Mom, that's James's dad. His biological dad."

"Huh?"

"James was adopted by his stepdad just after his biological dad died. James remembers his dad telling him stories about a Stelladaur, only he was too young to remember details."

There was a short pause. "What are you saying?" Her voice softened. "Are you sure?"

"Yes! So anyway, now James needs to see if his mom knows

anything else. Something that will help us to figure out what Travis is up to."

"But, Reilly—"

"Gotta go, Mom. I'll fill you in later."

He hung up the phone before his mom could say anything else.

"Do you want to call your mom now?" Reilly asked James as he held out the phone.

"I've got a phone, kid." James laughed. "No, she's probably just leaving work or stuck somewhere on I-5. I'll call her later. Maybe we can stop by before we head back tonight."

Reilly sighed. He shifted in his seat and turned to look out the passenger window. He stared at a dent on the edge of the side-view mirror and watched the traffic and people pass him in a blur. With every blink, he tried to consider what the next step might be. The fact was, he really didn't know what that would be. But he felt his Stelladaur's gentle pulse, reminding him that he would know when he needed to know.

"Looks like this is the place, kid." James glanced at Reilly before turning into the service entrance to the Fairmont.

Reilly tucked the stone back under his shirt.

"Good idea. You don't want everyone to see that." James pulled around to the loading dock and backed in. "Let's check out where we're supposed to bring this stuff before we carry it all in. They must have some kind of cart we can use."

They stepped out of the truck and took the side door into the hotel. No one was in the warehouse area, so they meandered down a hallway past the laundry and janitorial supply rooms. Turning a corner, they walked by the pool and sauna room, behind the elevators and into the main lobby. Next to the concierge's desk was a large display board announcing the big event.

Reilly and James stood side by side and read the sign silently.

Renowned Entrepreneur, Scientist, Philanthropist
Travis Jackson
Announces another new discovery for humanity!
East Ballroom — Tonight, 8:00 p.m.
(Invited guests only)
Broadcast Live on KING News

James rolled his eyes. Reilly read it over again, looking for anything that might be a clue, but he saw nothing.

"Which way to the East Ballroom?" James asked the concierge. "We've got a delivery from Blackberry Bakers."

"The ballroom is on the top floor, sir. Turn left off the service elevator. The back entrance door is straight ahead."

"Thanks."

Walking through the lobby towards the main elevators, Reilly caught a glimpse of someone standing in the elevator just as the door closed. The person looked familiar, but he couldn't place her. Impulsively, he sprinted ahead and pressed the up button, but the elevator had already started its ascent. Reilly watched the numbers flash, from L to 6.

"What's up?" James asked as he approached Reilly.

"Hold on. I want to see what floor that's headed to."

"Why?" James asked as they watched the numbers continue to flash.

Reilly didn't answer. He kept his eyes on the numbers until the elevator stopped.

"Tenth floor," Reilly stated.

"What is it, kid?"

"I'm not sure. I thought I saw someone I know. A girl."

"A girl, huh? Someone you're sweet on?" James nudged Reilly with his elbow. "I knew that shyness was just a cover-up. That's probably what all the girls like about you, anyway. And you thought it was your sexy eyes that caught their attention."

"It's not like that." Reilly felt his face flush, but he kept walking. "It's just that she—. Never mind."

He felt mildly annoyed with James and with the heat radiating from his face. They walked in silence down the hallway past the pool, the weight room and back towards the laundry room.

"Hey, sorry, kid."

Reilly gave him a half smile.

"That's okay," he said. To avoid any further questions, he added, "I'm not even sure it's who I thought it was. Forget it."

Reilly knew it was not the time to blurt out everything about the Stelladaur, the vortex and Jolka. Or about the girl named Norah. Though he couldn't explain it to James, or even to himself, Reilly was almost positive that he had seen Norah in the elevator. Everything inside of him hoped it was she. Suddenly his stomach felt like it dropped into his shoes, or like he'd just plummeted down an incline on an insanely steep roller coaster. No doubt about it, Norah took his breath away! *It must be her,* he thought, *but why is she here?* For the moment he didn't care why she was there; he just wanted to see her again.

Reilly and James found two carts in the warehouse and loaded the cheesecakes onto one and the breads on the other. Wheeling them up the ramp, Reilly almost lost a cheesecake but caught it with one hand as it slid off the bottom shelf of the cart.

"Good catch!" James said.

"Well, I may be shy, but I know when to catch something that's coming my way—and when to let it slide." He wasn't referring to James's teasing, and James knew it.

"Yeah? Like what?" he asked Reilly as they stepped into the service elevator.

"Like Travis Jackson. I'm going to find out what he's doing with fake Stelladaurs. *That* I'm not going to let slide." He pushed the button for the fourteenth floor. "We've got to find a way to hang out in the ballroom until after the broadcast. Maybe get some kind of pass or something, so we look officially invited."

"We could ask the concierge for a service badge."

"That's a good start but I don't want to hang out in the kitchen. We need to be in the ballroom." Reilly spoke with determination and felt his Stelladaur pulsating steadily. "We'll find a way to get in."

When the elevator door opened, they turned left and pushed the carts down the hall and then through two large doors.

"Wow!" Reilly began as he gawked at the ceiling fixture. "That's some chandelier. And the walls!"

The fabric-paneled walls with a red-and-gold paisley pattern and the cream-colored marble floor with black swirls made the room reek of opulence. Round dining tables dotted the room, each set with white linen tablecloths, crystal wine glasses, white china rimmed with gold trim and gold place settings. Each table had a square vase stuffed tightly with red roses tied with a black ribbon. Long tables draped with white linen and decorated with a colorful array of hors d'oeuvres, fruits, and cheeses lined the far wall of windows, displaying the lights of Seattle as an impressive backdrop.

"This guy spares no expense." James left his cart and wandered around the room.

Reilly was uncomfortable in the lavish setting. The door behind him opened and a bald man dressed in a black tuxedo entered.

"May I help you?" the man asked with a distinct British accent.

"Yes, we're here with a delivery from Blackberry Bakers. The breads and the cheesecakes?" Reilly said, looking at the trays and then back at the man.

James moved quickly from the side table, where he had been eyeing the caviar, and extended his hand to the man. "James. James Oliver." The man shook James's hand and gave him a wary look. "Where would you like us to put these?"

"You will see that each serving table has a large basket in the center for the assortment of breads. As for the desserts, those can go in the kitchen for now. They need to be cut and placed on individual plates. The media will be arriving momentarily, so please assemble those breads and then meet me in the kitchen. Come in through the side door."

"Of course," James replied.

The man returned to the kitchen and Reilly and James began to arrange the breads and rolls. A TV camera crew of three entered the room, shuffled some chairs at the back, plugged in equipment and set up a camera on a tripod.

After displaying a dozen croissants in the last basket, Reilly took the empty cart and James grabbed the one filled with the cheesecakes. They left through the side door to find the man in the tux.

"Yes, I understand. That is unfortunate, but it does put me in quite a bind." The man turned to look at James and Reilly as they walked into the kitchen and added, "Never mind. Plan B just walked in." He hung up the phone and grinned as he approached them, this time extending *his* hand.

"Mr. Oliver, is it?"

James nodded as he shook the bald man's hand again. "Yes?"

"And you are?" He reached to shake Reilly's hand.

"Reilly. Reilly McNamara."

"Ah, yes, Mr. McNamara. My name is Baxter. I am in desperate need of your assistance this evening, both of you." Reilly and James exchanged glances. "It seems my two other assistants scheduled for this evening's event—brothers, I might add—have come down with that dreadful flu that has been plaguing so many. It is rather unfortunate. Perhaps you would be willing to fill in?"

Reilly looked at James as if to say, *See, I told you we'd find a way.* James smiled at Reilly and then turned to Baxter.

"Of course. We'd be happy to help. What do you need us to do?"

"Mr. Oliver, I should need you to help me serve the wine. And Mr. McNamara, I need a good water boy. You must be on top of keeping everyone's water glasses filled. The caterers will restock the buffet tables, however, dessert will be served after Mr. Jackson's announcement. If you could stay for the entire evening, I should think we could use some help offering everyone that sumptuous cheesecake. Will that work for you?"

"Yes!" Reilly and James answered in unison.

"Fine. Then the first order of business is to get you both out of those grubbies and into something more suitable," Baxter said. He grabbed his lapel and held it firmly while he looked at James. "The in-house formal shop will have no problem fitting you, Mr. Oliver. But you ..." He stopped and turned to Reilly. "There will be no time for alterations, but I'm sure they will have something that will suffice. I shall call them just now, to alert them of your arrival. It is on the mezzanine level, next to the floral shop. Now off you go."

Hardly believing their good fortune, they left the kitchen and gave each other a high five when they reached the elevator. The woman in the formal shop was efficient. She had a basic black tux with a black cummerbund and white shirt in James's size, ready and waiting, as well as a black tie and silver cuff links. She set out two possibilities for Reilly. After holding up the first pair of pants, it was obvious they would be too long. The only other option was a black tux with a white cummerbund, white lapels and white bow tie. Reilly wasn't worried until he noticed that the jacket had tuxedo tails.

"This?" He scrunched his nose, flipping the tails.

"Well, dear, it really is the only option I have available for this evening." The woman tried to sound consoling.

Reilly sighed. "Okay. Whatever it takes to ..."

"Excuse me?"

"Just ... whatever. This will be fine."

They changed quickly, but the only shoes that worked for Reilly were a good size or more too big. He stuffed some tissues in the toes, figuring it would do the job. But with the tux tails flapping behind him, his shoes clomping on the marble floor and the bow tie strangling him, he scowled as they made their way to the elevator.

"I look like a penguin trying to practice Zumba," he muttered.

But when they approached the main elevator and saw who had been inside, waiting for the doors to open, Reilly choked audibly. It was Norah.

Chapter Fifteen

The Unveiling

Norah wore a long royal blue dress with flowing layers of lime-green chiffon and green and blue faux jewels on the spaghetti straps. It made her eyes look a brighter emerald color than Reilly had remembered. Next to her, and obviously her escort, was a man in a black tux.

Reilly didn't say anything to Norah, nor did she to him. They tried not to look at each other as Reilly and James stepped into the elevator. The man escorting Norah pushed the number 14.

"Good evening," James said, imitating the voice of a jovial butler.

Annoyed, the man said nothing in reply and closed his eyes in a long blink. Norah turned her head sideways and rolled her eyes, noticeably embarrassed by her escort's rudeness. James didn't bother making an attempt to converse any further. Reilly and Norah exchanged a quick glance and her mouth curved up slightly in a smile.

The ride to the fourteenth floor was uncomfortable. Reilly was thrilled to see Norah and knew it was no coincidence that she was there. But he needed time to clear his mind—and to breathe—without her stunning beauty distracting him! When the door opened, she and the man stepped out first and turned to the left. Reilly and James stepped out and turned to the right, looking for the back entrance to the kitchen.

"Who was that?" James insisted.

"Her name is Norah."

"Is she a friend from school? Why didn't you say anything to her?"

"No, she's not from school. I've never spoken to her before."

"How do you know her name?"

"I sort of saw her somewhere before. A friend showed me a picture of her, sort of … and, um … mentioned her name."

"Does she know your name?"

"I don't know."

"Well, it's obvious she thinks you're hot," James teased. "You do look handsome in that tux, Reilly, even if the shoes are a bit too big."

"I feel ridiculous," Reilly grumbled, pulling at the bow tie. "So you think she might like me?"

"Dancing penguins are definitely her style," James chuckled.

"Very funny. So, what should I do?"

"That's easy. When you're pouring her water just say, 'My name is Reilly. Please let me know if there is anything else I can do for you.' And then give her that adorable smile of yours."

"Whatever." Reilly tried not to smile, but he did. Entering the kitchen, he intentionally switched gears. "The most important thing tonight is to find out what Travis is doing. After that, I'm not sure. I can't go into details now, James, but Norah is definitely here to help us figure it out." They stepped up to the counter where Baxter was arranging the last few slices of cheesecake on dessert plates. Reilly turned around to look directly into James's eyes. "Trust me," he whispered before James could respond.

"Ah, you're back. Dandy!" Baxter chimed. "The guests are arriving. Mr. McNamara, the water pitchers are there, ready to go. Carry them with a linen napkin underneath to catch any droplets. You can fill them at the utility sink, and the ice is over there." He pointed to the pitchers, the sink and the ice dispenser, in that order. "You may start immediately. Mr. Oliver, come with me to the wine cooler."

Reilly filled the pitchers almost to the brim. He took a white linen napkin in his left hand and grabbed a pitcher in the other hand, gently resting it on his left palm. *No big deal*, he thought. *I've served coffee at the bakery lots of times. Just never in a tuxedo.*

The ballroom buzzed with people mingling and eating hors d'oeuvres. Reilly did a quick scan of the room to see if Norah was there, but he didn't see her. He filled the water glasses at the nearest table and then moved on to the next, where four people nibbled on shrimp cocktail, spinach-stuffed mushrooms and an assortment of cheeses and crackers. The combined aromas reminded Reilly that he was hungry. He scanned the room again but still didn't see Norah anywhere. He worked his way around the room, filling water glasses while people chatted noisily and loaded their plates with appetizers. By the time he reached the last table, most guests were seated. He looked up, searching again. This time he spotted Norah sitting at the head table, next to the man she was with in the elevator. Reilly noted that he and Norah were the youngest ones in the room. His thoughts were interrupted when a gentleman stepped to the microphone.

"Good evening, everyone. Please be seated." The man waited a minute while the remaining unseated guests found their way to their reserved chairs. "Welcome. Tonight you've been invited to participate in the unveiling of an unprecedented device offered by Imperial Plastics, Inc. Its founder, Mr. Travis Jackson, personally requested that you attend this auspicious occasion."

Reilly finished pouring the water at the last table and moved near the kitchen door, where Baxter and James waited. The host continued.

"It's a great honor to introduce to you the man whose inspiration, innovation and ingenuity have given hope to humanity in countless ways. Please welcome entrepreneur, scientist and philanthropist, Mr. Travis Jackson." There was a burst of applause as Travis stepped from behind a series of ornate room dividers that zigzagged across the front of the room. He wore a black tuxedo with a crimson red cummerbund and bow tie, perfectly coordinated with the fiery red lapels of his jacket, where a single red rose tipped in glittery gold was pinned. He stepped to the platform and gave his typical politician-style wave. He positioned himself in front of the microphone, taking his time to adjust it to the exact position he wanted.

"Thank you. Thank you very much," he began proudly. "I'm thrilled you're here this evening for the presentation of my greatest invention yet. Tonight you'll witness something that will change the way we look at ourselves, others and all life as we now know it." There was a hum of muttering voices. "This is indeed an historic night!"

"He looks like a cat ready to pounce on a bunch of mice," James whispered to Reilly as he nodded in the direction of the camera crew.

"Yeah, an evil cat and innocent mice," Reilly whispered back.

Reilly could feel his Stelladaur between his chest and the stiffly starched shirt. He inhaled deeply, gleaning some reassurance from the stone.

"Since I know you'll all soon be reaching deep into your pocketbooks—certainly getting on the phone to talk with your bankers—I figured the least I could do is offer you some fine Northwest cuisine before we get on to business. Please, enjoy your dinner." With that, Travis stepped away from the podium and descended from the platform to sit at the head table right next to the man who had been in the elevator with Norah.

Reilly went to the kitchen to refill the pitchers and bumped the toe of his shoe on the corner of the prep table. The tissue in his shoes had compacted, leaving too much space between his toes and the end of the shoes so they slipped as he walked. He tore a piece of paper towel from the dispenser near the sink and stuffed half in one shoe and half in the other, hoping none of the waiters who were busy dishing seafood entrées onto dinner plates had noticed. He washed his hands quickly, filled each pitcher with water and placed them on the counter near the door. Taking a fresh linen napkin in one hand and a pitcher in the other, he returned to the ballroom. Baxter and James were busy pouring wine while numerous waiters served everyone their meals. Meanwhile, the TV crew drooled, looking as hungry as Reilly felt. Reilly hoped he and James could eat leftovers later.

Starting at the back table and working his way towards the front of the room, Reilly filled glasses that needed to be topped up. Two tables away from Norah, he caught her staring at him. He held her gaze, reading panic in her spruce-green eyes. *Help! Get me out of here!* they begged. It wasn't a typical I-can't-handle-this kind of look. It was one of sheer desperation. Reilly shrugged slightly and bit his lower lip.

Travis finally noticed Reilly when he approached the head table.

"Well, Mr. McNamara, look at you. Everyone, this is Mr. Reilly McNamara. His mother was an invited guest but, unfortunately, was not able to attend." Sarcasm tainted the tone of his voice, but only Reilly and Norah seemed to notice. "She is also the one responsible for the lovely breads. Later we'll enjoy my favorite dessert, also from her bakery on Bainbridge Island."

Travis shifted in his chair to look directly at Reilly. "Reilly, I assume you assisted with the delivery for tonight's event, and that *that* is your purpose for being here?"

"Yes, Mr. Jackson, that's correct," he responded without hesitation. "However, as it turned out, the head waiter was short-handed and asked James and me to fill in at the last minute. I'm happy to help, sir."

"I'm sure. Always eager to be where the action is, huh, Reilly?" The sarcasm in his voice was now more than subtle. "Well, let me introduce you to my good friends and associates. To my left are Mr. Grant Dever and his wife, Trudy, then Mr. George Abbott, Mr. Peter Moss and his wife, Annie, and finally, the lovely Norah Gustalini and her father, Mr. Martino Gustalini. I believe Miss Gustalini is about your age."

Reilly smiled and nodded at each person as his or her name was mentioned. Norah smiled but still revealed a look of desperation. "Nice to meet you all. Would anyone like more water?" He could see that only Norah's glass needed a refill; the others obviously drank more wine than water.

"Yes, please," replied Norah. He walked around the table and stood between her and her father.

"Reilly, you may be interested to know that Miss Gustalini and her father will be occupying my guest house on the island for the remainder of the summer," said Travis as he swirled the red liquid in his glass. "We have some business matters that will be requiring our full attention, and she will likely need someone to show her around." Travis seemed delighted with the opportunity he had presented.

"That would be … great. Uhm … I'd be happy to show her around," Reilly said as he walked behind Travis and then topped off Trudy Dever's glass.

Reilly presumed that neither Travis nor Mr. Gustalini knew anything about Norah's knowledge of a Stelladaur. But he knew without a doubt, once again, that Travis must have ulterior motives. He felt his own Stelladaur pulsate under his shirt, confirming his thoughts. For the first time, Reilly recognized that he actually had a thought and believed it was accurate *before* he felt the vibration from the stone. Previously, the Stelladaur had sent a message before or simultaneously with a thought or feeling. But this time, it confirmed his thoughts after he was certain.

"Maybe you can come by the bakery tomorrow morning ... I'll be there ... my mom just hired me to help with the baking ... but I don't have to work until Monday, so ... yeah." Reilly knew he was stammering, and that the adults around him mistook it for typical teenage jitters, but he was glad no one suspected a previous connection between him and Norah. Norah smiled, then gave him another brief look of frustration that only he caught.

Reilly left the head table and meandered around the room, filling other glasses. He listened for comments that might give him further information, but nothing emerged. Most people talked about the fine accommodations, the lobster or the wine and their upcoming plans for the Fourth of July. He heard no one speculate about Travis's invention until he caught the middle of an interesting conversation.

"I'd be a fool not to, since every investment I've ever made with Imperial Plastics has been more lucrative than I had projected," said a robust man in a rather loud voice.

"Same here. As a matter of fact, investing shares in his Magic Eye gave us the capital for my project in West Africa," another gentleman said. "We've now done over 400 transplants. It couldn't have happened without Travis's innovation."

"Apparently what he's got now will completely change the way we all look at things," added another person at the table. "In the twenty years I've invested in his company, I've made more than I've made from most of my other investments combined. He's a remarkably talented individual. Always on the cutting edge of science technology."

Reilly filled each water glass slowly and lingered at the table as long as he could without being a nuisance. Then he retreated to the kitchen for another pitcher. One of the caterers offered him a plate of food. He shoveled it in, not wanting to miss out on anything in the ballroom. Baxter and James walked in as Reilly finished the last bite of crab-stuffed salmon roll. Baxter went to get more wine and James looked at Reilly's empty plate with wide eyes.

"Where's our food?" James asked as he scanned the area for whatever Reilly had just snarfed down. He spotted an open warming tray with several plates of extra food, moved quickly to grab one and then closed the lid. Baxter returned with two bottles of wine. He placed one on the counter next to James and told him to eat quickly before returning to the ballroom.

"I figured out something about Mr. Jackson that I didn't realize before," Reilly said.

"Yeah, what's that?" James asked with a mouth full of potatoes.

"People trust him."

"And?"

"Despite the fact that he's rude and loud and demanding, people still trust him. They trust him and invest in his companies because he's invented a lot of great things—things that have helped a ton of people."

"Get to the point."

"It's a false trust."

"What do you mean?"

"It's a cover-up. The fact that he stole a Stelladaur from a kid tells me he'll do anything, and at any cost, to get what he wants."

"He stole a Stelladaur? I thought you said he was making fake ones?"

"Never mind, the point is he doesn't really care about people. It's all about him. His fame. His fortune. And I think another motive, too."

"What else is there besides fame and fortune, both of which he has?" James asked as he speared a chunk of salmon.

Reilly opened his mouth to answer but was interrupted by Baxter, who burst through the door in a flurry.

"Dessert! They're ready for dessert! Mr. Jackson has requested that we serve the cheesecake *now! Before* he makes the announcement! Hurry, we don't want to keep him waiting."

Reilly raised his brow. James set his fork down. They followed Baxter to the far corner of the prep counter where carts filled with plates of cheesecake waited to be wheeled out to the guests. "James, you start at the back and I'll take the middle section. Reilly, you take the head table and serve Mr. Jackson first. Once we see that he has been served, we'll serve the others."

"Sure," Reilly said confidently.

Pulling his cart to a stop behind Mr. Gustalini, Reilly set a plate of cheesecake in front of Travis, who picked up a fork and bit into the dessert immediately.

"This is the best cheesecake on the west coast," he began. "My good friend here, Reilly, and his mother, are the dessert chefs. As I mentioned earlier, Monique McNamara owns a small bakery on Bainbridge Island. I like to do business with the McNamaras whenever possible." He took another bite and shot a glance at Reilly. The comment—and the look—normally would have made Reilly feel uneasy, especially as it related to his mother. But he felt his Stelladaur against his chest and let the comment go without the usual emotional response, also disregarding the comment Travis had made about Reilly being his "good friend."

He set a plate of cheesecake in front of Mr. Gustalini and then squeezed between him and Norah to serve her. As he did so, Norah reached up and slipped something in the pocket of his tuxedo jacket without looking up at him. Reilly simply picked up another plate of cheesecake and served it to Mrs. Moss. By the time he had served everyone at the table, most had followed Travis's lead and were eating the dessert, praising Reilly for his obvious talent. He smiled and nodded, moving quickly around the table without speaking. Noticing that most of the water glasses were now nearly empty, he excused himself to retrieve a pitcher.

As soon as he was in the kitchen, he reached into his pocket and pulled out Norah's piece of paper. It was a receipt from the hotel gift shop, with a short message scribbled on it: *Room 1015 A.S.A.P.!*

He stuffed the note back in his pocket, grabbed a pitcher and headed back into the dining area. The media crew waited in position while Travis stepped up to the podium. Reilly moved towards a nearby table and exchanged a brief look with Norah, giving her a slight nod. She acknowledged him with a half smile. Quickly scanning the closest tables, Reilly saw that only a few glasses still needed refilling. He paused to watch Travis reach for something under the podium. Travis placed a small box in front of him and cleared his throat.

"I hope everyone enjoyed dinner. Please feel free to finish dessert while we get started." He looked around the room, and when he spotted Reilly, their eyes met briefly before he continued.

"I assure each of you that you'll be quite amazed by what I'm about to reveal. Let me begin by saying I've spent my entire professional career searching for the opportunity to present this device to the world. It has the power to change the way we look at everything we do, every place we go and every idea we thought possible. For decades, Imperial Plastics has considered the implications of what I now hold in this box. Millions of dollars have been invested to bring it to you tonight. So, without further delay, I present to you …" Travis lifted the lid from an ordinary black box. "… the Realm Reaching ROCK!" Travis picked up the stone, which, from where Reilly stood, looked exactly like his own Stelladaur, except that it hung from a black ribbon.

Everyone oohed and aahed as beams of light reflected off both the crystal chandelier and the ROCK like a psychedelic laser show.

It was mesmerizing. Travis grinned as he watched the reactions of his guests. He twisted the ribbon to spin the ROCK, causing more miniature beams of light to shoot in every direction.

There were muttered inquiries: "What is it?" "Is it a diamond?" "What does it do?" Travis answered none of the questions as he dangled the ROCK. Finally, he stopped spinning his treasure and held it in his hand.

"No, it's not a diamond. It's a piece of rock we believe came from a galaxy far beyond our own, a miniscule chip of a star that exploded and drifted into our atmosphere some hundred million years ago. This particular one was found in Jamaica, and we have unearthed many more just like it. While we know the rocks landed randomly, we are finding them in clusters. Imperial Plastics has complete ownership of the region where this one was discovered. There are more such regions throughout the world, and securing those regions is our number one priority."

Again, Travis held the ROCK by the ribbon. "Now, what does it do? The Realm Reaching ROCK is so named because, with the aid of this device, you can literally reach into another realm. The acronym R.O.C.K. stands for Reaching Our Cosmos Kaleidoscope. It's a time-and-space travel device that has—"

"Let's see how it works!" a potential investor shouted.

Travis raised his hand in an attempt to put a stop to any further outbursts. "As I was saying, the device has unique properties which react in extraordinary ways to three stimuli: light, heat and salt. The right combination of those elements creates a vacuum that makes it possible for a person to be transported to another realm, far beyond this world. The technology used to facilitate this time warp is cutting edge and more advanced than any of the projects Imperial Plastics has spearheaded before. The Realm Reaching ROCK will change NASA's entire approach to space travel. It will make such travel available to anyone who is bold enough for such adventures!"

Reilly sensed that the last statement was intended to be a challenge, and as the thought came into his mind, he felt his own Stelladaur burn under his shirt.

"Allow me to show you evidence of one such adventurer." Travis stepped to the side of the podium and watched a full-size screen slowly descend from the ceiling. The lights were dimmed and random flickers of light shot around the room from the Realm Reaching ROCK, which glowed eerily. A photo of a hand-written document was displayed on the screen, and Travis read it aloud.

> "*October 21, 1969: I have taken this journey through time and space many times, and each time I returned with a greater sense of awareness and understanding of the planet that I now live on, and of my own existence and relationship with it.*
>
> "*November 29, 1969: Today the rock took me to a place called Jolka. I went in a purple tunnel through the ocean—how I'm not sure, but the rock propelled me through it.*
>
> "*February 16, 1970: It's been a discouraging winter, not being able to go through the tunnel for so long. But yesterday the sun was finally shining and I left work to try again. It was unbelievable! I look forward to the day when I can tell someone about this but I wonder if the world is ready for such advanced technology. As a kid, I used to think the year 2000 would find everyone flying around in hovercrafts and warping through space in time machines, like it was no big deal. It's definitely a possibility!*
>
> "*April 29, 1970: I just took a position at the University of Washington, starting this fall, in the physics department. I've decided to help each student adopt the following as a personal creed for their discovery through the world of physics: **Only by experiencing the unknown does one***

> *allow the remarkable opportunity to create endless pos-*
> *sibilities. Perhaps someday the power of this rock will be*
> *realized by many.*"

Another image was displayed on the screen. It was a sketch of the rock drawn on the same lined paper that the journal entries were written on.

"This sketch labeled 'The Rock' was found in the pages of the same journal we've just read from. It belonged to a brilliant physicist who received, at the age of twenty-one, the youngest professorship at the University of Washington. I have his journal here in my hand." Travis took the journal from the same black box and held it up. "The book has been carefully scrutinized for its authenticity. There is no doubt it belonged to the renowned scientist, Dr. William Jamison."

Reilly turned his head quickly to look for James, who stood on the opposite side of the room in front of the camera crew. James's jaw dropped and he stared at Reilly with disbelief.

Travis continued. "Dr. Jamison died in his mid-thirties but left us with a wealth of knowledge and information. As a matter of fact, much of his research was the catalyst for many of my inventions over the past couple of decades. I wish the man were still here today so we could collaborate together on this latest device. While he simply called it The Rock, we at Imperial Plastics have renamed it The Realm Reaching ROCK—Reaching Our Cosmic Kaleidoscope. As I know you are here to consider investing in this device with us, I'll now answer any questions you'd like to ask, as I'm sure there are many."

Arms shot up from potential investors and the media.

"If the rock you're showing us was found in Jamaica, where is the rock that Dr. Jamison allegedly used to go through time and space?" asked someone from the media.

"No one seems to know. His wife of only a few years contends that she knows nothing of the journal or any of his work on time travel," Travis responded.

"How did you obtain the journal?" asked another reporter.

"Dr. Jamison left it to me in his will. He knew of my own scientific research. As I said, we worked on other projects together. The will states that if he had not revealed his discovery to the world by the time of his death, he wanted me to do so at the time I thought the world would be ready for it. I've taken a bold step forward in making that assumption."

"How does the device work?" a potential investor asked.

"The ROCK is held in direct sunlight and then massaged gently. The rubbing action extrapolates salt and natural oils from the skin and creates a microscopic film on the ROCK. This film reacts to both the sun's ultraviolet rays and the ROCK's cosmic properties, creating a sudden vacuum around the person holding it. The vacuum carries the person through a wormhole, so to speak, to another realm." Travis spoke as if what he said should be of no surprise to anyone.

Reilly glanced back at James again, who was still noticeably stunned. He looked at Norah who gave him the same look of frustration he'd seen earlier in her eyes. Though he, too, had many unanswered questions, he remained calm.

"What realm?" another potential investor asked.

"According to Dr. Jamison, he went to a place called Jolka. We're not exactly sure where that is, except that it is beyond our galaxy and the universe as we now understand it. We believe it may be where the ROCK originated."

"And have you been there yourself?" someone called out from the back of the room.

"No, but I've been through wormholes which have taken me to other places, as have many of my associates. Though barely perceptible, each ROCK is a slightly different size; therefore, we suppose each ROCK may take a person to different locations and times."

"How was the one found in Jamaica?"

"As I mentioned before, I have spent my entire career searching for a time-and-space-travel device such as this. It would be impossible to give you all the details related to the discovery of this first ROCK in the time we have tonight. Suffice it to say that Dr. Jamison's work was pivotal in the discovery, and our team of experts have been studying it for decades. We now have a facility on location in Jamaica, where we are studying and searching for more ROCKs. The first few hundred are now available for private purchase."

"How much are they?" Trudy Dever asked.

"Though we suspect the price will go down as more are unearthed, these first few hundred will be sold at a premium: $1,000,000 each. Shares are now offered at $150 a share."

Numerous people raised their hands.

"Look, it's all in the prospectus, which a few of my associates are handing out to you now." Travis shifted his position at the podium. "Read it over and decide. For those of you who want to purchase one of the first few hundred, my broker will be available to handle the transaction and arrange for delivery of your own personal Realm Reaching ROCK. In conclusion, I would like to present one further photograph for your consideration."

The lights were dimmed again and an image appeared on the screen.

Shocked, Reilly nearly dropped the pitcher in his hand. Projected in full screen was a photo of Reilly's kayak, with a purplish beam of light, quite like an aura, arching from the kayak into the water. The faint hint of a person inside the beam looked like a ghostly silhouette.

"Transporting between here and there, to wherever your ROCK takes you, is a faster-than-the-speed-of-light experience.

Ironically, current camera technology cannot yet fully capture such an event, though an aura effect—which some would classify as paranormal—is evident in this photo. However, my expertise *and* experience would conclude otherwise. Here you will see that my photographer was able to get a glimpse of an image of … me … beginning my journey through one of the wormholes. As I said, it's all in the prospectus, including a signed copy of this image. That's all for now." With that, he stepped back from the podium, placed the ROCK inside the black box and secured the lid.

The camera crew continued to film as guests called out more questions. Travis only waved his hand and shouted, "It's in the prospectus. Get on board tonight if you want in on the best ground floor investment in history!"

Reilly briefly considered running up to the microphone to say something. Anything! *Mr. Jackson is a fraud and a thief! It's all a lie! I am the person in that photograph! And I really have been to Jolka!* But his feet felt like lead and his mouth had that stuffed-with-cotton sensation. Instead, he moved towards the head table to refill any water glasses that were less than full.

As he approached the table, a man behind him pulled away from his chair, bumping him from behind. Reilly raised the pitcher in the air to stop any sloshing water from spilling, but in doing so, he failed to notice the briefcase someone had placed in the aisle. He tripped clumsily over the briefcase and then over one of his too-large shoes. Like a juggler losing control of his apparatus, he fumbled as the pitcher sailed through air. It landed precariously on Mrs. Moss's lap and sprayed everyone in front of her, including Travis who stood a few feet away at the edge of the platform.

Reilly fell with a smack, face down, wearing only one shoe. Travis did not move from his position. Mrs. Moss sat motionless with a bewildered expression, and the gentleman with the briefcase muttered obscenities about the imprint of a shoe marring his Italian leather case. Norah jumped to her feet to assist Reilly.

"Reilly, are you all right?" Norah asked as she darted to reach him. She knelt down to support him at the shoulders.

"Ugh!" Reilly groaned. "I think I twisted my ankle."

A few adults, including James, Baxter and a cameraman, gathered around him.

"Here, let me help you up," James offered. He squatted and grabbed the underside of Reilly's right arm.

Reilly shifted slowly to his left side and pulled himself up to a sitting position.

Norah gasped! James stared at Reilly's chest while pointing to his own, and his eyes darted back and forth between his friend and Norah.

Two buttons had popped off Reilly's shirt. Bulging for all to see was his Stelladaur!

Chapter Sixteen

Discoveries

James grabbed Reilly by the shirt, covered the Stelladaur with his other fist and lifted his friend to his feet. Standing directly in front of Reilly, James stuffed the Stelladaur back under Reilly's shirt and pulled at the lapels of his jacket before buttoning it up.

"That was quite a blunder, kid," said James as he patted Reilly on the chest. Looking down at the unshoed foot, he added. "How's that ankle? Can you hop? Let's get you out of here."

Not waiting for a reply, James lifted Reilly by his left arm and hoisted him around his shoulder; Baxter took his other side. Reilly turned to see if Travis had noticed the Stelladaur. Nothing in Travis's look suggested that he had. Everyone's attention was scattered; most people seemed to be wondering what the kafuffle was all about.

Though his ankle was throbbing, Reilly knew the accident had actually prevented him from revealing Travis's deceit prematurely. *Timing is crucial for things like this,* he concluded. Confident that Travis had not seen the Stelladaur hanging from his neck—and hoping no one else had—Reilly decided that the mishap was actually provident. *I'm not sure how this is all going to fit together, but it will,* he thought as he hopped on one foot between James and Baxter.

James and Baxter set him down on a stool in the kitchen while Norah got a bag of ice. Fortunately, it was only a twist and not a full-out sprain. The swelling subsided with the ice and within ten minutes Reilly insisted he was good to go.

"Well, now, you had best head on down to the tux shop and put your own shoes on, young man," Baxter said as he handed Reilly the shoe that had come off his foot. "The cleanup crew will handle things from here. It's been a pleasure to meet you both and to work with you this evening. I will make sure accounting sends you adequate remuneration."

"Thank you, Baxter, it's been … great," Reilly said. He and James shook Baxter's hand and they turned to leave.

"I don't believe I've had the honor of meeting this young lady, though," Baxter added, extending his hand to Norah.

She took it and simply replied, "My name is Norah."

The three of them left the kitchen without speaking to each other until they were in the elevator.

"I need to show you something in our room before my uncle finishes with Mr. Jackson. They'll likely be another couple of hours or so, so you've got time to change," Norah instructed.

"Your uncle? I thought he was your dad," Reilly said.

"No, he's my uncle. I'll explain later. Now hurry." The elevator stopped on the tenth floor and Norah got out. "Remember, room 1015."

James pushed the button for the mezzanine level and began to pepper Reilly with his own inquisition.

"She's cute but kind of bossy … But what's going on here, Reilly? Travis Jackson knew my dad? And my dad knew about time travel? Why wouldn't my mom tell me about this? And why did she let him have my dad's personal journal?" James's voice rose higher with each question until it resolved in a final declaration of utter confusion. "This doesn't make any sense!"

"Here's what I know. Your dad was my dad's professor in grad school. They were good friends and they trusted one another. They both had a Stelladaur and your dad used his to go to a place called Jolka." Reilly spoke calmly and matter-of-factly. "And guess what, James? I've been there, too."

"*What?*"

"Twice, actually. That photo of the kayak with the purple beam of light … well, that's me. Mr. Jackson came up from behind me just as I was returning from my second visit. He must have taken the photo then."

"Whoa! *You've* actually been there? To that *Jolka* place?"

"Yes. But what I don't know is how Mr. Jackson got a hold of your dad's journal. There's no way he left it to Travis in his will. Most of what the guy said tonight is a lie anyway."

The door opened and they stepped out of the elevator into a crowd of people.

"My mom must know. We're going to see her tonight."

They changed quickly. Reilly was relieved to wear his own shoes again. It wasn't until they were headed down the hallway on the tenth floor that they had another chance to talk.

"So how does this Norah girl fit in to all of this?" James asked as they passed room number 1001.

"I saw her briefly the first time I went to Jolka. We never spoke to each other but someone named Fiala told me her name. We, uh, we just saw each other. You know, our eyes met. The next time I saw her was in a place called Just Beyond Jolka."

"There's a place past Jolka?"

"Yes, numerous places. Anyway, she was in a 3D virtual movie-scene thing ... sort of. But she disappeared behind a door." He stopped in front of Norah's hotel room and nodded. "It was this same door, number 1015."

Reilly knocked before James could ask any more questions. Norah opened the door wearing jeans, a yellow tank top, and a half-zipped orange hoodie. The colors made her eyes look lime green. Reilly opened his mouth to speak but instead uttered a deep guttural noise.

James rolled his eyes and turned to Norah. "Hi. I'm James. We haven't met yet."

"Nice to meet you." Norah shifted her gaze from Reilly to James and opened the door wider. "Come in." James stepped into the room first, and Reilly looked directly into Norah's eyes as he passed her, before she closed the door. He scanned the suite: two separate bedrooms, a kitchenette, a living room and a separate dining area. Piles of papers and folders covered the dining table, with boxes stacked underneath.

"Quite the accommodations," James said.

"Yeah, this is awfully nice," Reilly added. "And the view!" He walked to the far wall with floor-to-ceiling windows overlooking Seattle.

"It's just a room. I mean, who really cares?" Norah's tone was more annoyed than sarcastic. "Thanks for coming. I was hoping you'd be here, Reilly." She waited until he looked at her again before continuing. "I, uh, what I mean is, when I used the Chalk Drawing Rock in Jolka and then looked up and saw you standing there, I was startled because I had just seen you in my picture. You were paddling in a kayak. But when I jumped into the drawing, you weren't there. I didn't know what it meant until my uncle and I flew over the water this morning. It's the same harbor you were kayaking on in my sidewalk drawing."

James looked more confused than ever. "What sidewalk? And what the heck is a Chalk Drawing Rock?"

"Reilly, since you brought him with you, I assumed that he knows what's going on." Norah sounded a little concerned.

"I haven't had a chance to tell him everything. But he knows enough."

"Okay, well, you'll have to fill in the gaps for him later. Anyway, I need your help. I'm not sure what to do."

"About what, exactly?" Reilly asked.

"You and I both know Mr. Jackson only has one real Stelladaur. A stolen one. And that he has absolutely no idea of how to use it, so it's actually useless to him. He knows that." Norah began to pace the floor. "But he has enough evidence to know there must be others who know more about Stelladaurs than he does—Mr. Jamison, your dad, you, the boy in Jamaica, me. And others, I'm sure."

"You?" James interrupted her again.

"Of course me!" She unzipped her hoodie and revealed her own Stelladaur hanging from a golden chord. "No one except the two of you know I have this."

"What about your ... uncle?" Reilly asked.

"No. He doesn't know much about me and doesn't care to. I'm more a bother to him than anything, so he usually has no clue of what's going on with me." Neither Reilly nor James interrupted her this time. Norah stopped pacing in front of the window. "My dad is in prison. My mom left him eight years ago when she found out he was with the Mafia. He was arrested for smuggling drugs from Bogotá, and he's not up for parole for another twelve years. I was very young when he left, but he wasn't around much so I never missed him. Anyway, my mom died last New Year's Eve. They say it was an accident ... slick roads ... but I don't believe them. Uncle Martino, my Dad's brother, is my only living relative. The courts said I have to live with him until I'm eighteen. Another year and half." It was as if she had popped a painful blister and let the puss ooze out.

After a long pause, Reilly broke the silence. "I'm sorry, Norah. Where did you get your Stelladaur?"

Norah shifted to a non-venomous but still painful tone. "From my mother. She gave it to me for Christmas. She found it in our garden early last fall, when she was planting a bunch of spring bulbs. When she picked it up, she felt a powerful surge through her entire body. She didn't know what it was but said she had the feeling the stone was meant for me. Of course, at first I didn't know what it was either, but soon after she died, I started to get a few hints that it actually had powers. Or it gave me powers. When I found out that I had to live with my uncle, my Stelladaur told me I couldn't let him find out about it."

"The Stelladaur *told* you this?" James asked.

"Not in words. It sort of prompts my thoughts and helps me figure things out."

"How did you know it was called a Stelladaur?" James asked.

"Fiala told me. She said Stelladaur means 'Star Door.'" Norah zipped up her hoodie to cover the shining stone.

"Who's Fiala?" James continued.

"You sure ask a lot questions, don't you?" Norah looked back at Reilly and continued before James could reply. "We're getting sidetracked. Reilly will fill in the gaps later." She walked over to the dining table and pressed her pointer finger on the hard surface to emphasize her next statement. "The point is the Stelladaur led me to *this* very place, on *this* very day, with *this* very information staring me in the face. It's time to figure out what to do about it."

Norah picked up one of the files, opened it and took out a piece of paper, which she turned around and handed to Reilly so he could read it.

James moved next to Reilly and they both peered at the paper.

"What's Obsidian Industries?" James asked.

"It's one of Mr. Jackson's projects in Colombia. A rock mine where they excavate a black rock and pulverize it to a silvery powder. The powder is mixed with some of his plastic resin to create an adhesive stronger than any other bonding material invented. NASA uses it on their rockets and stuff," Norah said.

"And what does this have to do with the Stelladaur—or Mr. Jackson's 'Realm Reaching ROCKs'?" Reilly wondered out loud. But while asking the question, he began to see a connection. "Is he changing the color of these rocks somehow to make fake Stelladaurs?"

"He's using the powder from the rocks."

"The powder?" James continued to press for answers.

"Yeah." Norah picked up another file from the table. "I've looked through these but all I can find are invoices from a warehouse here in Seattle. This one is for a shipment of three dozen cases of OI's powder. Why would they be shipping powder here when the manufacturing plant for the adhesive is in Colombia?"

"You're right. That does seem weird," Reilly agreed.

"Maybe he's moving his manufacturing headquarters?" James suggested.

"I hardly think so. I did a Google search for this address, and it's in the middle of a rundown area that's basically abandoned. As a matter of fact, the city wants to tear down all the buildings within four blocks for some business revitalization project. Apparently the mayor has been holding it up; she says today's economy won't support it. Anyway, all of Mr. Jackson's other buildings for any of his companies are very prominent properties. He prides himself on social status and he spares no expense on his lavish manufacturing facilities."

"Wow, you've done your homework," James declared. "You're awfully smart for someone so young."

Norah responded sharply. "Age has nothing to do with intelligence. It's usually quite irrelevant compared with a person's passion, motivation and vision."

Reilly smiled, thinking about how much Norah would connect with Eilam.

"And what's your passion? What motivates you?" he asked her.

"Justice," she answered firmly.

"For who?" James asked.

"For all who've been cheated, deceived, wronged … or hurt." Norah lowered her eyes. "Like my mom." James did not respond. Reilly wondered if she'd been through the same cave in Jolka, and if the hooded creatures she saw were of Travis Jackson, too. But he thought it best to steer the conversation back to a less personal topic, at least for now, for Norah's sake.

"So we need to find out what's going on in that warehouse and more about the powder," Reilly said. When he moved to pick up another file, his foot bumped a box under the table. "What's in these boxes?"

"I don't know. They're all taped shut, and I didn't dare to open any. It's been tricky enough to keep these files exactly where my uncle had them." Norah took the file from Reilly's hand and placed it on the table just as it had been. "But they're from Obsidian Industries, too." She pointed to the logo on the box.

Reilly's eyes widened. "What's that?" He bent down for a closer look. "Whoa! It's a gargoyle!"

"That's a strange company logo," James said as he moved in for a closer look. It was an ink drawing of a gargoyle whose wide-open mouth was the entrance to a cave.

"Not really. It's making more sense every minute," said Reilly with a shudder, "for a company that mines a black rock similar to obsidian, and whose owner has a heart as hard as that rock. Yeah, it's just the kind of bizarre logo Mr. Jackson would use."

"Exactly," Norah agreed. "But no one would suspect anything unusual. Look at the tag line: *Obsidian Industries—Discovering Rock Solid Advancements for Humanity.* Mr. Jackson has received more awards for his inventions than just about anyone. He's even been nominated for the Nobel Prize, and more than once!"

"Prize-shmize," James interjected. "Let's see what's in these boxes." He lifted one of them to the table and ran his hands over the tape, looking for a ripping point.

"No, don't!" Reilly hollered as he stood up and pushed James's hands off the box. "He can't know we're on to him yet. Let's think this through a minute."

"Reilly's right. Believe me, James, I want to know what's in those boxes, too. But not yet." Norah stepped in front of the boys, picked up the box and put it back on the floor exactly where it had been. "Let's go check out the warehouse."

"Tonight?" James asked.

"Yeah, why not? It's perfect. Mr. Jackson will be with his key people, including my uncle, for a couple of hours. Besides, I told him I'd be down at the pool until it closes. We've got till midnight. I promise you, he won't come looking for me."

James glanced at his watch. "It's almost ten. What did you say the address of that place is?"

Norah reached for the file of invoices and gave him the address.

"That's not far from my mom's house. Let's stop by there, too. She's usually up late," James said.

"It's not that I wouldn't want to meet your mother, James, but frankly, getting to the warehouse tonight is probably a higher priority," Norah said rather snidely.

"Actually, Norah, his mom might have some helpful information for us," Reilly said calmly. "Dr. Jamison is James's dad."

"Oh, James, I'm sorry! I didn't know. That's horrible ... I mean, about your dad ... and that Travis Jackson has your dad's journal ... and is exploiting his work." Norah stammered with embarrassment.

"No worries. He died when I was a toddler. I hardly remember him." James tried to sound reassuring. "C'mon, let's get going. You obviously need me along anyway." James started for the door and Reilly followed with Norah behind him.

"Yes, we do need you, James. And for a lot more than your wheels," Reilly said firmly. "Hold on, don't open the door yet."

James stopped and turned around with his hand on the knob.

Reilly began again. "The three of us are in this together. Here's the way I see it. We've each come from a different place and, for some reason, have converged here in this room. From here on out, we're in this for the same purpose: to protect the integrity of each Stelladaur, however many there may be in existence. At any and all costs."

"Any and all costs," Norah agreed, reaching her hand out in a Three-Musketeers kind of handshake, while with the other hand she reached for her Stelladaur hanging from the cord around her neck.

Reilly pulled up his Stelladaur from under his shirt, and put his other hand on top of hers. "Any and all costs."

James dropped his hand from the doorknob and turned to look at both brilliant stones blinking in luminescent brightness. "I'm not sure why the two of you have a Stelladaur and I don't. Or why you're both so stinkin' smart, but whatever." He put his hand on top of Reilly's. "Any and all costs," he declared.

They moved their hands up once in unison and then back down, repeating the oath one more time.

James found the directions to the warehouse on his smart phone. It was in a rundown area of town between Pioneer Square and the shipping docks, next to a deserted housing project surrounded by a chain link fence. He saw a sign on the fence: CONDEMNED PROPERTY—KEEP OUT. To the left was a row of five badly dented and graffiti-covered boxcars on a short span of rusty tracks. Between the boxcars and the housing project was a dilapidated, three-story brick building, with no windows on the first floor, no light coming from the windows on the upper floors and only a single door at the far end. Surrounding the building was a high fence with a sign at the main gate: UNSTABLE AND DANGEROUS PREMISES—KEEP OUT!

"Looks like it's ready to crumble," James said. He pulled the truck up to the gate and turned off the headlights. The full moon cast an eerie beam in the darkness. "Reilly, grab the flashlight under the seat. Let's get past that gate."

Reilly felt around for the flashlight but found nothing. "We don't need a flashlight," he said.

"We can use the Stelladaurs." Norah nodded, and they both unzipped their jackets to reveal their stones, shining brighter now against the dark night.

When Reilly stepped out of the truck, the smell of wet rust and moldy wood made his nose twitch. Walking up to the gate, they found a thick chain wrapped three times around the gateposts and secured by a heavy padlock. Norah pulled on the chain. Immediately the lock gave way.

"That's lucky," James said, surprised.

"No, not luck." Reilly said, and he noticed Norah nod again in agreement.

They opened the gate far enough to squeeze through, and then wound the chain back around the post.

"Those things are awfully powerful," James said, pointing to Reilly's Stelladaur. "We can probably see fine without them. We won't want to attract any attention."

"Good point," Norah said. She and Reilly zipped up their jackets. The moon and the distant street lamps provided dim but sufficient light to the door at the far end of the building.

James tried the handle. "Darn. Locked."

"Let's try around back," Reilly suggested.

He led the way to the corner of the building and made a right turn into a dark alley formed by a cement wall that extended along the entire length of the warehouse. In the distance, they spotted a dim light coming from a low window, and Reilly barely made out another door. Instinctively, he turned to James and Norah and put his finger to his lips to shush them.

"I think someone's here," he whispered. With only a dumpster between them and the door, they moved single file, cautiously, along the wall for thirty feet. They stepped carefully on the dirt, trying to avoid the noisy loose gravel as much as possible. Reilly turned around twice, making sure both Norah and James kept close behind him.

As they approached the window near the door, Reilly heard a heavy whirring. *Likely a generator,* he thought. Straining to hear anything else, he turned his head slightly, looking away from the door. Norah kept her eye on the light coming from the window.

"Get down!" she whispered, as loudly as she dared. They leaped forward and dived for cover to the side of the dumpster.

"He wants it all out the door by morning," a man's voice bellowed above the clang of the metal door as it slammed shut. "The truck will be here at 4:00."

"But we're not even half finished yet. Jackson doesn't pay us enough for these all-nighters," another protested.

"Shut up. You'll get your share when the project is done." The lid of the dumpster screeched as he opened it. "Now throw it in."

Something heavy landed with a *thump* and echoed down the alley. Reilly, Norah and James froze and held their breath.

"Yeah, I'd better get my share. We're the ones doin' all the grimy work and he's gettin' all the glory."

"So what? Now you want the glory? It ain't gonna happen that way, punk." The man grabbed the kid and slammed him against the wall on the other side of the dumpster. "Jackson always gets the glory. He's the one with the power. No one else. You got that?"

There was a choking sound, and the kid fell to the ground as the man opened the door. Holding it open, he added, "Next time I hear you complain, you won't remember your name."

The kid got to his feet and walked into the building; the door slammed shut with a bang that reverberated off the dumpster. For a couple minutes, no one moved.

Finally, Reilly whispered. "Let's take a look in that window. And then check out the dumpster."

No one objected. They crouched around the dumpster, ducked under the window, and squatted with their backs against the wall. James was in the middle with his head inches from the bottom of the windowsill. Norah's head was barely higher than Reilly's. No one spoke as they turned to face the wall. Then Reilly slowly straightened his legs. He peeked warily from the side nearest the door, and Norah mirrored his actions from the side nearest the dumpster. Finally, James poked his nose past the ledge.

"Look at those boxes stacked to the left," Norah whispered. "They are the same kind of boxes as the ones in the hotel room."

"It looks like they're full of Stelladaurs," Reilly added, nodding to some opened boxes strewn across the room. "Fake ones, no doubt."

"What do you think is in those plastic containers?" James asked.

"It's all too far away. We need to go inside," Reilly added.

"You're crazy! We can't see where those guys are from here. They're probably in the next room." James gestured to the door beyond the pile of boxes.

"Reilly's right. We need to get inside," Norah said as she backed away from the wall. "Let's check out the dumpster first."

Reilly and James scooted away from the window. James lifted the lid while they peered in at a bunch of boxes, some flattened and some smashed by the weight of the fake Stelladaurs.

"Why would they be throwing a bunch of them away?" Reilly wondered out loud. Knowing nothing would make sense until they got inside the building, he stretched over the edge, reached into the dumpster and grabbed one of the rocks. He handed it to Norah before reaching in for another. "James, can you get that full box? I can't reach it."

James leaned in and pulled out a produce-size box. "They look similar to yours, but different, too," he said.

"Quite different. About the same weight and shape—and sort of brilliant—but they're covered in some kind of plastic lacquer." Norah made the distinction with a measure of disgust.

"James, you take this box to the truck. Norah and I are going inside. Make sure to leave the gate open so we can make a run for it if we need to."

"What? I'm not leaving you two here!"

"James, we've got the Stelladaurs. We'll be fine," Reilly insisted. "Besides, as you said, we need you to be ready to get us out of here fast!"

"He's right," Norah declared. "And we're shorter than you, so we can stay out of sight more easily."

"This isn't a Nancy Drew mystery!" James protested annoyed.

"Very funny." Norah sneered.

"No, it's not funny. These guys are real, Norah—and they're dangerous. The older guy basically threatened to kill that kid!"

"Okay, look. If we're not back to the truck in twenty minutes, call 911. Now get going." Reilly spoke calmly but firmly.

"Give me one good reason why I should listen to two kids nearly half my age, when this makes absolutely no sense at all?" James insisted.

Norah put her hand forward, palm down. "*At all costs*, remember?"

Reilly shot James a look of determination and waited for him to put his hand on top of Norah's. When he had done so, Reilly put his own hand on top.

"At all costs," they whispered in unison.

Chapter Seventeen

The Duds

Reilly and Norah didn't wait for James to disappear into the shadows before they peered through the window once more to make sure no one was in sight. Then they stepped up to the door. Reilly rotated the knob slowly, as far as it would turn, and held the position securely as he pulled the door open. Norah reached in and put her palm flat against the inside surface, and Reilly held the door open just enough for her to slip into the room. Grabbing the inside doorknob with his other hand and keeping it in a turned position, he backed into the room with his shoulder supporting the weight of the heavy door. Then he strained to let it close without a thud. Once the door was securely inside the doorframe, he gently released the knob.

They both scanned the room but saw no one. High stacks of boxes created a maze of cardboard tunnels they could barely see over. Most of the boxes were sealed and bore the same Obsidian Industries labels as the ones back in the hotel room. An unsealed box at the end of the row caught Reilly's eye and they moved in for a closer look. Reilly heard a noise above the hum of the generator. Turning towards the sound, he spotted an inside door that had been previously obscured by the stacks. The door was opening. Norah gasped.

"He's gonna be irate about all these duds!" It was the older guy shouting behind him as he came through the door.

Reilly and Norah ducked behind the long row of boxes to their right and crouched down low.

"Get the next batch right!" The guy swore loudly and continued muttering obscenities as he walked towards the very spot where Reilly and Norah had been standing just seconds before. He dropped something to the floor, turned around and went back into the room he had just come from. Reilly and Norah exhaled softly.

"That was close," Norah whispered.

Reilly nodded. "Let's take another look."

They peered around the row of boxes to make sure no one else was there. It was just the two of them again. They found another open box filled with the same plastic-covered Stelladaur look-a-likes as the ones James had taken to the truck. Reilly bent down and picked one up.

"So these are duds. Why?"

Norah picked one up, too, and turned it over in her hands. "Look at this odd seam," she said, rubbing her thumb over the back of the fake rock. "It's bumpy—not smooth like the rest of it."

Reilly looked at the one in his hand more closely. "Huh! Same with this one." He rummaged through the two open boxes on the floor and discovered that both were filled with fake Stelladaurs, each with a scar-like imperfection on its surface. Reilly checked a dozen or so quickly. Norah, still holding the first one in her hand, picked at the scar with her thumb.

"It feels like it's covered with some sort of resin. It's kind of gooey and warm," she said.

Reilly stood up and moved closer to her for a better look. Without warning, Norah's arms went limp at her sides and her legs gave way as she sank towards the ground. Reilly caught her under her armpits just before her knees touched the ground. He lowered her slowly to the floor.

"Norah? What happened?"

"I don't know." She shook her head and placed the plastic dud in the open box. "Suddenly I felt real dizzy and my head ached." She rubbed her forehead back and forth with her fingers. "I'm probably just tired or maybe hungry. I didn't eat much dinner. I was too busy trying to get your attention."

"Well, you've got it now!" Reilly squatted down beside her. "We'd better get out of here. Are you okay?"

"I'm fine. Really."

As she started to stand, Reilly reached his arms around her waist and lifted her up slowly. They stood for a moment in an awkward embrace with Reilly's hands on her waist and Norah's hands resting on his biceps. Reilly smiled as he held her gaze briefly. Flustered, she dropped her hands and stepped back.

"C'mon, let's take some of these with us," Norah whispered as she grabbed a couple of rocks in each hand and stuffed them into the pockets of her hoodie, under her jacket.

Reilly picked up a few more. "We can see if they're the same as the ones in the box James took to the truck."

"I bet they're all duds. But what does that mean?"

"Let's listen at the door," Reilly suggested.

They stepped to the inside door and stood facing each other, each with a hand cupped behind their ears, pressed against the door. They strained to hear the men's voices above the loud hum of the generator.

"That's the last of the powder. It'll probably make two or three more batches," the younger one said.

"It ought to be enough. We've only got a couple hundred more to do," the older man said.

"Can we get that many done in a few hours? What if we don't finish before the truck comes?"

"You worry too much, punk. And you talk too much, too. Just shut up and keep workin'. Make sure there ain't no more duds! Jackson said he wants us to dump 'em in the water. We'll take the first ferry over to Bainbridge and do it from the car deck."

"Why does he want the duds thrown in the water? Why not put 'em in the dumpster with the scratched ones?"

"How the hell do I know? I just do what I'm told. It pays well, ya know?"

"You keep telling me that."

"Look, man, Jackson said when this job's done, we'll have nothin' more to do until the next shipment comes in from Bogotá. He said that ain't gonna be for two more months. We'll have the summer to live it up in Aruba!"

The men talked and laughed about what they'd be doing in Aruba—and the women they'd be doing it with—cussing vulgarities like crude scoundrels. Reilly shifted his glance to the floor and both he and Norah blushed as they pulled away.

"We've heard enough," Reilly began. "Let's get outta here."

They walked back through the maze of boxes, opened the door as carefully as they had before, slid outside and closed the door quietly behind them. As they turned the corner at the far end of the building, they heard a loud clang and turned to see one of the men holding a large load, which he was about to drop into the dumpster. Norah slipped on some loose gravel and fell to the ground.

"Who's there?" the man shouted as he let his load fall. He turned and sprinted towards Reilly and Norah.

"Here!" Reilly held out his hand. Norah took it and held on tightly as they dashed around the corner and bolted for the truck.

Reilly felt the Stelladaur pulsating on his chest and pulled it out to signal to James. He and Norah heard the engine start and, with a burst of adrenaline, ran even faster. Reilly bounded through the half-open gate, pulled Norah through behind him and didn't let go of her hand until he'd opened the passenger door and she'd slid into the middle of the bench seat.

"Go!" Reilly hollered. "He's right behind us!"

James shifted into gear abruptly and peeled away while Reilly leaned out of the truck, clasping the handle and pulling hard to shut the door. Reilly turned back to see the younger man reaching the gate, holding the open padlock in his hand.

"Do you think he got close enough to get the license number?" James asked.

"No, he didn't." Reilly spoke with conviction and confidence.

"I hope you're right, kid."

"I am. Trust me."

"Trust you? Hey, I let you talk me into waiting while you guys went in there—and risked your lives! Now look!"

"We're fine," Norah said.

"I don't know how you guys can be so calm. I've been out here for almost half an hour, wondering what the heck was going on. I was just about to call 911 when I saw your light flashing. You scared me, kid!"

"Sorry."

"So? Did you see anything?" James began the questions. "Did you get a look at their faces? … They didn't see you, did they? … What else did you find out?"

"No, they didn't see us and we didn't see them. But we did get some good information," Reilly said.

"And we got some rocks—from a box of scratched ones. And some other ones they call duds," Norah interjected.

"Duds? What do you mean?"

"We're not sure. They're all dipped in some kind of a coating but the duds seem to be the flawed ones because they have bumps on the back," Reilly said. "They were thrown into a bunch of boxes."

"Rows and rows of boxes," Norah added. "Hundreds of them. All sealed and stacked."

"Yeah, but not the duds. They're dumping those in the Sound, off the first morning boat to Bainbridge," Reilly said.

"What?"

"We've got to wait around for that boat, James. Let's go see your mom, then take Norah back to the hotel. We'll just have to sleep in the truck for a few hours."

"But one of them saw the truck. We can't risk him seeing it on the boat," James objected.

Reilly wondered why he hadn't thought of that. "We'll figure that out as we go," Reilly said calmly.

"Figure it out as we go?" James replied, annoyed. "Look, kid, this is getting way too risky."

Reilly felt his Stelladaur vibrating against him. "It's all coming together, James. One thing at a time."

James didn't respond. Norah glanced at Reilly and smiled. They drove in silence until they reached the exit onto the West Seattle Bridge towards James's mother's place.

"It's not far from here," James said.

"Great," said Reilly. "Hopefully she'll be able to fill in some of the missing pieces."

"It does seem odd that Mr. Jackson would have your dad's journal," Norah said as she turned to look at James. "This must be really strange for you."

"No doubt, it *is* a lot to take all at once." James signaled and turned right into a subdivision. "But, hey, it's an odd coincidence that all three of us know what it's like to unexpectedly lose a parent."

"Eilam told me there are no coincidences in life," said Reilly. "He said those are magical moments when we're ready to receive what the universe has been preparing for us all along. It's a sign that our belief is catching up with what already is … with what always has been."

James narrowed his brow. "You really are unusual, kid. Sometimes you say the most annoying things. But then, I don't know … then you'll say something that just sounds right, in a weird sort of way. Does that even make sense?"

"Perfect," Reilly nodded.

"I'm glad it does to you because I'm still not sure." James frowned.

"You like me. You're glad we're friends." Reilly smiled and chuckled.

"Is that what I said? I don't remember saying that."

"Oh, yeah," Norah said, "that's exactly what you said. I heard it."

"You're both strange!" James laughed as he pulled into the driveway of a small, pale yellow stucco home. "But I *am* glad we're friends. Let's find out what my mom knows about Travis and Stelladaurs. And my dad's journal."

They walked up a rock pathway to the front steps and well-lit porch. James swung open the door with Reilly and Norah standing side-by-side behind him. A woman in her early fifties with dark brown eyes and shoulder length blondish hair jumped up from a chair to greet them.

"James!" His mom threw her arms around him. "What a surprise!"

"Hi, Mom." He hugged her in return. "Sorry it's so late." He stepped back and turned around. "This is Reilly and Norah."

"Nice to meet you both." She reached her hand out to shake theirs. "Please, come in."

She opened the door a little wider and stepped aside to let them enter the living room. Reilly made a mental note of the comfortable surroundings—an old home with wide planked floors, decorated simply but with exquisite taste. Reilly and Norah sat on a small camel brown couch with chenille fabric, and gold and green silk throw pillows. James sat in a leather over-stuffed chair that matched the caramel walls. His mom did not sit down.

"Can I get you anything? Are you hungry? What sounds good?" Where James got his zeal for incessant questioning became clear to Reilly. "Something to drink? I've got cranberry juice, coffee or tea."

"I'll have juice, Mom," James said.

"That sounds good to me," Norah added.

"Me, too, please," Reilly said. "Do you need any help, Mrs. Oliver?"

"Goodness, no. I'll be right back." She left the room but kept talking from the kitchen. "So, Reilly, where are you from?"

"I live on Bainbridge. My mom owns the bakery where James works."

"Oh, yes, I remember him mentioning that he met you a few months ago, shortly after he started working there." She spoke loudly from the other room. "And what about you, Norah? Do you live on the island, as well?"

"No, ma'am. I live in Chicago."

"Chicago? And what brings you to the Northwest? Are you a relative of Reilly's?"

"No, we're friends. My uncle and I are staying on the island for the summer. He has business in the area. I'm looking forward to exploring the beaches and stuff like that. You know, just relaxing."

"That sounds lovely," she said. "And Reilly, do you help out at the bakery?"

"Yes, I actually do some of the baking. I used to just do clean up stuff, but since my dad died a couple months ago … well, I've been learning how to bake."

James's mom entered the room carrying a tray. "I'm sorry, dear. That must be very difficult for someone your age."

"Yes, ma'am."

She set the tray on the coffee table and handed out the glasses of juice. Then she offered Reilly and Norah a plate of brownies. "Well, these aren't likely good enough to sell at a bakery, but hopefully they'll be edible."

"Thank you," Reilly and Norah said as they each took a brownie.

"James?" She offered the plate to him but he shook his head. Then she pulled up an antique wooden chair from the corner of the room, which creaked as she sat down on it.

"Mom, we don't really have much time. Norah needs to be back at her hotel by midnight," James said. He took a sip of juice and then jumped into the reason they had come. "Mom, why does Travis Jackson have my dad's journal?"

James's mother choked before replying. She looked directly at her son. "I saw the broadcast, James. But I promise you, I knew nothing about the journal."

"Well, how do you think he got it? Do you have any idea what's in it? Did anyone else know about it?"

"I have no idea what's in that journal, son. Until tonight, I didn't even know it existed. All I know is that after your dad died, someone offered to set up a scholarship fund in your father's name, and the philanthropist who donated the original capital wished to remain anonymous. The only stipulation was that he would retain full ownership of your dad's research files. I've always suspected it was Travis Jackson."

"Why?"

"Because of a conversation he had with your dad shortly before he died."

"What conversation?" James asked.

"The night before your dad's heart attack, he told me he had met with a student of his, a good friend, who had just told him about some kind of a time travel device—a stone shaped like a star.

Your dad was thrilled because he said when he was a child he had a similar device."

"What happened to it? Do you have it?" James pressed.

"No, I don't. I never saw it. Your dad said he misplaced it soon after we were married. It's not that I didn't believe him, but I was young, James. We were only together such a short time and you were so little. I was overwhelmed by what had happened and there were too many other concerns. I didn't really think much about it after he died."

Reilly swallowed hard, thinking of his own mom. He could tell that Mrs. Oliver was pained by the memories she was sharing, but he knew there was more to the story. He waited for James to reply. After a long pause, James spoke again.

"I remember him telling me about the star. As I grew up, the details became fuzzy and I assumed he was talking about make-believe wishing stars—nursery rhymes, you know? Or something like that." James sounded apologetic. "But I do remember him often saying 'It will bring you what you truly wish for.' What do you think he meant by that?"

"I don't know, James. Your dad was a dreamer. He said most anything was possible when science and imagination are combined. I loved that about him. I do miss that, but I never really understood it." She shifted in her chair and reached for the plate of brownies. Holding one in her hand, but not eating, she continued. "When I married Lee, I decided to put aside everything that had happened in the past. I had a new life, and I needed to forget any memories of magic stars, vague as they were."

There was a silence while James looked at Reilly and Norah for support.

"So you think Travis set up the scholarship fund to get possession of all of Dad's work?"

"Yes. After hearing the broadcast tonight, I'm sure of it. Your dad's journal must have been stashed away in the back of a filing drawer or something. I went through his office myself to retrieve any personal items, but the only thing I found of significance was the last family photo we had taken."

"The one of us at the park?" James remembered.

"Yes." She paused, and finally bit into the brownie.

"May I ask you a question?" Reilly said, looking at James's mom.

"Of course."

"You said James's dad had a friend, a student, who he talked with about the travel device. Was his name Kevin McNamara?"

"Why, yes, it was! How would you know that?"

"That was my father."

She choked on the brownie. "That is remarkable! What a coincidence!"

"No, Mom, not a coincidence. It's all part of the puzzle we're putting together." James looked at his friend.

"My dad had one of those stars, too," Reilly said. "He got it from my grandfather. It was called a Stelladaur." He felt his Stelladaur pulsating against him, but fought the urge to reveal it to Mrs. Oliver. "My dad told me he had a conversation with your husband about it. They realized Mr. Jackson was eavesdropping on part of the conversation, so they never got to finish it. My dad suspected your husband knew a lot more about the Stelladaur and what it could do, but he had no way of finding out."

Reilly felt Norah watching him intently; then she nudged him in the ribs. He knew she wanted him to pull the stone from his shirt and that if he did, she would, too. Still, he hesitated.

"The stone can bring a person their greatest desire," he said.

"Greatest desire? What do you mean?" James's mother asked.

"The stone will reveal to its rightful owner what he or she wants more than anything else, and then help that person get it. It could come as a suggestion or an idea, and it can be used as a time-travel device if the person desires that," Reilly said, trying to ignore Norah's elbow pokes.

"Now that does sound like William," she said with a melodic sigh.

"Yes, but the thing we're concerned about is that Mr. Jackson has used a stolen Stelladaur as a prototype to make fake ones. He's now mass-producing them and selling them to the public. But we're not sure why because they can't do what a real Stelladaur can do, nor will they function as a time-travel device. Only a real Stelladaur can do that."

"And you have personal experience with this?" James's mom asked.

"Yes, I do," Reilly turned and winked at Norah.

"So do I," she said.

Reilly unzipped his jacket while Norah unzipped her orange hoodie.

"Oh, my!" James's mom gasped. "Those are beautiful! Where did you get them?"

"This was my father's."

"My mother gave me this one."

"And you have used these stones as time travel devices?"

"Yes." Reilly and Norah answered in unison.

"I don't know what to say." Her eyes widened and she took a deep breath. "No wonder you're concerned about Travis's announcement. I was quite nervous when I listened to the broadcast tonight, but I'm not sure what I can do to help."

"Mom, you *have* helped. I just wish there was some way we could get that journal. I mean, without stealing it. Any ideas?"

"I could talk with Lee when he gets home tomorrow. He's been in Dallas all week taking depositions on a major case." Lee, James's stepdad, was a partner in a top litigation firm downtown. "I'm not sure I'll tell him about the Stelladaur, but once he knows about the journal, perhaps he can look into the negotiations regarding the scholarship fund. It was a long time ago, so I can't promise anything."

"Thanks, Mom. That would be great. The key to all of this has to be in that book." James stood up and placed his glass on the table.

His mother gasped and lifted her hand to cover her mouth. Then, slowly lowering her hand, she said, "Yes, of course … the *key!*"

"What key?" James asked.

"I'll be right back." She left the room and returned a few minutes later with her hands clasped together in front of her. Standing in front of her son, she said, "Your father gave this to me when we were married. He told me that no matter what our life together might bring us, we would be connected forever—and that this key would be the link to understanding connections to eternity. It never made sense to me."

She opened her hands and reached them out to James. In her palms she held a tarnished silver key. The handle was shaped like a heart, with a narrow stem about three inches long. The locking mechanism was flat and shaped like a capital E, with the top line of the letter longer and wider than the middle line, and the middle line longer and wider than the bottom line. Made of ivory-colored abalone shell, the E was encased by a thin beading of gold. At the top of the key was a solid bead of silver, the size of a pea, with a small ruby embedded at the tip.

"Mom, this is remarkable!" James whispered.

She lifted her open hand to him. "It's yours now."

James hesitated. She lifted the key from her palm and held it to her son's chest.

"Take it. I've kept it all these years, never really knowing what I would do with it. But now I know. It's meant for you."

James took the key and looked at it closely. "Thank you, Mom. This is a real treasure." He hugged her tightly.

James's mom reached for a clean napkin on the coffee table and daubed it at the corner of her eyes. "Well, now, it's late. You'd best be on your way."

"Yeah, we gotta go. Norah needs to be back at the hotel by midnight," said Reilly.

"When's the next boat?" James's mother asked.

"Actually, it's kind of a long story, but we need to wait and get on the 5:30 tomorrow morning," James replied.

"What are you going to do till then? Do you want to come back here and sleep?"

James looked at Reilly, who nodded.

"That would be great. We'll drop Norah off and be back before 1:00," James said.

"I'm going to bed, but I'll leave the door open and put some blankets out on the couch for you. Reilly can use the guest room."

Reilly and Norah set their glasses on the table, stood up and zipped up their jackets.

"Thank you, Mrs. Oliver," Reilly said offering his hand.

"Please, call me Rhonda."

"It was nice to meet you, Rhonda. And thank you so much for your help."

"Yes, it was a pleasure." Norah shook Rhonda's hand, too.

"Let me know what Lee says. I have so few memories of my dad. It would be awesome to have that journal."

"I will. Now you be careful. All of you." She stood on the front porch until they pulled away down the road. Everyone was quiet on the drive to the hotel.

It was ten minutes after midnight as they approached the hotel entrance. Reilly suddenly became aware of the predicament Norah would be in if her uncle had already returned to the room and she was not there.

"Do you want me to come up with you?" he asked.

"No, I'll be fine. I'm not concerned in the least," Norah said with confidence.

"Okay. Come by the bakery on Monday morning—Blackberry Bakers on Main Street. The side door will be unlocked."

Reilly opened the door and Norah slid across the seat. "Bye, James. I'll see you soon, too."

"Later, Norah," James said. "I live in the Waterfront Apartments. Here's my cell number. Call me if you hear anything you think might be important." He handed her a piece of paper.

Norah stepped out of the truck and stood directly in front of Reilly, reaching her arms around his neck. "Thank you, Reilly." She hugged him tightly. "I knew it was you … the minute I saw you in Jolka," she whispered in his ear.

Reilly was surprised by her sudden show of affection. But the hug felt good, so he put his arms around her and returned the embrace.

"Yeah, well, I'm glad we're friends now … and, uh … that we have the summer to hang out together."

"Good night. I'll see you Monday." She smiled as she pulled away. Then she turned and walked quickly into the hotel lobby. Reilly continued to feel the warmth of her body as he and James headed south towards West Seattle again.

Reilly sent his mom a text to let her know of the change of plans but turned off his phone after he sent it. He didn't want her to worry, but he also didn't want her asking more questions. It had been a long day and he had too much on his mind to deal with any more friction between them.

Reilly tossed and turned for over an hour, frustrated that he couldn't seem to quiet his mind. He hoped Norah was having the same problem. Finally, around 2:30, he drifted off to sleep with the scent of her hair lingering in his memory. Unfortunately, his dreams were not of Norah, but of hooded monsters surrounding him at every turn, groping at him with clawed hands, as he moved slowly through a dark tunnel towards a flashing light.

Reilly woke abruptly with his Stelladaur blinking in a slow rhythm, something it had never done before. He looked closely and intently between the steady blinks of light and the darkness. He saw nothing but the shadows of the closet door, a chair and a dresser a few feet away. He knew there was nothing else in the room except the bed he lay on. But he also knew he was not alone.

Gradually, the Stelladaur's beam of light projected a familiar form on the floor a few feet in front of him. It was difficult to make out at first because the form blended almost seamlessly into the Stelladaur's light. Reilly's eyes adjusted and two silver rays of light stared back at him. The creature was coming into focus. Then, materialized before him was Tuma.

"You need to go *now*," the dog said.

"Tuma?"

"Yes, you know it's me, Reilly. You must go to the ferryboat now! They will be on the starboard side on the lower car deck."

The Stelladaur stopped blinking and shone a steady but muted light. Tuma disappeared. Reilly reached for his jacket at the end of the bed and zipped it on as he dashed to the living room.

"James. James, wake up!" Reilly whispered loudly as he jostled James. "We gotta go!"

"Huh?" he moaned. "What time is it?"

"I don't know. But we need to go *now*."

James reached for his phone and squinted at the neon numbers. "Whoa, it's after 5:00!" He flung the blanket onto the floor and bounded off the couch. "My alarm didn't go off—what's up with that? We gotta race." They were out the door before he finished the sentence.

"Sure glad you woke up, kid. We gotta make that boat!" James slammed his truck door shut and thrust his key in the ignition.

"We will. Relax."

"Relax? You're not the one who has to drive like a madman to get us there!"

"We'll make the boat."

"Why are you always so chill at times when normal people panic?"

"So you don't think I'm normal?"

"No, actually I don't. It's not *normal* for a smart kid your age to be so intuitive, not to mention being immersed in dangerous ad-venture—*and* be so chill!"

Reilly could tell James was more perplexed than annoyed.

"So how did you wake up? I was so out of it, I didn't hear a thing and probably would have slept for hours. Did you sleep at all?"

"I slept okay. But I was having a strange dream and then my Stelladaur was blinking and it woke me up."

"Uh-huh. And you wonder why I think you're not normal."

"It was like a flashlight turning on and off slowly."

"I guess that would wake me up, too."

"It's never done that before so I knew there was a reason."

"See what I mean? You take out-of-the-ordinary events and make them seem very ordinary—not that a blinking jewel is ordi-nary. But you act like it's no big deal. You figure it's giving you some kind of telepathic message or something."

"It wasn't telepathic. It was holographic."

"*What?*"

"My dog, Tuma, was in the blinking light, and she told me we needed to go right away."

"Your *dog*? Your dog appeared and then she spoke to you. And this is *normal*?"

"Well, I'm not sure what normal is. Maybe it's different for differ-ent people. But it *did* happen." Reilly spoke confidently. "I'm always discovering more things that the Stelladaur can do. But that's the first time I've heard my dog actually talk! Kind of cool, huh?"

"Very cool," James said in a bewildered tone, shrugging his shoulders.

"Tuma and my Stelladaur have been like personal guides. I trust them as completely as I trust Eilam." Reilly could tell James wasn't quite absorbing it all.

They crossed the West Seattle Bridge only twenty minutes before the boat was scheduled to leave. Fortunately, it was Sunday so they didn't have to combat commuter traffic, but they took the first exit off the bridge to avoid any delay on the train tracks. Speeding along the old highway, they passed the warehouse district and saw in the distance the building they had been in just hours before. James checked the time and pressed his foot down on the accelerator.

Driving under the viaduct a block from the terminal, they spotted a parking space across the street from the taxi drivers, who waited anxiously by the curb for morning clients. James lurched into the empty space. He glanced at the time again.

"We've got four minutes before the boat leaves," he blurted. "Let's run, kid!"

The sun had come up over the Seattle skyline and city traffic indicated that summer tourists had begun their day early. Reilly and James darted out in front of oncoming cars, zigzagging towards the row of taxis across the street. They ran up the ramp to the terminal lobby as "last call for passengers to Bainbridge Island," blared over the loud speaker. James swiped the bar code twice over the scanner with his monthly pass and they ran through the security gate. Though they had time to walk down the breezeway before the boat left, James continued to run. Reilly followed behind until they bounded onto the deck of the ferry from the passenger loading-ramp.

"We made it!" James said, breathless.

"I knew we would," Reilly said as they walked towards the main doors. "I wondered why the rush."

"Very funny. C'mon, let's get down to the car deck and see where those guys are."

The mid-section of the lower deck was half empty and Reilly was glad they had decided to walk on the ferry because their truck would have been easy to spot and would have given them away had they driven on.

"You check things out on that side." Reilly pointed to the left. "I'll go this way." He held back by the service elevator, in the breezeway between the staircases at the bow of the boat. He peered carefully to the left around the corner, but saw nothing. Then, turning to the right, he spotted the two men standing at the side rail, facing each other and talking. Reilly quickly scanned the two rows of cars but didn't see anyone else. He figured people were either snoozing in their vehicles or they had gone up on deck for coffee. He ducked down and waddled along the parked cars until he got closer. Only one lane away, he crawled along the far row, inching slowly until he could see the guys' feet from under the car beside them.

"Let's wait till we're halfway between West Seattle and the island. It's deepest there." Reilly recognized it as the voice of the older fellow. "And it's far enough from any dive spots."

"I still don't get why we couldn't just put 'em in the dumpster with the rest of the duds," the other guy whined.

"I *told* you, you idiot. How many times do I have to explain this?" The man cussed and continued. "The ones with cracks aren't a problem, except that we can't sell 'em, cuz they *look* like duds. That's why we just threw 'em in the dumpster. As long as the resin is solidified, cracks or no cracks, nothin' can be detected. But these gooey ones, the ones that never hardened up right, they could be real trouble. Jackson said sea water is the only thing that'll dissolve the drugs."

Drugs? Reilly's mind raced as he began to put together the pieces that had been scattered until now. He inched closer and lay flat on his stomach; then he army-crawled under the SUV beside the thugs.

"Why couldn't we just put 'em in a tub of salt water and then throw 'em out with the rest? Why all this effort?" the younger guy persisted.

"Do I look like the scientist? Like I said, seawater is the only thing that'll dissolve any evidence of the drugs. Why do you ask so many asinine questions?"

They were silent for a few minutes. At their feet, Reilly could see two cardboard boxes like the ones he'd seen at the warehouse. A gust of wind blew dirt across the floor and under the cars. Reilly's nose twitched and he stifled a cough. He inhaled unexpectedly and barely caught a sneeze from exploding. It was trapped in the roof of his mouth, and he tightened his stomach muscles to release the muffled noise.

"What was that?" the younger guy asked.

"It's just the wind. Stop bein' so damn fidgety. Do you see anyone around here?"

There was a pause.

"No."

"*Riiiiight*," the older one said with a sarcastic drawl. "Remember, that's why we came over to *this* side. Sheesh!"

There was a longer pause. Reilly listened to the swooshing of the waves against the boat and felt the rhythm of the water as the vessel passed through it.

"Okay, this is good enough. Let's do it," the older guy said.

Reilly saw both men lift the boxes from the ground.

"On the count of three. One … two … three!"

Reilly couldn't hear the boxes hit the water, but he felt a sudden tightening in his chest and a stabbing pain in his lungs. It was difficult to breathe.

"That's it. Let's get some coffee," one of the men said.

Reilly thought it was the older man who made the suggestion, but he wasn't sure because the pain he felt in his chest distracted him. He leaned on his side slightly, hoping to relieve the pressure in his lungs, and watched the men's feet move around the SUV and down the aisle between the rows of cars. Though his Stelladaur had been trapped tightly between his chest and the car deck, Reilly knew something else had caused the pain and the feeling of strangulation.

He waited until he was sure the men were well out of sight, then inched his way out from under the car next to the railing. Standing up, he leaned over the rail to take a deep breath but still felt a dull aching in his chest.

Looking back towards Seattle, he noticed a black mist hovering over the surface of the water where the boxes had invaded the sea. The eerie mist spread out, increasing in intensity and forming a thick dark cloud. Reilly watched the cloud spiral upward like an inverted tornado and then dissipate into the morning air. He realized, painfully, that life below the surface of the water was suffering.

Chapter Eighteen

Insanity

R eilly found James and told him what he had witnessed. They headed to the galley, hoping to find the men there so they could eavesdrop again. There weren't many people on the boat, so it would be easy for Reilly to identify them by their voices. He walked past the center booth and saw them facing each other, drinking coffee. He glanced quickly but directly at their shoes and nodded a positive ID to James, who took a seat in the next booth down on the opposite side and nibbled on a brownie he'd stuffed in his pocket the night before. Reilly sat at the table behind the men and pretended to busy himself on his smart phone.

The younger man whined about his lack of sleep and pestered the other one about when they would get paid. The older one swore repeatedly and tried his best to end the conversation.

"Derek, you're the most irritating punk I know." The man stood up. "You don't know when to keep your mouth shut, do you?"

"Huh?"

"I'll be in the truck. We're just drivin' off and gettin' right back on." The man leaned over so he was only inches away from Derek's face and whispered loudly. "If I hear any more crap out of you on the way back, you're gonna be joinin' the duds."

Derek took a few more sips of coffee and then left.

Reilly and James rose and walked towards the doors to the main deck. Once outside, they stood near the rail, looking across Eagle Harbor.

"Derek looks younger than you," Reilly said to James. "He can't be more than twenty-one."

"Yeah. Looks like he's had a rough life. I wonder how he got mixed up in this mess."

"Who knows? But that other guy definitely threatened him."

"I don't think he'd have any reservations about getting rid of him," James said. Turning to look at Reilly, he added, "This is getting out of control. We need to call the police or something."

"No, we can't do that yet! It's not the right time," Reilly nearly shouted, but then lowered his voice. "We don't have any evidence. We're still not sure what Mr. Jackson is doing with those rocks. We've got to find out more information first."

"And how do you propose we do that?"

"I'm not sure." Reilly gazed out over the harbor. He could barely see Eilam's hut beyond the dozens of sailboats docked near the ferry terminal. "Let's talk to Eilam. He'll know."

The boat pulled into the harbor and a couple dozen foot-passengers walked off. As Reilly and James headed down the exit ramp from the terminal, Reilly saw the truck with Derek and the other guy drive off the ferry and make a U-turn to get back in line for the return sail.

"James, do you have a camera on your phone?" Reilly asked as they walked up the sidewalk.

"Yeah, but it can't zoom in close enough to get a decent shot of those guys," he said. "I've got a great camera at my apartment … it's just around the corner." Suddenly, James took off, running. "Wait there!"

Reilly found a bench inside the commuters' bicycle garage where he could still see the truck. He watched the first three rows of cars moving ahead to get on the ferry. Passengers passed in front of him, but Reilly filtered out the distractions and visualized James getting back before the truck boarded.

And he did. James zoomed in with the camera and shot a number of close-ups: the license number, a side view of the driver and a front shot of Derek. Then the truck eased along with the moving traffic and drove onto the boat.

Reilly knew Eilam wouldn't be at the kayak hut for another hour and that a conversation with his mom was inevitable, so they walked to the bakery.

"Oh, Reilly, I was really quite worried!" Reilly's mom jumped up from her desk and met him with a hug.

"Mom, there's no need to worry." Reilly pulled away without returning the hug. Touching his hand to the bulge under his jacket, he added, "As long as I have the Stelladaur, I'll be fine."

"So now it's a protector, too?" she asked with sarcasm.

"Actually, yes."

"And how, may I ask, does it do that?"

"I don't know how, exactly, but it does." He looked directly at his mom, trying to convince her of the stone's power. "And guess what else it can do?"

She folded her arms and jerked them to her waist without a reply.

"It's a great alarm clock," he smiled, trying to ease the tension.

"Come again?" She kept her arms crossed.

"It woke me up this morning with a flashing light. Tuma was in the flashes of light and she told me it was time to leave." Reilly's hope to tell his mom more details waned quickly as he watched her expression turn from irritation to disbelief. "We would have missed the boat and not found out what those guys were up to."

"He's right, Monique," James cut in. "Believe me. I know it's all kinds of weird. But we got some important information about Mr. Jackson. And the Stelladaur helped us out the whole time."

"I have half a mind to fire you, James." Keeping her arms folded, she scowled at him. "What kind of information?"

"He's making look-alikes out of plastic and coating them with a liquid resin that makes them sparkle and shine sort of like a real Stelladaur." Reilly sat down in a chair next to his mom's desk. "The ones that don't seal completely and that have cracks or bumps on them are thrown out. The ones that never solidified in the coating process are called duds. They're dumping the duds in the Sound between here and West Seattle."

"Why in the water?" she asked, finally unfolding her arms.

"Apparently sea water is the only thing that will dissolve any evidence of the drugs in the resin," Reilly said matter-of-factly.

"Drugs? What are you talking about?" she wailed.

"Mom, calm down." Reilly stood up again. "He's mixing some kind of drug into the resin. If the seal doesn't take during the coating process, then it stays kind of gooey, and anyone who knows enough about drugs would be able to detect the drug. If the resin solidifies there's no trace of the drug."

Reilly's mom stared at him with her jaw dropped.

"What we don't know is *why* he's putting drugs in the resin." James interjected.

A smile came across Reilly's face. "Yes, we do," he said, as he touched his Stelladaur. "I just figured it out."

"You did?" James asked.

"It's so obvious. It's a drug that falsely stimulates a person's imagination—to the point of hallucination."

"Hallucination?" Reilly's mom bellowed.

"What do you mean?" James asked, ignoring her.

"He announced to the world that his ROCK invention could be used as a time and space travel device. He couldn't just make plastic rocks that don't do anything. They'd never sell. So he's coating them with a resin to make them look like diamonds."

"But he said his ROCKs are *not* diamonds. Why would anyone pay a million dollars for one?" Reilly's mom asked.

"The resin has a drug mixed into it that makes people hallucinate and think they're traveling through space or something. That's what I'm guessing. Mr. Jackson is counting on those who have been investing in his companies for years to be the guinea pigs … to test them out." Reilly stopped to think about what he had just said. "It makes sense."

"With all his inventions, why would he want to do this? What does he have to gain?" his mom asked. "It's not like he needs more money."

"It's not about the money." The words flowed from Reilly's mouth now as if he'd known this all along. "It's about power. For more than twenty-five years, Mr. Jackson has tried to find the portal. Knowing now that portals actually exist and that others besides him know how to access them consumes him with jealousy."

"That's insane." Reilly's mom rolled her eyes.

"If knowing you'll never have something you want—even if it's because you're trapped in a hunger for greed or power—if that's insanity, then Travis Jackson is clearly insane." Reilly stated.

"But how does lacing a plastic-covered rock with drugs give him power?" James asked.

"If Mr. Jackson can't have what he wants, he doesn't want anyone else to have what they want. He thinks the Stelladaur is only a travel device, so that's what he's capitalizing on. But the drug will make people *think* they're traveling to another place, by some kind of hallucination." Reilly spoke confidently. "In the process, he's literally stealing the magic out of every soul who uses one of his ROCKs."

Confused, Reilly's mom interjected. "Stealing the magic?"

"Yes, of course …" James said. "Now I understand. How can someone be open to finding his own Stelladaur if there's no reason to look for one?"

"Exactly. Those who use the ROCK will be robbed of their desire to want something greater, or more meaningful. Desire is like magic. It makes all things possible by giving endless opportunities to ask. It's from the asking that all wishes, dreams and wants become realities. Desire creates the asking and asking manifests the desire." Reilly spoke with ease, yet he was suddenly aware that what he said sounded very much like something Eilam would say.

"What do we do now?" James asked.

"We call the police," Reilly's mom insisted.

"No, Mom! Not yet!" Reilly shook his head hard. "I'm going to talk with Eilam first."

"If Eilam doesn't have any answers, *I'm* calling the police!" She tightened her apron and walked into the dining area.

Reilly sighed as he and James followed her. Reilly loaded a plate with two scones, a blueberry muffin, a slightly browned banana and a bottle of juice from the customer cooler. James grabbed a sticky bun and some coffee.

"By the way," Reilly's mom said, wiping off the corner booth table for them to sit down, "your sister is coming to stay for a while."

"When?"

"On Wednesday. She's taking the entire month of July off. I don't think she had enough time here after the funeral. She just wants to relax and be home for a while."

"That's so great, Mom!" Reilly finished his last bite of muffin and swallow of juice. "James, you haven't met Chantal, have you?"

"No, I don't think I have."

"Well, you're gonna love her. She's awesome!"

"That good, huh? Is she hot?"

"She's gorgeous … and she's very single," said Reilly's mom, winking at James. Reilly smiled at his mom, happy that her mood had lightened.

"Excellent!" said James.

As they walked to the marina, Reilly told his friend all the reasons Chantal would be perfect for him. By the time they reached the pier that led to the kayak hut, Reilly had thoroughly convinced himself that it was destined to be. James laughed at Reilly's exuberance, but admitted he was looking forward to meeting Chantal.

Eilam had opened up the shop and was guiding a two-person kayak from behind the hut to the main loading dock. Tuma ran to greet Reilly. Reilly fell to his knees and wrapped his arms around his dog's neck, letting Tuma lick his face numerous times.

"Thanks for your help, Tuma."

Tuma barked.

"Hey, kid, it looks like Eilam could use a hand. C'mon." James sprinted down the ramp to the hut and Tuma and Reilly followed close behind. They stepped to the edge of the dock as Eilam looped the kayak's lanyard around a short spike.

"Hello, my friends," he said, standing to greet them. "I've been waiting for your return."

"You have?" James asked, puzzled.

"It is really quite easy to know a friend when you meet one," Eilam smiled. "Friends are quick to accept others and slow to judge them. I have felt that from you, James, during our brief encounters at the bakery." Eilam smiled again and then turned to Reilly. "And you are here to ask what is next for you?"

"Yes," Reilly said.

"Tell me what you believe you must do."

"I need to stop Mr. Jackson from harming others with his ROCK."

"And?"

"And I need to keep him from stealing the magic of imagination from anyone who's searching for their own Stelladaur, even if they don't know they're looking for one."

Eilam stepped closer to Reilly and put his crooked hands together at his chest, looking somewhat like a praying monk. "And is that a greater desire than wanting life to be as it was before your dad passed on?"

Reilly thought intently about the question. He felt his heart beating strong and steady, though his breathing was deep and calm.

"It's what my dad would do. And it's what I must do."

"And how will you do that?"

"I don't know. That's what I was hoping you could tell me."

"Ah, but if I simply tell you, then what need have you for the stone around your neck?"

Reilly pulled his Stelladaur out from under his shirt and held it in his palm.

"You are learning to hear what the Stelladaur speaks to you, are you not?" Eilam said.

"Yes, I am."

"Then continue to listen when thoughts come to you. But understand it is only when a thought also resonates in your heart that you will know what is next." Eilam put his hands under Reilly's cupped hand and held the stone with him. He looked deeply into Reilly's eyes and added, "Then you will have the needed courage to do it."

Tuma barked once and Reilly stepped away from Eilam, letting the Stelladaur fall to his chest on its cord, so he could stroke his dog's head.

A gust of wind blew past them, leaving the air noticeably still. Reilly saw a small blue feather at his feet and bent down to pick it up. He held it between two fingers, at the quill's point, so he could see the sunlight penetrate the threads that held it together. He turned the feather around in his fingers a few times, observing the blues change to black when the light refracted off of it.

"I need to go through the blue vortex," Reilly said, running his finger from the center of the quill to the edges of the feather. "And I think Norah should come with me." He looked up.

"I'd offer to go with you, but I'm not sure I'm ready for that time travel stuff just yet," James said as he raised his eyebrows.

"You might need your own Stelladaur anyway, James," Reilly suggested.

"Whatever. I think I'll focus on getting my dad's journal back from Travis first."

"Your Stelladaur will find you when you are ready for it," Eilam said.

"I'm confused," James added. "I thought a person had to find his own Stelladaur."

"Not exactly. The Stelladaur will appear when a person is ready to find his own greatest desire," Eilam said. "Then the stone will manifest what is wanted."

Four tourists approached and Eilam took a few steps towards them, but turned back to James.

"Perhaps you could spend the morning preparing," Eilam suggested. He didn't wait for a response.

"What does he mean by that?" James asked Reilly, frustrated.

"I'm not sure, but Tuma and I are going out on the water for a while. Later, after Norah arrives, we will come by your place."

"Okay." James sighed. "I'll wait to hear from you. I'm headed back to Seattle to get my truck."

Reilly watched James wave to Eilam as he passed the counter and walked slowly up the dock ramp. He thought James must be wondering what Eilam meant and whether his Stelladaur would just magically appear in his life.

The water beckoned Reilly and he slid down into his kayak.

"C'mon, Tuma. Let's go," he said, untying the rope and easing into the water.

Tuma leaped from the dock to the front opening of the kayak. Her white coat reflected like snow on a sunny winter's day, and her silver eyes glistened like stars on a dark summer's night. Reilly reached up to pet Tuma, who looked straight ahead, leading the way like a beacon on a lighthouse.

Reilly's blond hair blew behind him freely as he picked up speed in the kayak, moving towards the cove of the harbor. He breathed in deeply through his nostrils. After picking up enough speed to glide ahead effortlessly, he closed his eyes for a few minutes to allow the sun to penetrate his soul.

Then, as he slowly opened them again, he saw two bald eagles perched on top of a tall pine tree, holding perfectly still on the branch. He considered the fact that they had a clear view of the island and far beyond, and wondered if they could see the waves on the far coast—the ones Sequoran could see and had spoken to. Without warning, the eagles lifted their wings in unison and left the branch, causing it to bend noticeably.

Oh, to soar like an eagle! Reilly thought. The birds flew across the harbor and he watched until they became little specks against the blue sky, heading west towards the far coast.

He paddled steadily but gently to the end of the harbor, where he stopped to watch an otter and her three babies poking their heads above the water. Tuma barked, and the mother lifted her head higher, as if to nod hello. The critters disappeared under the water, and Reilly turned the kayak around to paddle east against the incoming wind.

In the distance, he could see his dad's sailboat, tucked in its slip at the marina, bobbing and rocking in the wind. He picked up speed, moving towards the yacht club, but gave no thought to possibly seeing Travis peer at him from the club's main window. He paddled hard until he was only twenty feet from *The Ark*, and then dipped the paddle deeply into the water, holding it firmly to bring his kayak to a stop near the dock.

Tuma leaped onto the wharf as Reilly looped the kayak's lanyard quickly around a post. The dog didn't wait for Reilly but ran ahead and waited beside *The Ark*, wagging her tail. Reilly walked towards *The Ark*, not really knowing why they were there, and pushed aside the thoughts of his mom forbidding him to get on the boat again. Tuma jumped aboard and waited for Reilly.

Hesitating only briefly, Reilly stepped on board. An eerie feeling crept over him, and he sensed they were not alone. Instinctively, he touched the Stelladaur with one hand and reached his other hand to his waist, where the top knob of his knife poked up above the sheath. He had made a habit of carrying it with him, but even in the pending danger at the warehouse, it had not crossed his mind that he might need to use it. Now he was glad he had it with him.

He walked slowly along the deck and stopped at the wheel, grabbing the top of it to brace himself as he stepped down into the boat's steering chamber. The galley door was ajar. He pushed it gently, and it opened with a slight creak. Tuma jumped in first and Reilly followed. The galley was empty. Reilly moved cautiously to the stern, with Tuma close at his side. He checked the head but it was empty. Then he put his ear to the stateroom door and heard a muffled sound—a guttural tone with intermittent non-musical humming. He put his hand on the doorknob and turned it slowly, opening the door a few inches and peering into the room, still unable to detect where the sound was coming from.

Finally, he flung the door open with one hand as he pulled the knife from the sheath with his other. Looking like a pirate ready to pounce upon his mutinous crew, he held the knife out in front of him, ready to attack. Then, he froze.

"Norah?" he cried, the knife still held out in front of him.

A girl was lying on the bed with her back to him. There was no answer when he called her name. Reilly moved slowly around the foot of the bed and saw that her eyes were closed. There was an iPod beside her, with earphones fit snugly in place. Her Stelladaur rested on the bed but was still looped around her neck.

For a long moment, Reilly stood and watched her breathe. He wasn't at all sure how to identify the rush of emotions. Astonished? Nervous? Excited?

Norah stirred and made a weird snoring-humming sound. Reilly reached out and touched her leg, just above her ankle. She jumped and opened her eyes.

"Reilly!" Norah sat up quickly, pulled the earphones from her ears and let them drop to the bed. "You scared me!"

"What are you doing here?" He still held the knife like a pirate.

Norah caught her breath, and then reached out to hold his wrist. "There's no need for this." She lowered his hand as she looked into his eyes. Then looking at the knife, she added, "But that's very cool."

"Oh, I'm sorry … I, uh, I thought someone was on board." Reilly quickly put the knife back in the sheath. "I knew someone was here. I just had no idea it would be you."

Norah giggled. "And who is this?"

"Tuma. Tuma, Norah."

Tuma gave a bark and wagged her tail.

"Hi, Tuma." Norah reached her hand out for Tuma to sniff. "Wow, she's beautiful."

"Thanks." Reilly scratched Tuma's head. "So, how did you get here, Norah?"

"My uncle and I came over with Mr. Jackson this morning on Mr. Jackson's yacht. He said he had business to take care of at the club. I knew neither of them wanted me hanging around, so I told my uncle I was going to go explore. You know, hang out at the beach or something. As usual, he didn't care and just told me to be back by 5:00 so I could change for dinner."

"But how did you know this was—"

"—your sailboat?"

"Yeah."

"Because I found this on the dock right beside your boat." She reached into her denim jacket pocket and pulled out a small orange feather. "When we were coming over, I stayed on deck and watched an unusual bird hovering just in front of me most of the way. It flew alongside the boat, like it was trying to keep up. When we pulled up to the marina, it flew off towards the end of the harbor. Anyway, I thought I'd take a walk to look for starfish on the pilings. There are tons of them, Reilly, did you know that?"

"Yes, but what about the feather?" He sat down on the bed beside her.

"Oh, yeah. As I walked along the dock and peered over the edge to see the starfish, I almost stepped on this beautiful little feather." Norah held the feather out for Reilly to touch. "I think it was from a young bird. Feel how soft it is." He touched it but his mind wandered from the bird to Norah. Looking at her, he wondered if her cheek was as soft as the feather.

"It is soft." Reilly dropped his hand to his side and looked away, hoping he hadn't been too obvious.

"After I picked it up, I walked to the bow to see if there was a name on the boat. I read the words *The Ark* out loud, and my Stelladaur rumbled against my chest. That's how I knew it was your boat."

"But I didn't tell you the name of the boat, did I?"

"No. But when I was in Jolka, I saw all of this in the Drawing Sidewalk."

"You saw all of what?"

Norah glanced quickly out the side window and then turned back to look into Reilly's eyes. "This beautiful place. The ocean, the trees, the forest, the seagulls … and your boat. I knew it was a place I would go to somehow, but at the time, I didn't know why. There's nothing like this in Chicago, at least not in the city. Actually, the first time I saw the ocean was while flying over Seattle." She paused and inched closer to Reilly. "It's so peaceful here."

Reilly tried to pay attention to what she was saying but was distracted, watching her mouth as she spoke. Suddenly nervous with the short distance between them, he stood up.

"I'm sure it's quite different from Chicago," he said. There was a long pause as he tried to think of what to say next. "Did you know that finding a feather in your path lets you know you're on the right track?"

"I didn't know that. But I believe it."

"How long have you been here?"

"Maybe an hour or so. I fell asleep listening to music—a habit of mine, I guess." She reached for her iPod and stood up from the bed. "It's weird, but living in the city with all the noise of the traffic and nothing but skyscrapers and cement to look at most of the time, well, I like to get lost in some good classical music. It calms me."

"Classical?"

"Uh-huh. I play the piano—really well, actually—but my uncle doesn't have one. And he sees no need to get one. As I said, he doesn't want to go out of his way for me at all." She picked up the earphones and finished her thought. "I figure if I can't play, at least I can listen."

Reilly silently vowed to help Norah find a way to get back to her music.

"Do you sing, too?" he asked.

"I wish," she said. "Sadly, I can't carry a tune."

Reilly chuckled as he realized the stifled, guttural sounds he had heard were from Norah humming to the music, half asleep.

"What's so funny?" she asked. "I suppose you sing or something?"

"Me? No, not really. I only play the piano a little. But I can whistle."

"Well, great! Maybe we can do a piano and whistling duet some-time." She laughed.

Reilly nodded, noticing the way her nose wrinkled when she laughed.

"Did you find out anything else last night?"

"Lots. Mr. Jackson's fake Stelladaurs are covered in a resin mixed with hallucinogenic drugs. The drugs are completely invisible, and when a person rubs one of the fake ROCKs, they hallucinate and think they've gone through some kind of time machine. At least that's what I think is going on. I don't know exactly, but it's not go-ing to take long for those shareholders who purchased ROCKs last night to get the word out. When they do, everyone will think Mr. Jackson has actually invented a time travel device. We need to stop people from buying them. Who knows what these drugs could do?"

"Reilly, that's terrible! Why would he do that?"

"Power and greed."

"What can we do?"

"We need to go back to Jolka, or wherever the next vortex takes us. I wish it would rain soon, but I checked the weather and it's supposed to be sunny all week."

"Why does it need to rain?"

Reilly could tell Norah was confused, but he didn't understand why.

"So we can get through the portal in the rainbow."

Norah furrowed her brow slightly and then relaxed her fore-head, giving Reilly a look that indicated she had had an epiphany of some sort.

"So you've only gone through a vortex on rainy days?"

"Yeah, after big storms. Didn't you?"

"No, it was bright and sunny both times I left to go to Jolka, just like today." Norah smiled. "C'mon, I'll show you!" She grabbed his hand and they darted for the door.

Chapter Nineteen

Affirmations

Norah let go of Reilly's hand when they reached the galley steps to the deck so they could squeeze through the narrow doorway. Tuma took the steps in one leap. Smiling and giggling, Norah walked ahead to the starboard side of the sailboat and leaned over the edge.

"Get back!" Reilly yelled as he moved quickly towards her.

"What's wrong?" She frowned.

"It's deep there!"

"I'm sorry." She touched his arm. "Of course."

Reilly looked into her eyes and knew Norah had not meant to stir up any flashbacks of his father's accident. Dropping her hand from his arm, she turned to Tuma.

"Hey, Tuma." She offered the dog the back of her hand. Tuma licked it repeatedly.

"She likes you," Reilly said.

"You really are the most beautiful dog I've ever seen." She cuddled Tuma with both hands and stroked her behind the ears. "Where did you get her?"

"Eilam said my dad sent her to me—from Tir Na Nog."

Norah stood up and looked into Reilly's eyes, smiling. "Then Tuma should know we can get through the portal on a sunny day." Tuma barked and wagged her tail.

"Well, she never told *me!*" Reilly frowned at Tuma.

Norah laughed and wrinkled her nose again.

"You don't have to wait for a rainbow. If the Stelladaur is wet the sun will create the portal wherever you are," said Norah.

"Are you sure?"

"Of course, I'm sure. Didn't Fiala tell you that?"

"No."

"Huh."

Reilly wondered what else Fiala had told Norah but not him. *How does a Stelladaur work when a person changes what he wants?* It was a question he wished he had thought to ask Fiala.

"It doesn't really matter," Norah said. "Let's get going." She took her Stelladaur from around her neck and dangled it over the edge of the sailboat. "You just have to make sure it's completely wet. C'mon, dip yours in, too."

Reilly took his Stelladaur and lowered it into the water, holding tightly to the golden cord. They leaned carefully over the edge of the boat, bobbing their Stelladaurs up and down a few times to make sure they were wet. The sun penetrated the water in brilliant streams of bright light, refracting off the stones and creating a small double rainbow.

"Let's see what happens when we dip them in the water at the same time," Reilly suggested.

He moved closer to Norah, pressing his left shoulder against her right shoulder as they leaned over the boat. She held her Stelladaur in her left hand and he held his in his right. They extended their arms forward, touching each other from elbow to wrist, holding tightly to the golden cords. They brought their stones together and lowered them like synchronized swimmers down into the water.

The moment the stones emerged from the water, a solid broad rainbow appeared. A beam of light struck the Stelladaurs with a bolt of energy that flashed blue sparks in every direction, an all-blue fireworks extravaganza. Mesmerized by the magical light display, their eyes sparkled like bright sapphire gems. Without further warning, the cords holding the Stelladaurs twisted around each other until they had become one with two stones dangling at the end. In a split second, the cord wrapped their wrists together and plopped the Stelladaurs into their cupped hands. With a final burst of blue, accompanied by a piano and a whistling duet of Debussy's *Clair De Lune*, they were elevated above the deck of *The Ark*. Simultaneously they swooped into the air and disappeared under the water like graceful divers slicing the surface without a splash.

Midway through the melody they bolted like a rocket through an azure vortex, their wrists still tied together and extended in front of them, their inside arms wrapped around each other's backs. The musical duet continued as they swirled through the tunnel. Though they both looked straight ahead, Reilly felt Norah's thoughts mirroring his own. In this vortex in space, it felt safe to admit to himself that he liked her.

As they twirled through the blueness, the cords unwound from their wrists and separated into two again. The stones still rested in their touching palms until, with a gust and a whoosh, both Reilly and Norah exited the tunnel and landed on their stomachs.

They faced each other, nose to nose, with the golden cords again around their necks and their Stelladaurs securely attached. The music stopped.

"My, my, you have arrived at last." A high-pitched but pleasant voice greeted them.

At first, Reilly and Norah could not see who spoke. Almost imperceptibly, a tiny girl with a youthful face but an odd demeanor of maturity appeared through a cobalt cloud. Her skin was a soft shade of white, not bright or translucent, but delicate and innocent. "I have been waiting for you both and am delighted you came together."

Reilly and Norah slowly stood up and Norah reached for Reilly's hand.

"Welcome to Glesig." The girl smiled with piercing cyan eyes. "I am Neela." She curtsied, holding two ribbons at her skirt, as an array of blue shaded ribbons swirled from her waist like gentle waves of the sea. Under the waves, she wore aquamarine leggings, cut just below her knees, and sapphire jewels adorned her bare feet.

Reilly and Norah bowed hesitantly.

Neela's mass of powder blue hair draped over her shoulders in two loose braids, trailing down a royal blue, smocked bodice. Nestled on her head lay a delicate crown of forget-me-nots interspersed with baby's-breath. "Glesig is a place to affirm the true essence of youth and learn to trust the heart of a child."

Neela curtsied again, as a thick cloud of blue seeped out of the ground. "We shall begin our journey." The cloud lifted them from the ground; they tumbled into it as if it were a giant feather bed. Slowly they moved into seeming nothingness, a mysterious place with no landscape, only blue space.

Relaxing into the cloud, Reilly and Norah waited for Neela to speak again.

"Here you will use your imagination as you have before, but also inner awareness to create affirmations. Every time an affirmation is clearly communicated, thoughts and feelings are intertwined to manifest that which is desired." Reilly looked at Norah again, trying to understand what the blue fairy-like creature meant. "There is no need to be confused. It is really quite simple. The Affirmation Cloud will help you understand the process."

Neela scooped up a handful of blue cloud, looked at it intently and drew in a breath to blow the cloud out of her hands. As the cloud dissipated to a mist, she spoke again. "I feel happy my new friends are here with me. We shall have a splendid time together." Her jeweled toes glittered in the sun.

A short distance from where they nestled on the blue cloud, a mirror image of them was suspended in the air in front of them.

Reilly laughed out loud when he saw the image of himself waving at them, though his own hands were at his sides, one intertwined with Norah's. The image of Norah laughed, too, and Reilly turned to Norah to see if her nose wrinkled with her response. It did.

"See how simple it is?" Neela said. "You simply state how you feel, and why, and then affirm what you would like to have happen. The Affirmation Cloud will do the rest. You try, Norah."

Norah's eyes widened. "Me? I'm not sure what to say."

"Gather up some Affirmation Cloud and listen to the child within you," said Neela. "Then speak it."

Norah tentatively pulled her hand from Reilly's and they both stood up. She reached out to scoop some of the blue cloud and looked at it carefully. Then she drew in a breath to blow the cloud from her hands, just as Neela had done. Norah surprised herself by saying something she had never said before.

"I feel sad that my mom died. I miss her. I want her to be with me."

At Norah's words, her mother appeared in the cloud, digging in a garden. Her mother uncovered a Stelladaur and held it up to touch Norah's chest. Norah lifted her hand to touch her mother's arm, but her mother vanished.

"Don't go, Mom!" Norah frantically grasped into the nothingness. Then she closed her eyes and rested her hands over her heart.

"Norah, what does the child want to say?" Neela urged.

Reilly could see Norah consider her thoughts and emotions carefully. "That's strange," she whispered, "my mom *is* with me.

She'll always be with me." With her hands still over her heart, healing tears flowed over her soul like a cerulean sea.

"You have affirmed it by listening to your heart," said Neela.

Neela waited until Norah dropped her hands from her chest. Then she turned and said, "Reilly, what will the Affirmation Cloud bring to you?"

Nervous after listening to Norah, Reilly knew he felt something different than he had expected. Resisting the feeling, he shook his head, *no*. Neela and Norah waited.

"I'm not sure. I don't—" Reilly took a step back. Norah moved towards him and gently pulled him forward. At first he resisted.

"It's okay," Norah whispered in Reilly's ear.

Reilly brushed his thumb across Norah's cheek to catch a lingering tear, then slowly stepped closer to the Cloud. He drew in a deep breath and extended his arms wide open, gathering a tremendous bunch of blue Affirmation Cloud. "I want to see my dad more than anything. But that's not what I want to affirm." He closed his eyes and lifted the Cloud to his chest, rephrasing his words. "I want to help others find their own Stelladaurs."

He took another deep breath and exhaled slowly as he watched the mist begin to take form. As the images came into focus, Reilly gasped in awe. Standing in front of them were hundreds of people—thousands—mostly teenagers or younger children, but also some adults. Each one held a brilliant Stelladaur, cupped in their hands. The light was blindingly bright. Reilly and Norah held their hands up to shield their eyes.

Suddenly, the blue cloud was infused with a tangible blackness that oozed and undulated around the images. The light from the Stelladaurs faded; some went out all together.

"Quick!" Neela said, "Affirm what you will do next."

With determination, Reilly reached for his own Stelladaur and held it out in front of him. Without hesitation, he shouted his affirmation. "I will not allow Travis Jackson to steal the hearts and minds of the innocent!"

There was a sparkling burst of every shade of blue imaginable. Reilly and Norah fell back onto the cloud and watched.

Neela stepped in front of Reilly and spoke above the clamor. "And so it shall be." When the noise had quieted and the sparks vanished, she added, "Now you are ready to learn the affirmations that will be most helpful to you and the others."

Neela began to dance and twirl on the blue cloud, her ribbon skirt flowing to the melody of another classical piano-and-whistle duet. She gracefully picked up bits of blue and tossed them into the air repeatedly, like a ballerina waving in arabesque.

"These will keep you steadfast in the cause of the Stelladaur and give you power to share them with others," Neela said.

Written in midnight blue across the vast sky was a list of seven affirmations.

Reilly and Norah read them silently.

Affirmations of the Stelladaur

1. I am eternal, without time or space.
2. I am imagination and creativity without end.
3. I am realization and manifestation as One.
4. I am all possibilities.
5. I am the open mind and gentle heart.
6. I am nature.
7. I am love.

"It is time for the Affirmations of the Stelladaur to be available to you always. Stand up, please, and read them in unison, loudly and clearly."

Reilly and Norah gazed at the shining blue writing and began to recite in unison.

"I am eternal, without time or space." As they spoke the words, the letters exited the sky and plummeted in two blue streaks onto the Stelladaurs that pulsated against their chests.

"I am imagination and creativity without end," they continued. Like a lightning flash, the words emblazoned the stones.

"I am realization and manifestation as One." The affirmation was engraved in the jewels. Five more times, reading each sentence boldly and solemnly, Reilly and Norah stood still as the words penetrated their Stelladaurs, and the meanings imbued their souls.

When all seven affirmations had been erased from the sky and seared into their Stelladaurs, Reilly and Norah stared in amazement. The first affirmation was engraved in tiny gold letters on the back. Reilly touched the letters, and the next affirmation appeared.

"Cool!" he said.

Norah did the same. "Wow!"

Reilly scrolled through them, one at a time, with the tap of his finger. Then he smiled at Norah again and reached for her hand.

"You both learn quickly," Neela said. "You are now ready to go to Gwidon."

With that, she exhaled—without any visible signs of inhaling—and the blue Cloud dissipated. Instantaneously, the Cloud transformed into a large, sparkling disc, a giant emerald gem turning slowly in circles in front of them.

"As Fiala explained to Norah, the Stelladaur can be used in more than one way to reach the portals through the Arc of Color. Water is the only element necessary to combine with the Sun's light. The Water will always respond joyously to those who respect and honor it." Neela raised her arms and multi-colored raindrops fell gently over Reilly and Norah. They looked up and let the rainbow shower wet their faces and then turn to clear water as it touched their skin. "Once you are inside a ribbon of color—as you are here, in Glesig—you can cross to the next without effort, provided you are ready to receive what it has to offer." She curtsied with the ribbons of her skirt in her hands, as she had when she first greeted Reilly and Norah.

Reilly and Norah listened intently, eager to absorb everything Neela said.

"I'm ready," Reilly affirmed.

"I'm ready, too."

They raised their arms to the rain and stepped onto the Emerald Gem.

There was no sense of falling or spinning. No moving through a vortex in the sea or somewhere in space. Reilly and Norah simply entered Gwidon through a magical doorway the moment they climbed on top of the giant green stone. The portal transported them from an endless cloud of blue to a lush field of green.

Oddly, no one was there to greet them. As far as they could see in every direction, there was only tall grass. No pathways. Nothing on the horizon. Just a sea of blowing grass.

"We should move ahead," Reilly said.

"To where?"

"Just ahead. C'mon!" Reilly let go of Norah's hand and sprinted forward, surfing over the rolling waves of green. Norah followed.

"Woo-wee!" Reilly shouted. "This is fun! I love it!"

Norah danced through the grass as she tried to catch up to Reilly. "Wait up!" She laughed.

Running for a couple hundred yards, the thick grass started to thin and mingle with clovers, some of them three feet high. Soon all the grass was gone and they found themselves in a field of huge four-leaf clovers. Reilly had never seen so many shades of green—emerald, jade, lime, forest-green, grass-green, chartreuse, melon, cucumber, tennis-ball green, pine, and so many more that he wondered if they even had names. The spectrum was endless.

Wherever he and Norah stepped, the imprint of their bare feet was only momentary because the trampled clovers sprang back up immediately.

"This is like breathing in all of Eagle Harbor and the Grand Forest at once. I feel like I can fly!" At the suggestion, Reilly raised his arms to his sides. He ran and laughed out loud as his body soared into the air. "Norah, lift your arms higher!"

Norah raised her arms to her sides, with her palms up, as she'd seen Reilly do. Up she went, too, flying above the strange place called Gwidon.

"Let's try flapping," Reilly said, still laughing.

They lowered their arms in deep, slow motions, increasing their altitude by dozens of feet with each swoop.

"Whoa!" Norah squealed. "This is so much better than I ever imagined flying could be!"

"I know!" Reilly hollered, and he turned the palms of his hands to face the ground. Like a stunt pilot at an air show, he spiraled and turned and plummeted. "Flip your hands back the other way!" He zoomed past Norah. "Try it!"

Norah giggled, then turned her hands upside down and veered off like a mini-rocket. They zipped and swooped, dipped and swooshed—loop-dee-looped like in Jolka.

Not wanting to stop, but wondering how to do so, Reilly maneuvered his arms and hands into other formations. He lowered both arms slowly to his sides and descended gradually, nose first. The ground approached faster than he expected it would. As if possessing bird-like instincts, he lifted only the palms of his hands, at a right angle to his forearms. Norah followed. With hands like flippers, they swerved right side up and hovered three feet above the ground.

Reilly opened his mouth to speak but gulped for breath as a mighty gust of wind overtook them. They turned towards the wind and saw streaks of bright green—a jet stream from something that had whipped by too fast for them to see. Then another whoosh of tremendous force blew past them in long streaks of green from the other direction. From behind them, someone spoke.

"I am called Jaida." It was a female voice, gentle and calm.

Reilly and Norah faced the creature and dropped their jaws, still surprised by the continual unexpectedness in the realms unknown to them before.

"I am the Guardian of Nature," she said, her long hair flowing with green threads of shimmering seaweed. "It is my purpose to protect the spirit of all living things." Fastened to uneven sections of her hair by green stems were flowers of many colors and varieties. Like strings of randomly twinkling lights, the blossoms transformed continuously into other flowers and buds. Jaida's two arms were moss-covered branches, and her hands were multi-pointed maple leaves. Though her shoulders were bare, her upper torso was covered in iridescent green scales, which blended into the feathered lower portion of her body. Reilly could not tell whether the scales and feathers were part of her body or her clothing. Tied about her neck was a flowing cloak, a collage of green leaves, which trailed behind her like an elaborate bridal train gathered about her in a sweeping fashion on the ground. Exquisitely camouflaged throughout the cloak—yet still appearing in their natural colorings—were small animals, birds, insects and reptiles, some poking their heads up slightly as if to see who Jaida was speaking to.

"This is Nebo," said Jaida, nodding to a bald eagle perched on her right shoulder. The bird's white head towered above Jaida. "He is the Guide of Wisdom, whose influence flows endlessly through all living things." The eagle blinked slowly as he, too, nodded to Reilly and Norah. They returned the greeting with a slight bow.

"Reilly, because you have an innate ability to listen to the spirits of other living things, your visit to Gwidon is primarily a reminder to you of what you already know within yourself," said Jaida, her scaly green breast rising as she spoke. "Norah, you, too, will learn from these same Spirits of Nature. They will aid you both in the healing of your souls and will offer simple treasures of delight, as you allow them. This is the purpose of Nature."

Reilly and Norah listened carefully, glancing occasionally at the creatures peering up at them from Jaida's cloak. Nebo continued to blink slowly and nod slightly.

"Each color of your journey has communicated specific knowledge. One adds upon the other. Violet is the portal to imagination—it links the Universal to the Individual through inspiration, creativity, and magic. Indigo is the bridge of mindfulness, creating awareness and inner consciousness of the connection between the finite and the infinite. It opens the third eye, offering clarity of inner self-potential." Jaida's own two eyes glistened like emeralds and her green fuzzy lips—reminding Reilly of a plant called Rabbit Ears that grew in his front yard—twitched at the corners. "Blue links thoughts and feelings by giving solemn affirmations. And thus reveals the heart of a child in all who honestly look." Jaida scrunched her delicate nose until it took the form of a conch shell.

Jaida moved her mossy arms gently as she continued to speak.

"Green reflects respect for life in all forms. It brings endless growth and fertility, creating perfect balance through the Spirits of Nature. When Nature's spirit is disrupted or harmed in any way, all other forms suffer as well. Most human beings are unaware of their power to create a peaceful balance with life." Jaida looked adoringly at the creatures nodding beneath her skirt. "Those who listen to the Spirits of Nature are more enlightened in their ability to create this balance."

"Can you repeat that?" Norah asked. "I don't know if I can remember all of that."

"You need only remember the feeling. Nature will remind you of all else." Jaida stepped forward and stood directly in front of Reilly.

"You have set your own desire aside, with an affirmation to prevent one called Travis Jackson from stealing the hearts and minds of other innocent living creatures. This is noble. This is for the greatest good of all. But it will require a greater sacrifice than you may have supposed."

Reilly's eyes widened. "What do you mean … a *greater sacrifice*?" he asked hesitantly.

"Do not fear. The Spirits of Nature will teach you. Listen."

Nebo left his perch on Jaida's shoulder and rose into the air with a single flap of his wings. A rushing wind swirled around them as the bird circled above, rising higher and growing larger with the ascent. With a magnificent plunge, the giant eagle swooped between Reilly and Norah, turning at a perpendicular angle and brushing past their bodies in a gust of air. Nebo landed on the ground beside them and tucked his wings at his side.

"Get on my back. The Spirits of Nature are calling for you," Nebo said.

Reilly laughed and did not hesitate. He climbed up close to Nebo's head, letting his feet dangle over the bird's wings. Then Reilly reached his hand out to Norah. She hoisted herself behind him and wrapped her arms tightly around his waist. Reilly gripped the thick feathers on Nebo's neck.

Suddenly, Nebo lifted his feet from the clover field and spread his massive wings. With one swoosh, they rose high above Jaida, who waved.

"Listen … just listen …" Jaida's whispering voice echoed in the wind as they flew away from Gwidon.

Chapter Twenty

Messages

Flying on a giant bird was quite different than transporting through an intergalactic vortex. The warmth of Nebo's downy feathers in Reilly's hands and the beating of the bird's heart against his knees gave him a keen sense of reassurance. He could feel Norah's heart beating between his shoulder blades as she pressed herself against him. *Finally, a friend my own age,* he thought.

Nebo soared through massive green clouds, then through clouds of blue, indigo and, finally, violet. Suddenly, the space around them turned pitch black. Norah snuggled closer to Reilly and he held her arms around him tightly.

"Where are we?" she asked Nebo.

"We are in Middle."

"Middle? The middle of what?" Reilly asked.

"A sliver of space between every *here* and every *there*. Middle is the place that connects the *now* in each moment."

The winged creature flapped his mighty wings again, leaving a glistening streak of light behind them in the darkness. Like a silver thread through a cosmic needle, Nebo instantaneously carried them through the warp of Middle. The darkness was infused with zillions of twinkling lights, many darting like a shower of shooting stars.

"Oh!" Norah said. "It's beautiful!"

Reilly drew in a breath. "It's amazing!"

"Each one is a Stelladaur," Nebo said. "They are Star Doors, waiting anxiously."

"Huh?" Reilly and Norah said together.

"A Stelladaur is created and prepared for each human soul by the great Star King and Star Queen." Nebo twisted his neck to look at the passengers on his back. "Every time a child is born on your Earth, a door opens and a burst of Stelladaur light beams to that child."

Reilly reached for his own Stelladaur and felt its warmth surge through his body.

"When the child within each human soul is ready, he or she will find a Stelladaur to hold and keep near, as you have Reilly, and you, Norah," Nebo said. Reilly turned his head to look briefly at Norah. She squeezed him and he placed a hand over hers.

"The human's search for light causes his or her own Stelladaur's light to gather behind its Star Door into a tangible form. Then it is transported through that Star Door to Earth. It reaches the precise spot where the one who summoned it will find it."

Nebo swooped around the stars as he spoke.

"Many throughout eternity have summoned their own Stelladaurs, creating a collective light that brings joy, peace and enlightenment to your Earth. But far too many humans have not done so. Thus, darkness remains and your world suffers."

Nebo soared effortlessly on the power of the last flap of his wings. Wide-eyed, Reilly and Norah were silent as they listened to the eagle.

"If your planet is to survive, there must be more light than darkness … more love than hate … more peace than war. More giving than greed … more understanding than intolerance. People must offer forgiveness rather than resentment, and share acceptance instead of exclusion. There must be more hope than despair … and more faith than fear."

"Is that possible?" Reilly blurted.

Nebo ignored the interruption. "Every Stelladaur summoned, found and honored will bring streams of this needed light. However," Nebo paused and twisted his head slightly again to look into Reilly's eyes, "it is the responsibility of each human who has found his or her own Stelladaur to help others find theirs—even those who are filled with the most darkness. Light not shared will dim and a world without Light will not survive."

Nebo looked ahead and thrust his wings to his side. He veered sharply, head first, as Reilly clung to the feathered neck and Norah gripped her friend's waist. They plummeted downward into another dark Middle, emerging into the sky above the Space Needle, and then veered west over the water between Seattle and Bainbridge Island. Nebo swooped down and joined a flock of seagulls hovering above a ferry.

Dozens of passengers leaned over the railing of the vessel to look at something in the water. Reilly nudged Norah with his elbow and pointed to an unusual area of black water spreading rapidly. He gasped as they moved in for a closer look. Floating on the surface of the water were hundreds of fish. Dead fish. And great clumps of dead sea plants and sea creatures, strangled with black seaweed. Reilly thought he heard choking sounds rise from the depths of the water, and muffled words: *A world without Light will not survive.*

"So the collective Light of all Stelladaurs connects all living things to each other?" Reilly whispered.

Nebo glanced at him and nodded.

Flying over Eagle Harbor, Reilly spotted *The Ark*, the kayak hut and Eilam, who was waving with both arms. They circled above Main Street and caught a glimpse of Blackberry Bakers and tourists walking in and out of shops. Reilly wondered silently if anyone could see them, but was not at all surprised when Nebo answered the question.

"They may see me as a large eagle but not as large as I really am. You, they cannot see. It is not that you are invisible. They simply do not look closely enough."

Circling around the harbor a few more times, Reilly wasn't sure where they were going to land, or if Nebo was going to drop them into the water. Nebo replied to Reilly's thoughts with a chuckle and headed southwest towards Gazzam Lake.

Approaching the lake, they saw Sequoran waving his upper branches. "Nebo, you have returned at last! Leave them with me now. I have a message for them."

Nebo hovered above Sequoran, who held out a thick branch for him. The bird landed gracefully and tucked his massive wings tightly to his sides. Reilly and Norah tumbled to the safety of Sequoran's outstretched canopy.

"You will not be returning to Gwidon again," Nebo said. "But look for me in the trees. I will be there when you need me."

With that, the great eagle lifted his feet from the branch and flew majestically into the distance, leaving Reilly and Norah standing on the top of Sequoran, towering above all the trees in the forest.

"Well, come on down," Sequoran said cheerfully. "Go easy on the smaller limbs. They haven't had anyone swing on them in a very long time."

Reilly and Norah each reached carefully for a branch as they stretched their legs to another branch and began their descent. Stepping cautiously, they made their way down the first ten feet.

"Oh, come now, have a little fun! I won't let you fall," Sequoran chuckled. "Jump out to my limbs and swing on them. I'll catch you."

Reilly plunged to grab a branch as if it were a trapeze bar. Sequoran raised his limbs to meet Reilly's hands as he swung from branch to branch and worked his way down the tremendous trunk.

"You look like a monkey," Norah shouted, still at the top of the tree.

"Oo-oo, ee-ee!" Reilly mimicked. "Try it, Norah. It's fun." Reilly kept swinging from the branches while Norah leaped towards a thick limb in front of her.

"That's the way!" Sequoran encouraged her.

Norah began her descent and caught up with Reilly near the tree's midsection.

"Now who's the monkey?" Reilly teased.

"Watch this." She dove forward for a smaller branch and spun around it like a gymnast on a high bar. The branch creaked. Norah screamed.

"As I said, go easy on my smaller limbs. They aren't used to all this exercise." Sequoran stretched a few limbs out further. "I've got you. I won't let you fall." The tree raised another branch to catch Norah. He curled the branch closer to his trunk and set Norah down on a thicker one. "Use this one."

Norah leapt and swung until she reached the ground. She sat back on her arms and looked at Reilly, still forty feet above her.

"Some monkey you turned out to be!" She laughed.

Reilly plunged to another branch with renewed determination and descended quickly, swinging from limb to limb. He released his hands from a branch twenty feet high, did a backward somersault in midair and landed on his feet with his arms held high. He bowed, begging for applause.

"Bravo! Bravo!" Norah cheered as she clapped. "That was definitely impressive." A dog barked behind her. Norah jumped. "Tuma!"

Reilly laughed, and he and Norah bent down to hug Tuma as if they hadn't all been together for a long while.

"Hey, good to see you, girl. Sorry to leave you on *The Ark* like that. Maybe one of these times you can come with me, huh?" Tuma lifted her ears and raised her brows slightly. But she did not bark. Reilly gave a sideways frown. Her non-response led him to believe she would not be joining him on any travels through The Arc of Color. "That's okay. I'm glad you're here. Let's ask Sequoran what's next, shall we?"

The dog barked once.

"The Waters of the far coast have been ringing a message for you through the wind," Sequoran said.

"What's the message?" Reilly asked the tree.

"The Waters have been violated. Poison strips them of their purity."

Reilly instantly recalled the two men throwing boxes of drug-laced duds into the water and the horrific scene of dead sea creatures they'd just witnessed. Closing his eyes, he saw the black water spreading rapidly across the Puget Sound. Then another image returned to him: a dark cave filled with hundreds of hooded monsters.

"Yes, I know." Reilly opened his eyes. "Many people will be robbed of their ability to imagine and believe. Some may die unless … unless we help. But, once again, I'm not sure what to do next."

"Yes, you do know, Reilly," Sequoran said. "Listen."

Reilly stood still. A gust of wind rushed through the forest, blowing his long hair in a blond wave behind him. He breathed deeply and exhaled slowly, his Stelladaur beaming steadily and spreading warmth over his entire body. A thought surged through his mind like a bolt of lightning and beat in his chest.

"I need to go see James. He has some information for me."

"Then go now."

Reilly looked at Tuma, who barked once, and then turned to Norah. "Let's go. It's a long walk to town."

"Why don't we call him?" Norah said. "I've got his number in my pocket." She reached into the back pocket of her jeans, pulled out the scrap of paper James had given her and dialed the number on her cell phone. "Drat. No service."

"That's okay. Let's start walking. We should have service by the time we reach The Treehouse," said Reilly.

"Where?"

"It's a café down the hill. C'mon."

Reilly headed down the trail with Norah on one side of him and Tuma on the other, but stopped after taking only a few steps. "Thanks, Sequoran," he said. "Thanks for the message from the Waters on the far coast. And for letting us act like monkeys."

The giant tree laughed. "You're welcome. As you know, not many visitors bother to stop and chat, or to swing. It was refreshing."

"Yes, thank you," Norah added as she waved. "I hope we'll visit again soon."

Reilly and Norah walked down the path and heard Sequoran whisper, "So few ever bother to say thank you when they visit the forest." Then the ground rumbled. The tree was asleep.

As Reilly walked through the forest, thoughts trickled through his mind like the early afternoon sunbeams peeking through the trees. His growling stomach couldn't drown out the phenomenon of time playing its haunting melody in his ears; though it seemed like days had passed, he knew his time in Glesig and Gwidon had not been very long. Only minutes or hours. He concluded that time is merely a warp, not a *warp in time*, as it's often labeled, but an actual warp. And not something he, or anyone else, can hold on to. It was just as Mr. Ludwig had said: *Time is an endless connection of one moment to another... and then another... and then another.* The irony was that now Reilly could be in the warp in various dimensions: forward, backward or parallel. Each warp was a moment of magic, and they were all linked together.

Reilly's symphony of time was interrupted by an unexpected *thwack!* Norah, who was only a few steps behind him, walked into a low-hanging pine bough protruding into the path and wrapped in a thick bunch of thorny blackberry bushes. The branch smacked her face and knocked her to the ground.

"Norah!" Reilly cried as he spun around. "Are you okay?"

"Wow! That hurt."

Reilly dropped to his knees beside her. "You're bleeding." He used his knife to cut a corner of his shirt and scrunched it up in his hand. "Here, use this." He gently touched her cheek with the fabric to catch the dripping blood.

"Ouch!"

"I'm sorry," He dropped his hand quickly. "You need an ointment or something."

"Ointment," she chided. "Why didn't I remember to bring some with me this morning?"

Reilly smiled at her playful sarcasm and suddenly remembered what Jaida had told him about the Spirits of all living things.

He turned to the thorny pine. "Do you know what could help Norah?"

"The needles of my neighbor, the blue spruce, can be crushed to make a healing antiseptic," the pine tree replied.

Reilly spotted a large blue spruce just beyond a cedar stump and walked over to it. He pulled gently on a low branch and scooped a handful of needles into his palm. "Thank you," he said.

"You're welcome. Crush the needles with a rock and then mix them with a few drops of fresh Water to make a paste."

Reilly found a large flat rock and carried it to where Norah sat on the path. He put the needles on the rock and found a smaller stone to grind them into a thick mush.

"Where's some Water?" Reilly asked the forest. He and Norah looked around but didn't see any signs of recent rain. Tuma barked in the distance. Reilly ran off and found his dog standing near a puddle of clear Water that had pooled in the hollow of a fallen tree. He picked up a maple leaf that had drifted to the ground and shaped it into a cone. He dipped the cup into the puddle, scooped some Water and carried it carefully back to Norah. He poured half the Water into the mush on the rock and used the piece of cloth to soak up the rest. Using his finger, he stirred the mixture until it blended into a salve, gathered a bit between his fingers and lifted his hand to Norah's cheek.

"I hope this doesn't sting." He dabbed the earthy ointment on her skin.

"It doesn't hurt at all," she said. "It's actually very soothing."

Reilly smiled and winked at her. "Good."

Looking into Norah's deep green eyes, Reilly gently wiped the drying blood from her cheekbone, along her jawline and towards her chin.

Norah dropped her eyes and lifted her hand to touch his fingers. "Thank you," she said. Looking back up into his eyes, she added, "Thank you for being here with me."

Reilly thought about kissing her. He really wanted to kiss her! But the truth was he had never kissed a girl before, so everything suddenly felt awkward, as if he was the only sixteen-year-old boy on the planet who hadn't had his first kiss yet, and she somehow knew it. So he pulled his hand away. "Uh, you're welcome. I mean … I'm glad we're friends." He immediately felt stupid for saying *friends,* as if he meant that was all he wanted their relationship to be. "What I mean is, it feels like we've been friends for … for a long time. Sort of weird that it's only been two days."

"Yeah, it is weird." She smiled.

"It's that time warp thing."

"Exactly."

"We've done a lot of time-warping in only two days. If you're on the island for the rest of the summer … maybe … well, I'm glad you're here." Still feeling like a stammering idiot, Reilly decided to change the subject. "How does your cheek feel now?"

"Much better."

"Looks like the bleeding has stopped, too. Are you ready to go?"

"Sure."

Reilly reached for her hand to help her stand up again. She held it tightly, giggling nervously. He laughed, too, watching her nose wrinkle.

As they walked along the path, he nodded to the pine and spruce. In return, a gentle gust of warm wind blew over them. Tuma led the way along the trail and down the steep hill.

"Are you hungry?" Reilly asked. "I'm starving."

"Me, too."

"Let's try James again and see if he can meet us for lunch."

"Great idea." Norah glanced at her smart phone and tapped it a few times to pull up the number. "Looks like I've got service here."

"Hello?"

"Hi, James, it's Norah. Do you want to meet Reilly and me for some pizza?"

"I've been trying to reach you guys! Where are you?"

"We're just headed to the Treehouse Café."

"I'll be there in twenty minutes."

Norah put her phone in her pocket. "He's on his way. He sounded anxious about something."

Reilly and Norah arrived at the café and ordered a large barbecue chicken pizza with added pineapple. Reilly filled two glasses with water from the self-serve pitcher on the counter and grabbed two straws while Norah found a table by the corner window.

"Great table! How did you luck out?" Reilly said, as he put the glasses of water down, and then bent down to pet Tuma under the table.

"I had to bribe some guy."

"What did you give him?"

"My Stelladaur," Norah answered nonchalantly. "I told him it could transport him to unbelievable places if he had some imagination. I think he thought I was loony. But he had pity on me because of the welts on my face."

"You what?" Reilly said loudly. Quickly scanning the room, he then noticed only two other customers in the café, seated in the far corner.

"Sit down, you goof." Norah chuckled. "Of course I didn't give anyone my Stelladaur."

"Hey, maybe I was so hungry I didn't notice we're basically the only ones here."

"I'm sure that was it," Norah teased.

Reilly pulled out his chair and sat down. "Weird, the place is so empty on a Sunday afternoon."

"It's such a nice day, maybe people are out on the water."

"I love the water. Being out on my kayak is the best."

"Coming over this morning on Mr. Jackson's yacht was my first time ever on the water."

"Really?" Reilly blurted, more loudly than he intended.

"That probably seems strange to you since you live on an island, but there's no waterfront in Phoenix and I haven't been to Lake Michigan since I moved to Chicago."

"Sorry," Reilly said more quietly. "Did you enjoy the sail?"

"Other than the fact that it was Mr. Jackson's boat, it was awesome. I loved the smell of the ocean and the gentle hum of the boat. Watching the sun sparkle off the waves." Norah poked at the ice cubes in her glass with her straw. "Yeah, I could get real used to that." She pushed the ice cubes down into the water and watched them bob back up.

Reilly didn't take his eyes off of her face. Clearing his throat, he asked, "Would you like to go with me? Sailing, I mean, on my dad's boat?"

"I would love that, Reilly!" Her eyes lit up with enthusiasm. "But do you want to—I mean, have you … been out sailing since … the acci—?"

"No, I haven't," Reilly interrupted. He poked his finger at the ice in his glass. "But I could. It would be fine. Really." He licked his wet finger, and added, "We'd have to go soon, though, cuz my mom doesn't want me to go on *The Ark* again. She put it up for sale." A twinge of guilt crept through him but he brushed it aside.

"I'm sorry, Reilly."

"Norah, how do you know about the accident? I didn't tell you about it, did I?"

"No," she said, watching the ice float in her own glass. "I saw it happen."

"What do you mean?"

"After my mom died, I felt like life was really unfair. I wished my mom hadn't died, you know? And that I didn't have to live with Uncle Martino. Actually, I wished I had died. There didn't seem to be much to live for. Anyway, I was sitting on my bed one day, looking into my Stelladaur, wishing I could see my mom. Then all of a sudden I saw this sailboat in the middle of a storm and a man pulling on some ropes or something. And then I saw … I saw you, standing over the edge of the boat. I heard you calling for your dad."

The lump in Reilly's throat made his glands ache. He blinked and looked down at the ice in his glass.

"I'm sorry, Reilly, I shouldn't have—"

"No, please, what else did you see?" He blinked hard and looked at Norah.

"Well, I obviously didn't know who you were but when I saw you in Jolka, I knew it was you."

"Why me? I would think you might have seen your mom."

"I don't know. But seeing you made me realize I wasn't the only one feeling the way I did and it's not like anyone can say his own grief is greater than another's. I just realized I wasn't alone." She sipped through her straw. "From then on, whenever I felt alone, I just thought of you."

"From then on? How long ago did you first see me in your Stelladaur?"

"Six months ago. I remember exactly because it was the first day at my new school in Chicago. As I said, I really hated life. It was January 12."

Reilly choked on his water. When he recovered, he looked at Norah, stunned.

"How can that be? Do you know what you just said?"

"Yes, I said it was horrible going to a new school in a huge city. I didn't know *anyone*!"

"No, Norah, listen. My dad died just over a month ago. It wasn't in January."

"You mean—?"

"Yes! Stelladaurs can show stuff in the future," he said looking directly at her. "Even without going through a portal."

"Reilly, you're right!"

Reilly took a few long sips of his drink. "How were you holding your Stelladaur when you first saw me? What were you doing with it?"

"I was sitting on my bed, crying," Norah said, staring into her glass. "I was thinking about my mom and how she found the Stelladaur. I remember wanting *her* to be there, not some dumb rock. I cried harder and I wanted to throw the Stelladaur across the room. But I just held it and looked into it."

"That's it!" Reilly insisted. "I know how your Stelladaur showed you something that would happen in the future."

Norah blinked and looked at him. "How?"

"It was your tears. Your tears must have fallen on the Stelladaur, which then responded to your emotions."

Norah stared at Reilly.

"It makes sense, doesn't it?" he continued. "The Stelladaur knew you were suffering and wanted to ease your pain."

"That's too weird." Norah chewed on her straw. "It's so much easier to think that a Stelladaur can just transport us to strange places outside our galaxy." She laughed.

"Yeah, but the pine tree wanted to help ... And what about Tuma, and Nebo? Why not the Stelladaur?"

Norah pursed her lips. "Are you suggesting that our Stelladaurs can breathe and feel ... like a plant or animal does?"

"Yes. That's what Sequoran meant."

"Huh!" Norah touched her chest where her Stelladaur hung on its golden cord under her shirt. "Do you ever feel like it's breathing with you?"

"Yeah, I do." Reilly touched his chest, too. "Sometimes it thumps right to the beat of my own heart."

"Mine, too."

"Other times it helps me feel calm or to relax. But sometimes it tells me to have courage and be strong." Reilly took another sip of water. "What else did your Stelladaur show you that day, when your tears were falling on it?"

Norah frowned. "I saw you ... in a dark cave with dozens of creepy monsters. They were the most gruesome creatures you could ever imagine. They were all trying to ..."

"To what?"

"To kill you."

"Why?"

"Because you were trying to protect a treasure they wanted to steal."

"A treasure?"

"A bunch of jewels on a boat." Norah's eyes lit up. "It was *The Ark*, filled with Stelladaurs!"

Reilly sat back in his chair, remembering his journey past Jolka through the dark tunnel with all the hooded monsters. And the multiple faces of Travis Jackson. "Did they kill me?"

"I don't know, Reilly. The scene disappeared and I never saw that one again. I remember thinking my life wasn't so bad after all, but I often wondered what it meant."

Reilly reached across the table for Norah's hand. "It means Mr. Jackson is trying to steal a priceless treasure from everyone he can."

"Their own Stelladaurs?"

"He doesn't know what a *real* Stelladaur is. His fake ROCKs simply mask reality and create a false world. With drugs, he's stealing people's need to find their own Stelladaur, or even know one exists for them."

"I'm not following you, Reilly."

"Mr. Jackson is stealing people's ability to use their own mind and listen to their own heart," Reilly whispered. "When that happens, the power of pure imagination is destroyed." His words hung heavy in the air and he felt the terrible weight of what he must do.

He looked into Norah's eyes, searching her thoughts. Her brow relaxed as she stroked his hand with her thumb, and her spruce eyes penetrated his soul. She knew his fear. She knew him. Together, they understood that their feelings for each other came from the place where heart and mind meet perfectly—and they knew perfectly that they were meant to be together.

Chapter Twenty-one

The Fireglass

Reilly left to check on their order. It would be another five minutes. He took the pitcher of water to their table and filled their glasses, letting a few ice cubes drop into both glasses. He returned the pitcher and then sat down. They sat for a minute without talking, bobbing the ice with their straws.

Reilly broke the silence. "To go through the Arc of Color together, like at the same time, I think our Stelladaurs need to be touching each other."

"Okay. We should go as soon as possible."

"Let's go now," Reilly said as he reached for his Stelladaur. "It's up to us, Norah."

"Here?" Norah looked around the café and saw the only other customers still at a table in the far corner. "That girl went in the back room," she said, glancing at the main counter. "Let's hurry." Norah pulled out her Stelladaur.

Reilly and Norah covered their Stelladaurs with both their hands and leaned across the table towards one another with their hands in front of them.

"On the count of three. One ... two ... three!" Reilly commanded.

They opened their hands and quickly touched their stones together. Nothing happened.

"Huh, I thought for sure it would work," said Reilly.

"Remember, they need water." Norah reached into her glass and scooped out a large piece of ice. "Let's try it again." They touched the stones together and Norah counted, "One ... two ... three!" as she placed the ice cube in the center where the stones met.

Immediately, a ray of sunshine beamed through the window and pierced the ice cube. With a cosmic vacuum force, Reilly and Norah warped into the melting ice. All that remained at the table were two glasses of water, two straws and a small puddle in between.

With the portal open, Reilly and Norah whizzed side by side through a blinding yellow vortex, connected by their Stelladaurs, whose golden cords were twisted together and extended full length from around their necks. The scent of lemon grass and lemon verbena filled the tunnel.

They landed with a jolt on the back of what appeared to be a yellow horse.

"I am Flavio Xanthipee," said the horse. "Welcome to Zora." Flavio's lower body and four legs were that of a horse, with a long tail of thick golden threads. His torso was that of a man with a smooth bare chest and a pale jasmine color.

"Zora is where the sun always rises, shining hope into every moment," said the horseman, his wavy yellow hair blowing behind him. "We will ride to the Well of Infused Light so you may learn how this is possible."

The horse-like creature lunged forward and burst into a full gallop. Reilly grabbed a thick yellow braid woven around Flavio Xanthipee's neck and held on firmly while Norah clutched her arms tightly around Reilly's waist. They rode across a meadow of blowing golden wheat fields and over hills covered in buttercups. The horseman slowed to a canter as they approached a sparkling waterfall made of shimmering sunlit jewels, cascading in strands from a high cliff. When the jewels reached the ground they vanished into a pool of clear water, as still as glass. Flavio Xanthipee stopped there.

"You may dismount," he said, swishing his yellow tail.

Norah slid off the creature first, followed by Reilly. They stood beside each other—between Flavio Xanthipee and the pool of clear water.

"Here is the Well of Infused Light. Look into the Water and it will reveal the secret to finding hope in each moment," Flavio Xanthipee said.

Reilly stepped closer and peered in. He immediately jumped back. As he had seen in Jolka, a vision of his father falling over the edge of *The Ark* reflected in the water. This time, he saw his dad's body sinking in slow motion down to the depths of the sea.

"Do not resist what is," Flavio Xanthipee implored. "What you resist will continue to scorn you, haunt and plague you—until you find the golden thread woven into it. Look again." Flavio Xanthipee took a step forward and nudged Reilly from behind. Although Reilly had felt great anticipation moments before, he was now equally gripped with fear.

"Move away from the resistance—into hope," the horseman said.

"How?" Reilly cried out.

"Find a reason to be grateful for the moment."

"Grateful?" It was too much for Reilly. Hadn't he already done his best? "Grateful that my dad died because I didn't do anything to save him?" Reilly shouted in frustration. Sadness and grief flooded his chest and shot down his spine. *"Grateful* for that?"

"Look for the golden thread." Flavio Xanthipee encouraged him kindly. "Just look."

Norah touched Reilly's arm gently. He jerked it away. Soon he turned back and looked into her eyes, searching for strength.

Taking a deep breath, he stepped to the edge of the glassy pool and slowly peered into the water.

A thin thread of gold arose out of the sea where his father had fallen overboard, and then out of the pool in front of Reilly. The thread formed a circle around a translucent bubble where Reilly saw himself surrounded by those he loved: his mom, Chantal, Eilam and Tuma. Others who were a source of strength and comfort appeared in the bubble, too: Sequoran, Nebo, Norah and his Stelladaur.

"I see a lot of things I'm grateful for."

"Yes. And your collective gratitude offers answers to the questions locked inside of you, but which can only be revealed upon your asking," Flavio Xanthipee said. "Look for the good that emerges out of difficulties, challenges and sorrow, and you will always find reasons to be grateful. Gratitude dispels the gloom of any dark moment and opens our hearts to hope."

Reilly continued to look into the bubble that now floated on the surface of the water. Sixteen years of happy memories with his family and Eilam flashed before him. He felt his heart swell with gratitude and thought his rib cage might burst from the expansion.

Flavio Xanthipee raised his smooth chest and drew in a deep breath, then blew it across the Well of Infused Light. The bubble vanished. "Norah, it's your turn," he said.

Norah stepped forward and looked at Reilly. He nodded with a smile. She peered into the Water and gasped, covering her mouth with both hands to keep from screaming. In the Water, she saw a man locked in a prison cell, sitting on a cot—a man she had known only vaguely. Suddenly, the years of longing to know her father and grieving over his absence in her life coursed through her veins. Her knees wobbled and she reached for Reilly to hold her up. He steadied her with one hand at her elbow and one around her waist.

"Can you see a golden thread of gratitude?" asked Flavio Xanthipee.

Norah looked further into the Water and saw a faint golden thread weave around the bars of the prison cell, circle above her father's head and then extend into a bubble above the Well of Infused Light. Someone she recognized stared back at her from the bubble.

"Uncle Martino?" she asked incredulously. "He doesn't want any more to do with me than my dad did. He's a greedy, selfish, power-hungry man," Norah shouted. "And I think he's the person supplying the drugs to Mr. Jackson. I've known it for a long while. I just didn't want to believe it." She started to cry.

Reilly tightened his arm around her. "Norah, it'll be okay. Some good must come from it." He didn't mean it to sound preachy but knew it did.

"No!" She pushed away from him. "There's *no* good. My dad is in prison because of his connections to the Mafia! Somehow my uncle is involved, too! If they take Uncle Martino, where will I go? I have no one else."

Norah crossed her arms firmly, but out of sheer spite took a step closer to the bubble. She took a deep breath and gazed into the bubble again. Gradually, her perspective began to change.

"I'm grateful … that … I can spend the summer on Bainbridge … with Reilly …" She did not look up. "… and for whatever comes of it," she whispered.

"Welcoming whatever comes is a rare thread of gratitude woven only into open hearts and minds." Flavio Xanthipee swept his tail up to his torso and held it in his hands. He pulled gently on two thick strands of the golden hair and held them up to the sunlight. "Give me your wrists."

Reilly and Norah held out their left arms. Flavio Xanthipee wrapped the threads around their wrists and tied them securely. "If you find yourself empty with ingratitude, these golden threads will help you shift focus."

"Thank you," Reilly and Norah replied together, neither knowing what else to say.

"You must return now. There is much to be done." Flavio Xanthipee pointed to a path that led to the yellow-jeweled waterfall on the other side of the clear pool. "The portal is behind the waterfall. Hold on to the golden hair at your wrist as you go through."

Reilly and Norah waved goodbye as they walked down the path towards the shimmering falls. Grasping the threads at their wrists, they stepped into the glittery shower of yellow and disappeared from Zora.

"Hey, I thought you two had left." The girl set the pizza on the table. "It was weird. I stepped into the kitchen for a few minutes … and when I came back, I thought you'd changed your mind about the pizza or something, so I took it back to the kitchen. I didn't know who was going to eat this." She smiled. "Anyway, here it is. Can I get you anything else?"

"No, we're good," Reilly said with a nod. "Thanks."

Halfway through their first slice of pizza, James showed up.

"Hope you like barbeque chicken," Reilly said.

"Smells good. Hey, Norah, I was surprised to hear from you so soon," he said as he sat down. "I thought you weren't coming over till tomorrow."

"Neither did I, but our plans changed. I've been here all morning. Sort of." She took a bite of pizza. James scowled but didn't ask her to explain.

"So, what's up, James? Norah said you sounded kind of anxious to see us."

"Yeah, get this. Baxter called a couple of hours ago and said a guy named Jordan Powell, a reporter for the *Seattle Times*, asked him if he knew who we were or how he could get a hold of us. He wanted to talk to you, Reilly. Baxter didn't have your number but told the guy your mom owned the bakery. Powell called your mom and she gave him both our numbers."

"I didn't get a call," Reilly said checking his phone. "Seems strange my mom would give the guy our numbers."

"Not really. Not when you hear what he wants."

"What does he want?" Norah asked, wiping sauce from the corner of her mouth.

"Apparently, he was at the hotel last night and got a photo of you—a full-on shot of your Stelladaur!"

"You're kidding!" Reilly choked.

"No, I'm not. As a matter of fact, he got a couple of different shots. He told your mom he was interested in the 'unusual necklace' you wore and said he could help bring Travis down if we worked together. That's basically the same thing that he told me when I called him back."

"What did you tell him?" Reilly demanded.

"I told him we'd be happy to meet with him. He's meeting us at the bakery on Wednesday after closing, around eight o'clock."

"I wonder what he knows about Mr. Jackson," said Norah. "Or those guys from the warehouse."

"He knows something, that's for sure. He sounded real nervous." James bit into a slice of pizza. "Almost scared. If this guy only cared about making the headlines, those photos would have already been in this morning's paper."

Reilly and Norah agreed.

After they finished eating, James dropped Reilly, Norah and

Tuma off at Reilly's house and said he'd see them in the morning at the bakery.

"This traveling through portals gives me a serious case of vortex-lag, or something." Reilly laughed. "I'm tired."

"Me, too," Norah said. "Do you want to take a nap at the beach? Get some sun?"

"Sure." Reilly winked at her. "I'll be right back." He left her on the front porch and went into the house to retrieve two beach towels, a Frisbee and some bottled water.

They played fetch and Tuma retrieved the Frisbee from the water. As Reilly chased Norah in the waves, she squealed, pretending she didn't want to get wet. Later, they spread the towels side by side on the sand to dry out their clothes and soak up some sun. Reilly closed his eyes but no longer felt tired. He turned on his side and watched Norah squirm and wiggle to mold her body into the sand. She settled in and turned her head to look at him. He leaned up on one elbow, reached his other arm across Norah's waist and pulled her closer to him.

"I might want to kiss you," he whispered, leaning towards her.

She giggled. "I might let—"

Just then Tuma poked his head between them and licked Norah's face.

"That's not what I was hoping for, Tuma," she grunted.

"Ugh!" Reilly groaned as he tried to push his dog away. "Tuma, what are you doing? Go away." Tuma stopped licking Norah and started to bark loudly.

Reilly and Norah sat up and looked around. A dozen people and a few dogs dotted the beach. Tuma kept barking. "What is it, Tuma?" Reilly asked as he slipped on his shoes. Norah quickly stepped into her sandals and they hurried to catch up with Tuma who was running down the beach.

It was low tide and they ran hard along the water's edge. At the mouth of the harbor, they slowed to a fast walk and rounded the corner with the Seattle skyline and Mount Rainier in full view.

They picked up their pace again when they saw Tuma stop beside something that had washed ashore. She barked loudly and incessantly at the object. Breathless, Reilly and Norah caught up and stopped beside a dead mother seal. Black seaweed was twisted around the seal's body.

"She was strangled," Reilly said with sadness in his voice. "Suffocated by the drugs Travis's men dumped into the Sound this morning."

"What should we do?" Norah turned away from the carcass.

"Report it to the Coast Guard. And to the police."

"Reilly, are you sure? What about that Jordan guy, and the photos? Maybe it would be better to wait."

"We can't wait. Who knows how many other fish and animals and plants will die, not to mention what could happen to those people who bought Travis's ROCKs! We need to tell the police everything."

Norah nodded. Reilly called James and told him to meet them at the police station. They ran along the beach all the way to the marina, where Reilly's kayak was still tied to the dock next to *The Ark*. Slowing to catch their breath, they looked around for signs of Travis or Norah's uncle, but didn't see any. People were busy cleaning their boats or relaxing on deck, and sailboats drifted in and out of the docking area, but there was no sign of Jackson or Gustalini.

Rounding the corner at the end of the first pier, Reilly and Norah saw *The Ark* and broke into a sprint with Tuma behind them. Halfway down the dock, they halted abruptly. Travis and Martino emerged from a boat slip and stepped right in front of them. Tuma growled.

"Mr. McNamara. I see Ms. Gustalini couldn't wait till Monday to have you show her around." Travis smiled wryly. "And your dog—always right by you." Travis glanced quickly at the dog then turned to glare at Reilly.

"Norah!" Her uncle scowled with deep frown lines in his forehead.

"I went for a walk on the beach. Reilly happened to be there, so we've been … hanging out."

"Why the hurry?" Travis pressed.

Norah thought quickly and said, "Reilly said he'd take me for a ride in his kayak, over to the ice cream shop … before it closes."

"They close early on Sundays," Reilly added. "We need to hurry."

"Be back here in an hour," Norah's uncle ordered her. "You obviously need to change before we join Mr. Jackson for dinner, and he shows us to his guest house."

"Perhaps Mr. McNamara and his mother would like to join us," Travis suggested slyly.

Reilly tried to appear calm. "That's very kind of you, Mr. Jackson, but my mother and I have made plans for the evening."

"Well, tell her hello for me, will you?"

"I will. We'd better get going."

Reilly and Norah walked towards the end of the dock without looking back. They slipped into the kayak and were halfway across the harbor before they spoke. Tuma swam alongside them.

"I don't want to go to dinner with that man," Norah said.

"I know. But for now, we need to act like we know absolutely nothing. Just a couple of kids happy to have the summer to hang out."

"That would be nice, Reilly. But what's going to happen if my uncle is arrested? I doubt I'll be spending the summer here. What then?"

Reilly put more power into his strokes as he paddled further from the dock.

"We don't need all the answers right now. We just take the next step, remember? Things will work out."

They glided the rest of the way across the harbor in silence. Eilam greeted them at the hut.

"You've been busy," he said.

"Very!" Reilly agreed.

"Good to have you here, Norah." Eilam smiled at her.

"Thank you. Reilly has told me a lot about you," Norah said as she climbed out of the kayak.

"He told me about you, too," he replied. "But, no matter, I know each One who has found their own Stelladaur."

Norah laughed nervously and her wrinkled nose distracted Reilly momentarily. Eilam smiled, noticing Reilly's attention to Norah.

"What you have learned thus far has brought you to this point," Eilam stated. "And now, you have decided to reveal your knowledge to allow further change, have you not?"

Reilly watched Norah squint her eyes and tighten her forehead.

"Yes, we're on our way to tell the police about the dead seal," he said. "And the guys at the warehouse, and the box of ROCKs James and I saw those guys dump off the ferry this morning." Reilly reviewed everything, even though he supposed none of the information was news to Eilam. "And about Travis Jackson."

"That is wise. Let others handle the things they are in charge of. Thus, you will have more energy to take care of your own responsibilities." Eilam took the rope from Reilly's hand and tied it loosely to the post on the dock. "Come back here after you report to the police. I will tell you the way through the orange beam of light. And then you will be almost ready."

"Ready for what?' Reilly asked.

"Ready to find Tir Na Nog."

Reilly gasped. He believed his father was in Tir Na Nog! And that his Stelladaur would actually bring him his greatest desire. Was he truly ready for that?

"C'mon. Let's hurry!" Reilly grabbed Norah by the hand. They ran down the long dock and through Waterfront Park. Five minutes later, they found James waiting on a bench outside the police station. After brainstorming their strategy, they came to a unanimous decision to tell the police everything *except* about Reilly and Norah's Stelladaurs. James had printed photos of the van, the license plate number, the driver and Derek, the passenger. Reilly had one of the dud ROCKs they had taken from the warehouse. With evidence in hand they entered the police station.

A receptionist directed them to an officer who was seated at a cluttered desk near the back of the room. The man did not immediately look up as they approached but shuffled papers until Reilly cleared his throat to signal their arrival.

"Make it quick, kids. I'm busy." The man said with papers in both hands.

Even with the dud and the photos, the officer did not take their story seriously. "The Coast Guard will check into the dead seal and the alleged boxes dumped into the water."

"Alleged?" James said.

The officer ignored the comment and rolled his eyes slightly. "The Washington State Ferries have already notified the EPA about the *possible* spillage that *appears* to be harming marine life."

With insistence from James, the officer said he would have someone look into any activity at the abandoned warehouse. But without additional evidence, the idea that Travis Jackson—world renowned scientist and philanthropist for humanity—was producing plastic rocks coated in drugs made the officer laugh out loud. He told all three of them to consider careers in acting because, were it not such a preposterous notion, their presentation would have been convincing.

James and Norah left the police station highly irritated with the officer.

"Don't worry," Reilly said. "Truth is difficult for some people. This is just the beginning of exposing Mr. Jackson—of revealing the truth about him to the world."

"Humph!" James sighed. "There you go again, being all calm, cool and collected. I just don't get it."

"Takes practice. But it does come easier with a Stelladaur."

"Yeah, well, I sure would like to know where mine is."

"Probably closer than you think."

"How's that? I don't even know where to start looking. I have an amazingly cool key, but absolutely *no* idea of what it unlocks. I've spent all day racking my brain, trying to think of how it could be linked to my dad and his journal ... and to finding a Stelladaur." James scratched his head nervously. "Nothing!"

"Use your imagination, James, and consider possibilities. Start telling yourself that it will come to you, and it will. When you're ready."

"And it will. When you're ready," James mimicked. "Are you *trying* to sound like Eilam, or does it just come naturally?" He sighed. "Seriously, kid, you can be *so* annoying!"

Reilly laughed as his broad smile flashed across his face. Norah smiled, too, looking at Reilly.

"Well, maybe you should spend some time at the water tonight. Head on over to the beach or something." Reilly patted James on the back. "Go sit on a log. Watch the sunset."

"Now that's profound!" James sneered. *"Go sit on a log."*

When Reilly and Norah returned to Eilam's hut, they found him sitting in his Adirondack, awkwardly rolling something shiny between his hands.

"What's that?" Reilly asked.

"A Fireglass," Eilam said, handing it to Reilly. The cylindrical object was five inches long and made of intricately carved, shiny brass. Reilly wrapped his hand completely around it and pulled on the small crystal knob at the end. The Fireglass extended to twice its compacted length. Engraved on the surface of the newly exposed brass was the symbol of a Stelladaur, continuously rotating around the surface of the brass.

"What does it do?"

"Look into it."

Reilly held the end of the Fireglass with one hand as he lifted the crystal knob to his right eye. Inside was a spectacular display of colored lights—a fireworks show unlike any he'd ever seen!

"May I see?" Norah asked. Reilly held the crystal end of the Fireglass to her eye. "Wow! Do we use this to go through the next portal?

"Yes," Eilam replied. "The Fireglass is one of Malie's treasures. It is used when one needs to accelerate passage through any portal, sometimes with the aid of a Stelladaur."

"How does it work?" Reilly withdrew the device from Norah's eye.

"The same fire that consumes a forest with only one spark also ignites a display of beauty that transcends all doubt. The Fireglass aids in welcoming change."

Reilly peered into the Fireglass again.

"Look for the orange Lotus flower in the fireworks on the water on the Fourth of July. It will flash only one time, in the middle of the finale, and the petals will branch out to form an orange butterfly that fills the night sky." Eilam spoke slowly, as if to emphasize the importance of what he was saying. "When you first see the Lotus, hold your Stelladaurs in front of the crystal knob of the Fireglass, and look through them together. Hold them securely until the butterfly takes you away."

Norah looked confused. "But there's only one Fireglass."

Reilly retracted the device and looked at Eilam for direction.

"Yes. Hold hands as you look through both the Fireglass and your Stelladaurs at the same time, and you will travel through the

Lotus flower together," Eilam said. "You will return at precisely the midnight hour, just as the Lotus petals separate from the stamen and trail to the sea."

A chilly breeze blew through the corridor of the hut, and Reilly knew if he intended to find Tir Na Nog, it would require a change he had not anticipated.

Chapter Twenty-two

A Hoax

Reilly and Tuma arrived at the bakery on Monday morning at 7:00 a.m. It had only been a few days since he and his mom made the cheesecakes for Travis's event, but so much had happened over the weekend. And lately, a lot seemed to happen in a matter of only a few moments. Sprinkling crystallized sugar on a tray of chocolate-chunk filled croissants, he debated talking to his mom about everything, but decided against it. Besides, if he went through as many time warps this week as he had the past two days, it would feel like an eternity before the fireworks show on the Fourth of July. How could he wait until Saturday to penetrate the next portal? And why bother trying to explain it all to his mom anyway? Too much had changed.

By 10:00 he felt as if he hadn't seen Norah in a month. Time had been playing with his mind—and now it was torturing his heart.

While preparing the last of the croissants, Reilly mentally reviewed his adventures through The Arc of Color, the creatures he'd met, the enlightenment they each shared and the haunting beauty that existed beyond Eagle Harbor. And he thought about how seeing Norah for the first time took his breath away. Now, just the thought of her did.

But even more pressing on Reilly's mind was the tremendous responsibility he felt to expose Travis. How was he going to convince people of the truth?

"Reilly, take a break," his mom said, interrupting his thoughts as she slowly pulled the tray of croissants away. "Go see if James is in yet."

"Okay." He set the jar of sugar on the counter. "Are you sure?"

"Yes. You've done enough for today." She smiled, but Reilly could see in her eyes that she wanted to say more. "As a matter of fact, you've got so much going on, why not just work a couple hours each morning. The bakery will always be here."

Reilly appreciated her recognizing that he had a lot on his mind, even though he didn't think she could possibly know what. "Thanks, Mom."

It was 10:35 a.m. when he stepped into the dining room filled with chatter and the ding of the cash register bouncing off the walls.

"If it's so great, why doesn't he make them more available?" A customer in line said to the person behind him. "Why just to the shareholders?"

"Who knows? The guy probably makes more money in a month than I'll see in a lifetime," said the other.

"Must be something to afford the luxury of time travel for a summer vacation. It's out of my realm, no pun intended."

Reilly glanced around the room and noticed an unusual number of people with their noses in a morning newspaper. He darted outside to the newsstand, put in three quarters and reached for a *Bainbridge Review.* Seeing the headline, he held his breath and sat down on a bench to read the article.

Jackson's ROCK a Huge Success

The unveiling of the ROCK, developed by world-renowned inventor and entrepreneur, Travis Jackson, was a huge success Saturday evening in downtown Seattle. Shareholders from around the country attended the event, hoping to execute promising investments. Such expectations were surpassed, according to those who have already used the device to travel through time and space.

"This is the most remarkable of Travis's work yet," said investor Peter Moss. "My wife, Annie, and I were amazed by how easily the portal opens wherever you are!"

Grant Nelson, another investor lucky enough to be among those who purchased a first series ROCK, shared how the device actually works. "You simply hold the ROCK in the sunlight and rub it. It sounds crazy, but it's almost like waving a magic wand that zips you through a kaleidoscope, out into the universe. I actually went back in time to a farm in Pennsylvania where I grew up as a kid."

Another stated, "Remarkable invention! Worth every penny!"

Dozens of reports from those who purchased a ROCK and have already used it reveal similar experiences. Each declared that the portal through time and space is accessed simply by rubbing the device in the sunlight. Some obtained successful results from standing under a sunlamp while rubbing the ROCK. Travel experiences ranged from going back in time as far as the seventeenth century to floating on intergalactic bubbles around stars and planets.

Jackson said he is thrilled with the response but not at all surprised. "It does exactly what I designed it to do," he said with his typical confidence. On Saturday, Jackson provided an image of a person in the process of transporting from a kayak in the Puget Sound to another realm with a ROCK in hand. Jackson declined to identify the user. "So far I haven't been able to figure out how a person can actually take a camera with them on their adventures through time and space. But I'm working on it. Hopefully such a feature will be added to the next production series of the ROCK, which will be available in late summer or early fall." Such a feature would allow even those who cannot afford the million-dollar price tag of a ROCK to enjoy some of the benefits.

Reilly stared at the photo more closely and was relieved to see that no one would be able to identify him. It was mostly a blur of white light above his kayak and a fuzzy outline of his backside. His Stelladaur looked more like a shadowy blob than anything else.

"Hey, kid, anything noteworthy in the *Review*?" Reilly looked up from the paper and saw James standing in front of him. He scooted over on the bench and handed James the paper without saying a word. James sat down and read the entire article. "Unbelievable!"

he declared as he dropped the paper to his lap in a crumpled heap. "What a hoax!"

"A hoax that will wreak all sorts of havoc unless we can get someone to believe us," Reilly said firmly.

"Our only hope may be that reporter, Jordan. I wish he wasn't out of town for two more days. I don't know if this can wait." James smoothed out the front page again. Glancing at an article at the bottom, he added, "Look at this, kid."

It was a short paragraph about the dead fish floating in the Puget Sound between Seattle and Bainbridge, allegedly discovered by a WSF captain on his first morning run to the island. Top EPA specialists made an investigation but concluded a boat fuel leakage had likely caused the harm.

"Didn't they see the black cloud rising above all the gunk oozing across the water?" James wondered aloud.

"People see what they want to see," Reilly muttered. "And they ignore what they don't want to see."

"True enough." James lowered the paper again, this time slowly. They watched people come and go for a few minutes.

Switching gears, Reilly said, "Did you go to the beach last night?"

"I did."

"And?"

"I watched the sunset, as you suggested. It was awesome. I should do that more often."

"What else?"

"What do you mean, *what else*?"

"Did you see anything else?"

James paused before giving his response. "It's so weird you would ask that question because something strange *did* happen. There were three massive cirrus clouds that made the sunset super intense. Then I thought I saw this bolt of orange light streak across the sky, but there were no thunder clouds anywhere."

"And?"

"And then I saw the orange streak again. It darted across the sky at an angle, landing in the water just off the tip of the island."

"Hmmm …"

"Hmmm? What's *hmmm*?"

"We should check it out."

"I won't have any time until Thursday. I'm working extra hours this week. The end of the month is always a crunch time for your mom to get the books and inventory done. Plus, with the holiday, she's got a lot of orders to fill on Friday and Saturday morning. Did I mention I also have a mid-term report due on Friday?"

Reilly was listening, but he grew distracted when he saw Norah coming their way. He stood up and took the paper from James's hand.

Late for his shift, James stood up and waved to Norah before going into the bakery. She giggled and waved back. Reilly watched her nose wrinkle.

"Hey," Norah said when she reached Reilly.

"Hi. Have you had breakfast?"

"Yes. Mr. Jackson's *personal chef* served us eggs benedict on the veranda." Sarcasm tainted every word, and she rolled her eyes when she said *personal chef*.

"Yuck. Here, read this." Reilly handed her the paper and they sat on the bench while she read the article. He glanced over her shoulder and reread it, too.

"What a bunch of malarkey. He's such a slime bucket." She handed the paper back and scowled.

"What's that look?" Reilly asked, noticing something more in the scowl.

Norah lowered her voice. "Remember when we were in the warehouse and I held one of the defective ROCKs?"

"Yeah?"

"I got dizzy and felt sick. And I thought maybe I was just hungry or something. Remember?"

"I remember."

"Well, the resin was kind of pliable; and the guy said the duds are the ones with seals that don't solidify, right?"

"Right."

"I had been picking at it and kind of rubbing it. I must have gotten some of the drugs on my hands, or in my fingernails or something. The heat from my hands started to activate the residue of drugs on the dud."

"Yeah, that makes perfect sense, Norah."

"We gave the officer one of those duds. If only he'd taken us seriously," Norah said. "If he doesn't have it analyzed in a lab, I doubt anyone will believe us. I wish we had taken a whole box of duds from the warehouse."

"Don't worry. James still has the box of scratched ones. Who knows what happened to the ones from the dumpster but we have a few more duds."

"We can't wait until Mr. Jackson gets that next shipment in from Bogotá. We've got to do something now!" Norah was no longer speaking softly.

Reilly took her hand. "Norah, there's only one thing we can do." He lowered his voice. "We need to tell Jordan about our Stelladaurs. It's time to show the world."

She stared at him, stunned.

"It's the only way." He paused and squeezed her hand. "But we won't have a chance to do that until Wednesday evening. In the meantime, do you want me to show you around the island?"

She smiled. "Yeah, that'd be great."

Inside the bakery, Reilly introduced Norah to his mom. She seemed pleased to meet Norah, but Reilly could tell she knew he was keeping something from her.

The rest of the morning Reilly and Norah toured downtown: the public marina, the library, boutique shops and more of Waterfront Park. They ate lunch at a Mexican restaurant and went to the matinee. On their way out of the theatre, Frank Bingham and Todd Petrowski came up behind them.

"Who's the hottie, Reilly?" Frank jeered.

Neither Reilly nor Norah turned around.

"Aw, c'mon, introduce us to your girl," Todd pressed.

"Her name's Norah," said Frank. "She's staying at my Uncle Travis's guest house for the summer. I've heard *all* about her."

Reilly and Norah kept walking past the concession stand and into the main hallway.

"No need to be standoffish," said Frank, as he and Todd continued to walk at their heels. "What? You think you're cool stuff cuz you've got a girlfriend?"

"Beat it," Reilly finally said. He held Norah's hand more tightly and picked up the pace.

"I hear her dad's doin' some serious time," Frank jeered right beside Norah. "Something about drug trafficking. Are you sure you want to get involved with folks like that, Smiley? You wouldn't want to ruin your nice-boy reputation."

At that moment Reilly decided even nice boys have limits. He whirled around and punched Frank hard in the stomach. Frank doubled over then looked up to see if Reilly was still there. Reilly popped Frank another good one in the mouth.

"Don't ever speak to her like that again," Reilly said, shaking his fist in an attempt to ease the pain, and holding the door open for Norah with the other. It was the first time Reilly had punched anyone. But it felt good.

"Thank you," Norah said once they reached the parking lot. She kissed him quickly on the cheek.

Monday evening, Norah joined Reilly and his mom for dinner at their home, and later they played fetch with Tuma at the beach. Reilly worked at the bakery again on Tuesday until Norah arrived in mid-morning. They took half a dozen muffins to Eilam and spent a couple of hours with him at the hut, where he told Norah the story of Malie the Magician and the gargoyle while Reilly whittled on his wooden feather. They spent the rest of the day kayaking to Blakely Harbor and back. Norah took to the sea as if she'd been born a McNamara herself. Until then, Reilly had never imagined he could be more enamored with anything than he was with kayaking. But Norah was quickly changing that.

On Wednesday, Reilly woke to the happy thought that Chantal was flying in that afternoon. He was even more excited by the thought that it was already halfway to Saturday—soon he and Norah would watch the fireworks together and look for the orange lotus flower.

Reilly and Norah met at the bakery for a late breakfast and brought Eilam some raisin-pecan bread at noon. They took the kayak out but this time without Tuma. Gliding towards the inner harbor and weaving the kayak between sailboats and cruisers pulling out of the marina, they spotted Nebo, perched at the top of a cedar tree near the end of the cove.

The giant eagle swooped down and circled the kayak. He asked Reilly and Norah if they wanted to see the water from the air, and then flew to the shore and waited for them to steer the kayak towards him. Reilly and Norah climbed on his back. This time Norah sat in front with Reilly's arms around her waist.

The take-off was effortless. With only three flaps of his wings, Nebo reached an altitude high enough for Reilly and Norah to see a breathtaking panoramic view to the south of Bainbridge Island, Vashon and the Tacoma Narrows Bridge. Whidbey Island and the Strait of Juan de Fuca opened up to the North, with the Olympic Mountains to the west and Mt. Rainier and beyond to the east.

"Now this is what I call a first-class flight!" Reilly laughed.

"It takes my breath away!" Norah sighed.

"You take my breath away," he whispered in her ear. The smell of her hair blowing in his face made him feel light-headed.

Nebo flew to Port Townsend and over the Admiralty Lighthouse. Here, Reilly heard the melodic Waters of the far coast echoing off the glass of the lighthouse.

"My waves are in continual movement, bringing constant change," the Waters echoed past Nebo's wings. "Even when I am still, somewhere around me or near me is the emergence of becoming. However, the sacred essence of the Waters remains the same and never changes, offering healing to all who honor and respect it."

Reilly wasn't sure why the Waters of the far coast had told him this, but he figured he'd understand soon enough, so he tried not to analyze it.

Nebo flew back over the Hood Canal Bridge, then the Agate Pass Bridge, and finally he veered east around the northern tip of Bainbridge Island. There, he circled a giant rock protruding from the water.

"At low tide, you must come to this rock with James and Chantal," Nebo said. "I am not able to carry four of you on my back, so you will have to hike in. Take the trail through the north woods. Descend on the rope ladder and then follow the beach until you come here. But be sure to come at low tide, or your efforts will be in vain. Bring a camera."

"Okay," Reilly said. "I suppose we'll know why we're there once we arrive, right?"

"You will know." Nebo blinked slowly. With five flaps of his massive wings, he returned them to Eagle Harbor, landing gracefully on the beach near the kayak.

"Thank you, Nebo," Reilly and Norah said together as they climbed off his back. They slid into the kayak and pushed out from the shore. Nebo ascended to his spot at the top of the cedar and watched them glide back into the harbor.

Tuma greeted them on the porch when they returned to Reilly's house. His mom was in the kitchen preparing ginger-chicken stir-fry.

"Hi. I was hoping you'd show up for dinner," she said. "Norah, would you like to join us?"

"That would be nice. Thank you."

"Norah is coming with me and James to the bakery tonight. To meet Jordan Powell. He's the reporter you talked to the other day." Reilly tried to sound nonchalant. "We're going to tell him about our Stelladaurs."

"What did you say?" His mom stopped adding soy sauce to the wok.

Reilly ignored her surprised response. "I hope he'll be more helpful than the police. Who knows, though, I guess people believe what they want to believe. Even if it's false. I mean, who'd take the word of a kid over a famous guy like Travis Jackson?" Reilly rolled his eyes at his mom but immediately wished he hadn't.

"I never said I didn't believe you, Reilly," she began. "I'm just trying to make sense of everything, too."

Reilly sighed. "Sorry. I know, Mom. Let's not get into it now, okay?" He shifted his eyes quickly towards Norah.

"Reilly, what you have to offer has the potential to change so much in our world," Norah said. "Perhaps all of humankind."

Reilly had never thought about it that way before. Until Norah spoke those words, he hadn't fully comprehended the power of the Stelladaur … or the responsibility that weighed on his shoulders.

Once the food was on the table, he scooped some rice onto his plate beside the chicken and began to eat, all the while doubting his decision to tell Jordan Powell what he knew. While it was true that he wanted to prevent Travis from harming anyone with his drug-laced ROCKs, he also realized the risk he'd be taking by exposing himself and his knowledge of the Stelladaur to the world.

He placed a hand on his chest to reach for the keystone.

"It's gone!" he screamed, fumbling at the neck of his shirt to find the golden cord. "It's gone! My Stelladaur isn't here!"

Norah quickly reached her hand to her chest, held her hand over her own Stelladaur, and breathed a sigh of relief.

"Where did it go? I haven't taken it off since the day I found it! How could it just be gone?"

"I'm sure it's not *gone,* Reilly," his mom said. "It will probably show up when you least expect it to."

"Mom, how am I going to convince Jordan Powell that my Stelladaur is real if I can't even show it to him? What if he thinks I just stole one of Mr. Jackson's *ROCKs?*"

"Reilly, just breathe," his mom said, touching his forearm. "Everything is going to be all right."

"Why do you always say that? *Everything isn't always all right!*" Reilly snapped as he jerked away from her. Embarrassed by his reaction in front of Norah, he turned away from both of them and stared out the kitchen window.

Regaining some composure, he said, "I need the Stelladaur to get through the other two portals. How will I find Tir Na Nog?"

Norah stepped closer to Reilly. "Maybe we could use mine—together." She still held her hand over her Stelladaur.

"That's an idea," Reilly said. "Before we meet with Jordan tonight let's ask Eilam if he thinks that will work."

"Eilam always has answers," said Reilly's mom. She served herself some stir-fry. "Now, should we eat dinner, so we can get going?"

Ginger-chicken stir-fry was one of Reilly's favorites, but tonight he hardly tasted it. He could only think about his missing Stelladaur. Norah talked with his mom about her own mother and her Stelladaur, but Reilly barely heard their conversation.

Then, snapping out of his anxiety, he interrupted. "Norah, you can't tell Jordan about your Stelladaur. You can't show it to him."

Both his mother and Norah set their forks down in surprise.

"Why not? I thought you wanted to let everyone know the truth," his mom said.

Reilly looked at Norah. "I do. We can tell Jordan exactly what we told the police, but nothing about *your* Stelladaur. We can't risk giving your uncle or Mr. Jackson any reason to keep you from seeing me."

Norah blinked in disbelief.

"Besides, they'd steal your Stelladaur, for sure, and then we'd have no way to get through the orange portal. We don't want it to even cross their minds that you might have one, at least not for a few more days. Not until after the fireworks." Reilly stood up from the table. "Or until I find *my* Stelladaur again."

He inhaled and let out a long sigh to release his anxiety.

After dinner, Reilly and Norah visited Eilam. It had started to rain. The water looked choppy across the harbor and the wind blew hard. Under the shelter of the hut's roof, Reilly told Eilam about his missing Stelladaur, the proposed plan regarding what they'd tell Jordan and more importantly, what they would *not* tell.

"Do you think that's a good plan, Eilam?"

"Good? Bad? Why is it one or the other?"

"I don't understand."

"Perhaps there is *good*, *better* and *best*. Or perhaps what you may consider to be bad is actually for a greater good."

"What do you mean?"

"You tell me."

Reilly thought hard. "It's *good* to keep Mr. Jackson and Mr. Gustalini from finding out about Norah's Stelladaur. At least for now. It's *better* if they *never* know about it. It's *best* to wait to tell Jordan anything different than what we told the police, until after I find my Stelladaur. Is that what you mean?"

"You tell me."

Reilly wished Eilam would just tell him what was best. "I'm confused."

"No, you are not confused. You know precisely what to do."

"But how will I know for sure without my Stelladaur? What do *you* think the right thing is for me to do?"

"*Right?* Who is to say what is right for another?"

"Eilam, *please!* No riddles! Jordan will be here in twenty minutes. What are you trying to tell me?"

Eilam put his hands on the boy's shoulders and looked into his eyes so deeply that Reilly thought he was looking right into his soul. Then Eilam lowered his right hand and placed it on Reilly's chest.

"Reilly, your Stelladaur is here. Inside of you. If you trust whatever your heart tells you, then whatever you do, or don't do, will always be right, because it will be best for *you.*" Then he added, "Even if you don't see how, it will be so."

Reilly wasn't sure he knew how to trust his own heart as much as Eilam believed he could. But he reminded himself once again that Eilam always spoke the truth. Reilly simply nodded and gave Eilam a hug. Stepping back, he reached for Norah's hand.

"Let's go," he said, and he smiled as they headed up the dock towards town.

Chapter Twenty-three

Interview

The ferry terminal was packed with evening commuters. Reilly and his mom waited with Norah for Chantal in the courtyard just outside the passenger breezeway. People moved past like a herd of cattle, but Reilly spotted Chantal the second she rounded the corner in the terminal. She pulled two very large suitcases with a shoulder bag draped around her body.

"Chan!" Reilly let go of Norah's hand and waved both arms to get his sister's attention. She nodded and Reilly made his way through the crowd to help with her luggage. Together they maneuvered through the crowd to the courtyard.

"Mom!" Chantal threw her arms around her mother. "It's great to be home!"

"Looks like you may be staying a while," her mom said.

"Yeah, maybe. I know it's a lot of stuff but I … uh … I thought I might stay for the summer. Or longer."

"What about work? Are they okay with that?"

"Things have been sort of awkward there lately, tense, I guess. I need to reevaluate the direction I want my career to take. New York is so big, after all." Chantal grabbed the handle of her bag again. "It's just good to be home on the island."

"Well I'm glad you're home, Chan," Reilly said. "We've got a lot to fill you in on."

"I see that." Chantal smiled at Norah. "And you are?"

"Norah. Norah Gustalini."

"Nice to meet you."

"And you, Chantal. Reilly has told me a lot about you and his recent trip to New York for the science fair—the man in the taxi … everything!"

"Everything?" Chantal looked at Reilly.

"Yes, Norah is the girl I told you about. She's the one I saw in Jolka. Remember?"

"You said you met her in Seattle," his mom interjected.

"Oh! That's *you?*" Chantal replied rather loudly.

"That would be me," Norah said, grinning.

"All right, then. I do need to be filled in," Chantal agreed.

"Hello?" Reilly's mom sang out, as she stared at Reilly.

"You, too, Mom."

Heading to the parking lot, Reilly walked beside Chantal, in front of Norah and his mom, and gave her an abbreviated version of the recent events. He couldn't help but guess that she had come home to look for her own Stelladaur, though he doubted she knew it herself.

The back door to the bakery was still open and the employee closing for the night was just finishing up. James sat at Reilly's usual spot, tapping a pen on the table while he read a newspaper.

"Hi. I'm glad you guys are here before this Mr. Powell guy arrives," James said.

He dropped his pen and jumped out of his seat when he noticed Chantal walk into the room, behind Norah and Mrs. McNamara.

"You must be Chantal." He extended his hand. "James ... James Oliver."

"Nice to meet you, James." Chantal extended her hand to shake his. "I understand you like hanging out with my brother. Pretending to be waiters ... checking out abandoned warehouses ... spying on dangerous men ... stuff like that?"

Reilly's mom shot her son another firm glance and then glared at James.

"Yeah," James laughed. "Never a dull moment with Reilly." James still gripped Chantal's hand in a solid handshake.

"Uh-huh," she said, looking down at her hand.

"Oh, sorry." James released his grip. "Nice to meet you, Chantal."

There was a tap on the glass front door. Looking up, Reilly recognized the man immediately, as images from the disaster at the banquet flashed through his mind: water splashing ... falling to the floor ... James trying to conceal Reilly's Stelladaur ... and the man to Reilly's left clicking a camera. Reilly knew the person waiting at the bakery door was Jordan Powell.

Reilly opened the door for the reporter.

"Reilly," Jordan said. "Nice to see you again." They shook hands and the man walked into the bakery.

"This is my mother, Monique McNamara, my sister, Chantal, and my friend, Norah." Reilly pointed to the three women sitting on one side of the table.

"Yes, I remember seeing you at the banquet," Jordan said with a nod to Norah. "Weren't you sitting at Mr. Jackson's table?"

"Yes, I was there with my Uncle Martino."

"And this is James Oliver. He was there, too." Reilly gestured towards James.

"James. I remember you, as well. You were the one assisting Reilly when he fell."

"That's right."

"Please sit down, Mr. Powell," said Reilly's mom.

"Jordan. Just Jordan works for me." He took a pen and paper from the briefcase he had set on the floor beside him. Then he held up a small recording device. "Do you mind?"

"No, that's fine," said Reilly before anyone else could object.

"Reilly, I'll get right to the point," Jordan said. "I'm here to find out the truth. I'm not the kind of reporter who likes to embellish stories at the expense of others. But as the saying goes, there's always more than one side to a story. And I've been in this business long enough to know when the *other* side hasn't been told accurately. Or told at all. Either way, it's about getting to the facts."

Jordan reached for his briefcase and pulled out a small pile of photos. "I hope you can help me understand the story behind these photos." He laid them in a row in the center of the table, each photo facing Reilly and James. There were more shots than Reilly thought Jordan had taken in the seconds before James shoved his Stelladaur back under his shirt.

Five of the images looked identical—they were close-up shots of Reilly, lying on the floor wearing a white tuxedo shirt opened at the third button. In full view was Reilly's Stelladaur. Reilly looked over each of the photos without speaking.

Chantal and Norah both gasped when Jordan placed the final two prints on the table.

One showed James from a side angle, in front of Reilly, with his hand over the Stelladaur. Light seeped between his spread fingers. The last image was of James's hand inside Reilly's shirt, at his chest, with no view of the Stelladaur—but with Reilly and James staring at each other with horror on their faces.

Reilly felt surprisingly calm as he perused the photos. He sensed James's anxiousness but hoped he wouldn't say anything just yet. Norah and Chantal held their breath nervously. Reilly's mom was looking at him, not at the photos.

After a few long minutes, Reilly changed his mind about telling Jordan only what he and James had told the police. "What would you like to know, Jordan?" he asked.

"Is that one of Mr. Jackson's ROCKs?" Jordan asked, pointing to one of the photos.

"No, it's not."

"What is it?"

"It's called a Stelladaur. The word means Star Door."

James nudged Reilly in the ribs and Norah's jaw dropped.

"What does it do?" Jordan asked.

"It's sort of like a personal GPS unit. It can tell a person which way to go, when and where to turn and when not to turn. It helps a person find what he's looking for."

"Do you plug it in to charge it, or is it solar powered?" Jordan busily scratched notes as he listened.

"Neither. But *you* have to be plugged in for it to work."

"Can you explain that?"

"As I said, a Stelladaur is a very personal device. It only works for someone who has learned to listen to it and trust it."

"So, it's voice-activated? It talks to you, like a programmed device?"

"Not like you're talking to me. It's more like something that teaches people how to listen to themselves. To be intuitive. It guides a person to listen to his or her own heart."

Jordan narrowed his eyes. "How does it do that?"

"I'm not really sure. It just does. The longer a person has one the more they know how to use it, to trust it."

"You said it helps a person find what he's looking for. How does it do that? Do you input what you want and then read a printout?"

"No. By learning to trust your own Stelladaur, you discover what you want most. And then it shows you where to find it."

"So … it's like a crystal ball?" Jordan chuckled. "Some kind of magic?"

"I used to think so, but no, it's not. It's magical, for sure, but it's not magic."

"Where did you get this Stelladaur?" Jordan asked, pointing to one of the photos.

"It was my dad's, and my grandfather's before that. This particular one has been in our family for generations."

"There are more?"

Reilly paused before answering, making sure he did not look up at Norah or anyone else. He kept his eyes on the photos as he answered the questions.

"Yes. Everyone has a Stelladaur made just for them." Reilly paused again and turned to look directly at Jordan. "But each person has to search for it, if he's going to find it. Everyone has to really look."

Jordan shifted slightly on the bench. "So you said you got yours from your dad. Did he give it to you or did you have to look for it yourself? Where did you find it?"

"I'm not sure if it's the same one my dad had or not, but I found it on his sailboat, a couple months ago … just after he died."

"My condolences," James said, looking first at Reilly, then to his mother and sister. Turning back to Reilly, he added, "May I ask how he died?"

"In a sailing accident," Reilly said.

Jordan quietly considered his notes before speaking again.

"Let's just assume this Stelladaur actually exists. What is a Stelladaur made of? Obviously it's a brilliant stone of some kind."

"It looks like a diamond but it's not like any other rock or jewel. You can't get it from a mine or anything. It's just *there* when a person is ready for it. Each Stelladaur would only be valuable to the person who finds it."

"So if I had *your* Stelladaur, it wouldn't guide me to where *I* wanted to go?"

"No, that's not how it works. Every person has to use his own Stelladaur."

"Yeah, you said that. I'm not sure exactly what you mean," Jordan said, "but I'll go with it for now." He flipped through his notes. "Tell me what else the Stelladaur can do. Mr. Jackson claims his ROCK is a time-travel device, something a person can use to actually go through time and space to other dimensions and other worlds. There are reports coming in from those who have purchased his ROCKs that would substantiate his claims. The Stelladaur in these photos looks identical to his ROCKs. That would lead me to believe that your Stelladaur can do the same thing Travis Jackson's ROCK does. Is that true?"

"Travis Jackson is a fraud."

"That's quite a statement against such a renowned individual."

"You said you were here to find the truth, isn't that right, Mr. Powell?"

Jordan glanced quickly at the others. Then he picked up the recording device and checked to make sure it was still functioning. "Yes, I'm here to find out the truth."

"Okay. Then may I ask you a question, sir?"

"Of course."

"What gave you reason to believe that what you see in these photos is different from one of Mr. Jackson's ROCKs?" Reilly inquired.

Jordan hesitated a moment. "A hunch. When I saw that stone around your neck, I figured there must be a connection."

"So you're here right now, not because of any real facts but because of a hunch? Something you *feel*?"

"A reporter's intuition is quite valuable, Reilly."

"You must be the kind of reporter who really *does* care about the truth." Reilly squared his shoulders to sit up taller. "Would you like to know why I believe *the great* Travis Jackson is a fraud?"

"Please."

Reilly and James told Jordan what they'd seen in the hotel room, at the warehouse and on the ferry, and about the piles of dead fish and the dead seal. Afterwards Norah added that she had witnessed everything they described. Reilly's mom just listened.

"The police said they were checking into the possibility of something poisoning the marine life, but they didn't take any allegations seriously," Reilly continued. "They told us they'd check out the warehouse, but I doubt they will ... unless they have more evidence."

"You're probably right. And I'm going to need more evidence before my editor will print any of this," Jordan added.

"Like these photos?" Chantal asked. James glanced at her and winked.

"I'm afraid these photos don't tell us anything about Mr. Jackson's alleged fraud. They only show a kid with something around his neck that looks like one of Jackson's ROCKs. I'd like to get your story out, Reilly, but I need more proof. My editor is going to be a lot more skeptical than I am." Jordan nodded his head and leaned over to get something from his briefcase. "What else can you give me?"

"What else do you want to know?" Reilly asked, frustrated.

"This—" Jordan set another photo in the center of the table. It was the same one that had been printed in the *Bainbridge Review* on Monday. "Is the person in that kayak you?"

In an instant, Reilly felt like he was in another time warp. His mind replayed scenes in Jolka, Just Beyond Jolka, Glesig, Gwidon and Zora. They were like pieces of a jigsaw puzzle scattered on the floor. He mentally scrambled to gather up the pieces while everyone else at the table seemed to be under a halting spell. Reilly subconsciously touched his hand to his heart to reach for his Stelladaur. Other than his T-shirt, the space between his hand and his chest was empty. But in that instant, Reilly was completely aware of what he must say. "Yes, I'm the person in that kayak."

Everyone else at the table stirred uncomfortably at the revelation.

"Are you saying that *your* Stelladaur can be used to actually travel through time—without any hallucinogenic drugs? It's a real honest-to-goodness time travel device?" Jordan asked with obvious skepticism.

"That's right."

"How does it work?"

"It reacts to rays of the sunlight—and usually with water—in very specific ways to create a frequency that opens various portals."

Jordan wrote feverishly in his notebook.

"Can you show me how it works?"

"Uh ... no. A Stelladaur only works as a travel device for the person it was created for. Remember? It's like a *personal* GPS."

"Okay," Jordan played along. "But obviously this photo suggests that others can witness it, right?"

"I guess so." Reilly shrugged. "But maybe a camera can only capture a blur of light during the transport. I don't know exactly."

"I've got my camera right here." Reaching again for his briefcase, he said, "Can we try it? If I took some shots before the portal opens, and then before and after you go through it, maybe we could capture more than just a blur." It was a challenge. Reilly couldn't tell if Jordan was mocking him or simply pressing for more information.

"I'm afraid that won't be possible," Reilly answered, still trying to sound confident.

"Why not?"

"I don't have it. I'm not sure where it is."

Jordan rolled his eyes. "You lost it?"

"I'm not sure."

"Was it stolen?"

"I hope not. That's what Travis Jackson did—"

"What do you mean?" Jordan demanded.

"He stole one from a boy in Jamaica, and used it as a prototype for his ROCK. No one can *make* a real Stelladaur, so he decided to create a counterfeit. But the thing is—he doesn't know that a Stelladaur only works for the person it was created for. Stelladaurs come from a realm and dimension far beyond our universe. Beyond all known galaxies." Reilly paused to give Jordan time for his last statement to sink in. "I don't think he designed the ROCK to actually take people through portals. Travis Jackson is only interested in the recognition of such a discovery."

"But he's as well known as Gates."

"Yeah, but Travis doesn't actually want to help people. He's using the ROCK to feed his craving for power and control."

"So you think he'd risk everything he's accomplished throughout his entire career just to say he invented the first ever time-travel device? And you believe he's risking people's lives to do it?"

"Yes. And yes, I do." Reilly answered both questions immediately.

The recording device beeped but Jordan ignored it.

"Is there anything else? Could you tell me more about going through the portals and your own experiences with time travel? For some strange reason, I want to believe you." Jordan put the lid on his pen and looked directly at Reilly. "But the evidence doesn't stack up and, quite frankly, I think the majority of people will have a difficult time believing your story over what they've heard from Mr. Jackson. He's so well respected in his field. The fact is, even these photos don't prove much. People could just say they were altered." Jordan frowned as he began to gather up the photos. "Most people will think your story is a fabrication, Reilly."

"There will always be critics, Mr. Powell. And there will always be people who don't believe the truth, even if it's staring them in the face," Reilly said. "It takes a wise person to recognize truth without visible evidence."

Jordan chuckled as he finished packing up. "You're an unusual young man, Reilly."

"Yes, sir. I mean, thank you, Mr. Powell."

"Jordan."

The reporter stood up to leave.

"Jordan? I have something else that may be helpful to you." Reilly reached into his coat pocket and placed a star-shaped chunk of plastic on the table. "It's one of the dud ROCKs we took from the warehouse. Maybe you could have it analyzed in a lab."

Jordan picked up the ROCK and turned it over in his hands. "Perhaps this will provide some concrete evidence."

"Be careful," Norah warned. "I did that with one of them and it gave me a real headache and made me feel sick."

Jordan set the dud down and asked James to hand him a napkin from the dispenser at the end of the table. Jordan wrapped the dud in the napkin and put it in his briefcase. "Fair enough. I'll get it to a lab first thing in the morning. Thank you."

"One other thing," said James, as he handed another photo to Jordan. "We gave a copy of this picture to the police but, as we said, they didn't seem to think it proved anything—just a photo of a guy sitting in a van, as far as they were concerned. Anyway, it's one of the guys who dumped the boxes in the water. We think his name is Derek."

"Thank you. This is great." Jordan zipped his briefcase shut. "Listen, I need to catch the next boat. However, if my editor gives the okay, I'll have the story ready for the Friday morning edition." Jordan and Reilly shook hands. "But don't hold your breath."

Everyone was quiet after the door closed. Reilly looked at the table where the photos had been. Norah looked at Reilly, as did his mom. James and Chantal looked at each other. Then Reilly stretched.

"It's been a long day, huh? I'm tired."

"Me, too," said Chantal. "What do you say we head home?"

"Yeah, I need to get going, too," James said, as he slid across the bench and started to push Reilly out of the booth. "I've got a midterm to study for."

"Norah, can we give you a ride home?" Reilly's mom asked.

"Yes, thank you."

James was still pushing Reilly to get up.

"Wait," Reilly insisted. "We need to go to the north end of the island tomorrow to check out a large boulder Nebo pointed out to Norah and me earlier today. He told us to go at low tide. Does anyone know when low tide is supposed to be?"

James checked the tides app on his smart phone. "Looks like the lowest tide will be around noon."

"We'll meet you here at 11:00 then," Reilly said.

"And you?" James asked Chantal.

"Of course. I wouldn't miss it!"

"Who's Nebo?" Reilly's mom asked as she locked the front door.

"Just a giant eagle, Mom."

"Right-O! Of course."

Chantal threw her luggage in the back of their jeep. Reilly sat in the back seat with his arm around Norah. The summer cottage where Norah and her uncle were staying was on the west side of the island. Reilly walked her to the door.

"Thank you for not telling him about my Stelladaur," Norah said. Then she hugged him.

"You're welcome," he said. "It didn't feel like it would be the best thing to do."

Norah pulled back and kissed him on the cheek. "Good night."

She turned and went inside. Reilly had wanted to pull her to him and kiss her gently on the lips. But he didn't want his first kiss to be seen in the beam of the car's headlights by his gawking mother and sister.

He simply whispered "good night" into the evening air.

By 11:30 the next morning, Reilly, Norah, James and Chantal were on a forest trail at the north end of the island. They stopped at a clearing on the edge of a cliff, where a notched-rope secured to an exposed tree root dropped down the high bank to the beach below.

"I'll go down first. Then you girls follow me," James said, puffing out his chest slightly. "Reilly can take the rear."

"Hmmph!" Chantal said, stepping in front of James. "What? You think you're Robinson Crusoe or something? I happen to be an expert rock climber." She stepped to the edge and carefully found her footing as she reached for the rope. Scaling the cliff with ease, Chantal was halfway to the ground before Norah nudged her way past Reilly and James to the edge.

"I'm no climbing expert, but I think I can handle this," she said as she grabbed the rope. James frowned and Reilly chuckled.

On the beach, they dodged spurts of water shooting up from dozens of small holes in the sand.

"Ahhh! What is that?" Norah squealed as water shot up her pant leg.

"Clams," laughed Reilly. "Geoducks. They dig deeper into the ground when they feel vibrations on the surface, creating a vacuum, which makes the water shoot up."

They jumped over the holes for a couple hundred yards, heading north until they spotted the giant rock

"That's it!" Reilly pointed. He took Norah's hand as they started to run.

Chantal looked at James. "Are we going to let them beat us?"

"No way!" James said as he grabbed her hand.

They sprinted ahead. The wet sand gripped at their shoes with a smattering of sucking noises. A flock of seagulls screeched above.

It was a tie. Breathless, they all bent over to catch their breath. Looking up, Reilly stepped closer to the massive rock, a mini sea stack, which had been under water earlier that morning. They walked single file around the rock to examine it. Aside from a few purple starfish and a long piece of kelp, they saw nothing unusual.

"Let's climb on top," Norah suggested.

"Yeah," Reilly said.

Chantal reached the top before Reilly and Norah were half-way up, while James searched for a firm hold to begin his ascent. Chantal called out encouraging words, but it only embarrassed him. On top, they looked out towards Seattle to admire the view.

Then Reilly began to look for clues. Before long, he spotted something at the far end of the rock.

"Petroglyphs!" Reilly said, gazing at a series of deep marks carved into a flat part of the rock's surface.

Chantal and Norah bounded over to Reilly. "Wow!" they both said.

"James, you brought your camera, didn't you?" asked Reilly. "Get over here and take some pictures!"

James joined the group and started clicking.

"Can you get all of it in one shot?" Reilly asked.

"Of course."

James let his camera dangle on the strap around his neck as he squatted down to admire the ancient carvings. Then he spotted something. "Check this out!" He pointed to a marking in the center of the others. "It looks like the key my mom gave me with the same heart shape at one end." James pointed more closely at the symbol on the rock. "See here … it has this E shape on the other end." They all squatted down for a closer look.

James touched the marking and immediately inhaled deeply and quickly.

"What is it, James?" Chantal asked.

"I don't know," James said. "I felt something when I touched it. Sort of like a surge of electricity. Not a shock, really, more a tingling sensation that shot through my hand and up my arm."

Chantal leaned in to touch the marking. "Huh! I didn't feel anything."

Norah and Reilly glanced at each other.

"Then it's a message meant for you, James," Reilly said.

James raised his brow. He silently counted the markings. "Seven. Plus this one in the middle makes eight."

"Hmmm," Reilly said.

"What?" James wondered aloud.

"Just thinking." Reilly looked intently at the message. "It could spell an eight-letter word. Or each symbol could mean something different."

"They're connected somehow," James said anxiously. "We need to find out how."

"We could research it online," said Chantal, "or see if the Bainbridge Historical Society has any information."

"I'd be surprised if you found anything," Reilly mumbled.

"Why?" James asked.

"James, finding your Stelladaur isn't something you can research."

"I thought you said a person finds his own Stelladaur when he's looking for it and when he's ready for it." He scratched his head.

"Yes, but looking for something doesn't necessarily mean searching through mounds of information that may, or may not, be useful. It means keeping your eyes open to possibilities. Kind of like Jordan's intuition. Anyone can *look,* but a person has to have an open heart and open mind to really *see.* That's what makes the person ready." Reilly felt Norah looking at him intently while he spoke to James. "And that's especially true when it's right in front of you. Like these markings, for example. James, we all *looked* at the same petroglyphs, but you're the one who was ready to *see* them."

"I *seeeee!*" James echoed, intending the pun.

"Just don't be disappointed if you don't find these symbols plastered all over the Internet, or if it's a mystery to the historical society." Reilly stood up. "The fact that the key-shaped one is in the center makes me think the message is hidden. Maybe only one person can unlock it."

"Sounds like a message for you, too, Reilly," Norah interjected. Reilly paused to consider what she meant, and subconsciously twisted the golden threads at his wrist.

They stopped at the Bainbridge Historical Museum on their way home. There were a few photos of the petroglyphs, as Chantal had suggested, but the records offered no conclusions about the age of the drawings. Speculations ranged from hundreds to thousands of years, or perhaps, simply modern graffiti. One theory shared by the docent was that the markings might have been used as some kind of ancient calendar with two markings representing each season.

Later, they spent almost three hours on the Internet. Finding nothing useful, James was discouraged. "Unfortunately, I've got to call it quits for today," he said. "I've got to cram for my exam in the morning."

"Yeah, time to finish up. Chantal and I promised our mom we'd help out early at the bakery tomorrow," Reilly said. "We're starting at 5:00 and working most of the day."

"She's barely started the float for the parade," Chantal added. "We've got so much work to do."

Reilly didn't sleep well that night. He had hoped to dream of looking for lotus flower fireworks with Norah. Instead, he woke numerous times from the same recurring nightmare—hundreds of hooded creatures were chasing him through a dark tunnel. Each time he woke, he sat up in bed gasping for air, and grasping for his Stelladaur, which no longer hung around his neck.

Chapter Twenty-four

Juggler

By 7:00 the next morning, an assortment of yummy smells wafted through the entire bakery and out through the open windows. More than the usual number of customers came in to purchase last-minute goodies for their Fourth of July picnics, barbecues and fireworks parties. For three hours after opening, a constant stream of customers formed a line that snaked out the front door and down the sidewalk. It wasn't until 11:00 that Norah showed up at the bakery kitchen with a newspaper in her hand.

"Have you seen this yet?" she asked, holding up the paper.

"No, it's been madness around here," Reilly said, glazing a batch of cherry turnovers.

"Read it to us, Norah," Chantal said as she wiped flour from her cheeks with the back of her hand.

"It's much shorter than I thought it would be. Very to-the-point, but I think Jordan covered it well," Norah said. "Here it is …

Travis Jackson's ROCKs: A Hoax?

Local innovator, Travis Jackson is under investigation for possible fraud after his recent introduction of the ROCK, purported to be a time-travel device, to the general public just one week ago. Traces of a hallucinogenic drug were found in ROCK samples taken from an abandoned warehouse in south Seattle, where three eyewitnesses—two of whom are minors—observed a crew of men conducting manufacturing operations. Anonymous sources and eyewitnesses reported seeing two men dump a couple of large boxes into the Puget Sound early Sunday morning off the side of a Washington State Ferry headed to Bainbridge Island. EPA officials are actively investigating reports of increased marine life deaths between Seattle and Bainbridge Island, including a dead seal that was washed up on the west shore of Eagle Harbor. Preliminary tests indicate that the waters contained traces of the same hallucinogenic substance that was found on one of Jackson's ROCK samples. Jackson's attorneys declined to comment on the investigation."

"That's it? It doesn't say anything about Reilly or his Stelladaur?" Chantal asked, putting down a rolling pin.

"No. That's all."

Reilly peeled off his disposable gloves, puzzling over the reporter's omission of information. "Maybe Jordan didn't think it was the right time to give all the information."

"Maybe," James said, "but he obviously had the dud analyzed in a lab, and someone contacted the EPA."

"That's positive," Reilly's mom said.

Reilly nodded. "I'm glad they're looking into it."

"Now what?" Chantal asked Reilly.

"Let's finish this baking and then work on the float." He put the tray of turnovers in the oven. "Tomorrow we take the day off and have fun. But let's keep our eyes open for Travis. I wouldn't put it past him to come after anyone he suspects could be an informant."

"Really?" Chantal asked.

"No doubt in my mind."

Reilly's mom shivered. "Reilly, you're grounded to the bakery, or home, until either this goes away or the investigation is complete." She wiped her hands on her apron. "I hope Mr. Jackson will be arrested soon."

"Grounded?" Reilly laughed. "That's funny, Mom."

"I'm serious!" She frowned.

"Mom, you're overreacting."

"Reilly, you know I've never trusted Mr. Jackson and I've got a bad feeling about this whole thing."

Reilly shared her foreboding feeling. Without responding, he reached for his missing Stelladaur.

Chantal chimed in. "Mom, we're all working on the float this afternoon, and tomorrow we'll be together all day. If anything seems out of the ordinary, we'll call the police. Okay?"

She clenched her jaw and sighed heavily. "All right. But I still don't like this."

Reilly smiled at his sister and mouthed the words "thank you" when their mom turned back to her work.

Reilly and Chantal made twenty dozen sugar cookies while Norah sat on a stool forming purple tissue-paper roses for the float. By mid-afternoon the baking was completed and they sat down to eat a late lunch. Reilly noticed Mrs. Claudette Morgensen, president of the Downtown Association, enter the bakery in an obvious panic.

"Oh, hello kids," she said, waltzing past them towards the kitchen. "Is your mom in the back?"

She reached the kitchen door but stopped abruptly and turned completely around to look at Reilly. Then she walked methodically towards their table, pointing at him and grinning widely. "You're just the man I'm looking for!"

"Me? You wanted to see me?"

"Yes, and your girlfriend."

"My girlfriend?"

"Well, this lovely girl is your friend, is she not?"

"Yes, she is … I mean … my friend. This is Norah. Norah, this is Mrs. Morgensen."

"Hello." Norah smiled.

"Reilly, how would you and Norah like to help out a frantic parade director?"

"What do you have in mind?" he asked.

"The Island Independence Day king and queen have just canceled. The king has the flu and the queen broke her leg in a soccer tournament."

"What are the odds?" Reilly pretended he didn't know what she was implying.

"The sponsor of this year's parade—Blackberry Bakers!—is providing the float to escort the royalty."

"We're working on it this afternoon." Reilly tried to ignore the inevitable.

"We can't very well have a royalty float without—"

"Without what?" Reilly interrupted without a hint of enthusiasm. Chantal snickered loudly. Norah sat up taller and flipped her hair over her shoulders.

"You and Norah would make a lovely king and queen!" Claudette exclaimed.

"Me? No way!" Reilly declared, shaking his head.

Norah stuck out her lower lip and frowned at Reilly.

"C'mon, Reilly, you two would be darling," Chantal teased.

"Shut up, Chan," Reilly said.

"Relax, brother. It's no big deal. You guys were going to ride on the float anyway."

"To throw candy!" he retorted.

"James and I will take care of the candy," Chantal said.

"Why don't you two be the stupid king and queen?"

"That won't work, Reilly." Claudette sighed. "The royalty are supposed to be high school kids."

"See?" Chantal chimed.

Reilly sighed. "What if there's just no king and queen?"

"Local merchants have paid top advertising dollars for various publications to be distributed during the parade. The sponsoring business receives additional signage and recognition," Claudette pitched, as she yanked papers from her oversized handbag. "There *has* to be a king and queen. It's been an island tradition for over fifty years!"

"How come I've never noticed?" Reilly muttered under his breath.

"Maybe you weren't *looking*," Norah chided as Chantal laughed out loud. Claudette looked confused.

"Very funny." Reilly scowled at both girls. "*Grrrrrrrrrr!* What do we have to do?"

Claudette clapped her hands with delight and grinned. "Norah, I've got a gown for you in my car. The girl who cancelled said she'd be happy to let the substitute borrow it. You may need to pin it here and there, but it'll be just lovely. Reilly, you don't happen to have a tux, do you?"

"Not so much." Reilly grimaced. "But I'm beginning to think I ought to just keep one on hand," he said under his breath.

"What did you say?" Claudette asked.

"Never mind." He sighed. "I'll wear a tux, but I'm wearing my own shoes."

Claudette frowned, confused. "No problem. I'll just take some measurements and pick one up for you this afternoon. I hope the shop has one your size. I don't have time to go over to Seattle." She rummaged through her handbag and whipped out a seamstress's measuring tape. "Stand up, Reilly."

Reilly rolled his eyes and glared at Norah. She giggled, making her nose wrinkle, and his annoyance fade quickly.

"I'll be back by 6:00 this evening with the tux and the dress. You'll need to be ready to go at 8:00 tomorrow morning." Claudette gave details of the parade route and added, "Just wave and smile!" She waved herself and flashed a big grin as she turned and exited the front door.

Reilly sighed.

"You're a good sport, Reilly," Chantal said. "Let's go out back and work on that float."

Reilly doubted decorating a flatbed trailer to look like a whimsical blackberry forest was going to make him feel any better, especially since he now had to ride on it looking all regal. Nevertheless, the three of them joined the crew of professional designers his mom had hired to oversee the job, and they gave Reilly the task of winding green raffia rope around hundreds of yards of heavy-duty florist wire for masses of mock blackberry bushes. Norah and Chantal worked on the thrones for the king and queen—high-backed wicker chairs that had been spray-painted a glittery gold. They tied purple and gold ribbons to the sides to serve as tassels, and then glued fake multi-colored gems to a piece of wood they attached to the top of the headrests to make the chairs appear much taller.

Reilly was elated when he saw James walking up the back alley to the parking lot.

"Wow, I'm sure glad to see you," he said. "I'm completely out of my element here."

James chuckled, seeing Reilly sitting in a mound of green wire.

"Looks like you've been busy," he said.

"You don't know the half of it. Norah and I are going to ride on this ridiculous thing in the parade ... as the Independence Day king and queen."

James burst out laughing. Reilly threw a ball of raffia at him.

"So, how did your test go?" Reilly asked, wanting to change the subject.

"I think it went well. Won't get the score till next week. But you'll never guess what happened on my way across campus." James sat on the edge of the flatbed trailer.

"What's that?"

"As I was walking past the Suzzallo, the main library, which I've done hundreds of times, I had the strangest feeling that I should really *look* at the library. I've looked at it plenty of times in the past, but this time I *really* looked—up! Way up. And I saw something I've never noticed before. At the very top of the building are large arched windows and other smaller windows, each shaped like a six-petal flower. Reilly, it's the exact same shape as one of the markings we saw on the petroglyphs! And inside each of the windows is a six-pointed red star—the same as another marking on the petroglyphs."

"Really? Did you go inside?"

"Unfortunately I couldn't. It closed early for the holiday, but it will be open on Sunday."

Reilly set down the wire in his hand. "We need to get there as soon as it opens."

"Absolutely. But, Reilly, that's not all," James said, this time more quietly. "I saw Norah's Uncle Martino walk up to the main doors. As soon as he noticed they were locked, he picked up his cell phone and made a call. He looked annoyed."

Reilly gasped. "James, we need to get inside that library before he does!"

"I know."

"Did he see you?"

"No. He walked off and didn't look in my direction."

"Here," Reilly said, handing James a spool of wire. "Help me finish with this stuff. And by the way, Chan volunteered you to ride on the float with her. To throw candy."

"Darn! I was hoping to be the king," James teased.

It was dusk by the time they finished. Reilly and Norah took a slice of strawberry-rhubarb pie to Eilam.

"I'm glad you found the petroglyphs," Eilam said. "Those are real icons of history. Ancient history."

"You knew about them?" Reilly asked, wondering at his own surprise. "Why didn't you didn't tell me sooner?"

"It was for Nebo to tell you."

"But you know I would have believed you."

"Yes, but that would have robbed Nebo of the opportunity to earn that same trust from you, and Norah, too."

Reilly didn't understand, but he let it go. "It's getting late. We've got to be at the parade first thing in the morning. Will you be there?"

"Perhaps."

Reilly lay in bed until after midnight thinking about Eilam until he finally drifted off to sleep. It was another night filled with hooded monsters chasing him through a dark tunnel. However, this time, Reilly saw himself in the nightmare, running through a large crowd of people and from Travis Jackson, who chased him only steps behind.

By morning, Reilly's worries had shifted from the fear of monsters lurking in his subconscious to feeling completely ridiculous and conspicuous in the white tux with a blackberry colored cummerbund, lapels and bow tie. However, when he saw Norah in her beaded deep purple gown, and her swept-up hair adorned with a rhinestone crown, he thought she must be true royalty. The golden cord of her Stelladaur hung from her neck as if it was part of the gown, with the stone itself tucked inside her bodice. Reilly suddenly felt honored to be escorting her.

Still, his thoughts vacillated between the contentment of being with Norah on the parade float and the nagging feeling that Travis lurked in a dark alley nearby. He also had an odd sense of responsibility to make sure Norah felt comfortable during the parade.

"Maybe no one will recognize me," Reilly said to Chantal as she adjusted his bow tie.

"Since when have you ever cared about what anyone else might think?" Chantal replied, stepping back to admire the finished ensemble.

"Only since I had to wear this! I don't exactly blend in."

"It's just for a couple of hours. What's the worst that can happen?"

"Yeah, kid, you're always telling me to *go with the flow … let things come to me … welcome opportunity …*" James nagged.

"I know, I know," Reilly agreed. "I just want to make sure Norah is … safe."

"*Safe*? Why wouldn't I be safe?" Norah asked, shifting in the throne-chair.

"It's nothing," Reilly said, lying. "This whole king and queen thing is definitely out of my comfort zone, that's all." He pulled his sleeves further down to his wrists from under his jacket. "But … I keep having this nightmare about Travis coming after me." Reilly noticed Norah's eyes widen and her chest rise as she drew in a quick breath.

"Reilly, relax. Try to have fun with this, okay?" James said. "Chantal and I are here and we'll help keep an eye out for anything unusual. Nothing's going to happen during the parade."

The float lurched forward, interrupting their conversation. The marching band ahead exploded into a lively rendition of "Yankee Doodle Dandy," and Reilly's mom drove her truck slowly, towing the float along the parade route. As they turned into the roundabout, Reilly looked at the throngs of people who lined both sides of the street, extending for a mile in front of them. Though colorful and festive, it had an eerie resemblance to the haunting, dark tunnel in his nightmare. He reached for Norah's hand and held it tightly at his knee, while she waved at the crowds with her other hand. Reilly smiled broadly, trying to appear in character, but he continually turned his head from left to right, looking for anything out of the ordinary.

Chantal and James threw candy by the handfuls and flirted with each other like teenagers. Reilly wondered why no one seemed to notice the inevitable dark abyss ahead of them. Was he the only one who felt impending mayhem? Yet he knew Norah was uneasy, too. Maybe he just felt vulnerable without his Stelladaur around his neck. Once again, unanswered questions probed his mind and heart as the Blackberry Bakers float rolled steadily down the street.

Norah let go of Reilly's hand so she could wave to parade enthusiasts on both sides of the street. Her smile did not leave her face and, as Reilly watched her for a brief moment, he forgot his concerns. When they rounded the corner on to Main Street, they both spotted Nebo circling high above the shops.

"What's he doing?" Norah said.

"I don't know. He's telling us something but I can't hear him through all this noise," Reilly said. "Have you seen Eilam yet?"

"No."

Half a block ahead, Reilly spotted a parade character he had not seen before, walking on painter's stilts. The character wore a crimson cape fastened at the neck, which fluttered in yards of billowy fabric and revealed a multicolored, polka dot clown suit underneath. Though its head was covered with a hood that draped over its face, the clown skillfully juggled five machetes.

"How can he juggle when his eyes are covered by that hood?" Norah asked Reilly.

Reilly didn't answer. Nor did he take his eyes off the juggler.

As the Blackberry float moved down Main Street, the juggler approached the truck that pulled it. Reilly could see the eyeholes on the hood of the cape covered with a mesh red fabric; he noted that a person would need to look very closely to see the holes.

Then Reilly grabbed Norah's hand and pulled her out of the queen's throne. "Stand up, Norah," he shouted, "and don't take your eyes off that juggler!"

Norah stood close to Reilly, her hand gripping his tightly. Reilly looked quickly towards Chantal and James, hoping to get their attention with a glance. They, too, had noticed the juggler and were watching him intently. Reilly scanned the parade-goers and noticed that many people were watching the juggler. Now parallel to the front of the flatbed, the juggler was only fifteen feet from Reilly and Norah. The machetes spun and twirled, dancing off the juggler's hands. With every turn of the blades, the juggling clown expertly caught each knife by its handle.

Suddenly, the crowd's attention was diverted by a second juggler, who emerged from the curb carrying three lit torches, maneuvering them like batons. The man wore all black and his face was painted like a mime's. The flames against the black silhouette left the crowd oohing and aahing, as the character stole their attention from the juggling clown. After two more rotations of the flatbed's tires, Reilly's eyes met the filtered glare of the red-hooded clown.

In that split second, a machete came whirring directly at Reilly and Norah.

"Get down!" Reilly yelled as he pulled Norah to the floor. She screamed and put her hands over her head as she fell down.

The machete flew past them, lodging at the top of the king's throne. The float kept rolling forward and the juggler continued to juggle as he moved passed them. With all the parade noise, no one but Reilly, Chantal and James heard Norah scream. The flame-thrower continued to distract the crowd. No one seemed to notice the machete stuck in the throne.

Before Reilly and Norah could stand up, Nebo swooped out of the sky. He flapped his wings, creating a tremendous gust of wind that blew out the flames on the juggler's torches. All heads turned to watch the giant bird fly past the float and grab the red hood of the machete-juggling clown, ripping it from the cape.

Reilly expected it to be Travis, but the man who threw the machete was no one he recognized.

Nebo held the fabric in his claws and circled around Main Street twice before disappearing over Eagle Harbor, shrinking to normal size as he retreated into the distance.

The torch-juggler ran into the crowd. Nebo's interference had caused enough of a distraction for someone to call an officer to assist with the commotion. Three police were soon at the flame-thrower's heels. The man tried desperately to unlatch his stilts before the police reached him, but to no avail. The parade halted as police ran in and out of the crowd and two more officers jumped onto the float.

"Are you all right?" one of the officers asked.

"We're fine," Norah answered.

Chantal nodded. "Yes, we're all fine."

"Did any of you see the bird that attacked that man?" The officer pointed to the guy in the hoodless red cape.

"If you look there, sir, you'll see it was that *man* who tried to attack *us!*" Reilly pointed at the machete lodged in the throne-chair.

The officer admitted that he hadn't noticed it. He walked over to the king's throne, communicating to the other officers on his mobile phone, but he did not touch the knife or the throne. Within minutes, backup cops on motorcycles lined both sides of the float and the parade continued down the street.

Reilly, his mom, Norah, James and Chantal were all questioned, more than once, at the station. They waited until late afternoon for Chief J. D. Gunderson, who had been spending the day with his family in Seattle, to arrive. Only the chief was authorized to remove the machete from the throne and bring it in to his office.

"There are two letters engraved on this knife. We believe they stand for the name of the manufacturer, Red-Herring Machetes," Gunderson stated. "Do you know what a red herring is, son?" Gunderson looked directly at Reilly.

"No, I don't, sir."

"Isn't it something that's used to distract the attention away from something else?" James suggested. Impressed, Chantal raised her eyebrows.

"That's right," said Gunderson. "It's strange, though, because none of the other machetes we confiscated have the initials R. M."

"Huh," Reilly muttered.

"I find it very interesting that those are also your initials," said the chief, still looking at Reilly.

"I … uh … *my* initials?"

"Reilly, do you have any reason to believe someone may be trying to hurt you?" J. D. Gunderson paused. "You can tell us the truth. We're here to protect you."

Reilly's heart pounded, but his head was clear. He didn't need a Stelladaur around his neck to know exactly who was trying to kill him. "The only person that comes to my mind is Travis Jackson."

"Travis Jackson? *The* Travis Jackson?"

"Yes."

"Why would you say that?"

"Because of what James and I told the police here last Monday. They didn't take what we told them very seriously. Now maybe they will."

Reilly repeated everything he, James and Norah had told the other officer earlier in the week, filling in the story with some of the same detailed information he had given Jordan Powell—but leaving out the part about his own Stelladaur, as well as the fact that Norah was wearing one around her neck at that very moment. Norah realized that on Monday they had forgotten to tell the officer about the boxes her uncle had stored in his hotel room in Seattle, the week before. She decided to tell the chief about them.

"Did you happen to take any photos of them?" Chief Gunderson inquired.

"I didn't have a camera. As I said, James and Reilly came up to the room right after the banquet, and neither of them had a camera either."

"You don't have one on your phone?" Gunderson pressed, sounding somewhat annoyed.

"I guess we didn't think to take pictures," Reilly offered.

"But you're each a witness of what was in that room?" Gunderson clarified.

"I wasn't there," Reilly's mom said.

"Sir," Norah said, "some of those boxes were brought over to the island Sunday morning on Mr. Jackson's yacht, but I don't know if they were taken off the boat."

"And did you tell the officer this in your report on Monday?"

"No. I guess we forgot to mention that part." Norah frowned.

"Hmmm …"

"But we did give the police some photos of the van, with the license number, and of the two men in the van," James said. "Before the ferry returned to Seattle, I ran home and grabbed my camera, since I just live a couple of blocks from the terminal. I took the photos of the men when they were in the ferry line. The younger guy's name is Derek."

"I see. So … no pictures at the warehouse *or* the hotel room?"

"Unfortunately not, sir," James said.

"Blake?" Gunderson hollered at an officer in the next room.

Blake entered the chief's office. "Sir?"

"Get me the file on the report these kids gave on Monday. Who took that report?" Gunderson was annoyed and impatient.

"I'll find out, sir, and I'll get you that file." He left the room.

"I think his name was Officer Mitchell," Reilly said.

"Yeah … Mitchell … that was it," said Norah.

Blake returned with the file and a plastic bag with a ROCK in it. He handed both to the chief. "Looks like it was Mitchell, sir," he said.

"Right," Gunderson said as he opened the file. He picked up the photos and flipped through them. "Get him in here. Now!" Blake turned and left the room.

"Chief Gunderson?" Reilly said.

"Yeah, son."

"I've got a few more of those duds that we took from the warehouse. At my home."

"That'll be helpful."

"And I've got a whole box of similar ones we took from the dumpster," James said.

"Great. I'll have an officer pick those up immediately."

The chief confirmed that they had been working with the EPA about the water situation, but according to the file in front of him, no other follow-up had been done.

"We'll be in touch with Jordan Powell, as well," said the Chief. "We'll find out where he had those duds tested and get to the bottom of this as quickly as possible."

Norah looked at Reilly, and he knew she wondered if Jordan would tell the chief about their Stelladaurs. Reilly shook his head, letting her know he was sure Jordan wouldn't say anything.

"We'll take it from here. This attack with the machete may be the very thing that puts all these pieces together," Chief Gunderson said, as he stood up from the chair behind his desk. "However, for the time being, and until we gather further evidence, you'll be under full police protection."

"Police protection?" Reilly blurted. "What does that mean exactly?"

"It means wherever you or your family members go for the next few days or so, an officer will escort you. There will be an officer at your home around the clock until I say otherwise. And one at the bakery, as well."

"Thank you, Chief," Reilly's mom said.

It was early evening when everything finally wrapped up at the station. Everyone was famished. Officer Blake, who was assigned the first shift as their escort and bodyguard, accompanied them to the only Sushi restaurant on the island to get some dinner before the fireworks show. The officer stood beside their table while they ate and then escorted them home.

Not bothering to change out of their formal clothes, Reilly and Norah walked across the backyard to sit on the grass overlooking the harbor to watch the fireworks. The officer moved to the edge of the deck railing so he could keep his eye on them.

"I don't think I told you, but … you really look great in that dress," Reilly said, trying not to sound too corny. "Actually, you look beautiful."

"Thank you. And thanks for being such a good sport about the whole tux thing. You look great, too." Norah reached for Reilly's hand. "We're supposed to be holding hands when we see the lotus flower, right?"

"Yeah. And then you hold your Stelladaur directly at it, right?"

"Apparently so."

She reached for the cord around her neck and pulled out her Stelladaur, glancing back at the officer to make sure he didn't see it. However, she knew the officer was far enough back that if he did see a bright light, he'd likely mistake it for a light from a boat in the harbor, or perhaps a reflection off the water.

"Reilly, guess what my Stelladaur did today?"

"What?"

"It saved your life."

Reilly waited for her explanation.

"When the machete was coming right at us and you pulled me down, I felt some kind of an energy field, a magnetic force, pulling the machete off its course. It was headed directly towards your heart, Reilly. I saw it all happening in slow motion. But my Stelladaur steered it away from you, just before it struck your chest, and redirected it above our heads." Norah turned to look directly at Reilly. "What do you think that means?"

Reilly paused to consider the possibilities before answering. "It could mean a few things. One, our Stelladaurs can be used in various ways to help others. Two, sometimes a Stelladaur can protect another's life—as well as our own, of course. And three, it protects someone even if the person isn't aware of it." Reilly put his arm around Norah and pulled her closer to him. "Maybe it means that when we're close to someone—like when they're really good friends or something—then one of them can use his or her own strength to help both of them, even if the other person isn't aware of it at that very moment."

"I like that," Norah whispered as she snuggled up to Reilly.

The fireworks began and they watched intently, waiting for the lotus flower to appear in the sky.

Chapter Twenty-five

Inevitable Change

T he finale was spectacular, with a steady stream of colorful explosions. Norah held her Stelladaur with her right hand while Reilly held the Fireglass in his left, ready to look through them both when the lotus flower emerged above. Reilly held the Fireglass in its fully extended position about six inches from his face. The brass device glistened with reflections of the fireworks while the rotating symbol of a Stelladaur accelerated on its surface faster and faster, until it was only a blur of light, whipping around the neck of the device. Norah held her Stelladaur in front of the Fireglass, touching the crystal on the tip of it. With their cheeks barely touching and their hands entwined, they held the devices in place, waiting and watching.

Suddenly, a mighty boom echoed across the harbor and the orange lotus flower burst into the sky. Reilly and Norah pressed together, looking through their devices. Emerging before them, a brilliant butterfly of orange lights filled the sky like a cosmic metamorphosis.

With the portal now open, the massive butterfly lifted Reilly and Norah from the grass and carried them through the lit sky. On the other side of the finale, everything changed.

"Welcome to Som," said a dwarf with rust-colored skin and fire opal eyes. He wore a felted tunic in various shades of orange. "I am called Kokumo. I help those who have already found their Stelladaur to understand and prepare for impending and inevitable change."

Reilly and Norah looked around. They stood on a white beach, with sand as fine as sugar, that stretched as far as they could see. The water looked like rolling flames from the reflection of the orange ball of light in the sky.

"Impending?" Reilly asked.

"Change occurs continuously for all. A change that will happen in the moment immediately following this moment is an impending change. Therefore, change is always impending," Kokumo said.

"And inevitable?" Norah asked.

"There are some things one can change. Some things one cannot. And some things change regardless."

Reilly looked out over the water. "Like the waves. They change continually but they do it on their own. I can't change them."

"When you experience enough change within yourself, you will understand the spirit of Water. Perhaps then you can change it, too, simply because you ask, and the Water welcomes the asking." Kokumo clapped his hands twice and spread them out to each side. The orange ball of light above and the waves turned a sea green color. He clapped again, and they turned purple. "These are changes that you can see. What about those you cannot see?"

"Like what's inside the water," Norah asked. "Or what it's made of?"

"Learning to welcome the changes you cannot see, and trusting they will bring you those which you can, is one of the keys of understanding never-ending change. The waves know this, and they do it. As does all of nature."

Reilly considered carefully what Kokumo had said. He knew this moment in Som was not about what he saw before him, but about what had been happening inside of himself for quite some time. Though he had no idea where his own Stelladaur was, Reilly knew he no longer needed to carry it around his neck.

"Soon after your return, you will both see much change. At first you may not welcome it. But remember, these changes are an opportunity to become like the waves. Ever growing. Ever moving. Yet inside, ever still."

Reilly felt a calmness fill him with courage, but he had one question for Kokumo.

"Will I still find my dad, even if I don't have my Stelladaur with me?"

"You do not need to see either of them to find them."

Kokumo clapped his hands again, twice. The Water turned a piercing azure blue, and the horizon changed to an endless rim of fire, whose flames danced and spun in the sky. It was the most exquisite sunset Reilly and Norah had ever seen. One of the dancing flames jumped right out of the sky, rolled into a ball and landed at their feet in the white sand, still burning. Directly above the fireball, multi-colored droplets rained down, extinguishing the flame. In its place a large fire opal rested on the sugary sand. The rain stopped.

"Pick up the fire opal and throw it as far as you can into the Water," Kokumo instructed. "When it lands in the Water you will see beautiful colored rings spreading continuously from the point where the opal penetrated. Run into the Water, and then jump over each ring until the center comes to you. There, dive into the Water and the red portal will open."

They thanked Kokumo, and Reilly picked up the fire opal. He threw it as far as he could. The gem skipped off the surface of the Water five times, emitting a tremendous spark each time it hit. Reilly reached for Norah's hand and they ran into the Water together. It was warm and shallow. They jumped and leaped over the colorful rings as each expanded outwards. Though they moved quickly, the rings continued to emerge from the point where the fire opal had landed.

"The rings will keep coming until we step over them without touching them," Reilly said. "But we need to wait for the rings to *come* to us." Reilly stopped, as did Norah. They stood still and watched the rings pass over them, just above their ankles. Standing on one foot, he added, "On the count of three, lift your right foot and wait for the next ring. Quickly jump over it but land in the same spot we are on. Let the rings come to us."

They tried it. Soon they had successfully jumped over nine rings without touching any of them. The center approached them, growing bigger with only three rings to go.

"I know the Water looks shallow now," Reilly said to Norah, "but it's not. As soon as the last ring reaches us, dive over it into the Water. Don't wait! Just go for it!" he said.

"I will."

Standing still, they waited for the last ring, an orange one, to come to them. When it was inches away, they bent their knees and dove into the portal. The colored rings that had spread across the water retracted, shrinking until they merged back into the center and followed Reilly and Norah into the portal.

Like two dolphins rising above the surface, Reilly and Norah emerged on a velvet mass of red sea-moss. They were completely dry. The water receded into a shallow beach of rubies.

Coming towards them on a path in the middle of the rubied sand, a young boy, less than half Reilly's age, approached. The boy wore a crimson wrap around his lower belly that hung to his knees. His hair was long and wavy, like Reilly's, but it was a soft reddish color. His black eyes were piercing, and he had a third eye in the center of his forehead—a brilliant ruby. Around his neck he wore a lei of exquisite red flowers. The boy walked onto the mound of moss and stood in front of Reilly and Norah.

"I am Aka-ula, meaning red reflection. This place is called Bozka, or Divine Gift."

The boy took the lei from around his neck, and another immediately appeared in its place. Aka-ula lifted his arms to Norah. She bent down so that he could garland her with the flowers. "Welcome," he said. As he removed the lei around his neck for Reilly, another appeared in its place.

"Whatever we give to another will always come back to us," Aka-ula said. "These flowers represent continual giving and receiving."

"Is that the Divine Gift of Bozka?" asked Reilly.

"The Divine Gift is love. Love is the most precious of all virtues. Without it, there would be no life. Many in your world have learned something of this love. Come and see."

Aka-ula led the way along the path from the red carpet of moss and through the rubies. "Look at this one." He pointed to a particular stone at their feet. Inside it, they saw the image of a nurse holding the hand of an elderly man; she was listening to him talk about his wife, who had passed on decades before. "And this one." It was a child sharing a cupcake from her lunch bag with a classmate. "And this one." A man in a grocery store checkout line handed the customer in front of him a ten-dollar bill to cover the cost of the items she wanted to purchase because she did not have enough money.

They looked into several more rubies, each showing gestures of kindness to a person or an animal.

"And this one," Aka-ula added. A woman smiled at a homeless man as she walked passed him.

"But she didn't give him anything," Norah said.

"She gave a smile," Reilly said.

"Yes," Aka-ula agreed. "Perhaps it was all she had to give. But Divine Gift never judges or condemns. It is always genuine, given freely, with no expectations."

Norah nodded her understanding.

Aka-ula picked up a ruby and held it in his cupped hand. "Many suffer in your world because no one gives them the Gift. Yet it is within every living thing to do so. When the Divine Gift is not honored in life, a Spell of Darkness descends, leaving only despair, misery and sorrow."

Reilly suddenly remembered Malie's story of the evil Gargoyle. *Only one thing can break the spell of all evil. Only love,* Eilam had said.

"Until your Earth feels true compassion from and towards those inhabiting it, it too, will suffer. And it will die …" Aka-ula lowered his eyes. "… and all living things on your Earth will cease to exist."

"Only love will break the spell, right?" Reilly asked.

"Yes. Every time a person extends love and forgiveness to another—no matter how insignificant they suppose it may be—the collective consciousness of the Earth is increased. A bit of the darkness is dispelled by the illuminated light of love. At that moment, all life on Earth is extended," said Aka-ula. "But the evil Spell of Darkness will only be permanently broken when the Divine Gift is realized by all."

Reilly and Norah looked out across the sea of rubies.

Reilly breathed in deeply and closed his eyes as he thought of those who had shown him kindness. "Red is the color of the Divine Gift," he said as he opened his eyes.

"Yes," said Aka-ula, "but it is also the color of hatred, war, revenge, blood and bitterness. Such contrast will always exist on your

Earth, without which there can be no power to choose. The choice of your heart determines which will prevail."

Aka-ula gave the ruby in his hand to Reilly. Then he picked up another one from the ground and placed it in Norah's hand. "Hold these to your heart and say out loud, *Divine Gift overcomes all.*"

Reilly and Norah faced each other, held the jewels to their hearts, and repeated the words in unison.

It was precisely the midnight hour when the last fireworks exploded across the sky—a burst of red flowers formed in a circle around a giant red heart. Reilly and Norah still held hands as the last flickers of light faded into the darkness. On Reilly's lap, he found one of the exquisite red flowers from the lei Aka-ula had placed around his neck. He picked up the flower and carefully tucked it behind Norah's ear. Her warm breath at his cheek mingled with a sweet floral scent and made him feel dizzy with desire to hold her to him. He lowered his hand from her ear and slid his fingers gently down her shoulder and upper arm. Then he pulled her to him, his hands tenderly sculpting her neck, and slowly leaned forward to meet her lips.

"Where did you kids go?" Officer Blake bellowed, interrupting the moment—and destroying the perfect first kiss before it actually *was* a kiss. Norah jumped and backed away from Reilly, who dropped his hands, but kept his eyes on Norah. "Somewhere in the middle of the finale," the officer continued, "... well, one second you were here, and then you were gone."

"Uh, the fireworks were awfully bright this year ... I mean ... that was quite a finale and all. The lights must have temporarily, uh, blinded you, or something," Norah said, looking at the officer.

Reilly shook his head to snap out of the euphoric moment that had ended too soon. "Yeah, as you can see, we're right here," he sighed.

"Uh-huh. Well, it's time to take Norah home. It's been a long day and I suggest everyone get some sleep," Blake said.

Reilly escorted Norah to the police car parked in front of the house. Blake walked behind them.

"I'll see you tomorrow. The library doesn't open until noon on Sundays," Reilly said. "We'll pick you up at 10:30."

"Sounds good." Norah gave Reilly a quick hug. "I'll see you then."

As he walked back towards his house, Reilly put his hands in the pockets of his sweatshirt. His fingers touched something round and hard, the size of a small pebble, and immediately he knew what it was. He smiled as he pulled a ruby from his pocket.

That night, Tuma slept at the foot of Reilly's bed, as usual, but Reilly did *not* dream of dark tunnels and hooded creatures. He dreamed of lotus flowers … rubies … and kisses.

Chapter Twenty-six

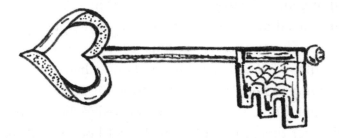

Links

R eilly woke early the next morning, wishing he was still dreaming. He wanted to zip through a portal back in time, so he could replay the night before—precisely at midnight. This time, *without* Blake interrupting!

Instead, he showered and dressed quickly. In one pocket of his jeans he stashed the ruby. In the other he tucked the Fireglass. At his side, he looped the sheath holding his knife to his belt.

Chantal was still sleeping and his mom was at the bakery. He couldn't find the bodyguard anywhere.

Reilly had an hour before they needed to pick up Norah, so he went for a morning kayak ride with Tuma. The water was unusually still, like glass. He dipped the paddle through the water with precision, as if threading a needle. A few geese honked overhead and numerous birds twittered repeating melodies. Music to Reilly's ears. He paddled slowly and pulled up to Eilam's little shack. He stepped out of the kayak, wondering why Eilam wasn't standing in the doorway to greet them as he usually did. Tuma jumped aboard and waited for Reilly to open the door.

"Eilam?"

It took only a single sweep of the place to see that Eilam was not there. Reilly checked the outside perimeter of the hut. Eilam's kayak was gone. Reilly went back inside for a closer look and on the table, found a note.

Dear Reilly,

I am sorry I was not able to see you in the parade. I have left Nebo to watch over you and trust he will be there when you need him. Of course, Tuma, as well. Please take care of the kayak hut in my absence. Perhaps James will be able to assist you. Remember everything you have experienced through the portals of The Arc of Color. Always be willing to share your knowledge to help others find the light that shines from their own Star Door. Remember that a person's greatest desire changes as his vision, understanding and imagination expand. Keep your heart open through this process. And Reilly, know that your Stelladaur will always be within you.

Eilam

Reilly reread the note. He looked at Tuma, but his dog was silent. "Why wouldn't he say good bye?"

Reilly had known Eilam his entire life, and he trusted him. But this turn of events was entirely unexpected. Had he been so enthralled—distracted even—by Norah that he hadn't caught any clues Eilam may have given about the change that was coming?

Or was the whole situation with Travis taking a twisted toll on his intuitive nature, to the point that he didn't have even an inkling of Eilam's impending departure?

Reilly read the note a third time; then he folded it carefully and put it in his pocket next to the ruby. He sat at the table, in Eilam's chair, and felt a wave of abandonment seep through the cracks in the walls. Too stunned to move, he stared out the opened window at the ripples in the harbor, imagining them to be tidal waves threatening his destruction.

Just then, the door blew open. A gust of wind whooshed past Reilly and out the window, spreading over the water and around the small abode in huge rings. Blinking to clear the dust from his eyes, he spotted Nebo swooping down and gliding just above the water past the marina. He ran to the door and waved, still filled with sadness, as the bird circled above the trees and disappeared into the distance.

But it was enough. Reilly decided to put his thoughts of Eilam—and why his friend would desert him when so many unanswered questions remained—aside.

Reilly and Tuma returned home and then left with Chantal to pick up Norah. Arriving at the summer cottage, Reilly immediately sensed that something was wrong. He knocked, but no one answered. He knocked again more loudly. Tuma barked. Still, no answer. He tried the knob and opened the door.

"Hello?" Reilly called. "Hello? Norah?"

"Maybe they're around the back," Chantal said.

"I don't think so," Reilly said, "but let's take a look."

Seeing no one in the backyard, he scanned the beach. No one was taking a Sunday stroll. Reilly opened the patio door and called for Norah. Still, no answer.

"Was she going to meet us on the boat?" Chantal asked. "Maybe she went to breakfast with her uncle and she'll meet us on the boat."

"She would have called. Or left a note. Or something!" he said. "Let's look inside."

The kitchen and living room showed no signs of anyone even having been there. The study looked as if it had been locked up since last summer. Both bedrooms were cleared out, and there was nothing in the closets. The dressers were empty.

Not only was Norah not there now, but it looked as if she had *never* been. More than ever, Reilly wished he had gone back in time and changed whatever had happened so it would somehow be different now. He shuddered at the familiar thought. Just then he remembered what Kokumo had told him and Norah the night before: *There are some things one can change. Some things one cannot. And some things change regardless.* For some inexplicable reason, Reilly knew this was a change that had to happen. But his heart ached.

Reilly opened the front door of the cottage to leave and looked down. There, on the threshold, lay the exquisite red flower he had put behind Norah's ear at midnight. He was sure the flower wasn't there when he arrived and called Norah's name. Or had he just missed it?

He picked up the flower. It was perfect. Tuma barked and looked directly at Reilly.

"I'm sorry," Chantal said.

Reilly smelled the flower deeply and then lowered it to his side. Back in the jeep, he put it on the dashboard and sat in silence until they pulled up in front of James's apartment.

"Just honk," Reilly said. "We need to make that boat." Chantal honked the horn. She waited and honked again. The third time she pressed the palm of her hand on the horn for a few seconds.

"What's taking him so long?" Chantal fretted. "We're going to miss the boat."

Reilly glanced at the flower on the dashboard. "We'll make it," he assured her, pointing out the window. "Here he comes."

Reilly took the red flower from the dashboard and crawled over the seat to sit in back with Tuma. James jumped into the front.

"Sorry to keep you waiting. Have you been listening to the news?"

"No! What's going on?" Chantal pulled on to the street.

"The police checked out the warehouse last night. Travis Jackson was arrested around midnight."

"No way!" Chantal squealed.

"And Martino Gustalini was charged with smuggling drugs from South America. He was arrested this morning about 6:00."

"And Norah?" Reilly asked.

"The report stated a minor was taken into protective custody early this morning and would be returning to Gustalini's home state of Illinois." James shifted to look at Reilly. "With her father in prison and now her uncle in jail, too, my guess is Norah will be placed in foster care."

Reilly reached for Tuma and put his arm around the dog's neck. He stroked her with one hand and stared at the red flower in his other one. He was glad that Chantal and James didn't say anything else.

After a few minutes, he cleared the lump in his throat and put the flower in his sweatshirt pocket. "Let's make that boat. We need to get to the library."

Their car was the last one on the ferry. Reilly sat quietly on the ride to the mainland, stroking Tuma and sorting things out in his mind. As they pulled into a parking spot on campus, he finally spoke.

"You brought the key with you, right?"

"Of course," James said, taking the key from his shirt pocket.

"May I see it?"

James handed Reilly the key as they stepped out of the jeep. Reilly ran his finger over the inlaid ivory-colored abalone. Holding it up to the sunlight, it looked like iridescent stained glass.

"Your dad told your mom that this key would be the link to 'understanding the connections to eternity,' right?" said Reilly.

"Yeah, I think that's exactly how she said it."

"Link? … Link." Reilly repeated the word, trying to find its truest meaning as he looked at the key. They approached Red Square, a giant redbrick courtyard on the campus in the center of several old university buildings. Reilly gasped as the Suzzallo Library—respectfully named the Soul of the University—came into view. It was a massive structure of cast stone and brick, with Gothic-inspired statues, terra cotta arches and buttresses, and monumental stained glass windows—a cathedral that commanded reverence.

"Look at those windows … at the very top," James said, pointing as they walked. "See the ones that look like a six-petal flower? And the red star in the middle of each one of them? It looks just like two of the petroglyph symbols."

Reilly took a photo from his shirt pocket, and they stopped in the center of Red Square to compare the petroglyph image with the design in the window.

"You're right," Chantal said. "That's amazing!"

Reilly gazed up at the towering building, looking carefully at the detailed carving in the crest-shaped stones at the top of every column. Each had an inspiring message related to science, math, history, philosophy or other knowledge, most inscribed in Latin and many with dates carved at the bottom.

Reilly peered at three stone statues above the main doors: an ancient Greek god whose body was bare except for a cloth draped around his groin area, a winged angel looking upward and a bearded sage who reminded him of Eilam. Reilly wondered what stories they would tell if they could speak.

Walking closer, he noticed more details of the arches. Each stained glass window was divided in half by a vertical stone column, creating two more narrow windows; there were twenty-two in all. Halfway up each one were circular windows displaying different symbols: a sunburst, a lobster, a shell, a bell, a bird, a fish, something similar to a yin-yang symbol and others. Reilly looked at them more carefully.

Where is the symbol of a key?

As he walked under the arch that framed the massive doorway, he did not see the three statues shift on their posts and follow him with their gaze.

The expansive stone foyer was empty except for a girl sitting behind the information desk. She looked up and smiled but said nothing.

"She must not have noticed Tuma," Chantal whispered, looking down at the dog.

"I don't think anyone will notice her," Reilly added.

Just then a student walked out of the restroom and right past the dog without acknowledging her at all. "See," Reilly added. "Not only can Tuma speak and appear in a hologram, but she can be invisible, too."

Two sweeping stone staircases spiraled up at the end of the main foyer, and they took the one to the right. As each step echoed off the walls and the distant ceiling, Reilly took a moment to gaze up. Continuing on, he silently counted the steps: thirty-nine, forty, forty-one. He stepped on the top landing and turned to look at a row of floor-to-ceiling windows that replicated the exterior windows on the west side. They took a few steps and spotted, above the left doorway into the reading room, a round stained glass window. Inside the window was the symbol of two crisscrossed keys, both exactly like the one Reilly held in his hand.

"There it is, James!" Reilly whispered. The words reverberated off the steps.

Reilly pointed to the window and stared. Chantal gasped. James took the key from Reilly's hand and held it up to compare it to the one twenty feet up. "That's it! Exactly the same key!"

"But why are there two?" Chantal wondered.

Reilly looked at the other round window above the doorway. It was designed to look like a balance scale held up by chain links. "If the key will help us understand the connections to eternity, one of the links on the chain of the scale must be related to the hearts." He studied the symbols, looking back and forth between the two windows. "Love. Love keeps all opposites in balance. Love *is* the key."

"What do you mean, Reilly?" his sister asked.

"It's the only thing that will break the spell," Reilly answered with a smile.

"What spell?" asked James.

"The spell of doubt, despair, discouragement—all the destruction that torments our Earth."

"And this key will do all that?" James asked skeptically, waving the key at Reilly.

"No, it's only an object. But it's leading us to a greater understanding of that love, just like a Stelladaur. A Stelladaur is really only a stone. It's rare, but what makes it so precious is the power generated from the love of the one it belongs to. Love is a power stronger than all other virtues."

Chantal and James looked at each other, perplexed. Their creased foreheads told Reilly they didn't really get it.

"Somewhere in this library there's another link between here—this moment and place—and eternity. And they are linked by love."

Reverently, Reilly stepped into the reading room and stood still. Sunlight penetrated through the colorful windows. He inhaled deep and long. The smell of exotic wood, oiled and polished, and of fine leather—as intoxicating as the salty ocean air he breathed every morning—filled his lungs.

To him the room was an omniscient sanctuary with voluminous bits of knowledge and wisdom waiting to be devoured. A feeling of magnificence filled his soul. He knew an impending and indescribable change was occurring. No one spoke.

He walked slowly to the right, down the center of the cathedral room. Only Reilly, Chantal, James and Tuma were in the room. They passed rows of long tables on both sides of the room. Reilly noted the intricate carvings of fruit, flowers and leaves along the top of the bookshelves lining the entire length of the room on both sides. Twenty-two bronze and gold-lighted chandeliers hung from the domed ceiling, painted in a myriad of designs. Another chandelier was suspended in front of each window on the east and west ends of the room, where a commanding display of high windows circled an enormous alcove. Both alcoves were lined with fourteen solid wood doors, intricately carved, giving the curved wall a paneled façade.

In the center of the alcoves was a lighted globe, secured on long chains and dangling in the air at an angle, as if spinning. Each globe was enclosed in a bronze filigree ring such that they appeared to be suspended in the rings. Bronze Zodiac signs, symbols of nature and Greek mythological creatures had been crafted around the rings.

They approached a low wooden wall with a half-door that led into the alcove. Reilly noticed an inscription carved in stone above the door. He read it aloud in a whisper.

"Good books are a priceless possession. They reveal the minds of creative man and enrich life with fine experience."

"Very inspiring," Chantal whispered.

"I've been in this library dozens of times, but I never noticed that before," James added, staring at the inscription.

"There's always more to see when a person looks up," Reilly said. James nodded in agreement.

Reilly craned his neck to see as far up as possible. The domed ceiling was built of beams positioned in the shape of a half star. Reilly suspected the ceiling of the alcove at the other end of the room would reveal the other half. He turned to view the entire length of the room and reached to stroke Tuma who was still beside him.

"Let's take a closer look at the window with the key symbols," he said. He and Tuma walked towards the middle of the room and stopped precisely in the center. They turned to face the stained glass key above the entrance.

"May I have the key?" he asked James.

James nodded and handed the key back to Reilly. Reilly held it out in front of him, glancing back and forth at the window. He turned the key upside down and held it by the abalone end, then looked through the inverted heart as if he were looking through a magnifying glass. He moved the glass up gradually at a higher angle until the symbol of the crisscrossed keys came into view. Extending it further from his body, but still looking through the inverted heart, he positioned it directly at the point where the keys on the window intersected.

Immediately a beam of sunlight seared through the window, through the inverted heart in Reilly's hand and straight behind him to land at a spot on the bookshelf. Tuma's silver eyes glistened like diamonds. Reilly turned to face the beam, holding the key out from his body to allow the light to penetrate it. He and Tuma followed the stream of light towards the bookshelf. Chantal and James walked slowly behind them, their eyes transfixed on the spot of light.

Reilly stepped closer to the bookshelf, holding the key in position.

"Move in and take a closer look," he said to Chantal and James.

They stepped from behind Reilly, each on one side of the beam of light, and approached the shelf. The light cast a heart-shaped glow that illuminated on the spine of a brown leather tome. James reached for the book and pulled it from the shelf.

He gasped as light poured out from the space on the shelf. He handed the book to Reilly and reached his hand into the empty slot. His eyes grew wide as he slowly pulled out something that had been tucked between the books.

"A Stelladaur!" James whispered.

"It is!" Reilly said.

"Wow!" Chantal stepped up to take a closer look.

"Unbelievable!" James said.

"Actually, quite believable," Reilly laughed. "And look." He pointed to the space where James had found the Stelladaur. A bright light still shone from the shelf. Chantal peeked into the space and drew in her breath quickly. Then she reached in and another brilliant Stelladaur emerged.

"Extraordinary!" Chantal said.

"Quite," Reilly agreed.

Both Stelladaurs were attached to the same sort of golden cord as Reilly's.

"Is this yours?" Chantal asked Reilly, offering the Stelladaur.

"No, it's yours, Chan. Obviously James isn't the only one who's been looking for a Stelladaur. And obviously you're both ready."

"Ready?" James and Chantal said together.

"To discover your greatest desire."

As Reilly said the words *greatest desire*, he felt a surge of energy zap him gently from the book in his hand. The book had no title. He opened it to the first page and read the hand-written words out loud: "*Finding Tir Na Nog* by Charlotte Louise McKinley."

"Tir Na Nog? *The* Tir Na Nog?" Chantal asked. "Where Great Grandpa Alistair traveled?"

"It must be." Reilly flipped through the pages.

"Charlotte Louise McKinley? That name is so familiar," James muttered.

"That's exactly what I was thinking," said Chantal. "I'm quite sure Great Grandpa's wife was a McKinley. I vaguely remember doing a family heritage project my junior year of high school. I had to draw up a family tree. A lot of our ancestors on Dad's side were McKinleys." She held her Stelladaur in one hand and touched the corner of the book with her other.

"That's too weird," James replied.

"What is?" Chantal asked, still looking at her Stelladaur.

"We must be distant cousins or something. Charlotte Louise McKinley was *my* third-great grandmother."

"You're kidding?"

"It's true. My dad's older sister, my Aunt Charlotte, was named after her. I don't know exactly *why* she was named after Charlotte Louise McKinley, except that my grandma remembered meeting her when she was a small child. She was fascinated by her. Grandma used to say she was so enamored with the woman's stories of adventures to magical places that she wanted to name her first daughter after her, in the hope that she would inherit some degree of imagination. So she did."

Chantal shook her head in amazement.

Reilly continued to turn the hand-written pages. Then a piece of paper, folded in half with a stiff crease, fell out and drifted to the reading room floor. Reilly picked it up carefully. Written on parchment paper in calligraphic ink was a letter.

Reilly imagined Charlotte Louise McKinley's voice echoing from the past as he read aloud:

May 1908

My Dear One,

I imagine you with soft cheeks, perhaps dimpled like your father's, a bundle of yellow curls and bright emerald eyes the color of the hills here in coastal Ireland. Perhaps it is silly to imagine such things. However, a young mother-to-be spends many hours wondering . . . waiting . . . wishing. She wonders who the child she carries will be. She waits for the arrival with great anticipation and a hint of trepidation. She wishes for her child all the goodness of life. Remember, my little one, goodness is abundant. It is all around you. And if you look with imagination, you will find endless delight. This treasured book is filled with stories of such delight, a collection of adventures my great grandmother had in a magical place called Tir Na Nog. Each time I read it, I, too, go to that place of magic, if only in my imagination. Soon we shall spend countless hours reading it together. Finally, my love for you is endless.

Momma

Reilly blinked. His heart pounded. He breathed deeply and slowly before he replaced the letter in the book. He read the very first sentence of the first chapter: "Books are To be read wIth imaG-ination, that theiR wisdom may iNterpret events ANd their ideals inspire wOrthy action."

"Another profound quote." Chantal placed her Stelladaur around her neck.

Reilly read it again silently. "It is." He paused. "But how these letters are written is more profound."

Chantal and James peered over Reilly's shoulder while he pointed at the formation of some words. "Look at the capitalized letters: B-T-I-G-R-N-A-N-O."

"It doesn't spell anything," James said.

"Look more closely." Reilly pointed at the page as James and Chantal leaned in for a closer look.

"Of course, the first letter in a sentence would be capitalized," Chantal reasoned. "But even if you disregard the B, it still doesn't spell anything."

"True. But why do you think the G is written in bolder ink?" Reilly asked, trying to get them to solve the puzzle he had figured out in a moment.

"Maybe it's the first letter? No, G-T isn't the start of any word I know of," James concluded.

"Maybe it's the last letter," Chantal said. Her eyes lit up and she clapped her hands as she read the letters out loud: T-I-R-N-A-N-O-G. It spells Tir Na Nog! That's so cool!" She jumped, startled by the echo of her voice in the room.

"Charlotte Louise McKinley is telling us to use *this* book and *this* message to actually find Tir Na Nog—the place. She says in the letter that the book is filled with adventures inspired by imagination. And always to look with imagination. We need to do that here, now, in this reading room." Reilly's voice was filled with fervor.

He and Tuma started to look around the room, then slowly walked towards the alcove at the south end.

James began to read the titles of a few books on a high shelf. Chantal noticed some drawers at the bottom of the same shelves and began to pull the handles. None of them opened. James and Chantal walked to the opposite side of the room where a large door wrapped in leather beckoned them.

The door was in the middle of glass-cased bookshelves with wooden drawers on the bottom half. The entire section of wall resembled a walk-in closet, with dark picture window panes.

Chantal pressed her nose to the glass and peered through. "That's odd. There are no books on those shelves." The closet was filled with empty shelves, and not a single book. She stepped over to the door and tried to turn the knob. She pushed and pulled on the door.

"Darn, it's locked." She peered through a small window on the door. "Nothing here, either," she mumbled, disappointed.

"Let's try the drawers," James suggested. They pulled the handles of all the drawers, sixteen on each side of the door. None of them budged. James reached for the Stelladaur around his neck and touched it. "Nothing is opening up."

"Try your key!" Chantal said with renewed enthusiasm.

James's face lit up at the suggestion. "Reilly has it!"

They turned and saw Reilly standing on a table in the center of the south alcove. He was holding the key up and looking through it again as if it were a magnifying glass. He was so focused that he did not notice Chantal and James approach. Reilly positioned the heart of the key under the globe above his head. Suddenly, brilliant streams of light shot from six red stars at the top of the towering stained glass windows on the upper walls of the alcove. The beams of light converged on a flat disk that hung from the bottom of the iron ring around the globe. Cut out in the center of the ring was an outline of an eagle in flight. The six beams of light converged through the disk at once, merged into one beam and projected straight through the heart of the key in Reilly's hand. The light continued to the wall and lit up the stone letter T.

James and Chantal looked quickly at the message carved in the stone. It was the same sentence that Reilly had just read in Charlotte's book.

James read it out loud again. "Books are to be read with imagination that their wisdom may interpret events and their ideals inspire worthy action."

Etched by flames, one by one in succession, each lower case letter of the words "Tir Na Nog" was transformed to a capital letter. By the time James finished reading the quote, the already capitalized and bold G was lit with fire.

Then, without warning, a burst of multi-colored lights ricocheted off the windows—a laser show unlike anything they had ever seen. Though the explosion of lights streaked across the room from every direction, it did not create a booming sound. Instead, a musical masterpiece filled the room. Reilly closed his eyes to listen to the exquisite melody.

"It's my song," Reilly whispered without opening his eyes.

"What did he say?" Chantal nearly shouted at James so he could hear her above the music.

"I think he said 'It's my song.'"

Reilly opened his eyes and watched as the lights extended through the heart and burned into the stone until the entire phrase, *Tir Na Nog*, was illumined in fire against the grey stone.

Then the music changed and a completely new movement began. String instruments carried the melody, but a female vocalist echoed a haunting Celtic descant. The multi-colored beams of light disappeared and the flames on the letters diminished to amber embers, one at a time. Then each letter began to turn to solid gold. The room darkened, as if the clouds outside had covered the sun. But the gold letters shone a glistening light in the alcove.

Strangely hypnotized by the music, Reilly stepped down from the table. Tuma was at his side, and Reilly smiled broadly while he pet his dog.

"Reilly? Are you all right?" Chantal asked.

"It's my song," he said, watching the embers on the last few letters change to gold. "It was written just for me the day my Star Door opened. That's when I first heard it. And I heard it again when I found my Stelladaur on *The Ark*."

The gold letters cast a shadowy beam of light on the paneled door in the center of the wall in the lower half of the alcove.

Tuma barked. The sound echoed loudly throughout the great hall and blended perfectly with the music. Reilly turned and looked deeply into Tuma's glistening eyes. At that moment, Reilly knew he could *see the everlasting and perceive the door*, just as Eilam had said the dog would help him to do.

"I need to go—before my song ends," Reilly declared. He and Tuma walked towards the shadowy beam. Chantal and James looked at each other, perplexed.

Nothing about that moment perplexed Reilly. He did, after all, see things quite differently from most. And for the first time since his father had died, the pieces fit together perfectly.

Reilly moved to the paneled door and put the key in the lock. Turning it to the right until he heard a click, he released his grip from the key, turned the handle and slowly pushed the door open.

Together, he and Tuma walked through the portal to Tir Na Nog.

Stelladaur

Book Two

Fading Heart

Chapter One

Vantage Post

eilly tried to move but the weight of the beam pressing on his thigh and across his chest made it nearly impossible. Inhaling was difficult. A searing pain in his upper left leg intensified with each shallow breath. The euphoric melody he heard as he went through the portal in the reading room only moments before had vanished. Instead, the screeching and screaming of people running past him sounded like familiar haunting wails—though he didn't know why—and made him shudder from the neck up. Thunderous cracking sounds as great wooden beams crashed to the ground made him wish he could jump to his feet and run. But he could only cover his ears in an attempt to keep the cacophony from breaking his eardrums. His nose twitched from a pungent smell—thick and spicy—that added to the queasy feeling in his gut. It wasn't the invigorating aroma of leather, plank floors and oiled hardwood in the old library. Reilly wondered if he had tripped going through the portal and banged his head. Or maybe he hadn't made it through at all. Was the paneled door he had stepped through just the entrance to a large storage closet? Did a massive earthquake hit at that moment? Flinching, he twisted slightly as another beam crashed to the ground only feet away. He grunted as he pulled himself up on his elbows, and he felt the wood slide down his chest a few inches. He strained to lift it off his legs, but it barely budged, and he fell back down in pain.

"It's coming down! We're going to die!" someone yelled.

"No!" another protested. "Run!"

Turning in the direction of the voices, Reilly saw a throng of people racing towards him, but they passed by as if he didn't exist.

"Hey! Somebody help!" he shouted. But no one seemed to hear him above the clamoring sounds of the shaking earth and falling debris.

Blinking to clear his blurred vision, Reilly spotted a clump of strange red mushrooms poking up from a cluster of matted ferns. Again, he strained to lift himself up on his elbows, despite the pain, and gripped the beam lying across his legs to support his upper body. His fingers slipped on the damp, mossy wood and he realized it was not a beam but a large tree branch. Panicking, and now fully aware that he was neither in the old library nor in the portal, he called out for his dog.

"Tuma! Tuma, where are you?" The albino dog that had mysteriously come to Reilly earlier in the summer, and at the worst time in his life, was nowhere to be seen.

Another thick branch crashed down, landing crisscross over the one on his leg. Then it rolled off, causing the one that pinned him to the ground to scrape down to his shin with a mighty force. He screamed in pain but barely heard himself above the rumble and violent shaking.

Slowly, Reilly sat up, relieved to be able to do so, and he breathed more deeply. Blood seeped through his torn pant leg and stained the fabric. Pulling it back, he saw the culprit—a piece of wood piercing his thigh like a giant sliver. He yanked it out and yelled even louder. As the blood began to gush a strange odor permeated his nostrils, and he covered his mouth to keep from retching. Feeling dizzy, he hung his head to his chest, letting his tangled hair cover his eyes. It was difficult to breathe again, and he couldn't tell if the reeling motion came from inside his body or from the moving ground. Still trapped at the ankle, he fell back again and closed his eyes.

It's so much easier to close my eyes. Everything seems quieter and more still this way.... Where's Tuma? She was with me when I left Chantal and James in the reading room and when I walked through the portal.

Reilly opened his eyes again and scanned his surroundings. Massive branches continued to fall to the ground. If Tir Na Nog was anything like what he had imagined, this was not that place. He felt his eyeballs retreat into their sockets.

It was supposed to be a beautiful place. I thought my dad would be here.

His eyes rolled forward again and he watched the blood on his leg continue to ooze. It was difficult for him to know if he was thinking clearly, not only because he had no idea where he was, but also because he wasn't sure if he was alive.

Can I think if I'm dead? Can I bleed?... I'll just lie here—in my kayak—and glide across Eagle Harbor. I love the gentle bobbing of the vessel as the ripples of water dance around me. I'll stop paddling and breathe in the salty air for a moment.... The nausea will subside....

I think I see an otter poking his head above the surface of the water
… and diving back under, humping his little back playfully. I'll just
paddle gently until I reach Eilam's Kayak Hut.… Ah, there it is.… I
don't see Eilam, but that is not unusual at mid-morning. Eilam has
been my best friend … for as long as I can remember. He has been a
part of our family since before I was born. Most people in our island
town think Eilam is a crazy old man. They don't know he doesn't
even have an age. He's from another place in a completely different
dimension from the Pacific Northwest. Eilam knows about portals,
Tir Na Nog, talking trees and where people go after they die—and
how they ought to live before they die. But he doesn't talk all that
much. He mostly listens, and that has the weird effect of helping me
figure things out.…

Tuma showed up at the kayak hut one day after my dad drowned
in the sailing accident, and Eilam said it was my dad who sent her
to me. I don't really know where my dad is. After sixteen years of liv-
ing on Earth, you'd think a person ought to know something about
where people go after they die. But if someone's close friend or rela-
tion has never died, it might not consume his thoughts the way it
does mine.… Ah, I have reached the dock of the hut. I'll get out and
secure my kayak.…

The hut seems still … strangely . At this time of day, there's only
one other place Eilam could be—the bakery in town … just down the
ramp and over the hill …

None of the vehicles are moving. There are only empty cars, some
deserted in the middle of the main road. The silence feels peculiar …
uncomfortable. People are standing in the bank and the barbershop
and the drugstore, but … There it is! I see the bakery ahead …

The entrance looks the same as always … but the brass bell above
the doorframe sounds eerie. Why does no one glance at me as I walk
in? They look like wax statues … with perfectly painted expressionless
faces. I hear the regular clap of the door shutting behind me … but
suddenly it sounds like an explosion of firecrackers is reverberating

off the walls. I'll walk to the back room … Oh, my! A mannequin figure is pouring coffee from a pitcher to a mug, and the liquid has stopped in mid-flow, like a frozen black waterfall.

I push open the swinging kitchen door.

"Mom?"

No answer. I'm the only one in the room. I feel relieved that my mom isn't in this bad dream. She's been dealing with her own nightmares lately—there is no need for her to be in mine.

Eilam is nowhere to be seen in the bakery.

The brass bell sounds eerie again, as the door closes behind me. I don't see Eilam on the street … I must get back to his kayak hut …

After the accident, I never wanted to take out the sailboat or my kayak again. But that changed when I found my Stelladaur … and then the portals … This place feels even stranger than before …

I've got to get out of here! Now! My only escape is the water … in my kayak … I push hard against the dock with my paddle … and drift out into the harbor.…

Reilly opened his eyes wide.

"What was the last portal?" he blurted, as if he was answering the final question on Jeopardy.

Something warm and wet touched his lips.

"Shhh. Drink this." A girl pressed a cup to his mouth. "Quickly, there isn't much time." She held the back of his neck and poured the warm liquid between his parted lips.

"Uh …" Reilly muttered, but he did as she instructed. The clear liquid trickled down his throat like a thick cough suppressant, leaving a salty black licorice taste on his tongue.

"Good," she smiled. "Now, can you get up?" She pulled at his arm without waiting for a response.

Reilly looked down at the gash in his leg. He was no longer pinned to the ground. Since the girl was the only person who had acknowledged he was there, he played along. "Yeah, I think so." The pain had subsided into a dull throb. As he struggled to stand, he clicked his tongue with the lingering taste of licorice. "Am I dead?"

"Not yet." She almost laughed. "But we will be if we don't hurry! Come with me!" She grabbed his hand and they moved to go. Reilly limped for a few feet, and suddenly his legs regained their full strength. "Keep your eyes open for more falling branches and be ready to jump over large limbs," the girl warned.

She led the way as they ran. The forest looked like it had been hit by a tornado. Hurdling over debris Reilly became aware that the thunderous noises had quieted to a soft rumble and the ground beneath his feet had become stable. Within a few minutes, they reached a giant willow tree.

The girl released her tight grip on Reilly's hand and pushed her fingers against the trunk of the willow.

"Our elevator was originally designed to hold five but it's smaller now, so it's a tight fit." The trunk gave way to a camouflaged door and they stepped inside. "I saw you from our Vantage Post and figured you must be new to the Great Forest. I mean … well, it was obvious the way you somersaulted right in front of that huge falling tree. Were you *trying* to get yourself killed?"

"No … I, uh, I just came through the closet door at the library," he said, shaking his head.

"The Library?" she whispered. "How did you escape without being captured?" She pushed a brass button on the elevator control panel and they ascended with a gust of air whooshing through the cracks in the wooden walls. "We've got to hide you before they find out you're here, or my whole family will be in danger," she whispered more softly.

"I'm sorry. I didn't know—"

"Shhh!" She interrupted, her silver eyes glaring at him. "They may already have seen you coming, and besides, our elevator has been synched!"

They rode in silence for half a minute, long enough for Reilly to assess his surroundings. The walls of the hollow trunk were lined with rough wood planks. There were big gaps between the planks and splintered wood protruded in some spots. The elevator rose so fast that everything beyond the cracks was a blur. Reilly glanced up to see that the ceiling, covered with dripping moss, was crawling with insects, bugs and worms. He stepped closer to the girl, wondering what creatures lived under the dirt floor beneath them.

The elevator lurched to a stop and their feet sank into the soft floor, leaving footprints as they stepped out. Reilly followed the girl down a rough, narrow wooden hallway lined with high sunlit windows. As they approached another door, he saw a green woodpecker perched just above the doorknob.

"Katell, this man escaped from the Library," the girl said to the bird. "I must get him inside quickly."

Man? I'm just a kid! Reilly thought.

"Stalwart 59," the girl commanded. The bird uttered a shrill staccato sound and flapped its wings as it gripped its claws to the perch.

Katell turned to face the door. After hammering a series of long-short-long pecks with its beak, the door opened.

Reilly and the girl entered and walked up a spiral staircase made of twisted tree branches and a chartreuse wooden handrail as smooth as polished jade. When they reached the landing, the space opened up to a gathering room with neatly arranged furniture: chairs, a couch, a piano and end tables in a cozy arrangement on top of a colorful wool rug. Paintings hung on the walls—pictures of the sea and coastal cliffs—and for a moment it reminded Reilly of home.

"Please be seated," the girl said. "I'll find my mother." She flipped her long, white-blonde hair over her shoulders as she left him alone.

Reilly sat down on the couch and scanned the room. Leaves draped the high ceilings, ivy framed the windows, and oddly shaped doorways made of intertwined branches dispelled any question in Reilly's mind about where the elevator had stopped. He was sitting in a very large tree house.

"Welcome to our home." The woman rolled her *r* and tightened her vowels in a strong Irish accent.

Reilly turned and rose to his feet. The mother looked like the girl's twin but with shorter hair and a few wrinkles curved around the corners of her mouth.

"My name is Brigid," the woman said with a warm smile. "My daughter, Lottie, tells me you have escaped from the Library. Please, sit down."

Brigid sat next to Reilly on the couch and Lottie took the nearest chair.

"Aye, you must have had quite a fright," Brigid said, taking Reilly's hands in hers. "You are safe here, at least for now."

Her hands felt warm and firm, and Reilly didn't resist her holding them. But his mouth had the stuffed-with-cotton feeling he'd felt when his father died and he couldn't find the words to make sense of it.

"Uh ... I ..."

"Take a deep breath, lad. You will be just fine with us, at least for now." Brigid patted Reilly's hand repeatedly. "Why don't you start with your name?"

He took her advice and breathed in slowly and deeply, then exhaled long and loud.

"My name is Reilly. Reilly McNamara." The girl looked at her mother with wide eyes, but Brigid remained focused on him without the slightest change in expression. "I really have no idea where I am, or how I got here."

"How did you escape after the Deceptors began to torture you with their lies?" Lottie asked.

"Deceptors? What's a Deceptor?"

"Oh, dearie me," Brigid said, shaking her head and patting Reilly's hand more quickly. "This is worse than I thought. They have completely erased their identity from his mind."

"No one has erased anything from my mind!" Reilly declared and pulled his hand away. "The portal was supposed to take me to Tir Na Nog. Am I in Tir Na Nog?"

Brigid turned and looked at her daughter. They both sighed.

"No, my dear, you are in Ireland," the woman said. "Tir Na Nog is but an ancient legend. Though we like to believe it exists, no one knows for sure that it does."

Reilly scowled.

"But some of the other Stalwarts have had experiences with portals," Lottie said. Reilly assumed she meant to sound encouraging, but then her voice lowered. "Our family has not been so lucky."

Still, nothing made sense to Reilly, but he told them he lived near Seattle.

"Aye, the coastal settlement discovered by a European explorer—a George Vancouver, was it? He first visited just before the turn of the century." Brigid leaned in a bit closer. "That is a very long way to travel—and through a portal, you say?"

"The turn of the century?" Reilly said, his voice cracking. "What year is it?"

"It's 1896." Lottie frowned. "What year do you think it is?"

Reilly breathed in deeply and closed his eyes. He released the air slowly from his inflated lungs before he looked at Lottie again. "It's 2015. As I said, I found a portal in the library. My dog came with me but something must have gone wrong." Without warning, his breathing became shallow and he began to hyperventilate. "My dad died … in a sailing accident a few months ago.… I thought I'd find him here.… This can't be happening to me."

The room started spinning. He saw Lottie leave and then return with a mug in her hand.

"Take a sip of water," she said.

He took the cup and gulped down the cool liquid.

"My friend, Eilam, left for no reason …" His dizziness increased. "And my dog is lost. I don't know … what to do." His head drooped to his chin and he blinked rapidly, trying to stay awake.

Reilly drifted off as he heard Brigid's soothing voice. "Poor thing." Then she added with notable conviction, "The Deceptors have already begun the Detachment Processing."

The  Academy

Where Young People ARE the Difference

〜 Educational Enrichment 〜

〜 Character Development 〜

〜 Self Discovery 〜

〜 Creative Renewal 〜

〜 Diverse Scholarship Opportunities 〜

Visit our online campus at
www.stelladauracademy.org

About the Author

S. L. WHYTE has written short stories, poetry and song lyrics since she was very young. *Finding Tir Na Nog* is her debut novel. "When I write, I see more clearly, feel more deeply, and share more truthfully. Children do this innately, but somewhere between pre-adolescence and adulthood, these creative qualities are often buried or abandoned. I hope the Stelladaur Series ignites the magic of your imagination as a means of self-discovery and creative renewal." S. L. Whyte lives with her husband on a small island in Puget Sound, Washington.

About the Illustrator

KONOHIKI PLACE says, "I have always enjoyed the creative process. As a young boy living in Hawaii, I spent a lot of of time sculpting and sketching. I especially liked drawing dinosaurs and comic book illustrations. Family members, friends and sometimes strangers encouraged me to develop my artistic skills. Seeing others experience joy from my work inspires me to create over and over again. Now a family man with four young boys, I am amazed by their ability to bring their own interpretations of the world into tangible form through various art mediums. This propels me all the more in my world of art."